Mosaic Souls

Mosaic Souls

DOUGLAS ROBINSON

Meeting

I hate these things, she thought, picking up a plate from the front of the buffet line.

Weddings were bad enough, but weddings with buffets were worse—especially when you were overweight. Standing in the line of shuffling guests, waiting for her turn while the people behind whispered speculations (real or imagined) about how much the fat girl was going to take or whether or not she'd come back for seconds, was maddening.

Emma shuffled forward, feeling the weight of their stares heating up the back of the uncomfortable gown she wore to this godforsaken reception. Her self-consciousness, which always worked in overdrive, just about reached the redline every time she thought about the gown.

Made of a ruffled, silky material that shimmered when the light hit it just right, it would've been nice—pretty even—except that, being overweight, Emma preferred to blend into a crowd rather than draw attention to herself. Glossy pink ruffles did not blend easily.

The shiny material, Emma thought with a touch of self-depreciating sarcasm, *is probably rayon, a fabric made by forcefully pushing the cellulose of plants through microscopic fiber holes and that's exactly what the fucker feels like it's doing to me—forcefully driving my cellulite through the miniscule fibers. I feel like I'm literally* oozing *out of this thing.*

Even though the oozing might have been in her head, the overflowing was not, the dress being a size or two too small for her. Although she usually fit comfortably, if a bit snuggly, into a size 20, the tag on this dress stated directly above the dry-cleaning instructions that it was an 18. Her breasts, double-D cups, spilled out of the low-cut front, constantly requiring her to tug at the top of the gown to pull it back up. Every time she adjusted the plunging neckline, her breasts were thrust together, creating a five-inch crevice of cleavage.

Continuing down her pink-encased anatomy, beneath the cliff of her bust, was Emma's waistline, where her belly stretched the limit of the gown's material. But in this area at least, the tightness of the dress worked to her advantage by acting like a girdle and restraining as much of her as it could. Emma could only hope that when she sat down to eat her meal, the zipper running the back wouldn't burst open. If it did, the air in her already-nonexistent ego would deflate even further, if such a thing were possible.

Under her belly and across the expanse of her hips, the fabric pulled taut enough that the ruffles looked as though they had been ironed out—the dress was as smooth as silk, so to speak.

The hem was of the appropriate length for a person her height as it ended an inch above the knee, which was fine while she was standing still or shuffling forward with her plate in hand, patiently waiting her turn at the troth. The problem, however, reared its ugly head whenever she was in full motion. Then, the gown rode.

Emma could live with being overweight. In fact, she found herself attractive in a plump sort of way, even if members of the opposite sex did not. With her weight evenly distributed throughout her frame, she was quite curvaceous and yet still retained a very feminine physique. Except for her thighs. The only curves on her thighs were rolls, rolls of fat, and they were decidedly unsexy, her inner thighs and outer shanks bulgy and covered with deposits of cottage cheese. Emma never wore shorts no matter how hot or humid the summer could become. That was one creed she held mandate in her life, an addendum to which was only wear a skirt or dress when it was absolutely, positively necessary. Since she'd been raised by an old-fashioned mother, weddings fell into the category of absolutely, positively.

Hence the dress.

A dress that rode.

Every time Emma took a full stride, the dress pulled taut across the swell of her leading thigh and the crest of her rear one. Since it was constructed of a non-elastic material, the dress had no other choice for self-preservation except to seek higher ground and move upward. Sometimes it would creep, exposing the vast, creamy flesh of thighs beneath, their pockmarks clearly visible through the nude-colored pantyhose. Other times, the son of a bitch would roll, which was far worse than sliding because she couldn't feel when it happened. If she didn't see it right away, the dress could roll over on itself two or three times before she caught it, leaving her cratered legs exposed to the world for who knew how long.

Emma shivered with the thought, consciously tugging at her hem. Of course, pulling on either end conversely caused the opposite end to shift, the result producing a two-step shuffle of pulling down on the hemline then immediately pulling up on the bust and vice versa. Emma's usual routine was to do one on the bottom and one at the top, followed immediately by another on the bottom and another at the top. The two-step shuffle, repeat if necessary after every forward movement—even while in a slow-motion buffet line—if habit so forced you.

She just knew when she received the invitation to this thing that it would be a buffet instead of the more conventional sit-down meal usually served at weddings held in halls. Not that this was much of a hall. No indeed. This reception was taking place in a *fire* hall. The Brakes County Fire Hall, to be exact, with capital letters beginning each word in the title to stress the importance of such a great, celebratory venue, as she was sure *all* fire halls across the United States required of their names. Formal venues necessitate formal titles, after all. From the cornfields of Kansas to the orange groves of Florida, from the open plateaus of New Mexico to right here in the suburbs of Philadelphia, the great fire halls of America— God bless 'em—where would we be without them? A nice, cheap reception area attached to the local firehouse, with its ladders and pumpers ready to run at the first sign of smoke where maybe, just maybe if you're lucky, you can pet a real live Dalmatian; where else would you rather celebrate your child's graduation, your family reunion, St. Patty's Day, or the joining together of two young souls in marital bliss?

Nothing said class like a party in a fire hall.

Satire aside, Emma was sure that somewhere, there must be a couple of fire halls that were indeed grand and splendorous. However, this was not one of them. In fact, *hall* might be too strong a word for this place. *Large room* would aptly cover the description in the brochure . . . if there was such a publication. No lobby, no coatroom (four racks on wheels with non-removable hangers secured to the overhead bar stood in a corner for guests to hang their own coats on), and no dance floor, per se. What area there was for dancing consisted of whatever amount of dark brown and scarred wood flooring was left unused after the buffet tables were set up, which wasn't much.

What the hall did have was a small dais for the DJ, a bar with the total walk-up capacity of six people, tended by one man, and two tiny closets, each marked individually as "his" and "her" bathrooms.

The overall impression of the place was one of claustrophobia. Emma looked around and could feel the paneled walls closing in on her. The lawful occupancy sign over the entrance indicated that the legal number of bodies allowed to be crammed into the room was 120 people. At present, Emma was sure there were at least a buck-fifty in the room.

Although they were all milling about like cattle in a pen, the general emotion was one of festive gaiety. Everywhere she looked, she could see happiness on the faces of the gathered; handshakes and hugs for long-missed uncles, kisses and hugs for the aunts, smiles for everyone. All around her people were glad for the sheer fact of being with other people they loved, and everybody conversed with someone else, adding his or her own hot air to the already-overheated stuffiness of the hall, where it rose to join a cloud of cigarette smoke forming like a thunderhead at the ceiling.

And Emma stood alone among these people she did not know, a giant island the color of Pepto Bismol, awash in a sea of dark suits and matching dresses. *I hate these things,* she thought again and took another tiny step forward in line.

She wasn't going to come to the wedding at all until her mother insisted it was mandatory that she attend. After all, wasn't Sheila the best friend she had had growing up in the old neighborhood?

The answer to that question was a big fucking *no*.

Being overweight as an adult was hard, but being overweight as a child was unbearable. Throw in the fact that she was an overweight *girl* and that, in a child's view, ranked just about one degree below leprosy.

Everyone knows that little girls are made of sugar and spice and everything nice, but the part edited out is the viscous, scathing tongues they have. Being still a little shy with the fairer sex during the developing ages will keep most (but not all) of the males from talking about an overweight girl in her presence. Once the blubber's gone, however, she becomes fair game; let the snickering begin.

Female children, on the other hand, are remorseless and have no need for decorum—they'll call anyone anything they can think of, right to their face. They'll even use their underdeveloped mastery of the English language to try and rhyme a person's name with an appropriate adjective. Fortunately for Emma, her peers, via their lack of imagination, couldn't think of anything that rhymed with her name, so they had to resort to calling her "Fat E," which was pronounced all as one word—*fatty*—thank you. Ah, the wonderful memories of childhood, may they rest in peace.

With the thoughts of an unpleasant youth ringing around her head, she reached the point of the buffet table where a man dressed in a tall paper hat and white button-down smock of a chef stood carving roast beef to specification.

The smocked mock-chef looked at Emma but did not say anything. He stood waiting for her request with a smug expression on his face, suggesting that he could read her like a book, that he could sum up her entire existence from this, his first glance at her. He was just another man deeming her valueless simply because she was overweight.

Emma Anderson glared back at him. She wanted to scream: *That's right, I like to eat, so what? Now cut me off a slab of beef, and I'll be on my way, asshole!*

Instead, a civilized request arose from her mouth. "I'll have a little off the darker side, please," she said. Not too bad, except that she couldn't bite off the rest of the statement which came forth as if in self-defense for doing something as primal as eating: "I'm trying to cut back."

The chef took his carving knife and sharpened it along a thick leather strop attached to the table. He glided the edge up one side and down the other until he was satisfied. Using a fork to hold the sizable roast in place, he sliced off two pieces of beef and placed them gingerly, reverently, upon the outstretched plate. He had cut them thin as if to say he knew she would be stopping off a McDonald's on her way home tonight.

"There you go," he said around a sly smile and mirthful eyes.

Emma thanked him and continued on to the vegetables.

*　　*　　*

Growing up and throughout high school, Sheila was the closest thing that Emma had to a friend. Even though they spent a lot of time together, theirs was more of an acquaintance than a friendship—they occupied a space together but never really knew each other. The real reason Emma even socialized with Sheila at all was to keep her parents off her back. Just like any good parents, the Andersons were constantly harping on their little girl about what was best for her. She could still remember some of their favorite bickers like snatches of lyrics to long-lost one-hit wonders.

So to keep the folks happy (and quiet), Emma put up the façade of a "normal" childhood (no matter how shallow it might've been) by sticking close to the only acquaintance she could stand, Sheila Oswald.

Sheila was a nice-enough person but at the same time a tough nut to crack. Not an openhearted or touchy-feely girl, or the type to confide in anyone, young Miss Oswald is best described by thinking of her as a marionette: wooden, but functional. And those were the attributes that appealed to Emma. If Sheila's "closedness" were a flaw in her character, it was one Emma admired.

When Sheila would call her Fat E, she didn't do so with malicious intent; she did it as if calling her by her given name. Although she wouldn't dare say there was anything resembling respect involved, Sheila at least treated Emma as a person. And that's the only reason Emma even considered going to Sheila's wedding when she found the invitation sitting in her mailbox like a coiled viper ready to strike, five years after graduating high school and their last conversation together.

As Emma left the vegetable area, she turned to look at the head table where the bridal party was eating. There was Sheila, sitting in the center next to her new husband, Paul something-or-other, and dressed in virginal white, a color that may or may not be appropriate for her to be sporting. As unusual as it sounded to be unsure concerning such an intimate detail about someone considered to be a friend, Emma had no way of knowing if Sheila was still a virgin. During the high school years, Sheila had several different boyfriends, but it was heretofore unknown if she'd had any sexual relations outside of the soon-to-, if you'll pardon the pun, come wedding bed.

Emma and Sheila may not have been the closest of sharing friends, nor had they always seen eye to eye, but definitely in this one area Emma was in complete agreement with Sheila's keep-it-to-yourself ideals: Emma never kissed and told.

Not then, and certainly not now.

Emma believed strongly in that because every time she'd been with a man, it'd been horrible. There had been a total of four times, two in high school and two since. Some people excel at certain things and some people do not; this is called talent. And Emma was sure that she had no talent for sex.

For her first sexual experience, she's not quite certain, but she thinks she was raped.

During junior year at St. Tiburtius High School, some acquaintances that hung around with Sheila (and consequently with Emma) decided that Emma should go to the prom.

"Come on, it'll be fun," a girl named Stephanie urged. "We'll rent a limo."

"My brother will get us some beer," said Stacey.

"Yeah, we'll get really trashed and dance our asses off," said Karen, who immediately jumped off the bed and shook her rump for everyone else in the room.

"And besides, you don't have to marry the guy you take to the prom," continued Stephanie. "It's only a social function. I mean, it's not even the *senior* prom."

Emma looked at Sheila, seated behind the desk in her room she used to do her homework. Sheila shrugged her shoulders and said, "It can't hurt."

With that, Emma conceded and went.

The guy her friends found to escort her was named Stuart James III, and boy, if that didn't make her mother happy. Mrs. Anderson went on and on about how she knew Mrs. James, and that they were a nice family, and that they have, drum roll please, MONEY.

What her mother did not know was that little Stuart James III was a pervert and a possible rapist.

If enough people say the same thing again and again, you'll start to believe it—repetition will wear down a psyche like a stone in a river. After continually hearing from her mother and her friends about how much fun she would have, Emma began to look forward to the prom and what was essentially her first date. By the time the extravaganza arrived, Emma was brimming with anticipation about going to the gala with James III.

And of course, it was a disaster.

The entire time in St. Tibby's gym, where the prom was held, Emma felt out of place. Watching the other kids didn't help either. They all bumped and grinded to the beat in ways that made Emma feel self-conscious about dancing, but she did it anyway. Stuart pressed himself close to her body, trying to sway it to the music, and every once in a while, he would cop a feel—a handful of ass here, a little brush of breast there, and the obligatory rubbing of his thigh against her pubic bone.

Mercifully, the prom was only scheduled to be four hours long. Emma decided she could outlast the four hours and then go home intact and climb safely into bed in the sparse, neat bedroom that was her haven. It didn't quite go as planned. When she did finally make it home to her bedroom a little before dawn, she was no longer intact.

After the final drum loop faded out and the lights came up in the gym, the five girls and their respective dates crammed into the white stretch limo. Alcohol was passed around, further plans discussed.

"Let's go to Atlantic City," someone near the rear said.

"Can't. I have to work in the morning," returned a female voice.

"Me too," said a male.

"Let's drive around the city; we've got the limo till 6 a.m."

"We've got to go to Smitty's party," added someone else.

And then, above the din of the other amalgamated suggestions, came the most reasonable and damning idea that Emma heard that night. Until this day, she still doesn't know who suggested it. "Let's go down to the river," the disembodied voice said.

A democratic (or should it be *demon*-cratic?) vote resulted in consensual agreement—motion proposed, seconded, and ratified in the flutter of a heartbeat. Further supportive comments were made about how nice a night it was for a walk and how the air coming off of the river smelled so good this time of year.

To Emma, it sounded like a shitty idea, but with the fear of not fitting in, she kept quiet and went.

It took them a half hour to get to the parking lot that ran alongside the Delaware River, a mile or so off Frankford Avenue. On the way, Stuart continually pounded beers along with the rest of them. When they reached their destination, Stuart was unconditionally drunk. They had the limo parked and gave the driver instructions on how long they figured it would be before they'd be ready to go home, then everyone in the group paired off and went in separate directions.

Emma and Stuart walked south along the bank of the river. They made small talk, accompanied by the sound of water slapping against stone. During their stroll, they saw two other limousines arrive, and a solitary police car gave the area a once-over. The officer did not get out to hassle anyone. Emma guessed he knew it was a prom night and, having been a teenager once, was willing to overlook minor infractions, as long as they weren't being done blatantly out in the open.

After a few minutes, Stuart and Emma crossed out of the parking lot and into a small wooded area. At his suggestion, they took a break and sat down on a nearby boulder. He said he wasn't feeling so good and the rest would give him time to clear his head.

"You want one of these?" Stuart asked, producing two bottles of beer from the outer pockets of his tuxedo jacket. She shook her head no. He sat one down on the rock beside him and opened the other.

"We'll be seniors next year. Amazing, isn't it, how fast it all went?" After a deep pull from the longneck, he asked, "What're you going to do after high school, Emma?"

"My father wants me to go to school up at State. It's where he went, and he's got that old alma mater pride," she shrugged. "So I guess that's an idea anyway. Something to do, at least."

"You don't sound really enthused about it."

"That's 'cause I'm not. I'm not enjoying high school that much, and another four years in college sounds awful right now."

"What aren't you enjoying about high school? St. Tibby's is a blast."

"I don't know. I don't think I fit in real well."

"Why not?"

For all Emma knew, he sounded genuine, so she opened herself up to him and, with her defenses down, became an easy target. "I'm not sure if people like me that much," she said in a small voice, her head down.

"I like you a lot."

"Really?" she asked, a shy smile crossing her face as she brushed a lock of brown hair out of an eye and tucked it behind her ear.

"Really," he said, his own bright blue eyes dancing with a glee that made them glitter like ice. "That's why I had Stephie and Stacey ask you to go to the prom with me."

"You're kidding! They never said you were interested in me. They led me to believe I had a responsibility to go, and that it was their responsibility to find someone to take me."

Stuart shook his head. "Nope, you're here because I wanted you to be," he said, while looking into her eyes. After a pause, he bent over and kissed her.

Emma was so overwhelmed by what he had said that she let herself be kissed before the usual reservations and fears grabbed hold of her. It had all progressed so quickly that she didn't even have a moment to realize that this was the first romantic kiss of her life.

And that it was good.

She accepted his lips onto hers, and at first, they were moist and cold, it being the middle of the night and still only late April. After a few more kisses, they became warm with wetness, but not too wet, not sloppy at all, but rather nice. Her mouth opened, and his gently probing tongue was there. She responded in like with her own tongue, finding a sweet and bitter taste inside his mouth, which was the remnants of the beer. A small weight nestled in her stomach, and all was right with the world.

Then things went wrong in a hurry.

Before she knew it, she was lying up against the rock, her feet still on the ground. He had unzipped his fly and pushed up her pink prom dress all in one motion. The expression on her face had gone from contentedness to blankness, while his had gone smug. It was his smugness that brought her back to herself, down from her high, to remind her that this was not what she wanted, not like this.

Later, bathed and dressed in a flannel nightgown, snuggled deep in the safe, embracing comforts of her bed, she was positive that she had said no. Many times in fact, but she couldn't remember hearing herself actually saying it aloud.

Emma's body went rigid as Stuart positioned himself above her. A detached feeling came upon her with the pain of the first thrust. She remembered shaking her head in negation that this can't—and won't—happen to her, while the rest of her body tried to push away from his. But happen it did, a horribly symbolic prom-night dance, twirled to the repetitious beats of punctuated grunts and thrusts.

Even as it was happening, she tried to prevent it. At the apex of each backward motion, before he plunged again into her depths, Emma shoved her hips forward in an effort to bounce him off, while her back simultaneously tried to push itself through the unyielding coldness of the boulder. While their torsos remained fixed in position, their bottoms swung in concert, like the pendulum of a grandfather clock. To her dismay, everything Emma did was to no avail; it seemed as though she and Stuart were locked together by a four-inch chain of flesh.

Then it was over. Just as fast as it started, it ended.

With one final thrust, he was up and off her. She watched as he pulled a condom (*When did he put that on?*) off his penis with a wet snapping sound and slung it deeper into the woods. He zipped his pants and picked up the open beer he had placed on the ground when they first started to kiss. "Whoa," he said and drank deep.

He had turned his back to her and was looking out over the water, as she pushed herself up off the rock.

"After high school, I think I'm gonna join the Navy," he said, as if nothing had happened in between the fragments of their conversation. The casual way he picked up right where they left off, as if nothing out of the ordinary had occurred, was what caused Emma to doubt herself, what made her think that maybe she hadn't wanted him to stop. It made her question if she had been raped at all, or if this was just the way sex was supposed to be.

"Yeah, I think it'll be the navy. I just love the water," he said and threw the empty bottle into the Delaware River to prove it.

*   *   *

Of course, Emma never mentioned the "rape" to anyone.

After prom night ended, she continued to live her life just as she had before, never regretting not telling anyone. What was the point? She was still the same person; having sex, warranted or not, hadn't changed her. Revenge would have been just, but the added pity of being a rape victim would've rendered any retribution worthless. She never looked back on that night as a "what if" night but instead accepted it as another fact of life. After all, it was just sex, not anything meaningful.

So here she was, alive and healthy (some would say *extremely* healthy) and again wearing a pink gown.

As she walked toward the numbered table she was designated to sit at, she wished that her parents had been invited. Even though they caused her grief most of the time, she would've liked to have had someone to talk to. Technically, Emma could have asked her mother to attend, the invitation having been for Emma and a guest. But it probably would've looked even more desperate for her to bring her mother rather than going stag, so she had RSVP'd with a false-advertising, skinny little 1.

Oh well, she thought, balancing the food on her plate as she made her way through the throng of guests. *I'll eat in silence, chat only when necessary, give the card to Sheila when she makes her rounds, then make a quick getaway and be home safely in bed before ten.*

With her mind imagining an easy escape and her senses occupied by the food on her plate, Emma did not notice the man standing in front of her before she ran directly into him.

As her right shoulder impacted with the man's left arm, her "getaway" thought was answered by another thought from the less sympathetic (more realistic?) part of her brain: *Safe in bed, just like you thought you'd be after the prom.*

Emma heard this thought so clearly in her mind that she imagined it had been spoken aloud by the man she had run into.

A tiny little yelp of a scream escaped from Emma Anderson's mouth as she looked into the man's dark, haunted eyes.

Psychosis

1

*H*is dark, haunted eyes stared at the inky blackness of the spring night, behind his glasses, the irises the deepest shade of brown. Because he had been standing in total darkness for the past long hours, brooding, thinking, his night vision undisturbed by any light, the irises had occluded the whites, turning his eyes into small pieces of onyx.

Looking out the front window of the bottom unit of the duplex, Michael Dedaker knew that tonight was one of those special nights, one of those nights in which he would transcend himself.

He could detect it in the particular smell that wafted in the window, a smell that could only be associated with a city street after a passing shower had just misted the ground, wetting the toxins without being strong enough to wash them away. To Michael, that smell was a conflicting odor of hope and hate, an odor that seemed *hasty*—the smell of the city. Putting his nose directly against the screen, he inhaled deeply.

Yes, tonight was one of those nights.

When his lungs were filled, he held the breath for as long as he could before releasing it slowly through his mouth, breathing it back out into the street in its new form. The air had been changed by him and he by it; such was the way of the world—each thing, alive or inert, reacting to every other thing in every moment of time.

Dedaker was a man who believed he was someone who dictated the path of the world, as he was born to do by the Creator. He did not think the world revolved around him, knowing it was impossible for the universe to spin on something as inconsequential as one human being. But he did believe that it was every man's responsibility to alter the course of life around him. It had been God's plan to create the heavens and the earth as complex levels of existence; God presided over his heavens, and he had created man, in his image, to preside over the earth. Therefore, it was man's responsibility to interact, using his God-given abilities, with the things around him, altering and changing what needed to be. Through these changes, man transcended to holiness, to godliness.

Dedaker pulled the window shut, closing off the smell of the street. The slight rain had added a thick humidity to the already-dank night, and with the windows closed in this part of the house, it would become uncomfortable very quickly. Dedaker enjoyed the heat while he was working; he did his work naked, and the sweat from his body—mixing together with hers—created a musklike oil that permeated the apartment with its sweet, animal perfume.

He let go of the corner of the curtain, and it silently draped his view of the sleeping street. Stepping away from the window, Dedaker walked across the thick plastic tarp covering the near-empty living room. It crinkled as his bare feet trod over it. The sound the plastic made would always be one of comfort to Dedaker. He felt it a private sound, one which only he could associate with his own inner thoughts.

Halfway across the clear plastic of the tarp, he stopped at the podium, one of only two pieces of furniture in the room with the other being a four-foot-long bench that had complemented a small wooden picnic table Michael had never seen—having spotted the weather-beaten bench one night, sitting curbside amongst many bags of trash awaiting the following morning's collection.

Dedaker walked around the podium and looked inside. Satisfied that the tools (clean) and the charcoal (plentiful) he would need for the remainder of the evening were there, he retreated back into the unlit recesses of the duplex to go upstairs and get dressed.

*   *   *

Ten minutes later, wearing all black, Dedaker emerged through the second-floor door. Michael, who owned both the top and bottom apartments of the duplex, chose to live on the second floor while keeping the first to practice his art. The only access into the house from the outside was through the door Dedaker had just exited—both doors on the ground level were kept locked from the inside and out simultaneously. To gain entrance to the bottom level, one had to unlock first the exterior side and then go in through the top floor to unlock the inside, or be an armed locksmith with the tools and knowledge to break in. And such feats were only possible with the rear door, anyway.

When he had purchased the duplex from the previous owner, the man had been living in the quarters now occupied by Dedaker and renting out the space below to a young married couple. He had sold the duplex with six months still remaining on the downstairs lease. Dedaker—well aware that he didn't want the couple to have a vivid memory of him—hadn't made any waves with them about breaking the lease. The three of them cohabited in the same building for the next six months in harmony. Sixty days before the termination of the original contract, Dedaker officially notified the couple in writing that their previous lease would not be renewed. The husband, whose name Dedaker had heard and read but never retained, had knocked on his door one day to see if there was anything they could do to sway him into re-upping. The man pleaded their case by stating that he and his wife both liked the neighborhood and that the lease was within their financial means. Dedaker amicably declined and lied, saying he had family members ready to move in. The man thanked him for his time. Six weeks later, a big yellow moving van pulled up out front and parked with two wheels on the sidewalk as the couple loaded up their lives and took them elsewhere.

Once the house was completely his, Dedaker began to make the special alterations he required. First, he cut a three-foot square hole in the floor of his dining room, creating a passageway to the lower unit so that he could get from one to the other without having to venture outside. Each level of the duplex had two restrooms: one full bathroom connected to the master bedroom and a powder room between the kitchen and dining room. When needed, Dedaker fastened a length of rope around the toilet in the upstairs powder room and ran it down the access hole into the apartment below. The rope was used to travel between floors. He chose the toilet for an anchor because it was the sturdiest thing in the apartment that could handle his weight without having to add any further support—support that could be noticed by any surprise visitors, seeing as no one would ever be *invited* here. By fastening the rope around the base of the toilet, he assured himself that he could simply untie (or cut, in an emergency) the rope and store it in a closet, away from prying eyes. The access hole itself was not a problem. He had made it, so it could be concealed beneath a small china cabinet with an expensive collection of plates that had been his mother's mother, given to her on her wedding day shortly before the outbreak of World War II. Even with the plates in it, the cabinet was easy enough to move with minimal effort applied.

After creating the access hole, he went down into the lower unit to take care of the doors. There was no question about the front door, which looked out onto the street—it had to be sealed. Besides the normal knob lock and deadbolt, Dedaker took long nails and drove them through the door, into the jamb. Not satisfied with the locks and nails, he added cement. From the local hardware store (which has since been put out of business by a large chain store the size of an airplane hangar) he bought the cement and mixed it in a paint roller tray. He then took a flat putty knife and smoothed the gray substance into the space between the door and its jamb.

The back door was another matter entirely. Dedaker knew he could not secure that door the way he would like because he had to transport his finished products out of the duplex's bottom unit somehow. It was easy to get them in by dropping them through the access hole, but they were too impossibly heavy to retrieve the same way. The back door was the only logical exit to take care of such a maneuver since the driveway that led to the alley behind the row of duplexes backed right up against the door. So for this reason, he could not seal the rear door as securely as he could the front.

Dedaker reluctantly had to settle for typical locks for the rear door. Three safety chains inside, two deadbolts (keyed on both sides) outside, and the knob lock; any more would've looked suspicious, thereby defeating the purpose. There was one set of keys for these locks, and it was always, always kept in the upstairs apartment. The danger of the locks being opened from the inside was as great as if they were opened from the outside, perhaps even more so because the person on the inside knew what was happening, while the people outside did not.

Dedaker, who now stood directly in front of the door in question, looked at the three locks. He still wasn't satisfied with the situation, but there were only so many possibilities, and preparation had to end somewhere and action had to begin.

Deactivating the alarm on his nondescript midsized sedan, he got in. This was not the car he used to obtain his quarry. That one was a black 1969 Cadillac hearse. Built in the years before all the elaborate details were added to comfort the survivors, the hearse he owned resembled nothing more than a slick-looking station wagon. The wagon had belonged tongue-in-cheekily to the police coroner's office before its transmission went. Michael bought it at auction for a song then had a transmission, two u-joints, and a transfer case installed for the over-the-barrel price of four thousand dollars. After the repairs, the wagon was once again in excellent running condition and was the perfect form of transportation he required with its elongated cargo space big enough for a body. It was overly ostentatious, of course, and maybe even an eyesore, but he couldn't resist. Michael Dedaker loved his hearse and its irony.

Although his love ran deep, he did not dare keep the hearse at his house, on the off chance that someone might be able to identify it from an obtaining scene. To counteract that possibility, he kept it locked in a large storage garage at a monthly rental facility. He drove in with the sedan, parked it in the rental, and drove out with the station wagon. He wasn't concerned that this would be overtly suspicious because he only did the transfers at night. If he were ever questioned about the macabre-looking wagon, his at-once ready reply would be that he was trying his hand at restoration, and the old lady (fictional) wouldn't let him keep the creepy (her word) car at the house.

For his purposes, Dedaker was thankful the facility was here, even though he couldn't fathom that there was a need for such a thing as "public storage." To him, it was unbelievably wrong how people living in the American culture put so much effort into obtaining material possessions. He thought it ridiculous that beings with a full understanding of their own mortality wasted so much of their precious short years acquiring material things. Man was the only creature on the entire planet that knew of his own impending doom, and yet he still chose to piss away what little time he did have frivolously. You wouldn't see an *animal* wasting its life looking for a Louis XIV chair or a rookie baseball card of someone who had died a generation before the seeker was even born. Fuck, no. Animals were smarter than that. The only things they looked for were their next meal and their next lay. They provided, protected, and reproduced; they do not sand furniture.

So then, was the knowledge of mortality what really separated man from animal? Or was it the stupidity of the humans?

Accomplishments were what people should aspire to, not the gathering of old bits of junk. But gather they did, and they did it with gusto. Dedaker had even seen a bumper sticker (another godforsaken art form for which he had a whole diatribe) that read "The one who dies with the most wins." Wins what? There were no winners in the afterlife, dead was dead. And life should not be considered a game but an experience. An experience of evolution. If you can't evolve—if you *don't* evolve—you won't be ready for what's next. Did people actually believe that heaven was going to be a place that didn't need things done, that it was going to be a place where you laid on your ass, floating on a cloud? Dedaker couldn't imagine that St. Peter was going to stand at the gate and say, "Oh, you were a ditch digger who didn't take the Lord's name in vain, drank eight glasses of water a day, and paid your taxes on time? Go right in. Wing fitting and harps to the left, floating clouds to the right." Dedaker supposed heaven needed ditch diggers too, but with everybody vying for the same *after*life, he was sure mundanely squandering your *actual* life was not going to be enough to secure admission. Heaven is not a reward, it's a privilege—now there's a bumper sticker for ya. A privilege that not only had to be earned but also maintained, or it could be revoked. Yes, there would be a lot of requirements in heaven, and he for one would be ready with an accomplished resume and a zest to perform whatever was required of him.

To display such vigor in this life, Dedaker's job on earth, bestowed on him by the Father, was to assist people with *their* change, *their* evolution; he was to help those too blind to help themselves so that they may be forgiven and their privilege to ascend granted.

He started the sedan and shifted to drive. Easing on the gas pedal, he inched the car up the inclined driveway, toward the alley. At the top of the driveway, he braked to make sure no other vehicles were coming. When he did, the rear door of the downstairs apartment was momentarily splashed red.

Then he was gone.

2

$\mathcal{I}$t had been a long night, and her feet were hurting.

Her name was Sherry Dasher, and she was a dancer. If that wasn't poetic justice, she didn't know what was. She could just imagine the jokes if her friends knew what she really did for a living. She could almost hear the improvised start to the jingle for "Rudolph, the Red-Nosed Reindeer." "You know Dasher the Dancer . . ."

Hardy, har, har.

But it didn't matter because nobody knew, and that's the way she intended it to stay. If her family ever did find out, it certainly wouldn't be a jovial subject—no jokes about live, nude dancing would be made around the Reverend Dasher's dinner table, that's for sure.

Sherry was a practicing Protestant, and her father was one of the nicest men on the face of the earth, but he was serious about his religion. Cross the word of God, and her father could become one mean sonovabitch. Sherry was sure that if Dean Dasher ever found out about the Hippy Hippy Shake, he would yell fire and brimstone, and Sherry would find herself sleeping out of doors, homeless at age nineteen.

Not that that would matter with what she was pulling down as a dancer. She'd only be homeless for as long as it took to drive to the nearest hotel, where she would reside until she found a suitable apartment. A week, ten days at most, she figured. But that wasn't what she wanted to do. She enjoyed living at home in the spacious house with two parents that loved each other and a sister who was her best friend. She didn't want to jeopardize that in any way. As a business major at Rutgers University, with a three-seven GPA, she considered dancing as only a temporary gig that paid the bills, anyway.

For her legitimate job—the one she could tell people about—she was the manager of the local Stop Mart.

But being a cashier at a convenience store wouldn't suffice for a college student. Once tuition became an issue, she knew she needed to make a move. Sherry's sister was four years older than she was and had graduated from State at the same time Sherry graduated from high school. Sherry had watched as Denise filled out loan agreement after loan agreement. Her sister—who had lived the first two years at home but spent the last two years living on campus—was almost $100 K in the hole before she even got out of the starting gate. Sherry saw this and mulled her own future. She knew that there would be no tuition help from her parents, and she refused to dig herself such a hole just to get an education. She considered every possibility and finally decided that being a dancer (read: stripper) was the easiest way to the lost city of gold she sought.

With that in mind, she began working on dance routines. She took the money she saved from the Stop Mart and bought some strutting clothes, some vibrant makeup, and a car.

Now, aged nineteen, Sherry Dasher knew the value of a buck (and other assorted rhyming words). And she knew how to invest it. Well. In a year and a half (she lied about her age to get the job) at the club, she earned just under $150,000, two-thirds of which she did not claim on her 1040. Approximately two grand a week over the last eighty weeks, and except for the tuition she paid Rutgers, almost every cent of it was earning its weight in gold in mutual funds and bonds.

Great, fast money, working short weeks consisting of four—or five-hour shifts, and the work wasn't hard, if you had the stomach for it. The average shift was comprised of six fifteen-minute shows. She started semiclothed and shimmied and shook until she shed down to almost nothing. Sherry figured that she could make even more if she went to work over in Jersey. Pennsylvania had a statute that required all adult entertainers to remain clothed in public establishments. Otherwise, the Department of Health would shut them down, heavy fines would be imposed, and the liquor license would be revoked. Of course, if you read between the lines and followed the statute to the letter, it simply stated that clothing must be *worn* at all times; it didn't state *how* you had to wear them. So you did exactly what was required and no more. As long as you were wearing clothes, you could adjust them any way you wanted. So what if your breasts and nipples were exposed because your top was pushed down to your waist? It didn't matter, as long as the top was on your body. The same went for the bottom. The regulation was a pain in the ass, but one that could be worked around. The only other alternative was to dance at a BYOB place, where, since no food or drink was being sold, the DOH had no control over what the people inside were wearing. Sherry could opt to work at one of those, but they tended to get seedy.

At the Hippy, her dance routines were then followed by a half hour of "working" the customers around the bar. She walked from man to man (very rarely would there be a woman in the company of these men, her being a friend thrown in the mix for shits and giggles; even rarer a lesbian), made eye contact, and flashed a lot of flesh. Stroked their egos—and occasionally their cocks—and they slapped down green-backed bills. After she collected as much as she thought the market would bear from each john, she came to the final ritual act of the business—she solicited.

Solicitation. There it was, the evil word, one her father would definitely think was the devil, but one that separated the women from the girls; and the only one that would make or break a career in dancing, something Sherry preferred to think of as "gold mining." Dancing was lucrative, no doubt, but your employer—who's cut off your earnings even steeper than Uncle Sam's would've—would not retain you if you weren't willing to provide "other services" for customers. And there was no incentive for him too because there were always fresh faces getting off buses somewhere who were willing to make a quick buck by turning a quick . . . well, you get the picture. These fresh faces had needs the employer was willing to take care of, as long as the young ladies in question were willing to set scruples aside. And you'd be surprised how cheap scruples are going these days . . . or maybe you wouldn't.

Anyway, the brass ring was there for those willing to wrap themselves around the brass pole to get it. The other services were merely how you kept it.

It started out simple enough. You asked every person in the crowd you worked if they wanted a lap dance, which was a version of what you did onstage, only done behind a wall, and done *on* the customer. When you got a bite, you lead the individual toward his special seat, where he paid admission to a big, burly guy standing just outside the entrance of the partition. The burly fellow was there to protect the working ladies from any overzealous customer getting out of hand. He was also there to protect the owner's cut of the wealth. Behind a wall, money could change hands without being seen or services rendered at incorrect rates or the like. The thug struck the balance; otherwise, he struck whoever needed to be struck.

Now that your prey was perched, you went to work. If you were good, and he was interested, you could keep building him up and building him up—something that had to be done carefully and skillfully, so as to keep him at the height of desire without pushing him over the edge. If it was done correctly, you could work him for every last dollar he had and still send him home to his wife with blue balls, where it became her problem, not yours. A fool and his money, indeed.

All of this ran around Sherry's head as she sat on a metal stool in the dressing room at the rear of the Hippy Hippy Shake. She had been a "closer" tonight, which meant she had worked from 9 p.m. until the bar closed at two. It was now quarter to three in the morning, and she still had to go home and look over a paper that was due for her Human Development Psych class tomorrow. She had been working for six straight days between the club and the Stop Mart, along with attending class and writing the paper in her spare time.

Sherry was tired.

And her feet hurt.

She sat on the stool in nothing but a pair of panties. They were thongs, of course, and the cold metal of the stool sapped her body temperature. She shivered as she rubbed her aching feet.

That's it, she thought, *I'm never going to buy another pair of cheap heels from that fucking* Walking on Air *store again. No way. My insteps are killing me, my heels feel like they have spurs, and it's all because of those goddamn shoes.*

She picked up the six-inch open-toed black leather heels by their ankle straps and tossed them underhand toward the battleship gray trash can in the corner. Surprisingly, the trash can was nearly empty, and both shoes banged home for two.

She shook her hair out and stood up in front of her locker. The coolness of the painted concrete floor felt good on her tired feet. To her left was a mirror that took up the entire length of the wall. She glanced at it, admiring her figure in the emptiness of the locker room.

She was a five-foot-ten brunette, her breasts a smallish C cup (natural, thank you), and they would still be winning the fight with gravity for another ten years to come. Her hips were slender and her tummy tight. She didn't like jewelry and only wore makeup while onstage. Altogether, she found herself an attractive woman who did not resemble a stripper, nude dancer, solicitor, or fornicator.

Sherry liked the reflection she saw but still wondered how long it would last. Then she shrugged her shoulders because how long it would last ultimately did not matter. In two years, she'd have a degree and a large-enough nest egg to jump-start her career. That meant no more hand jobs in the dark for dirty old men, cooing them on while the smell of stale cigarette smoke and sour beer filled her nostrils. There was even a young fellow at school she was interested in, and she had a feeling that he was just as interested.

But those were pipe dreams for the future, and this wasn't the future; this was the present, and the only dream the club felt like was one inside a stagnant pipe. A present that consisted of pumps that hurt her feet and random ponderings about whether or not she should change her dance song (currently the seminal "You Shook Me All Night Long" by the quintessential sex, drugs, and rock and roll band AC/DC, subtle huh?) to something with a sultry dance loop rather than a pounding backbeat.

She sighed, reached into the locker for her shirt, and pulled it on, sans bra. At two forty-five in the morning, who was going to be looking?

After she dressed, she slammed the locker door and shouldered her pocketbook. There was a time clock (the dancer's base rate was equivalent to that of a waitress's—the tips were the money was, honey) by the emergency exit that led to the rear parking lot. She punched it and pushed open the door.

The sound of the alarm buzzer followed her out into the night.

*   *   *

Sherry Dasher's much more comfortable sneakers made a squelching sound as she walked across the parking lot, still damp from the earlier rain, to where she had parked her car, a late-model Toyota Camry. There were five other cars in the lot, four of which she knew belonged to people still inside the club, but the fifth one she didn't recognize.

The unknown car was a long black Caddy that looked a lot like an eerie old hearse, parked between her and her Camry. For a minute, she worried about the presence of such an odd car in the lot and slowed her stride. Sherry was suddenly completely aware that she was a lonely female in a dark, empty parking lot late at night, one who had just been brazenly naked and sexually suggestive in front of a large, faceless crowd of horny men, to boot. Her fright elevated, for there were no security cameras hooked up to survey the lot, and not for the first time did she wish that the Hippy employed escorts to walk the dancers to their cars at night, as other clubs did.

A second later, the small panic attack passed as she remembered the new bartender Vic recently hired. Tonight was only his second night, and the odd car could be his. All of twenty-one and partial to tight white undershirts with the short sleeves rolled up to his shoulders, he looked the type who would drive a hearse. Yeah, it was probably his car.

Resuming her pace, she continued toward the Camry.

Out of the corner of her eye, a tiny flash of light appeared. She turned her head to see what it was and realized that it was the interior light of the hearse, which came on when the door opened. It had only been a brief flash before the bulb had been blocked by the person getting out. Her heart skipped a beat as she saw the silhouette of a man rise up next to the car.

Sherry stopped, staring at the man standing next to the hearse. She swallowed hard and asked, "Who's there?"

No answer.

Fuck, it's a creep. Why did I ever do this? How'd I ever get involved in a life like this? Thought I was being so smooth, so smart, making money hand over fist, but I should've known nothing ever comes easy; everything has a price, and now I'm going to have to pay mine. I'm going to be a dead, raped statistic found in a parking lot.

Dead, yes. Raped, yes. But not in the parking lot.

*   *   *

Michael Dedaker stood beside his hearse, looking at the woman he'd been waiting for, the woman he'd seen dancing onstage. For the last three hours, he had watched her gyrations from a small corner in that rank local franchise of Sodom and Gomorrah. While Dedaker watched the woman who called herself Desiree Sheer, he noticed how the other people in the room watched her also. He watched as she paraded herself for the perusal of these people with their hungry, soulless eyes, people who looked at her with a total lack of respect, looked at her as if she were just a plaything there for their personal amusement. Those looks were bad, but the looks that were even worse were the ones she hadn't been getting— the ones not of desire but of disinterest.

The casual, offhanded way some of those men *didn't* look at her had Dedaker seething. There she was, showing them her most intimate person, showing them the only possession that she could ever truly own in this life, her body. In a world in which these same bastards made material possessions their most honored treasures, they had the nerve to *not* look upon the singular beauty that this woman had offered to show them, the one possession in which she alone had control. Instead of awe, disinterest resided in their eyes as they laughed and joked amongst themselves, acting as though what this beautiful young woman was doing was commonplace.

The uninterested way in which some of them *refused* to look at her was rude, and it had infuriated him. He would personally take care of that. He would show them the beauty of this woman.

He would have everyone speaking her name tomorrow, after he helped her transcend.

Michael Dedaker was so enraged that he hadn't heard the woman he knew as Desiree Sheer speak to him. The second time she spoke, he was jolted from his reverie.

"Fucking creep," she said in a voice younger sounding than he had expected. He imagined her voice would be husky and deep, as if years of smoking and drinking had taken their toll, when in fact, Sherry did not partake of either vice. "Not going to talk to me, huh? You think I'm just going to lie down, spread my legs, and let you mount me?"

She had come to a complete stop and stood in a defensive posture a few feet from the rear bumper of the hearse.

"W-what?" he stammered. "No. I don't want to . . . do that. I didn't mean to . . . That you should . . ." Dedaker's eyes shifted to the hearse, as if he were bashful. Finally, "I didn't mean to scare you."

While his head was down, Sherry looked him over. She remembered seeing him in the club earlier.

Around thirty-five, he stood six feet or so with an average build, brown hair, glasses, and dark eyes, the exact color of which she couldn't see in the dimness of the parking lot. She guessed he would weigh in at 170 and thought she might be able to give him a good fight if it became necessary. She definitely knew she could outrun him, tired feet or no. When she finished assessing him, she felt a little more at ease, a little more in control. With a semblance of control back in her grasp, she decided to give him a piece of her mind.

"You did scare me," she said. "What'd you think you were going to do, getting out of a car like that in the middle of the night? What was I supposed to think?"

"I'm sorry. I only wanted to meet you."

"Well, you've met me. Now I have to go." She turned to stalk away.

He held out a hand. "Please don't go."

She looked at him, the defiance flashing in her eyes.

"I'd like to buy you a cup of coffee or something," he said, then quickly added, "are you hungry? I know a diner that makes a great Western omelet."

Sherry smiled in spite of herself, in spite of the ire still roiling a pool of bile in her mouth. *A Western omelet, that's kind of cute.* "No, thank you. I'm not hungry," she said, still with an edge but duller.

"Another time maybe."

"Yeah, another time."

"Would it be rude of me to ask for an autograph?"

"After all the rude things I get asked in there," she said, cocking a thumb back at the Hippy, "asking for an autograph would be the kindest compliment I've gotten all day."

"Then, formally, may I have your autograph?"

Sherry laughed a little at his innocuousness. "Sure."

"Let me get something to write on." Ducking back into the hearse, he bent to rummage, the pale whiteness of the car's dome light shining on his face. It was a good-looking face, clean lines, smooth skin, handsome. Liking what she saw, she let her eyes roam, checking out the rest of his body. Wide shoulders, broad back, narrow waist, tight buns, and what looked like muscular thighs encased in jeans. She even liked his glasses; they gave him an academic look. All in all, he was a person she could find attractive. Sherry decided that if he ever showed up at the club again—and had the balls to ask her out for a Western omelet a second time—she might go, which wasn't something Sherry would usually do. In fact, she had never gone on a date with a patron of the club before.

Fuck it, there's a first time for everything, she thought. *Here he was, waiting in the middle of a rainy night—a* Tuesday *night at that—to meet me. He says hi and offers dinner, and the best I can do is be rude to him. Jesus, Sherry, he didn't ask you to blow him, like most of the other slobs that come here do. All he wanted was to be nice because he's got a crush. Is a crush such a bad thing for someone to have on a woman like you? I don't think so. Imagine the courage it had to take to try to court a stripper the old-fashioned way, when he only had to throw down a little cash to get his fill, then head home, no strings attached.*

Yeah, if he asked again, she just might go.

The man was getting back out of the car. He had a book in his hand as he walked toward her. He smiled, and she returned it. It was a warm smile, one Sherry found alluring.

"A book, huh? You a reader?" she asked, chitchatting.

"Absolutely ferocious. Can't get enough of it."

"Really? Me too. Are you sure that's what you want me to sign?"

"Yep."

She placed a hand over her heart, feeling her braless chest beneath her shirt, and cringed inwardly at being dressed-down. "I'm honored that you'd want me to sign your book. You want some catchy little quote, like in a high school yearbook? Or do you just want my name?"

"Just your name."

"Do you want me to inscribe it? You know, like 'To so-and-so'? Hey, that reminds me, I don't even know your name."

"It's Michael."

"Michael," she said, feeling the roll of it. "I like that. You look like a Michael, not a 'Mike' or a 'Mikey.'"

"Thank you."

"You're welcome. Would you like it written 'To Michael'?"

"Nope. Just your name."

"All right, do you have a pen?"

"No. I was hoping you did."

"I think I have one in my handbag. Let me set it down, so I can find it with all the junk in here."

Sherry Dasher stepped over to the car on her left, a white Ford LTD belonging to a poor bastard named Ricardo who had the unsavory job of mopping up all the wasted highs of retched puke and spilled beer and dried semen inside the club. He worked without complaining throughout the night and into the early hours of the morning, and it just went to show that no matter how bad your job was, it could always be worse.

Sherry laid the book and her handbag on the age-faded white paint of the hood. Unzipping the bag, she began to fish around in the detritus for a pen.

Michael Dedaker watched her. He said, "I think you're a very intelligent woman."

Sherry was flattered but said anyway, "No, I'm not. If I were half as intelligent as I thought I was, I wouldn't be here."

"Here with me?"

"No, here working at this dump. I'm better than this."

"I know you are. That's why I'm here tonight. To show you—and everyone else—that you're better than this."

With her hand still buried up to her elbow in the bag, Sherry turned to look at Michael. "Wha—," she started. But before she realized what was happening, Dedaker had grabbed her by the hair and, using all of his strength, slammed her face into the hood of the car. She hit with such force that on impact the steel dented. With the first hit, Sherry's nose broke, and her left cheekbone shattered; crimson blood erupted from her nostrils and splattered across the off-whiteness of the hood, Pollock style.

Sherry was so caught off guard and shocked by his sudden action that she couldn't comprehend what was happening. Dedaker yanked her head back up by her hair, pulling a clump out by the roots and sending it fluttering down to the rain-slicked asphalt of the parking lot.

Sherry did not scream. If she had, it might have saved her life because at that very moment, Ricardo was sitting on the same metal stool Sherry herself had used to change her shoes just minutes ago inside the emergency exit of the club. Nightly, after the dancers went home, Ricardo went into their dressing room to clean it. While he cleaned, he took his time and looked through their personal belongings, their lockers, their shoes, their clothes, their underwear. He touched these things, liking the feel of the cotton and the silk and leather against his body. He smelled them, inhaling the sweet aromas of perfume and soap, the bitter aromas of sweat and cunt. Sometimes he pleasured himself; sometimes he didn't. Tonight was one of those nights he'd take himself in his hand.

While Sherry was being accosted, Ricardo sat on her stool holding the discarded shoes he fished out of the trash can. He was looking at them and dreaming. If she had screamed, Ricardo might have heard her. Instead, Sherry tried to speak, tried to ask the man named Michael why he was hurting her. What emanated from her mouth wasn't a question but an inarticulate gurgling sound.

For his part, Dedaker didn't even hear the sound Sherry made. He had already reached the zenith of his backward momentum and was beginning to thrust her head forward again.

Her face hit the second time with the terrible sound of meat striking metal. Because she had been trying to speak, her mouth was open at the moment of impact, her top incisors and cuspids striking the steel directly. Before all four of them broke off at the gum line, they chipped the ivory paint, leaving a small bite mark in the hood. The hard bone behind her upper lip broke in three places. In conjunction with her already-shattered nose and cheek, her facial structure turned to mush, giving the impression that her countenance had sunken into her skull. Her mandible—which struck the unyielding metal of the car a nanosecond after her teeth—received a hairline fracture, the force of the hit causing it to become dislodged from the hinges it sat in at the base of her skull.

Suddenly, her head was pulled backward again.

There was a moment at the apex of the pendulum when she found herself looking straight up at the night sky. She noticed with dazzled wonderment that the sky had cleared and that she could see the winking starlight of the Big Dipper hanging in space exactly where it should be, as well as a glittering array of six stars in the form of an isosceles triangle nearby. So perfect and beautiful, it was funny that she had never really noticed the stars before. She had a rudimentary knowledge of their composition and knew the location of some of the constellations from school, but she had never really *noticed* them before.

At that precise moment, before the next forward thrust of her head, Sherry wished upon a star. Her wish was that she would live through this so that she could learn what it was like to fall in love beneath the stars, to sit in a field under those tiny jewels with a man's strong, loving embrace wrapped around her. She looked at the stars, and she wished. With amazing alacrity, her vision began to surge forward, the stars blurring as if she were in a science fiction movie and had just made the jump to light speed.

The forward momentum blew a light breeze across her broken face, slightly chilling the warm, runny blood to a thick, tacky paste. Sherry closed her eyes in anticipation of the sudden stop her face would come to shortly.

And come it did. Sherry Dasher's face struck the hood of Ricardo's practically ancient 1976 Ford LTD for the third time. The hit caused further structural wreckage as well as intensified the already-considerable damage inflicted upon her once-beautiful features, the previously fair and unblemished skin blackened by contusions. On impact, a blood vessel ruptured in her left eye a centimeter from the iris, immediately causing her to lose peripheral vision on the left side of her body, an impairment that didn't register at the moment, though, because the rest of her vision was quickly fading away with her consciousness. There was an immense flair of pain in the misery her face had become when the impact grated all the broken bones together, the splinters creating a sound in her head like that of chalk drawn across concrete, and the fragments behind her upper lip separated from each other, forming a tear along the roof of her mouth and splitting her hard and soft palates almost in half. Her lower jaw—already floating loosely—was smashed upward, an audible click heard as her teeth unintentionally clamped together, causing her molars to bite the inside of both cheeks.

There was a fourth hit, but Sherry Dasher did not notice, having been rendered unconscious by the previous one.

After the final hit, Dedaker let go of the woman's hair, and she crumpled to the ground, the hand she had been using to look for a pen raining the contents of the handbag down on her.

Dedaker looked at her prone body. She had landed in a fetal position, with the remnants of her face covered by hair that stuck out in haphazard cowlicks, the patterns of which were caused by the way he had gripped her while incapacitating her.

Dedaker looked at her for a moment as she lay there. He watched as her breast rose and fell in an irregular breathing cycle which, although irregular, meant that she was still alive. He had never gone too far with one of his intended before, but he felt that one day he might.

Yes, one day he might.

He could see that clearly. It was just so easy to overpower the unsuspecting infidels. They were so far off the path they should be walking that they couldn't hear the approaching footsteps of change—the footsteps of the transcendentalist.

Through the infidel's ignorance, he could one day go too far. The power of change ran through him so strongly that he sometimes felt he did not have complete control over it. Those times were usually during the hysterical moments while subduing an infidel, the excitement causing him to lose his senses, causing him to lose control. Out of control was a state he regularly entered the moment he wrapped his fist around the neck of one of the devil's serpents. Once control was lost, Dedaker might push it too far and accidentally kill an infidel in cold blood. If a serpent were killed before she was transcended, it would make him a murderer.

That final thought struck him like a splash of water in the face, waking him up. Dedaker scanned the empty early-morning parking lot. No one else was in the area, just the woman and himself. But he didn't know how long it would remain that way; these other cars belonged to people who worked inside the serpent's lair, people who could come out at any time. There would be time for reflection later; this was the time to act quickly.

He strode the couple of steps to the hearse. Having unlocked the rear gate earlier when he'd taken the car out of the public storage garage, he pulled up on the handle, and the gate opened in two parts—the solid bottom door swinging outward, the glass top rising like a hatchback. When he had both parts of the door open wide, he went over to pick up the woman.

Bending, he shuffled her in such a way that he could wiggle his hands under her armpits. When in position, he wrapped his arms around her, clasping his hands across her breasts, and lifted. The contents of the handbag lying on top of her fell off and scattered around the area. Although she was—dare I say it—dead weight, she didn't weigh so much as to prove a burden for Dedaker. He was able to carry her, her feet dragging, across the small expanse of parking lot to the hearse. While he carried her, he did not look down at the bloody mess her face had become.

At the hearse, he sidestepped a little and placed her torso against the bumper. Holding her up with his right hand, he reached down and cradled her buttocks. In one full motion, he lifted and shoved forward at the same time. Her body slid along the small rollers built into the cargo area for the exact purpose that he had just used them—to slide a body into or out of the automobile.

Dedaker fastened two of the three seatbelts bolted to the car's floor across her body then slammed both parts of the door shut.

And just like that, the transcendentalist had caught an infidel.

Dedaker, feeling the need to hurry, rushed over to the spilled contents of the handbag. He gathered everything he could and stuffed it into the maw of the bag—keys, wallet, tampons, some makeup. He left the change on the ground.

When he thought he had everything, he quickly gave the area the once-over. Everything was to his satisfaction, except for the dents in the hood. And the blood. But there was nothing he could do about those. Once noticed, Dedaker knew something would be suspected, and what was suspected would be confirmed when the woman did not show up for work anymore. But he didn't see any need to fret, sure that there wasn't anything that could directly point anyone to him. And if he could get at least a day's head start to take care of the infidel he bagged tonight, everything else he had planned would fall into place anyway: he was almost ready to tip his hand at the airport, which would lead to the grand finale on Purser Street.

Dedaker jogged back to the hearse. The driver's side door was still ajar. He tossed the handbag in and got in after it.

3

$\mathcal{T}$here was a sense of falling.

She thought she must've been having one of those dreams, one in which she dreamed she was falling only to suddenly jar awake and find herself wrapped snuggly in her blankets, perfectly safe in her own bed.

She floated and dreamed and waited for the jarring that would bring an end to the falling and wake her up. With an intense burst of pain she had never experienced in a dream before, the jarring stop came. Instantly, she awoke. But she wasn't sure she wasn't still dreaming, not recognizing her surroundings. She wasn't lying in her bed, as she had expected. Instead, she was lying on her right side on a rough-hewn, nappy carpet the off-yellow mustard color of baby shit.

There didn't seem to be any furniture in the room, but she couldn't be sure, having woken up three feet from the wall to her right and being unable to see to the left at all. Her vision to the portside looked like the screen of a monitor with its horizontal control turned all the way to the opposite—there was a vivid picture on the right half and then absolutely nothing but blackness to the left.

And there was the pain. A lot of it.

When she landed and awoke on the carpet, she did so in such intense pain that she sucked in her breath, holding it With a deep, slow exhale through her mouth, she released the used air from her lungs. Once the old air was out, she tried to draw more in through her nose and found that she couldn't.

Oh my God, I can't breathe, her frightened mind alerted. Before she could reason it out on her own, her subconscious took over, breathing through her mouth for her. The breaths came in short gasps—in and out, in and out. She took sips of air rather than large gulps, hoping that it might hurt less by making as little movement as absolutely necessary. The air in the room was stale with a hint of copper, but it was the sweet air of life.

Now that she was breathing again, she decided it was time to take a physical examination of the rest of her body. The first step was to roll from her side to her back. Summoning up all her courage and using her arms as pistons, she pushed against the rug, feeling the paisley pattern beneath her palms. Since she pushed gently, the roll was controlled enough to allow her to ease over. When she came to a stop, she could see from where she had fallen. Directly above her was a square hole in the ceiling. Somewhere on the floor she was on, there was a light burning, but up through the hole she could see nothing but darkness. She didn't know what was up there or why she had been up there, but she was sure it was through that hole that she had gotten down here.

Must have not seen it in the dark.

But that didn't seem quite right to her. If she had been awake and moving and then fell through a hole, she'd probably be able to at least remember the moments before the fall. She couldn't remember any of it, making her positive that something else had happened. Just what was anybody's guess.

What she was sure of was that her head was splitting, and along with her sight problem, her face didn't feel right on her skull, as if it didn't quite fit anymore. Sherry closed her eyes and began an assessment of her body, starting with her feet. She didn't feel any pain in them, even though she could distantly remember that they had been aching her before . . . this.

When was that? Last night? Last week? Last YEAR? She didn't know, but in light of everything else, they felt all right now, snug in a pair of sneakers and dry. She moved them side to side, and they complied without any pain.

Nope, definitely didn't fall, she thought.

Continuing up her legs and over her groin, she found everything to be where it should. She lifted her hands, opening and closing the fingers. Sherry rolled her shoulders; nothing wrong there. She took her hands and felt along her torso, lifting up her shirt, pressing against her belly. A sheen of sweat covered it, but it was intact, the organs beneath free of pain. Evaluation to the moment: nothing broken, nothing bleeding.

Sherry found no problems until she got to her neck. At first, she tried to turn her head and found that she couldn't move it. She tried twice, once left and once right. With each movement, pain radiated up and down the length of her neck. Her hands gingerly caressed the sides as though giving herself a message. She could feel tenderness and two little knots at the base where her neck met her shoulders. The knots were in her muscles, indicating neck strain.

She swallowed and it hurt her throat. For one fleeting moment, as the parts of her body were reporting positive results, she had begun to think that her situation wasn't as bad as it seemed. Now that she had felt her neck, she knew that it was bad. Very bad.

Sherry was scared to feel her face, scared of what she would find.

She swallowed again even though it hurt to do so because she needed to do something to steel her nerves enough to touch her face. With her eyes still closed, Sherry very slowly brought her hands up.

Using just her fingertips, she gently traced the contours.

She thought that it would be bad, but just how bad she could never have imagined.

Her fingers first traced along her jaw, which was out of line and tilted to the right. By the way it hung, she knew it would list from side to side if she tried to stand up, even though standing up was the farthest thing from her mind at the moment.

As she continued upward, her fingertips began to brush flakes off her face. They were crusty and easily peeled from her skin to seesaw down to the nap of the rug. From the way they put up no resistance to her fleeting touch, she knew that it wasn't her skin flaking off but some other dried substance, most likely blood.

Then she got to the center of her face, where her petite nose should have been. A centimeter or two farther, she found the crumbled cartilage that used to be the slender bridge.

Her fingers grazed the landscape like a blind person trying to visualize her beauty. Instead of finding beauty, Sherry discovered the unintelligible lumpy mass that was her mangled face. She was surprised that there was no pain there, at what was essentially ground zero, just raw distant numbness; all of the pain she felt was deep within her head, deep within her mind.

As Sherry felt the remnants of her face, two burning tears squirted from the corners of her closed eyes, eyes she squinted tighter and tighter in grief and fear. A low moan crossed over the broken stumps of her teeth, filling the empty room around her.

Finished with her assessment, Sherry gently covered the horror her face had become with both her hands. Exploring the disaster had sparked the memory of the parking lot. There had been a man who she'd thought was a nice guy but apparently wasn't. She had been talking to him, and then he hurt her. He must have beat her unconscious then brought her here.

Sherry was in big trouble, and she knew it.

Lying on the floor of Dedaker's lower duplex apartment, hiding behind the protective covering of her hands, Sherry began to sob.

4

$\mathcal{D}$edaker tugged on the rope to make sure it was fastened tightly around the base of the toilet. When he was satisfied with its fastidiousness, he stood, hands on hips, staring at the soiled coil of rope lying on the tiled floor of his powder room. He was wondering why he hadn't tied the rope before he went out into the night. He had known he would obtain an infidel this night, and yet he hadn't been prepared. Dedaker had always adhered to strict guidelines before this, never missing a step. The unprepared man made mistakes. And yet, here he was, attending to a last-minute detail while the woman was downstairs (*Downstairs right! If there were stairs, he wouldn't even* need *the rope he'd forgotten*) in the apartment below, free to roam about.

That was an issue.

His tools were downstairs. And his tools had sharp edges. What if she had gotten to them while he was wasting time with the rope? He could unsuspectingly descend and not find the docile snake he had put in his garden but rather an asp with many sharp teeth poised to bite and inject its evil venom into his soul. Going down to find such teeth would be like descending into a nest of vipers.

Then there was the window.

Dedaker had taken many precautions in securing the lower apartment, but he had never completely secured the front window, the one that looked out on the street. That window was a weakness, an Achilles heel, but one he could not work—or live sanely—without.

He had boarded up all the other windows, then, after painting the boards black, he hung very thick, deep blue velvet drapes. Both the drapes and the boards kept the sun out and the sound in. He had been extremely thorough, but he just could not bring himself to board up that final window, else he'd feel trapped in. There were some days he couldn't even go into the lower duplex for this very reason. Down there he could feel the still air and the heat pressing against his skin. He knew it wasn't physically possible, but sometimes he could feel the walls of the duplex getting closer, closing in.

Dedaker supposed he had a touch of claustrophobia. If it were true, he didn't care.

Only because of that one unsecured window.

He needed that window, needed to see it. He needed to feel the perfect smoothness of the glass, to open it from time to time. He needed to see the sunlight shining on the floor, creating colorful prisms in the clear, oily plastic of the tarp. He needed to feel the occasional puff of air blow across his naked chest. He needed his window for all of these reasons.

Then, of course, there were the ghosts.

Michael was very happy in the work God had chosen for him. But sometimes—usually after a long lull in between doing God's work—he thought he could hear things down there. Noises, movements Voices. He would be in the upper apartment, sitting on the couch, eating at the dinner table, or trying to sleep, and he would hear things below him, down there. Things would fall over or bang. Boards would creak as if trod upon. There would be whispering; *their* whispers, the women whose lives he had taken in the apartment below. It was rare for him to hear them because they were soft, almost like breezes blowing through the eaves, but when he did, he listened, fascinated by them, wanting to know what they were saying. The whispers frightened him.

Who were they talking to?

What if it was God they were talking to? What if God was here in his house, talking to those women? What if their souls had to remain where they had died to await the trump of judgment? What if they had strayed so far from the path that even he, Michael Dedaker, hadn't been able to help them, their eternal salvation denied, and it wasn't God they were whispering to but the *other one*?

Those thoughts scared him, and for that he had his window. He needed to know that he would have a way out of the apartment if the ghosts ever started speaking while he was down there, working or not.

Dedaker heard a murmuring sound coming from below. It locked him in place, scared that he had conjured the voices by merely thinking about them. A cold shiver ran his spine and chattered his teeth. He stood in the second-floor powder room, holding the rope and straining to listen, to hear what they were saying.

The sound was low and rhythmic, unlike the sounds he normally heard. He recognized this sound. Not the quiet murmuring of ghosts talking but water dribbling over pebbles—the sound of crying. The woman was awake. He had work to do.

With that, he stripped off his clothes, leaving them lying on the powder room floor. Stark naked, he shouldered the coil of rope anchored to the base of the toilet.

5

*S*herry's hands were still over her eyes when she heard the footsteps above. Immediately, ice-cold fear overtook tearful sorrow. She stopped crying, ceasing to be concerned about the ruins of her face, and instead thinking about survival.

Spreading her fingers wide as if playing peekaboo with a child, she looked up at the hole. She had heard the footsteps approach and knew that someone was standing just above her. She knew it was probably her assailant, but hope being the ever-elusive bitch that she was, Sherry prayed that there might be a slim chance it was someone who would help her.

Odds warred within her. Should she call out, hoping it was a Samaritan, or should she remain silent, crossing her fingers that the person up there had other things to do before coming down, giving her time to think of something?

After a quick moment, Sherry decided that whomever fate had put in this house with her, that person had already heard her crying in the quite stillness and was now alerted to her wakefulness, leaving no reason to play possum. Sherry called for help, the words formed by her devastated mouth, heartbreaking to her ears.

"Who's there?" was what she asked. Being unable to move her jaw or use her tongue to form the words because of the split in the roof of her mouth, it came out sounding mushy and toneless, but surprisingly articulate. At least it sounded articulate to her. Then, "Help me."

At the end of *me*, her voice cracked from the strain of talking through her ailing throat. The crack tickled the top of her esophagus, cascading into a choking, coughing fit that produced the worst pain Sherry had ever experienced in her life, which, on this night, was saying a lot. She coughed and coughed for what seemed like forever, the force of which caused her abdomen to contract, making her double over and sit halfway up. The sit-up strained her neck again; the coughs ripped her throat raw. With each hack, blood spurted from her mouth and what was left of her nose, her jaw flapped excruciatingly with every motion.

Finally, mercifully, the coughing ended. Sherry did not as much lay back as fall back to the carpet.

Two tiny, simple sentences, four words in total; it was pathetic, but it was all she had—the pain from coughing had silenced her. Sherry couldn't summon up any more energy or courage to speak through her useless mouth again. Bathed in sweat, all she could do was stare at the dark square above her and wait for whatever was to come.

What came was a rope.

It tumbled down out of the darkness directly above her. She watched as the rope uncoiled its length, anticipating the pain that would flair in her face when it struck her. But the pain never came. The rope had stretched to its full length, ending a scant three inches above her. She looked at the tiny fibers in the weave, not believing her good luck. It *was* a Samaritan up there. He had heard her crying and had gotten a rope ready to pull her up. Thoughts of safety (and a much-needed hospital visit) ran through her mind until she saw the head that emerged from the darkness above, a head that belonged to the guy from the parking lot.

With the darkness surrounding him, as well as the ambient lighting from the floor she was on, the man looked like the most frighteningly kitschy image ever to be embossed on a black-light velvet poster.

He smiled at her.

Sherry would have screamed, if she could've.

6

*W*ith quick, hand-over-hand motions, the man had climbed down and was now straddling her prone body, his face right up to hers. When he spoke, she felt the breath of each word. For some reason she couldn't fathom, she wondered how his breath would smell. She would know if she still had the capability to smell, but it had been diminished when he broke her nose. The fact that he was naked chilled her to the bone.

"If you cooperate, I promise to make this as quick as possible If you choose to fight, I will have to hurt you some more. Do you understand?"

"Why are you doing this?" she managed to ask. It came out sounding more like *wire ewe dooig iss?* She knew she was risking another round of coughing fits by attempting to talk, but she had to know.

"I'm doing this for a very important reason. It's a reason you wouldn't understand at the moment and couldn't comprehend through your pain, but believe me, what I'm doing, I'm doing for you."

"For me?" Sherry wasn't sure she understood what he said. *Why would he be doing this for me? I didn't ask for this. I don't want to be hurt like this. Nobody in their right mind would.* And there it was, all the answer she needed: nobody in their right mind would be doing this.

"Yes, for you," he said. "One day, in the next life, you might thank me for my sacrifice."

"Oh please, let me go."

"I would if I could, but you chose your path in life, and now you must walk it."

Tears had started to fall from the corners of her eyes again. "Fuck you," she slurred as vehemently as she could.

Michael Dedaker stood up, grabbed Sherry Dasher around the ankles, and dragged her down a hall toward the front room of the apartment. As she slid across the carpet, her shirt pulled up, exposing her back to rug burn from the hard-napped paisleys.

Sherry had believed him when he said he would continue to hurt her if she resisted, but what was she supposed to do, just let him rape and kill her without putting up a fight?

For the first few feet, she let herself be dragged, keeping her good eye fixed firmly on her assailant, watching and waiting for an opportunity. As they approached a corner that led to an entranceway with no door, he turned his head to guide their way. She made her move.

With the grace of a dancer, albeit a self-taught one, Sherry pirouetted. She flipped onto her belly—causing her ankles to cross in his hands—and retracted her legs at the same time. Amazingly, her feet came free. Catching him off balance, she had managed to twist from his grasp. When her legs hit the floor, she pushed herself up onto all fours and began clawing at the carpet to expedite her effort. She had no idea what the next move was or how she would escape him, but she had to try something.

With the quickness of a cat, Dedaker was standing in front of Sherry, blocking her forward progress, a contrast of control and vulnerable nakedness.

Still crying, she veered to the left to go around him. Dedaker took the opportunity to kick her with the arch of his instep in her unguarded ribcage. With a whimper, Sherry collapsed to the floor, her drive for the great escape snuffed.

"Did you think I was kidding?" he asked the crying woman on the floor as he kicked her again and yet again.

There was no response, but he hadn't expected one. He circled her and roughly took up her feet again. With his hands firmly clamped around her ankles, they resumed their journey into the front room. This time, being dragged on her belly, Sherry did not resist.

From her inverted position, she couldn't see where they were going, but she knew they had arrived when they crossed over a threshold, the baby-shit-colored rug ended, and a clear plastic tarp began. One of the buttons on her shirt caught in the gold-plated strip of tin holding down the edge of the rug and popped off.

Beneath the tarp she could see a parquet hardwood floor. This new room was noticeably cooler than the other, with the absence of the rug. But that didn't matter. What mattered was the tarp. Sherry could think of only one good reason to have an entire room covered with a tarp—to protect it from spilled liquids. And she didn't think it was paint or iced tea her assailant was worried about.

Sherry thought it was blood.

Specifically, her blood.

In a tear-soaked voice, she tried to beg for mercy. "Oh please, oh please, don't hurt me." This time her words were pure gibberish, but she continued anyway. "I'll give you anything you want. I've saved a lot of money. I'll give it to you, just please don't hurt me anymore."

Dedaker either didn't hear, didn't understand, or didn't care. He continued dragging her until they were in the middle of the room, where he stopped beside a podium. He reached into the podium and withdrew a pair of scissors. Not the ordinary type of scissors found in a household but a pair specifically bent where the blade met the handle. Sherry knew what scissors like those were used for from watching medical dramas on TV. They were used to cut the clothes off trauma victims, the bend so that the patient wasn't punctured while doing so.

Sherry watched him come toward her with the scissors but was too physically broken to do anything about it. Still Sherry still lying on her belly, he cut off her clothes. Beginning at the cuff of her right pants leg, he effortlessly ran the scissors up until they cut through the waistband. Then he did the left. She was not wearing panties, the thong she had worn onstage earlier sitting on the bottom shelf of her locker at the Hippy Hippy Shake.

Her shirt was still bunched up at her chest. He grabbed it all at once and cut it in half in one quick snip.

The scissors went back into the podium, and out came another length of the same rope currently hanging down from the upper floor with its mocking promise of salvation. She watched as he took it down between her legs and, after roughly pulling off her sneakers and socks together in one hooked finger motion, tied some kind of slipknot laxly around her ankles.

With the casual toss of a shortstop flipping the ball to second for the force-out, Dedaker looped the free end of the rope over a pipe that spanned the entire width of the room, near the ceiling.

Winding the dangling end tightly around his fist, he stepped backward and hauled Sherry Dasher up to her final destination, the knot tightening as she went.

7

Exactly one week and one day after she was reported missing, Sherry Dasher was found.

A man by the name of Art Fleuridor was replacing light bulbs at the southern end of runway two of the Northern Philadelphia Airport when he had to take a piss.

The NPHIA was rated for planes as large as 707s but was mostly a small-craft airport that handled private jets and helicopters. It had two runways, the first running east to west, the second north and south. Along with one terminal to service both tarmacs, there was a flight training school and a trendy restaurant/club on the grounds. The NPHIA, while much smaller than an international airport, was of a higher scale than a one-runway mom-and-pop.

The light towers needing Art's attention this morning were called RILs. The runway independent lights were a single line of five white strobes that led to the beginning edge of each runway tarmac, and the ocher-colored ground lights that outlined them. Due to the September 11 incidents—and the stepped-up precautions that followed—security patrolled the entire grounds every four hours or so, reporting any problems they found on forms called NavAids. RILs were directional lighting, and problems dealing with such were directed to the electricians in the maintenance department. The NavAid that Art had stuffed in his breast pocket, written up by the security patrol, stated that all five of the RILs on runway two were out. A quick check in the 13-2 room (which stood for 13,200 volts) at the electrical panel showed that the circuit breakers had not been tripped—the RILs were receiving juice. Art expected a bigger problem lying in wait for him, but he took five bulbs from the maintenance storeroom to rule out the simplest solution first, dead bulbs, before heading out into the field.

The RILs reported malfunctioning were over a half a mile from the communications tower. Art had driven the maintenance rover (which was actually a roofless golf cart with NPHIA MAINTENANCE stenciled on its side) out along runway two until the cement stopped and the grass started. At 6:50 a.m., with the sun finally high enough to see by, he pulled the rover off to the side and walked the rest of the way to the closest tower needing repair.

The first light tower—the farthest one from where the runway started—was located across approximately forty yards of mown lawn from a Cyclone fence which surrounded the perimeter of the airport. Beyond the fence was a dense thatch of woods. In this neighborhood, the fence was more to keep the deer population off the runways than hooligans.

Normally, RILs were located on the ground, as they were on runway one. But out here, just after the leading edge of the runway surface itself, the ground began to slope downward as it headed toward a small creek located somewhere in the woods on the other side of the fence, making it necessary to elevate the lights so they could form a flat, straight line of illumination for inbound planes. For higher work, the maintenance crew had a cherry picker, but these towers only stood eight feet in the air and had rungs that ran to the top. Art gripped the first rung and began ascending with the replacement halogen held tight under his arm. At the top, the tower's steel post was capped off, creating a flat surface that he used to rest the bulb on while he went to work unscrewing the old one.

That's odd, he thought. The bulb currently in the socket had not blown out; it had been shattered. Art glanced over to the next tower from this higher vantage point. It too looked as though it had been smashed. And the one beyond that. *What the hell was going on here?*

There could only be one explanation—someone had deliberately broken the lights. *Why would anyone want to do that? Maybe the hooligans* were *starting to spread this far north of the city. Ah, well, at least it's a problem I can fix.* The other possibility was something he didn't want to consider, some sort of first-stage terrorist activity.

Once the broken bulb was out, he swapped it with the new one. Art repeated the process four more times until he had replaced all the damaged bulbs. At the top of the fifth and final tower, with the last shattered bulb sitting on the flat surface that served as an impromptu work table, Art reached into his back pocket and pulled out a walkie-talkie.

The handheld radio was a black Motorola, with the identification number M-3 etched into its casing in a squiggly-handed script. The M-3 indicated that it was the third of six units belonging to the airport maintenance department. Art's supervisor, Steven Mellot, routinely warned Art about carrying the radio around in his back pocket. Just this morning, as Art took the unit out of the charger, Mel had said something about it.

"One day you're going to sit on that damned nickel-cadmium battery and give yourself a jolt right in the ass," Mel had said.

"You know what, it still won't be as strong as this shitty coffee you make," Art fired back, taking a sip of the dark, steaming brew from the same unwashed mug he used every day.

"Yeah, yeah, it's all fun and games until they have to put a pacemaker in your chest to regulate your heartbeat. We'll see who's laughing when you're a piece of fried chicken."

Without another word, Art took the radio and stuffed it into his back pocket, then left the warehouse on his way to see about the RILs.

Holding the radio in his hand now, Art smiled at Mel's admonishment. He knew the boss meant well, but who gave a fuck. Art was sixty-one, eleven months away from retiring and moving to the warmer climates of Georgia where his only daughter was a newspaper columnist. He had worked at this airport for twenty-five years, having carried a radio in his pocket for every damn one of them, and never once got a shock.

Art used his thumb to key the radio's mike. "Maintenance to Comm Tower," he said, after it squawked.

"Comm Tower, go ahead Maintenance," replied a professional female voice which Art recognized as belonging to Jamie Culver, a cute young thing who recently graduated to become an air traffic controller. She was from Washington—State, not DC—and wished to return home when a job opened up. In the modern computer age quickly making dinosaurs out of blue-collar workers, you had to go where the jobs were or, in Jamie's case, where you were assigned.

"Morning, Jamie."

"Morning, Art. What can I do for you this early?" There was a static click before her voice died out.

"Just replaced some bulbs on the strobes out on two and need you to light her up for me so I can make sure they're working." The RILs at the Northern Philadelphia Airport were manually run by the Comm Tower, only being turned on when a plane was landing or taking off. The rest of the time, they were kept in a standby mode, keeping the bulbs dark, but holding the electricity right on the cusp of flowing just in case an emergency should arise and the lights were needed quickly.

"Roger. Stand by."

A half mile away from where Art was hovering eight feet in the air, Jamie Culver flipped a switch, and the runway independent lights came to life.

Art could feel the electricity vibrating through the steel pole of the tower. When the lights came on—including all the bulbs he had just changed—he could hear the hum of the electricity flowing into them with each strobe. It sounded like a thousand angry bees swarming around a hive, or a mob scene at an electrocution.

"Okay, Jamie, you can shut 'er down now. All the lights on this approach are in operational order," he said into the radio.

"Roger. Out."

A second later, the bulbs were dark again, the vibrating hum gone.

Now a jolt of that would turn you into fried chicken, but it still would be no match for that coffee. That was a pretty good one. He would have to remember it for when he got back to the shop. Mel's wasn't the best-tasting cup of java in the world, being strong and tart with a dash of salt in it, but fun-poking aside, Art really didn't mind because it was a good kick-start first thing in the morning. Even at sixty-one, he still had trouble shaking off the cobwebs. That's where Mel's coffee came in.

The only problem was that it ran right through him. As a matter of fact, he had to take a squirt right now. Art climbed back down, carrying his radio and the final dead bulb with its broken glass. *What the hell had happened to them?* With all five bulbs found broken at the same time, there was only one answer: someone had deliberately done it. But why?

Since he was outdoors and could still remember growing up on his father's farm in Virginia, Art decided that he'd relieve himself over by the woods rather than wait till he got all the way back to the shop.

He walked over to the rover and sat the dead bulb with the rest of them in a wire-frame basket attached to the back of the cart, then he walked the forty yards to the fence line where he planned to stand and urinate into the trees. If he had gone to his right instead of his left, he would've found a hole large enough for a man to walk through cut into the fencing. But he didn't. He went left.

At the fence he was ready to take care of business.

Holding onto the fence with the same hand that held the radio, he undid his belt, lowered his pants slightly, and fired off into the woods.

When empty, he went to hitch his pants back up, the act of which required the use of both hands. Art let go of the fence only to watch as the antenna of the radio got caught in one of the diamond-shaped holes.

With the reflexes of a man much younger than sixty-one, he tried to grab the radio before it hit the ground and possibly damaged one of the transmitting crystals inside.

Instead of catching it clean, he bobbled it right through the fence hole, where it came to a rest on the other side, six feet from where he stood.

"Son of a bitch," he said to the offending radio sitting in the rough grass, the scrawling designation M-3 below the speaker holes condescendingly glaring up at him. In retrospect, he'd rather have been caught bare-assed than with his proverbial pants down. That he could've explained; how was he going to explain this?

The only way to explain it was to not explain it. He would have to get the radio back, right now, before someone tried to contact him on it.

He finished fastening his pants as he gauged the height of the fence.

As he saw it, there were two options. One was to take the rover all the way back to the entrance of the airport and drive it all the way around to the beginning of the woods on the other side. From there he would have to eyeball the location of the radio, which wouldn't be too hard because he could use the light towers for markers. Then he would have to trek through the trees, with the underbrush poking and prodding him, to retrieve it. Time consuming, but possible; the only drawback being that in order to get to the airport entrance, he would have to drive right by the shop, keeping his fingers crossed that Mel wasn't looking out his window at the exact moment he drove the golf cart by. The chances of that were slim to none, since Mel's desk sat facing the window.

That left the other option: climbing the fence.

At least there's no barbed wire. Or electricity. Art had only been at work for an hour, and he had already thought about being electrocuted three times. What a day.

With a sigh, he began climbing.

* * *

Jamie Culver was seated in a swivel chair at her console when the radio squawked in her ear. She'd been filling in times on her flight log when suddenly a panicked voice transmitted over the headset.

"OHMYGOD! OHMYGOD! OHMYGOD!" the voice yelled over and over again in a harried state, splicing the words together.

"This is the Comm Tower. Please identify yourself," she replied, as trained.

"Jamie . . . Jamie, it's Art."

"Art? Calm down. What's wrong, Art? Art?" Jamie, like all ATCs, had been schooled to remain calm during a crisis. In her business, a state of emergency was intolerable. Thousands of lives were literally up in the air at any given time, all of them depending on her to be able to keep her head when the shit storm flew.

There was no response from Art. Still using the same calm tone, she tried again. "Art, what's wrong?" Nothing but the slight hissing sound of unused airwaves. "Art, are you there? *Art?*"

When there was still no response, Jamie adjusted the numbers on the repeater to the frequency for the maintenance department.

"Comm Tower to Maintenance," she said.

"Maintenance, go ahead."

"Mel, is Art there?"

"No, he's out in the field."

"I've just received an abnormal transmission from him. I think he might be in trouble. Did he contact you?"

"After the conversation he had with you about the lights being fixed on two, I haven't heard from him. But I stepped away from the desk for a minute."

"Roger that. I think you better send someone out to see if he—" Jamie's transmission was cut off as Art's voice broke in.

"Jamie? Jamie?" He sounded out of breath, like he'd been running. "There are a lot of them . . . Can't tell how many . . ." There was a sound of retching, followed by a hiss of dead air.

"A lot of what, Art?"

Nothing.

"Art?"

She toggled the radio frequency switch again.

"Mel, you there?"

"Yeah."

"There's definitely something wrong. He's panicking out there. I don't know if he's hurt or not, but it sounded like he threw up," she said. They were both thinking about the old-timer's ticker.

"I heard, Jamie, thanks. I've already sent a couple of guys out to the runway. I'm heading out there now myself."

"Roger that. I'll notify security." She tuned to another frequency from memory. "Comm Tower to Security," she said.

"Security, proceed Tower."

"We may have a problem out on runway two. Something happened to a maintenance employee. Don't know if he's sick or what." As an afterthought, "He's older."

"Okay. We're on it."

Just then, Art was back. "I can't tell how many there are . . . Could be half a dozen . . . They're all together in one pile. It's the worst thing I've ever seen. The smell is horrible."

"Art, I've notified security. Mel's coming your way with some guys too."

"Good, Jamie. You'd better call the police too."

"Art, what's out there?"

"People."

"People? What do they want?"

"They don't want anything. They're all dead."

8

The police couldn't tell how many there were, either.

"Hoover, over here," Captain Korzenowski said.

Detective John Hoover had just arrived on the scene. He lifted the yellow caution tape and bent under it to enter the marked-off circle. He was glad to see that the first officer had taped off the crime scene properly, even one this deep in the woods. It was a good tape job too; from where Hoover stood, he couldn't even see the far side of the circle.

It hadn't been hard to find the scene in the woods. The NPHIA was located near an industrial park, and there was a feeder road adjacent to both the airport and the warehouses. As soon as Hoover turned onto the feeder, he could see the flashing reds and blues. Along with the patrol cars and the unmarked cars, there were four orange GMC Suburbans with their own flashing lights (yellow) and AIRPORT SECURITY painted across the doors. There were also three golf carts.

If the traffic jam wasn't a sure sign of police activity, then the uniformed officer stationed at the precipice of the woods (to redirect the press and keep them out from under the cops' feet and off the crime scene) was a definite indicator.

Hoover had gotten out of his personal car and walked toward the woods. The uniform did not stop him. The man knew him on sight, and Hoover had his badge and ID clipped to his brown sport coat anyway.

Hoover did not need to ask which way into the woods the scene was, there being a fresh path trampled into the grass by a hundred flat feet to lead him, and he could easily follow the sounds of the commotion.

"It's right over this way," Captain Korzenowski said, waving him over with his left hand while pointing to the location of the bodies with his right, the pose making Korzenowski look like a crossing guard.

The grass was still damp with dew, and Hoover's shoes were getting wet. He hoped it wouldn't soak through to dampen his socks. Any didn't mind any other article of clothing, but he hated when his socks got wet—the feeling was uncomfortable, and the toes became disgustingly pale and puckered with wrinkles. He sighed and asked, "What do we have?"

"What do you know?"

"Not much. Was on my way to the city to report for duty when a text message scrawled over the cell phone. I called in and was told to respond here for 'multiple 5292s.'"

In the fifties, a code system was instituted for all police activity in the city. This code system, a form of radio shorthand, was put into use to cut down on the amount of radio traffic by making conversations as succinct as humanly possible. It was also intended to cut down on interference from the press or the public in a time when it became fashionable to have a police scanner in the home. But it wasn't long before the meaning of the codes became public knowledge, rendering the codes passé.

So slowly, ever so slowly, the codes began fading out of existence as new generations of recruits weren't made to strictly adhere to their use. But even today, some of the old code numbers have survived and were still viable, one of them being 5292—dead bodies found.

Korzenowski was Hoover's captain out of the homicide division. In the Municipal County of Philadelphia, there were six independent detective divisions, other than homicide, that served the twenty-three local police districts. The divisions—separated geographically and named for their locations—were Northeast, Northwest, West, Central, South, and East. Each detective division responded to crime scenes within its jurisdiction, but once it had been determined that wrongful death had occurred, the case got turned over to homicide.

For the entire city of Philadelphia—a city of roughly 1.6 million people and 129 or so square miles—there was but one homicide division to investigate all suspicious deaths. The homicide dicks worked out of police headquarters at Eighth and Race streets, a building more commonly referred to as the Roundhouse because of its architectural shape. Constructed in the form of two adjoining circles, forming a close approximation of a figure eight, every office and hallway within the building had walls that were curved. The sixty or so detectives working in the homicide division hailed from the second floor, room 104.

Between Hoover and Korzenowski in the chain of command were two sergeants and a lieutenant; the fact that the captain was on the scene indicated that whatever was in the woods was serious.

"Multiple is an understatement," said Korzenowski.

"How many are there?"

"Don't know, can't tell."

"Guess."

"More than six, less than twelve."

Hoover whistled. Korzenowski was an experienced officer and had a good eye for crime scenes; if he said he couldn't tell how many bodies there were, then there was a sound reason why he couldn't. Hoover didn't push the issue as he would see the bodies for himself any second now. Currently, Hoover and Korzenowski, on their way to the epicenter, were gently shoving through plain-clothed and uniformed officers When they pushed past the last man, Hoover caught his first glimpse of the bodies.

"Jesus Christ," he said before covering his mouth with his hand.

In the middle of the short expanse of woods stretching approximately equidistant from both the feeder road and the perimeter of the Northern Philadelphia Airport was a pile of human carnage so grisly Hoover had never seen anything like it before in his eighteen years on the force.

In a thick growth of spring grass surrounded by a small ring of trees lay the decaying remains of several human bodies in varying states of decomposition, the pattern of which seemed to be the most recent on top and descending down the timeline from there.

All of the bodies were naked.

The one on top, Hoover could tell on sight, and the two directly beneath it were female. He had no way of knowing what the other ones were, their sexes so far gone they would have to wait for the pathology report; or at the very least, for the medical examiner to reach into the pile and pull them apart enough that some distinguishable traits could be identified.

The woman on top had been a slender brunette, the other two recognizable females both blonds. There were other tufts of hair visible to the eye—clumps of dark, light, and red strewn among the flesh and bones—but Hoover couldn't tell what hair went with which body, the effects of the weather having settled them so much that he couldn't see where one ended and the other began. Protruding from the pile were arms and legs, hands and feet, heads and chests; none of it an easy sight to look at, but the hardest were the skins.

The skins were a mottled, rainbow hue of rotting colors.

The shade of flesh on the uppermost body was that of a recently deceased female Caucasian—pale and dead, but retaining a slight touch of pink. Adipocere—the slick, greasy sheen that forms on the skin of a body after the fat has begun to hydrogenate into fatty acids from being left exposed to moisture in the air—had only just started to develop. From there down the skin rot darkened. It went from pale to ash, from ash to gray, from gray to black, and from black to the mossy green of growing mold.

Mother Nature had had her way with the exposed flesh of the bodies, some she froze until the skin had cracked and split, some she baked in the heat of summer until they simmered and then cured into parchment. All had been dampened with moisture from rain or snow or both, sometimes enough to cause the skin to slide off the body, leaving denuded bone in the wake.

Festered with maggots and flies, the odor was unbelievably fetid, the gaseous stink that arose that of the putrid funk of spoiled meat.

Finally Hoover had to look away. Korzenowski had been right. The number of corpses was undeterminable.

*   *   *

The hierarchy on the scene always went like this:

The call came into 911, police radio. They then dispatched a district squad car to investigate and ascertain if the call was real. If the call was founded and determined to be legit, the first officer's job was to protect life, property, and then the scene in that order. On a big-enough crime, the officer radioed in, and an immediate supervisor, the district commander, responded. The DC would either be a captain, a lieutenant, or a sergeant, depending on who was working what swing shift at the time of the call. The DC would then proceed to notify the appropriate geographical detective division, in this case the Northeast dicks If the nature of the crime involved dead bodies, the DC would also notify homicide and the ME's office. Once the ME declared the body (or bodies) dead of misadventure, the DC and the detectives dropped the whole investigation into the hands of homicide.

The tenth district commander who responded to the crime scene in the woods was a lieutenant, a big, beefy Italian named Speziale. "Looks like you guys got yourselves a high-priority case here, huh fellas?" Speziale said to Korzenowski and Hoover.

"Oh, you're a fucking ME now, Speziale?" asked Korzenowski.

Speziale shook his large, shaggy head to indicate that, alas, he was not, but he did have a huge, toothy grin on his face. "No, but I like the way that sounds—ME Spez-i-al-e. It's kind of got a ring to it, don't'cha think? Either way, this here," he casually gestured to the bodies, "looks like a homicide to me. Get it? Me. M-E. Ha."

Speziale was a guy who liked to break your balls, but he was a good cop—even if he did wear black sneakers and a pink shirt under his brown suit. If you could overlook the fashion impairment (what was a man supposed to do, raising four kids on a cop's salary?) underneath was a man you could trust. A man who kept his word, as well as his mouth shut. Korzenowski originally broke in among the ranks of the tenth, under Speziale. They were old-time friends and they bantered like it. Hoover stood off to the side, watching their vaudeville routine.

"Homicide? How the fuck you figure that?" Korzenowski asked in an imitation startled voice.

Speziale threw a thick arm over the captain's shoulder, as if he were about to impart some great wisdom on him. "Well, you see, there's a bunch of dead people over there."

"Who told you they were dead?"

"Hypothesis."

"*Hypothesis?* An educated guess? From you?"

"You don't have to have an education to guess that those people are dead, just a nose." Speziale drew a deep breath into his lungs.

When he inhaled though his nostrils, the hairs of his salt-and-pepper mustache ruffled in the breeze. "You smell that, Captain? That is the sweet smell of pine cones and homicides."

"There you go, throwing the H word around again. So there are a few dead people; what makes you think they were killed?"

"Oh, I don't know. Maybe it's the fact that I've never seen a suicide that resulted in a dozen corpses."

"Really? Maybe they were a cult who decided to off themselves, like that one in California with the Kool-Aid."

"Okay, that's a point for your side. But why would members of a cult kill themselves one by one over a *loooong* span of time, Korzenowski? Clearly, even an ignoramus like you can see from the different states of decay that these people didn't all die at the same time, am I right?" Speziale was stroking his mustache as if he had just connected with a solid one-two to the head.

"Who the fuck knows what these sick bastards think? Maybe it was some sorta ritual they performed every three, four months. Seasonally, you know, for the trees or some shit."

Speziale was nodding his head in understanding. "You might be onto something there, Korzenowski." The literal translation of that meant Speziale was impressed with Korzenowski's take of the scene. The captain had come up with a plausible scenario to account for the absurdity of these being time-delayed deaths that Speziale hadn't thought of, and Speziale was giving the other man a professional compliment the only way he knew how.

Speziale looked hard at the bodies with narrowed eyes. Finally, he said, "I don't think so. The bruises on the face, as well as the number of cuts and the pattern of the locations, indicate to me that the woman on top was murdered. If it was a sacrifice for the trees, then someone else sacrificed her."

"I agree," said Korzenowski. "What we have here are homicides." And the two men shook hands smiling. "How the hell you been, Loot?"

"Good, good. I see you did well for yourself. Captain of homicide," he said, making it sound like a comic book superhero. "Who would've thought that an officer I had to wake up twice, three times a night on last out would ever amount to anything?"

"I learned from the best. Damn, what's it been about nine years since I left the Tenth?"

"Yeah. I read about your promotion, but you haven't kept in touch. No calls, no Christmas cards, nothing," Speziale said, bent right into Korzenowski's face, the bristles of his upper lip nearly brushing the captain's cheek.

"Didn't think I had to. You used to run a safe district, not many stiffs turning up. What were you doing, saving them all up to drop on us at once?"

"You're a cocksucker, Korzenowski."

"Best you've ever had."

At that, both men burst into laughter. An outsider watching two men have a jovial conversation over the dead might not understand how they could be so nonchalant. But then, an outsider wasn't a cop. In the line of duty, death was just another fact—desensitization set in minutes out of the Academy.

Korzenowski turned to Hoover. "Salvatore Speziale, meet John Hoover. Hoover's going to be the lead on this case." Hoover shook hands with Speziale, the lieutenant's gigantic paw engulfing his in a tight grip. They pumped twice, then let go.

"How you doing, huh?" Speziale asked in a heavy South Philadelphian dialect.

Hoover nodded his status quo. As of that handshake, he had still been doing fine. That was all about to change in a hurry.

"You got anything for him to start with?" Korzenowski asked.

"Nothing but what you see here. We've only been on location what, twenty, thirty minutes, notified the examiner's office as soon as we saw the mess. But you can see for yourself that the ME is just now getting around to poking through the pile. After he's done, it's all yours."

"You're so nice to me, it's a wonder I ever left your command."

Speziale laughed. "It's been good seeing you, Korzenowski. I have to get back; shit like this generates a bitch load of paperwork."

"Yeah, tell me about it."

"Give me a call sometime. The wife and I will take you and Lydia out to dinner some night," said Speziale.

"Be careful what you wish for," Korzenowski warned.

Still laughing, Speziale walked away.

For a minute or two, Hoover and Korzenowski watched as the pathologist looked over the bodies and a member of the crime scene unit snapped photographs that would later be labeled and then added into the case file, a copy of which would eventually find its way to Hoover.

They stood in the early-morning dew watching as the surreal silver light from the high-powered flash on the CSU's camera continually popped, visually documenting the scene. *Flash.* Hoover stared at the injustice of murder. *Flash.* He looked at the lushness of the newly reborn green grass surrounding the dead. *Flash.* He took notice of one vibrant yellow dandelion standing by itself, engulfed by a million blades of grass. *Flash.* A dandelion that thought it was bigger, prettier, stronger than the grass around it. *Flash.* A dandelion that was nothing more than a weed. *Flash.* A weed that kills grass like a cancer spreading through the field. *Flash.* Hoover envisioned that dandelion as a representation of his job here. *Flash.* He was looking for one single weed among the verdant hordes of society. *Flash.* A sociopath who stood out in stark contrast to the field of sanity that surrounded him. *Flash.*

A dandelion in the grass.

Flash.

"Hoover?" Korzenowski was talking to him.

"Yeah, Captain?"

"You and DiSilva were up on the wheel for this one."

"The wheel" was the term the detectives of the Philadelphia Police Department used for the rotation of job assignments. The rotation was written on a piece of paper and kept on the desk of the detective working the phones in the office. At the start of each shift, the names were written down in the same order they ended the previous day. When a job came in, the names at the top of the list were assigned to the case and were then scratched off and rewritten on the bottom, awaiting the next rotation. When Hoover left at nine-thirty last night (his shift actually ended at four, but in this job you can't just punch the clock when the whistle sounds, you have to follow a lead until it got cold, no matter what time it was), he noticed that he and DiSilva were first up for the next day.

When your number was called for a job, that job was yours whether you were in the office or not. Hoover had been on his way to work this morning when the call for this particular job came in, and since it was as close to his eight-o'clock starting time as it could get without actually being eight o'clock, his name was penciled in for the assignment—the deskman always did his best not to screw the outgoing shift.

Hoover could already see where Korzenowski was going. He and his partner, DiSilva, had been working a B&E case in which the guy who broke into the house had shot and killed the husband and wife, an elderly couple named Sullivan, before taking off with some of their jewelry. The perp was nabbed trying to pawn a necklace that had been personally designed by a store on Jeweler's Row for the late Mrs. Sullivan's mother (who was still alive and kicking at eighty-eight), which she in turn passed on to her only daughter.

The mother, outraged by the death of her daughter, had provided descriptions of the missing jewelry along with the specifications of the handmade necklace to the police, who then distributed the list to the local pawnshops. Four days after the murder, a young black male was apprehended trying to move the necklace. The shop owner stalled him while looking the piece over until the cops arrived. When the male was asked to produce some ID, he produced a gun instead. After he was apprehended and processed, ballistics reported that the weapon he had drawn on the cops had been the same gun used in the B&E murder of the Sullivans. Fingerprints in the house matched; they had the right man.

From there it was only supposed to be a matter of putting on the finishing touches for the prosecution. Hoover and DiSilva had caught the initial squeal and were ready to testify to their findings in court, when it was brought to their attention via a late-coming witness to the scene that there might've been another perp in the house on the night the Sullivans were offed.

As it turned out, further investigations showed that the latter information was only a smokescreen. But it had made the papers, and the department had taken a lot of heat for what was supposedly a fucked-up investigation. An exposé had been written about the slipshod work being done by the police, and the race card was trumped throughout the local media because the person the long arm of the law had singled out for the crime had been an African-American, while the second, heretofore unknown perp was reported to be Caucasian. The bold-typed headlines had a field day with that, and the mayor got hot under his starched collar.

The result of all the bullshit was that the open-and-shut case of the Sullivan murders became high profile almost overnight. Under a pressure cooker of a microscope, the case was scheduled to have its day in court at eleven this morning, which was why Hoover and DiSilva had worked late into the previous evening, making sure they were ready for the morning's high-wire circus act.

What Korzenowski was about to tell him was that DiSilva was going to go to court and bat for the late Mr. and Mrs. Sullivan, and he, Hoover, was going to work this new case with a different partner. There was a bad taste in his mouth already.

"Look, Hoover, you know what a pain in my ass the Sullivan case has been," Korzenowski started.

"I know," he said, having been on the same hot plate as his boss because of it. He also knew that along with more responsibility came more heat, so he could sympathize somewhat with his boss. But from the way Korzenowski was trying to break it to him gently, Hoover was thinking that *this* case was about to become a pain in *his* ass.

"We're very thin right now. I don't have any other choice but to do this to you."

"Who is it?"

"It's Beverly."

"Shit," Hoover said under his breath. He knew it. "It has to be her? There's nobody else?"

"Nope. I'm sorry, John."

"Excuse me, Captain, are you in charge of this one?" It was the ME. His name was Ezekowitz, and he looked his part in a long black coat over a black suit and a stethoscope draped around his neck.

"Yeah, Zeke, I'm in charge."

"Everyone in the pile is dead," he said, as dry as a desert. Neither Korzenowski nor Hoover needed a doctor to tell them that, but it was protocol; homicide detectives were not allowed to move or touch any bodies before they were pronounced dead at the scene by a medical examiner.

"How many?" Korzenowski asked.

"Uncertain," the ME said. "The weather played hell with them. They're all kind of stuck together, so I won't have an exact count until they've been separated. But as for now, there are no signs of life from the exposed areas."

"How?"

"Unofficially?" ME's don't like giving guesses without having all the facts.

"Of course."

"From the top couple, I would surmise they died from loss of blood due to antemortem wounds—cuts made with a sharp instrument." He turned, his black coat swirling like a cape as he walked back to the scene where the CSU technicians were walking a grid pattern, looking for trace evidence.

"What about Jasner?" Hoover asked when they were alone, continuing the previous conversation.

"He won't be back until Friday."

"Yeah, right, I forgot. So there's nobody else, nobody at all?"

"How many times do you want me to tell you? No, there's no one else."

"Let me work it myself then."

Korzenowski pointed to where the pile of bodies lay. Six stretchers had been aligned in twos next to the dead in preparation for transporting them to the coroner's van. "Are you fucking kidding me?" he said. "I'd never let anybody work this by himself; there wouldn't be enough time for one person to even scratch the surface on this one. You know how quick the wheel turns, how swamped we are, new cases coming in every day. Just because we're overloaded with work doesn't mean the assholes out there are going to stop killing each other while we get caught up. In fact, there's so much to be done here I'm not even going to let the *two* of you work it by yourselves. I'm assigning three teams of two detectives each on this."

"Sorry, Cap, you're right." And he was, but that didn't change the way the new partnership bode with him. "But it has to be Beverly? What happened to her partner, Cathy Delaney?"

"Just started maternity duty. She'll be working indoors for the next six months, then goes on leave for birth." Korzenowski shrugged his shoulders and puffed his lips, blowing out air. "I know you and Bev had a little problem when you worked together in the past, but goddamn it, this is important. I need you to get past it

and work as a team. Be a professional, for Christ's sake."
Korzenowski was pulling rank without actually giving an order.

With another sigh, Hoover said, "Okay. You're right. I'll work
with her."

"Good. It's settled then."

"Does she know yet?"

"I haven't come right out and told her, but she's not stupid.
She knew who was up on the wheel for this one, and she surely
knows that her partner is pregnant. When she was dispatched to
the scene, it added up, I'm sure."

"She's here now?"

Korzenowski pointed. "Right over there."

Hoover looked to where Korzenowski indicated.

With all the activity of the people working the scene, Hoover
hadn't noticed her earlier. Or maybe he had a blind spot for her.
Either way, there she was.

Beverly was standing next to a man in a gray shirt and navy
blue pants. There was a white patch over his left breast. Hoover
thought it was probably a nametag but was too far away to
read it. The man was talking and gesturing to all ends of the
earth. Hoover figured him for an employee of the airport that
was supposed to be around here somewhere but whom Hoover
hadn't seen a lick of yet, hadn't even heard a plane roar by
overhead. All he had seen so far were trees. And of course, the
dead.

Hoover watched as the man explained the minutiae of his life
to Beverly Farrell. She listened as if what he was saying was the
single most important thing in her life. That was one of the great
things about Bev—she was an excellent listener. No matter what
you were talking about, she hung rapt on every word. Not reading
or watching TV, or politely waiting her turn to speak, but *listening*.
When the need arose to jot down notes while someone was talking,
she waited until they were finished. What she did was listen with
her ears *and* her mind while maintaining continuous eye contact.
She was doing precisely those things with the employee right now.
Hoover used to love it when she would pay attention to him that
way. He found himself a little jealous at the personal attention she
was giving the stranger.

Don't be an ass; you can't afford to fuck it up this time. She's not doing anything but her job. Good listening habits are a natural trait for a cop.

Hoover tried to shake the pang of jealousy but couldn't quite make it go away. He decided to wait for the conversation to end before approaching her, thinking it rude to interrupt. He watched and waited.

Beverly Farrell was strikingly beautiful in a demure sort of way, as she was not one to play it up by highly accenting her features with a lot of makeup or flashy clothes. Instead, her beauty was displayed in the way she carried herself. Today she was wearing a high-necked, form-fitting black sweater, gray slacks, and a pair of matching flat business shoes. Earrings were permitted, but she never chose to wear any while on duty.

At five-foot-ten (an even six in heels) her height gave her the confidence to look people right in the eye. She had the tight physique of a swimmer, with firm breasts and very feminine hips. The skin of her flawless complexion was slightly pigmented, giving her the appearance of always being tan. Her fingers were long and slender, the nails kept short. She had high cheekbones with just a hint of rouge on them, thin eyebrows, and an ever so slightly crooked smile. Her dark brown eyes were large and warm and inviting, the size and color giving them the appearance of being deep. A man could get lost in those eyes. Hoover knew because he had been such a man.

Beverly reached out and touched the airport employee on the arm. This was an indicator that she was done with him. The touch was a way to dismiss him reassuringly, by making him feel he had been very helpful and would not soon be forgotten.

Unexpectedly, she turned toward Hoover, and he found himself looking directly at her.

Damn, you just got caught leering, he thought. To his surprise, though, Beverly raised a hand and gave him a wiggling finger wave. He waved back, smiling. She returned it with her cute, crooked mouth. He could just see the tip of her tongue poking out between her teeth, teeth he had always found sexy because her front right incisor overlapped her left by the tiniest fraction. When she smiled at him, he looked into her eyes to see if it were genuine. It was; her eyes shone with it.

"Let's go over there," said Korzenowski.

Hoover was startled a bit when he spoke. He had completely forgotten that the captain had been standing right next to him the whole time. Hoover found it a little intriguing that Korzenowski had also waited until Beverly finished talking before deciding to go over to her. Korzenowski walked through the damp grass toward Beverly, and Hoover followed.

When they got to where she stood, Korzenowski started right in as the Captain of Homicide. In other words, he was telling her how it was going to be, rather than handling her with the kid gloves he used on Hoover. Hoover knew this was because Beverly was a woman. It wasn't out of disrespect—and it certainly wasn't because he was a sexist—but it was definitely because Beverly was a woman. Korzenowski acted in such a way because it was the only way he knew how to. Like many others his age, he'd become a cop when it was still a man's job. He accepted women in uniform but still found it awkward; women police made him uncomfortable, and it showed. Beverly made sure she didn't notice.

"Farrell, I've decided to put you on this one. You're going to be working with Hoover here. Make sure the i's are dotted and the t's are crossed, both of you. I don't want any screwups on this one, understood?"

"Yes, sir," they both said in unison.

"Good. Get to work." Exeunt Korzenowski.

There was a heavy pause. Hoover could feel the strain of its weight, but he was going to wait for her to make the first move. He had to, so he could see which side of the net the ball would fall on. Would it be in her court or in his? If he started, he would definitely let a foul. The two of them hadn't spoken directly to each other in over eighteen months. They worked in the same squad—on the same shift even—but their paths had crossed minimally. If this was a conscious action on both their parts, he wasn't aware of it.

"Hello, John," she said. She spoke the words without venom. To him, they sounded like the sweetest words he had ever heard in his life.

"Hi, Bev." That was all he could come out with. He had a million things he wanted to say to her but didn't know how to broach them. It was best not to overwhelm her. If he wanted to say anything in particular later, he would have to ease into it slowly, over a period of time. He would tread lightly. "Are you okay with this?"

She shrugged. "It's a job. We were both assigned to it. If I make a stink about it, we'll both end up with egg on our face. What else can we do?"

Analytical, professional, surgical; it cut him to the bone.

"There's nothing we can do," he agreed, "so let's get started."

"How do you want to handle it?"

"The way I figure it, we'll alternate the lead, depending on who we're questioning, you know, because of the nature of the crimes." Statistically, murders of this type were committed by men. Breaking the news to a father that his baby girl had been found naked and dead in the woods was not something any man wanted to hear, even less so from another man. "You take the sensitive ones, and I'll do the ones that seem unruffled."

"Fine by me," she said.

"What do you have so far?"

"I haven't been here that long, but I just took a statement from that guy over there." She pointed to the man Hoover had seen her talking to. From this distance, Hoover could read the patch on the man's shirt. It was white with black stitched letters that read Northern Philadelphia Airport, Phila, PA. Above that was a cursive "Mel." Mel was currently having a conversation with someone in a security uniform.

"He's the supervisor of the maintenance department here at the airport," she continued. "Said that an employee of his by the name of Arthur Fleuridor was the one who found the mess while replacing bulbs on some light towers just on the other side of the fence. The supervisor says it's impossible that all the bulbs would go out at the same time, and it looks like they've been tampered with."

"Tampered with?"

"Smashed. There's a six-foot hole cut into the fence about a hundred yards to the east. The techs are checking it out. They already took the bulbs into custody."

"Think it's related?" Studies have shown, and statistics have corroborated, that people who commit murder want to be caught. With this in mind, Hoover had just asked her if she thought it was their unknown suspect who intentionally broke the bulbs.

"I believe so," she said. So did he.

"Why's the opening so far away from the scene?"

"Tree coverage. The hole's in the closest area clear enough of vegetation to make the cut."

"Where's Fleuridor now?"

"They took him back to the maintenance office."

"How do we get there?"

"Hey, Mel," Beverly said.

"Yes," Mel replied. It was "yes," not a "yeah" or "yo," the typical Philadelphian responses. On top of that, it sounded flowery. Beverly had cast her spell over this man too.

"Can you take us to Art?"

"Sure. I'll drive you up there. Come on over to my rover. It's parked right over here." Mel led the way back through the woods to the feeder road. A few minutes later, the three of them emerged from beneath the foliage and into the bright morning sunlight. The uniform was still there, and he still didn't have anything to say to Hoover.

Mel went over to one of the golf carts parked among the rest of the airport vehicles and the police cars. There were only two seats in the cart. Deferring to the lady, Hoover got on the back, lowering his rump into a basket. Reaching below his seat, Mel turned the ignition switch. The little electrical cart sparked to life. The transmission lever had only three positions: D, N, R. Mel pushed it forward into the D slot, made a huge, sweeping U-turn around the other vehicles, and drove off. Instead of heading down the blacktopped feeder road, Mel stuck to the grass on the shoulder.

The little cart was surprisingly quick as it bounced over the rough terrain of the airport grounds, the wind whipping the hell out of their unprotected faces. Hoover had to squint to be able to keep his vision, and even then could only see the back of Beverly's head from where he sat. He couldn't tell how she was handling the gale, but he knew she wore contact lenses. The thin lenses had to be kept moist, and he wondered how fast wind shear like this would dry them out. For protection, he guessed she had her eyes closed.

Hoover tried to glimpse as much as he could off to the sides, through narrow slits of eyes, as they drove north toward the maintenance facilities. To his right were several large buildings, some constructed out of unpainted concrete cinder blocks, some out of brick, all utilitarian looking. Warehouses.

To the left were the runways. Although he was sitting considerably higher than the front seats, Hoover could not see the tarmacs from the golf cart. What he could see, however, were lights, and they were beautiful. Even in the dazzling sunlight, Hoover could see a plethora of different colored lights spread in many helter-skelter patterns: royal blues, scarlet reds, whites, yellows, every one holding significance to a myriad of people, all with lives depending on them.

The grounds themselves were spacious and flat. Off in the distance, he could see the miniaturized skyline of the city, which was more than twenty miles away from where he currently was.

Having been raised by lower middle-class parents, vacations for the Hoover family had been day trips to the Jersey shore, or no-frills camping sites that were barely more than balding dirt patches in the Pocono Mountains. Hoover had just realized that he had never before seen an airport, other than on television, in all of his thirty-seven years.

The cart bounced along until it came to a break in the fence that could be closed off by a gate. The gate stood open at the moment, a heavy chain and padlock dangling from the hook. Hoover suspected it was secured during nonbusiness hours.

Mel drove the rover off the grass and over a dip that went down to a gravel driveway. The dip roughly bounced all of the passengers in the cart, nearly jarring the teeth right out of Hoover's head and giving him the somehow sickly, somehow pleasant feeling of his stomach dropping into his balls. Mel never even slowed down. The gravel crunched under the cart's wheels until they reached a building that looked like a tin shack. There, Mel stomped on the rectangular brake pedal. The front wheels of the cart locked, and they slid to a halt that would have impressed Popeye Doyle.

The three of them debarked. Hoover checked to make sure that his gun—a two-inch-barrel, .38-caliber, six-shot revolver made by Colt and called a Detective's Special—was still in its holster under his left armpit. Hoover was right-handed.

"Hey, Mel, you realize those bodies out there are dead, right?" Beverly asked as soon as she was standing on firm ground again.

"Yes, ma'am," he said proudly, awaiting her approval for all the assistance he was giving the police. Beverly lowered the boom.

"Then what was the rush?" she asked. "Why'd we have to drive so fast?"

"W-w-well I-I-I, you know, thought that, um, you were in, like, a hurry," caught off guard, he stammered. Mel looked at Hoover for some support, but found none. When he realized Bev was going to let Mel have it, Hoover turned his head away to hide his smile. What he found himself looking at was the tin shack they had stopped in front of.

Hoover imagined that if there were a fourth little piggy in the story, his house would've looked something like this. And the wolf certainly would've had no problem huffing and puffing it down.

The tin was a shiny silver on all four sides of the building, Hoover supposed, based on the two sides facing him. There were two doors, a small one for people to enter and a larger one, about the size and shape of a typical garage door, for machines or vehicles. Both doors were painted sky blue. A sign on the people door proclaimed this to be the Northern Philadelphia Airport Maintenance Shop. It also stated that "No Unauthorized Persons Permitted."

Mel was about to stammer another unintelligent sentence in an attempt to regain some face, before Hoover saved him from further embarrassment. "Is Art in there?" he asked.

Mel turned his attention from the woman. "Yeah, he's in there."

"Can we just walk in?"

"The door's not locked. You can go right in."

"Thank you, Mel." This was from Beverly. It was gracious, following the reprimand. "Would you wait here so we can hitch a ride back with you." Not a question.

"Yes, ma'am" This time it sounded dejected.

"Come on, John. Let's go see the famous Art."

"Yes, ma'am," he said quietly, so only she could hear it. Hoover walked alongside Beverly as they entered the maintenance shop.

*   *   *

The first thing they noticed was the smell of oil.

Hoover had no idea where it was coming from. He looked around the shop and couldn't readily see anything leaking. He thought that maybe the odor was coming from *everything*. The entire shop seemed to be greasy and grimy; the smell of oil probably worked deep into the foundation.

The color palate in the shop was gray on gray. Every tool, fixture, and wall was gray. The only dash of color was from the calendar, which depicted a buxom woman in a bathing suit straddling the hood of a classic pickup truck painted fire engine red. The woman's one-piece—as well as her lipstick and nail polish—matched the paint to perfection. Other than that, stepping into the maintenance shop was like stepping into a void.

Even Art looked washed out.

They could tell he was the person they were looking for by the way he sat slumped in his chair. His complexion was pale, his uniform shirt ripped up the front; there was a gash running across his forehead that he applied pressure to with a rag. All of these things combined (other than the fact that he was the only person in the room) were enough to indicate that this was the guy they were looking for. But the flashing neon arrow was the look on his face. Art wore a mask of fear and looked as though he'd seen a ghost. Or perhaps, the dead.

"Are you Arthur Fleuridor?" asked Hoover, redundantly by the book.

"Yeah, I am," the man replied. His voice sounded strong, so Hoover continued with the questioning, thinking that the guy only looked the way he did because it had been a hard morning on the old boy. Art sat in a battered chair he had swiveled toward the detectives, springs and stuffing poking out of holes in the fabric. When he was fully facing them, he leaned back, the chair letting out a squeal like rusty nails being pulled as it reclined so precariously far that it stopped a scant inch from the desk that was its mate in life. If Art had been on the heavy side, he might now have a gash on the back of his head to bookend the one in front. Art did not offer any of the unoccupied chairs to the two detectives, and they remained standing.

"I'm Detective Hoover. This is my partner, Detective Farrell." Art didn't have a response, so Hoover went on. "You found the bodies out there?"

"Yeah."

"What happened to you? Why are you bleeding?"

As if Hoover's questions made him think of it, Art removed the rag to check on the status of the wound. All three of them looked down at the rag in his hand—it seemed to be clean, if a little dingy from being washed too many times without bleach. There was a spot of blood about the size of a quarter on it. The blood hadn't dried yet but wasn't exactly fresh, either. The cut itself was superficial. Art didn't look either satisfied or not. He reapplied the shop rag to the wound.

"When I saw what I found," he said, "I tripped and fell. My head must've hit a rock or something."

"Did you lose consciousness?"

"No."

"Do you feel well enough to talk to us now?"

"Yeah, I feel fine. What do you want to know?"

"Tell us what you saw; tell us how you came upon the bodies."

Art told them the whole story: the light tower, the radio, taking a leak, climbing the fence (his shirt got snagged on the top, ripping it), and finally, the bodies.

"About what time did this happen?" Hoover asked.

Art looked at his watch, "'Bout an hour ago. Right before we called you guys. Jamie will have the exact time written down on her log, if you need it."

"Who's Jamie?"

"Jamie Culver. She was the air traffic controller on duty when I found them."

"I see. Did you approach the bodies?"

"Yeah. As I picked my radio up from the ground, I noticed what I thought was a dead animal, a dead deer. I walked over to take a look and found out that it was no deer."

"Did you touch the bodies?"

"No fucking way." Art's eyes darted to Beverly. "Excuse me," he said to her, ashamed. "No, I didn't touch anything. I got spooked, and that's when I tripped and fell. When I got my feet back under me, I ran back to the fence. I wanted to go get help, but I couldn't find the energy to climb; that's when I remembered the radio. I called the Comm Tower and waited for someone to come."

"Did you see anybody else out there?"

"You mean more bodies?"

"No, living people."

"No."

"Do you think someone broke those lights on purpose?"

"I don't think it, I know it. What else would've happened to them?"

"What can you tell me about the hole in the fence?"

"Nothing, I didn't see it. Didn't even know there was one till Mel told me about it."

"Previous to today, when was the last time you were out that way, by the fence?"

"I don't know, maybe a month ago. Mel has to keep a log of all the work we do. I'm sure you'd be able to look up the date."

"Do any of the other maintenance employees go out there?"

"Sure, sooner or later everybody that works in the department goes out to the runways for one reason or another."

"How many are on staff?"

"The maintenance staff or the whole airport?"

"Just maintenance."

"Twenty or so. A couple of guys work the night shift, a couple the evening and weekends; the lion's share is seven to four, though, Monday through Friday. I tend to start a little earlier since my wife passed."

"All right. Is there anything else you think we'd need to know about the incident this morning?"

"Nope, told you all I know."

"Thank you, Mr. Fleuridor. That's all for now. If you think of anything you might have forgotten, would you give us a call?" Hoover handed him a business card. Art looked at it then stuffed it in a pocket. He rechecked the rag as the detectives left.

Escaping back into the Technicolor world, Hoover and Farrell found Mel sitting in the front seat of the golf cart, waiting for them like a curbed dog.

"Mel, I understand that you're the maintenance supervisor," said Hoover.

"That's right."

"What I need you to do is make up a list of names and phone numbers for everyone that works here at the airport."

"You mean in my department?"

"No, the whole airport."

"That wouldn't be my job," he balked. "I only take care of the maintenance department."

"You just said you were a supervisor. I would expect a supervisor would be in a position to be able to contact the proper people in human resources who'd be privy to the information I need. If they don't have anything, then go to payroll. I'm sure they'll have a list of names and addresses there."

"You're really going to go through all that? That's a lot of people," Mel cautioned.

"So is that pile out in the woods."

Trailing a faint scent of oil, the detectives got back into the golf cart and had their driver return them to the location of the bodies.

9

After another two hours in the woods, followed by a forty-five-minute drive into the city, Hoover and Farrell entered the Roundhouse through the only unlocked entrance, off Cherry Street, at the rear of the building.

The police headquarters building consisted of the main lobby, three floors of offices, and a basement where the holding cells (thirty-two male, sixteen female, and the overnight tank) and armory were. The décor of the main lobby, as well as the rest of the building, was done in '70s-style dark wood paneling beneath flickering, pale fluorescent lighting that made everything look even darker, and scuffed tile flooring.

There was a uniformed officer (presently a corporal) in the lobby behind a bulletproof, sliding glass window. To his left was the arraignment court, to the right the lobby proper and the elevators. Beyond the lobby were the cafeteria and the private elevator for the commissioner and the deputy commissioners. A wall next to the main elevators displayed a photograph of every cop lost in the line of duty over the last four decades, along with the date and a facsimile of the person's badge. As Hoover incessantly pushed the button, trying to make one of the two elevators arrive quicker, Beverly gazed at the pictures.

Man, that poor bastard bought it on leap day, she thought, wondering if he'd still be alive today if it hadn't been a leap year.

With a whoosh, the door opened, and they stepped into the beige car. When it came to a creeping stop on the first floor, they got off and made a right. Walking along the curving hallway, they passed room 102, a bathroom, and entered room 104, homicide.

Homicide was a large area that took up a third of the entire floor; the other two-thirds contained the narcotics offices and the labs. When they entered the homicide office, they were in a small anteroom that served as a waiting area. Here there were two benches and a desk manned by a civilian who verified reasons for admittance to the office beyond. Currently, six people were cooling their heels on the benches.

Immediately beyond the anteroom was another door which separated the general public from the inner workings of the office. Behind that door was the slatted wooden railing that was the original barrier between the waiting public and the working detectives.

Hoover pulled open the three-foot-high gate (which swung both ways, and many a joke being made about that) and held it for Beverly to enter. To the left of the semicircular room were four holding rooms, furnished with metal chairs that had handcuffs bolted to them and the prerequisite one-way mirrors used for interrogating suspects. On the far wall of the homicide den was the captain's office.

After that, all planning gave way to chaos.

The rest of the large open area contained fifteen haphazardly placed desks and many, many filing cabinets scattered around the room, standing upright in every nook and cranny they could be wedged.

Because there were sixty detectives spread out over four squads (three squads worked the three eight-hour shifts of the day, while the fourth had the day off), there were not enough desks for each of the detectives to have his or her own. Since it was just after noon on a weekday—a weekday containing a high-profile murder case—all of the desks were occupied by detectives clacking away on typewriters (computer age or not), save one. The empty desk sat in the far corner next to a window. For safety's sake, no window in police headquarters was opened in case some perp decided to take a leap or had enraged a member of the force bad enough that he or she assisted the individual out of the building the hard way. Hoover and Farrell walked over to the desk with its scenic panorama view of the other glass and concrete edifices claustrophobically penning PHQ.

Hoover sank into a chair very similar to the one in which Art Fleuridor had sat. In the lap hole, his shoes squelched, and his toes were cold from being wet. He hated that.

Beverly sat to the side, facing Hoover. "You don't think these deaths have anything to do with the airport, do you?" she asked.

"No, the airport was a dumpsite."

"Then why the list of employees?"

"Just coving all the bases to keep the captain happy. Remember, I'm one of the detectives involved in the Sullivan case. Fate nailed me as the lead on this one, and I want to make sure I investigate every possibility, no matter how insignificant," he said, but didn't add that if he stumbled a second time on the road to Golgotha, no one was going to help him carry his cross. And he didn't want Beverly to be crucified with him. "DiSilva's in court right now trying to clean that mess up."

"I know. You make it sound as if I don't work One Squad with you, right here in this very office."

"Sorry. It's been so long since I've talked to you that it seems to have slipped my mind how close we work."

"Don't go there, John. Stay focused on the case."

Hoover didn't say anything. He pushed back from the desk and went to retrieve the appropriate forms that needed filling out.

* * *

While Hoover typed, Farrell found out who was on the rest of the investigating unit. Besides her and Hoover, there were two other pairings consisting of Meltzer and Sako, Holmes and Whaat.

Hoover had completed the preliminary reports (the more detailed ones would have to wait for the ME's filings), when Captain Korzenowski pushed open the railing.

"Hoover, gather your teams and meet me in the interrogation room in twenty minutes," Korzenowski shouted before disappearing inside his office. There was no need for Hoover to gather anything; everyone in the oversized room had heard Korzenowski clear enough.

The specific interrogation room Korzenowski meant was the only one that had a rectangular folding table set up for lawyers to meet with their clients and/or the detectives. The room had several uncomfortable, hard plastic chairs on one side and the metal holding chair with its attached handcuffs on the other. The plastic chairs had been purchased in bulk in the same late '70s when the building had been paneled, and were all bright orange, which clashed severely with the faux-wood walls. The only other things in the room were two trash cans overflowing with Styrofoam coffee cups and balled-up wads of paper, and a vast amount of stacked boxes of files.

Five of the six detectives were seated in the plastic chairs, the one-way mirror to their backs, when Whaat came in carrying four pizzas and a fistful of napkins. With all of the morning's hustle and bustle, no one had gotten a chance to eat. He sat the pizzas directly in the middle of the table, throwing the pile of napkins down next to them, the napkins intended to serve double duty as facial wipes and fine dinnerware.

"Get your food quickly, Teddy was on the phone right outside the room when I came in," he said, causing a feeding frenzy to break out around the pizzas reminiscent of sharks attacking wounded porpoises. In a matter of seconds, three of the pizza boxes were emptied and tossed to the floor in the general direction of one of the trash cans. The Teddy whom Whaat had been referring to was Captain Korzenowski, whose first name was Theodore.

"Where's this from?" asked Holmes in reference to the pizza, his voice a rumbling baritone. He was a solidly built black man who still had the body of the college football player he once had been at Temple University. The only indication of his age was the male-pattern baldness that had untimely struck in his midtwenties. What remained of his hair capped his skull in a horseshoe shape, stretching from ear to ear across the occipital ridge, the rest of his head devoid of even a stray follicle. In an age when it was considered chic to shave your head completely, Holmes refused to because it made his skin, as he said, "bump up."

"Shit, Holmes, just eat the fucker," said Whaat as soon as Holmes spoke up, knowing the question was going to come.

"No, I'm serious. Where's it from?"

"Some place below Chinatown."

"Sure, blame the Orientals," said Sako—a Japanese—dryly.

"What difference does it make where it's from?" asked Meltzer. "You know it's not going to be good. Just look at it. It's Greek-style." Greek-style, a description that had caught on in the city, was used to describe pizza made with a very thick dough and very little sauce, and mozzarella that had been cut with feta. The pizza was cooked in a pan rather than on an oven shelf, causing the bottom of the pie and the crust to remain soft and underdone. This seemed to be the preferred method of pizza making in shops whose owners happened to be of the Greek nationality. "For pizza to be any good, it needs to be made by an Italian, preferably one right off the boat," Meltzer opined.

"I agree," said Beverly who, with her dark hair and dark eyes, was partially Italian. "This is tasteless. You know why? Because when the dough is kneaded into a pan, the secret ingredient is left out. The secret *Italian* ingredient."

"What ingredient's that?" asked Holmes, a fierce Greek-style detractor, looking at her as if she were the Muse of Pizza.

"I don't know; I'm a cop, not a pizza cook. But I'll tell you what; my opinion is the secret ingredient's in the air." Beverly pointed upward, smiling. "It's added to the pizza when it's tossed."

"It's probably the stale garlic coming from the old mama-mia's breath when she breathes through her mustache," said Sako in a decent Italian accent. All the cops in the room broke up at that, except Beverly, who crinkled her nose in a mock grimace. Sako was born in Japan, but he came to the States when he was less than a year old. His perfect English was so natural it went unnoticed, but hearing the Oriental speaking in a goofy Italian accent was amusing.

"What do you think this cheese is made out of? Goat's milk?" Holmes asked, chewing.

"Fuck you, guys," huffed Whaat, a small smirk on his face. "If God made those pizzas himself, you ingrates would complain that it was too *heavenly*. Next time one of you gets the fucking pizzas."

"Whaaaaat? Whaaaaat did you say? Whaaaaat?" Meltzer jested.

"Some jokes never get old, do they?" said Whaat, looking at the ceiling for serenity.

"No, they don't," mumbled Holmes through a mouthful of pizza.

"Hey, where's my change?" Meltzer asked.

"Change! Bitch, I had to throw in two *extra* dollars, and I was the guy who went and got it," Whaat said, taking his first bite of the pizza.

During the banter, Hoover had remained silent. He wasn't in a mood to be jovial. However, he was ravenous no matter how many decomposing bodies he had seen today. He ate three slices, Greek or not.

After a few minutes, while the six detectives ate silently, Whaat tossed a crust rind to the table and said out of nowhere, "Man, this does suck." The laughter was long and loud.

"All right, ladies and gentlemen, let's get serious," said Captain Theodore Korzenowski, who had just opened the solid wood door and entered the interrogation room. Behind him walked Lieutenant Stevens, a sour look on his face.

As the pneumatic elbow pulled the door close, Korzenowski made his way down the table to stand behind the metal holding chair. He was carrying a large manila folder, which he slapped down in front of his chosen seat. Korzenowski opened the remaining pizza box and looked in.

"Shit," he said, "Greek pizza." The room broke out again. "Settle down, people, settle down. This ain't the Comedy Cabaret," he said as he removed two slices. He slapped them down on the table right next to the folder, not worrying about using a napkin or plate before sitting down on the uncomfortable metal of the holding chair. Lieutenant Stevens stood silent sentry behind him.

"Hey, Cap, you gonna kick in for that?" Holmes asked.

"The only thing I'm gonna kick in is your ass; you keep asking me stupid questions."

"I don't ask for myself, sir, but Meltzer there," Holmes pointed at him with a long, thick finger, "wants to know how much each slice cost him."

"I just don't see how it balances out," Meltzer protested. "Five dollars for three slices of pizza; it doesn't add up."

"You want to know what doesn't add up, Meltzer? Nine. Nine doesn't add up. What were nine bodies doing out in those woods?" Captain Korzenowski asked everyone at the same time and no one in particular. He then opened the manila folder to the freshly developed CSU photos of the bodies. There were many snapshots taken from many different angles. Some of the photos were of the whole collection of bodies while they were still in situ; some were from after they had been separated. The remainders—individual shots—were taken in the morgue itself.

Sitting side by side with the meager sauce of the pizza, the pasty whiteness of the exposed flesh and the dark smears of dried blood would have been enough to make even the strongest of hearts a little nauseous. Korzenowski wasn't affected at all, not even giving it a passing thought as he picked up a slice of pizza with one hand and doled out photos with the other.

"Those of you who weren't out at the airport, take a look at these. This is what you're up against," Korzenowski said when everyone had a photo in their hands. "The unofficial preliminary report from the ME cites 'wrongful death caused by sharp instrument drawn across the neck, causing trauma to the carotid artery and the jugular vein.' To make matters worse, the ME says these women were all bled."

"What do you mean 'bled'?" asked Sako.

"It means that there was hardly any blood left in the bodies. Due to decreased indication of lividity, what Zeke believes happened was these women sustained all the rest of the cuts seen in the pictures *before* their throats were slashed, killing them. In other words, the prick let them bleed from the other wounds before he finished them off. Somewhere there's a big puddle of DNA lying around, waiting for us to step in it."

"Damn," Holmes whispered under his breath as quietly as he could. For him that was almost the volume of a normal conversational voice.

"That's right; our boy doesn't get queasy easily. It also means that the kills were premeditated. Murder-first. When we catch this guy, he'll get the chair." Korzenowski spoke figuratively. While the Commonwealth of Pennsylvania did sentence capital punishment, it was administered by lethal injection rather than electric chair.

"I don't understand," said Sako. "I see the cuts on the front of the bodies, but I don't see *any* lividity. If they were bled, then there should be some indication of where it ran out of them?"

"Sharp eye, Sako. You can't see any apparent lividity because they weren't lying down while they were bled. They'd been strung up. He cut them while they hung by their feet, ligature marks around their ankles from ropes. The lividity—what little there was—was under their hair, on the scalp, and on the crowns of the shoulders, the dead blood drawn to those spots by gravity."

"This is one sick bastard," Meltzer said.

"Yes, he is. And because of that, you can imagine this is going to be a highly publicized case. There'll probably be pictures, graphs, charts, exposés, you name it. I wouldn't be surprised if some asshole eventually wrote a book about it.

"But regardless of how the public sees it, we don't work for them. The citizens of this great city might pay our salaries, but we report to the people upstairs." He was referring to the fourth floor of the Roundhouse, where the commissioner and other police brass had their offices. "I just came down from up there, and they want to see some serious action on this one. They requested that I personally supervise the operation, so you're going to bypass Lieutenant Stevens and both sergeants for the time being and report directly to me." That explained Stevens's sullen expression. "That is not a reflection on your immediate supervisors," Korzenowski told them, "but only a precautionary measure that one of the deputy commissioners suggested. I don't have to remind anyone about the heat the department's been getting from the media over the Sullivan case."

"That's bullshit," said Holmes.

Korzenowski held up his hands, palms outward, indicating that this was not the forum for debate. "Wrong as it may be, people believe what they read; what can I say? But this is our chance to make our star rise again. The pressure is on. That's the bad news. The good news is that we have positively identified each of the dead bodies."

"What, already? How? They were nude."

"Thank you for pointing out the blatantly obvious, Detective Whaat."

"Anytime, Cap'n."

"Yes, as Whaat's sharp detection pointed out, the bodies were naked. But believe it or not, they were all carrying a photo ID."

"You're kidding me."

"Yeah, I'm fucking kidding you, Whaat. I've got nothing better to do than perform stand-up for One Squad," Korzenowski snarled.

It was out of character, and it let every cop in the room know that the brass must've come down pretty hard on their captain.

"Sorry, Captain."

"You *are* sorry," he said, shaking his head. "Anyway, eight of the nine women had a driver's license stuffed up their snatches." Korzenowski's eyes shifted to where Beverly sat. He scratched the top of his scalp and said, "Pardon my French, Farrell."

"I've been working this job for a while, sir. I've heard the word 'snatch' before," she said.

"The other woman . . . ," he checked the folder, "one Melissa Griffin, had a student ID from State inside her. We'll have to cross our fingers and hope that she attended one of the satellite local campuses. If not, someone's going to have to take a trip upstate, into God's Country, the farmlands of Pennsylvania, and that could get hairy with jurisdictions. I for one do not want to involve Barney Fife, if I don't have to." Korzenowski began handing out sheaves of paper. "These are copies of the licenses. They're in order of decomposition, the freshest on top, most rotten on bottom, just like they were in the pile."

When Hoover got his, he looked down at the nine names and photos:

> Sherry Dasher
> Leta Hursch
> Kristen Fiorella
> Melissa Griffin
> Andrea Hustead
> Heather Plunkett
> Tammy Allensworth
> Haley Goldberg
> Judith Kasay

Korzenowski continued speaking. "Unfortunately, I don't think we're going to have much more to go on besides the identities. I don't have anything official yet, but the techs on scene said they hadn't found much. There weren't any prints on the fence or light towers other than those belonging to the maintenance guy who found the bodies, and the weather played hell with the integrity of the surrounding area. The best that can be hoped for at this point is some DNA from the vaginal canals and the pubic region. As for now, all we have to work with is the women themselves.

"There are nine bodies and three teams here. The math says each team has to pound the pavement on three of the victims. I don't care whose identity you tackle, except that Hoover drew the short straw, so he's the lead investigator. I want him and Farrell to take the freshest corpse, which is one Sherry Dasher," he said, consulting his own copy of the IDs, "and the earliest, which is one Judith Kasay.

"Also, I don't want them to take the girl from State College. We can't afford to have them taking three-hour drives up to the main campus, if it need be.

"Hoover, I'm sure you know, but I'm assigning you Dasher and Kasay because the lead will be the warmest on the last person to turn up dead, Dasher, and because Ms. Kasay might've sparked this spree somehow—the killer could've been a friend, lover, enemy, whatever.

"Now all nine of these women have at least one thing in common, someone killed them. I assume that the same guy killed all of them, but you know what you get when you assume. Find out if they have anything else in common. If they do, it'll point to our man. First thing in the morning—and every morning thereafter—we'll meet right here and we'll throw together what we have. Every piece of the puzzle, no matter how small, will eventually come together to show us the complete picture, understand?"

Everyone at the table understood.

"Good. Now as you can see, I have half of the squad working on this one. I will try to keep the wheel spinning and keep the incoming jobs off you guys for the next couple of days; the rest will have to pick up your slack. So gentlemen—and lady—please work quickly and efficiently. That's it, get to work."

He closed his folder and took it with him as he left, Lieutenant Stevens trailing behind.

10

$\mathcal{T}$he IDs are what bother me," said Hoover. They were driving in a department-issued Ford Crown Victoria, heading to the former residence of Judith Kasay.

"Why do you say that? I thought it was kind of gracious of him to save us from having to wait for the dental and fingerprint results. Even then, there might not be a match. This way is much more convenient," Beverly argued good-naturedly, poking at him to try to keep it light between them.

"No, he left us those IDs because he wanted us to know who those women were; he wanted us to know whom he killed. He's trying to make a statement. If he's trying to make a statement, he's not some sick pervert; he's got an agenda. He killed those women specifically. He killed them on purpose, not randomly."

"He's also sticking it in our faces. Showing us he's not scared of us," Beverly added.

"That too."

They drove on in silence, twisting and turning their way through a residential area.

Finally, Hoover asked, "What was the address again?" Beverly opened the pocket-sized notebook she was holding and read him the address. Hoover bent to look out his window. "There it is, third house up on the left." Hoover parked the car and they got out, finding themselves standing in front of a single rancher-styled house constructed out of brick and surrounded by a Cyclone fence. There wasn't much to the house. From the outside, there looked to be about five or six rooms total in the whole domicile. And since it was a rancher, it only consisted of one floor.

"This is probably going to be yours," Hoover said to his partner.

"I know," was all the response she had. In a job that rarely had any high points, the nadir was breaking the news of an untimely and usually horrific death of a loved one. Every homicide detective, at one time or another, wondered why there wasn't a special team of psychiatrists set up for such a thing. A sleep-deprived cop in a rumpled Brooks Brothers suit, who had seen the final remains of the said loved one firsthand, should not be the person to deliver such terrible news to the family. Yet that was part of the job.

They let themselves in the gate, approaching the front door. Beverly pushed the button, and from inside, a soft doorbell could be heard chiming.

After a minute, a man in a worn-out, button-down flannel shirt and a pair of jeans answered the door. Because it was mid-April, the spring air still had a little nip to it; the man could get away with wearing the flannel for now, but in a month it would be T-shirts and shorts. In this part of the country, it seemed as though every year the seasons were blending together in such a way that the spring and the fall were being boxed out—the temperature went from cold to humid in the span of a week.

Standing directly behind the man and wringing a dishtowel in her hands was a woman of approximately forty-five. She was tall and slender and the spitting image of the driver's license photograph they had of Judith Kasay, the earliest victim found in the woods of the Northern Philadelphia Airport. The only recognizable differences between the two women were twenty years and the breath of life.

The detectives held up their badges and identifications. "Mr. and Mrs. Kasay," Beverly said.

"Kasay," the man corrected. "Edward Kasay, both *a*'s are hard. This is my wife, Miriam." The woman said nothing.

"Sir, ma'am," Beverly said, "I'm Detective Farrell; this is Detective Hoover. May we come in and have a word with you?"

"It's about Judith, isn't it," Mr. Kasay asked.

"Yes, sir, it is."

He held the door for them to enter as Mrs. Kasay began to cry.

The front door opened directly into the living room. Hoover would guess that the room measured about twenty feet by fifteen—not much space—but it was tastefully decorated with a country motif, the rugs a nice shade of jade. There was a couch, a love seat, and an entertainment console containing all the standard electronic appliances, lining three of the four walls. The other wall was covered entirely in framed photographs. A quick glance at the pictures told the detectives all they needed to know about them; the photos were a still-life chronicle of the lives of the Kasays and specifically that of Judith Kasay.

"Please, have a seat," Mr. Kasay said, showing them to the couch at the far end of the room. The husband and wife sat down on the love seat to the left of the detectives. Mr. Kasay leaned forward so that his knees almost touched Beverly's.

Immediately, Mr. Kasay jumped into it. "Have you found our baby girl?"

"Yes, we have."

"Is she all right?" His voice cracked with emotion at the end.

"Uh . . . Mr. Kasay," Beverly began and looked at his wife, who was crying into the dishtowel.

With stony, staring eyes, he said, "Whatever you have to say, you can say it in front of my wife. She has a right to know what happened to her daughter." He was right, of course, but it still didn't make it any easier for Beverly to give voice to the terrible end the precious life this woman had brought into the world had come to. When Beverly paused, Ed Kasay drew his own conclusion. He broached the subject himself by saying what Beverly could not. "Judy's dead."

"Yes, sir, she is," the detective said in what was almost a hushed whisper. Upon hearing confirmation for what they had long suspected, Mrs. Kasay began to sob harder into her dishtowel almost uncontrollably. Edward looked at his grieving wife. He put one hand on her knee to console her, but the rest of him remained all business. Either he had come to terms with this reality before the detectives had shown up at his door, or he would wait until they left to cry it out.

"How did she die, Detective Farrell?" he asked through the small tight line that had become his mouth.

"She was murdered."

"By whom?"

"Well, sir, we don't know yet. That's part of the reason why we're here. We've begun an investigation into the murders—"

"Murders? Plural? What do you mean murders?"

"Judy wasn't found alone."

"Somebody else was with her? Somebody dead, I mean."

"There were eight other people, all women," she said.

"*Nine* bodies?"

"Yes, sir."

"I don't understand. Why were there so many? Was there some sort of an accident?"

"It seems that your daughter was the first victim in a rash of murders," Beverly said while looking Edward Kasay right in the eye.

"You mean a serial killer?" Kasay looked at Hoover to corroborate, as if checking with the man to make sure what the woman said was true. It was Beverly who answered his question.

"Yes, sir, a serial killer."

"You're sure that this was our Judy?"

"Her driver's license was found with her body." At that, Mrs. Kasay began to cry even harder. Her husband sat back and put his arm around her, drawing her close to his chest, holding her tight.

"Was it vicious?"

"Yes, it was."

"What'd he do to her?"

"She was cut many times. She bled to death."

"Was she raped?"

"At this point, we don't know. The pathology report hasn't come back yet."

"Pathology, Christ," Kasay whispered, looking at the ceiling, questioning God or holding back his tears. "Our little girl."

"We're truly sorry, sir," Beverly said.

He nodded, then asked angrily, "What are you going to do to find this fiend?"

"First, we need to ask you some questions about your daughter."

"What do you need to know?"

"Her full name was Judith Marie Kasay, born August 1, twenty-one years ago this year." They already knew this, but Beverly wanted one final confirmation before delving further. Since man had first developed an opposable thumb—and wielded the first weapon—

mistakes have been made in the question answering afterward. Beverly wanted to make sure that none were made today.

"That's right," Ed told her.

"Can you describe her for me?" Beverly asked, and Hoover pulled out a notebook, waiting to write down what Kasay told them.

"She had blond hair and blue eyes. She was tall and thin—"

"Can you be specific about that?"

"I don't know. Five-seven, a hundred and twenty pounds."

"Did she have any out-of-the-ordinary physical attributes such as scars, tattoos, any elective surgery?" In the day and age of liposuction and implants, it was a question that needed to be asked.

"No surgery, but she did have a tattoo."

"Where?"

"On her pelvis."

"Do you have a picture of it?"

"No."

"Can you describe it?"

"No, I never saw it. My wife told me about it. I never mentioned to Judy that I knew she had it."

"Ma'am, could you describe it for us?" Beverly asked, addressing Mrs. Kasay, who, it appeared, had run out of tears.

"Sure, but why?" she asked in a timid voice.

"We're looking for anything that could possibly tie your daughter with either a suspect or one of the other deceased women."

"Oh, I don't think her tattoo will help with that. It was on her right hip, a cherry with a flag on the stem. There was a date that was personal to Judy inscribed on the flag."

"What was the date?"

Mrs. Kasay told them and Hoover wrote it down.

"Do you know what the significance of the date was?"

"Yes," Mrs. Kasay said with a sob, "it was the first time she'd had sex." Apparently, there were still more tears in the well.

"I'm sorry, ma'am. I know it's hard, but I have to ask these questions. And please believe me, I wouldn't ask them if I didn't think they would help us find the person responsible." Beverly was fully a woman, but with a cop's sense of authority. The duality was both comforting and reassuring, as if passionate, but in control.

"I understand," Miriam Kasay said.

"Was this with a boyfriend or . . . ," Beverly let it hang.

"Yes, a boyfriend. David Stanton. They dated throughout high school. After graduation, they went on a trip down the shore to Wildwood, New Jersey. That's where they . . . they did it. The next day, she got the tattoo, while still down the shore. They remained an item that whole summer, but then he went away to college and dropped out of the picture."

Beverly and Hoover were both sure that the tattoo was a dead end, but Mr. David Stanton would still have to be looked into, out of the picture or not.

"Any other boyfriends?"

"None that she ever brought home."

"Could you give us the names and addresses of all of Judy's friends, including Mr. Stanton's?"

"We'll give you what we know," said Ed, "but she went to visit her friends by herself, so we don't know many of their addresses."

"When was the last time you saw your daughter?"

"She had gone to work one night and hadn't come home. This was last May, the twenty-first." Edward had resumed answering Beverly's questions.

"What time did she leave?"

"Around four-thirty in the afternoon."

"Did she leave alone?"

"Yes. She drove her car."

"Did she pick anyone up to give a ride to work?"

"Not to our knowledge."

"Where is the car now?"

"After she left with it, we never saw it again. We reported it missing, hoping that if they found the car, they'd find Judith."

"What kind of car was it?"

"It was an old, beat-up Dodge Caravan."

"Can you describe it for me?"

He did.

"Where did your daughter work, sir?"

A glance passed between Edward and Miriam Kasay, who were still nestled together for support. "Judy told us she worked in a shoe store at that large outlet mall off Route 63. I can't remember the name of the mall. Do you know the one I'm talking about?"

"We do," Beverly answered for both of them.

"She said she worked in a store called Walking on Air, said she was a sales manager in training."

"But you don't believe she worked there?"

"No."

"Why not?"

"She seemed to have too much money to be working a job at a mall. Plus there were the hours she worked, evenings and nights. What salesperson starts work in the evening, after normal business hours? Then she'd be out until all hours of the night. I asked her about it one time, and she said that she wasn't doing direct sales, and the late hours were because her job consisted of doing the paperwork for the sales that were made throughout the day."

"If not the mall, then what did you suspect she was doing?"

"We could only guess. Neither of us ever asked her directly. We were only thankful that she kept coming home safely." Mrs. Kasay started to cry again as her husband talked. "And then one day, she didn't. I'm ashamed to say it, Detective, but I hold myself responsible for Judy's death. If I had been the father I should've been, and demanded that she tell us what she was up to, Judy would still be alive today.

"You have to understand, though," he almost pleaded, "we raised our little girl with a free will. We taught her to look to her conscience for the answers to moral questions. I thought that that was the way God intended it to be. He made humans in his own image, then gave them a free will. Don't get me wrong; we're not Bible thumpers, but . . . I don't know. It just sounded like the right thing to do. But it wasn't, was it?

"If either of you have any children, watch them carefully. They might think they know everything, but they don't. Even after they become adults—as Judy was when she disappeared—watch them. They'll give signs when they need you. No one will know your children better than you, because they are *you*. You'll know when something isn't right. That's when you have to be strong, be a parent, even if it hurts to do so. When my time came, I wasn't strong enough, and I let Judy slip away from us. I wish I could make this right, wish I could do it all over again, because now I'd be able to be strong enough for her. But I can't, can I? There won't be a next time. There won't be any way to right this terrible wrong, will there?

"Don't let what happened to us happen to you," Kasay said. "The world is an unforgiving bitch."

*   *   *

The detectives wrote down what little information Judith Kasay's parents had on her friends, which did not include David Stanton's address, then left with one of the deceased's hairbrushes in a cellophane bag for the lab to extract strands of DNA for proof positive on the body. Back out on the street, they walked in silence to the car. They drove off in that same sorrowful silence, with only their private thoughts to rationalize what Ed Kasay had just said.

11

*H*oover sat in darkness.

One small source of light spilled into the living room from the next, the bedroom, but the ambient lighting was not wide enough to reach the easy chair where Hoover sat. The detective was off duty, or as off duty as a cop could get. He sat in a relaxed posture even though he was anything but relaxed. His sport coat and tie were gone, his shirt unbuttoned and pulled from the waistband of his pants, a strong bourbon and soda in one hand rested on the arm of the chair.

Beverly and Hoover had gone to the other two houses after they left the Kasay residence. The second house they visited hadn't been as bad as the Kasay's in one respect—there had been no crying, no suffering. Other than that, it had been terrible just the same.

The house itself had been a ransacked row home that sat squarely in the middle of a run-down street. Toys, clothes, and food were strewn equally about the interior and exterior. The house had once been the residence of a young woman named Andrea Hustead. Her placement within the assemblage of bodies indicated that she had been the fifth victim.

When the detectives broke the heart-wrenching news to her father, George, he didn't seem to care. He hadn't batted an eye when they explained the grisly details of what had happened to his daughter. George Hustead, whose wife had run off and left him to raise Andrea and her three sisters alone, stated that he always knew that one, meaning Andrea, was going to amount to no good. He said she had probably finally pissed off the wrong person and got what she deserved. His callous statements would have put him in first place on the probable suspect list, if the detectives thought it even remotely possible that he had any contact with any of the other victims. As it stood, he would be looked at through a microscope but would probably turn up clean. A dickhead for sure, but clean nonetheless.

When they pushed him for details on his daughter's life, he pushed them out the door, saying that he was late for work. The only real information he had was that he had last seen Andrea sometime in November, this he knew because she had taken her sisters out for Halloween. After that, he couldn't recall exactly. He didn't know any of her friends but had seen some of them from afar and could tell they were bad news, up to no good. When the detectives asked him to elaborate about Andrea's life, he said she was a junkie and a whore.

"Literally?" Hoover had asked.

"Yeah, literally," he answered.

"Did she have a job?"

"Sure, she had a job. She was an *entrepreneur*. Her job was buying and selling."

"Buying and selling what?"

"Her mind and her body and her dope." That was it, then he left.

As bad as the Hustead house had been, the next visit was worse. It had been to the Dasher's, the most recent victim's family, which had therefore made their sorrow all the more poignant, since there had been such little time between the disappearance and the realization of their worst nightmare.

Sherry's mother, father, and sister had been sitting down to a late dinner when the detectives showed up on their doorstep. Because Sherry had only been missing for a little over a week, the Dasher family hadn't given up hope yet—at least until Hoover and Farrell dealt them the crushing blow. Once it was out there, all hell broke loose. All three of them, parents and sibling, cried and wailed. The Dashers were strict Protestants, the patriarch a reverend at their church, and all three of them repeatedly invoked the name of God and quoted scripture. Neither of the detectives could get a feel for how to play this one. They settled for sparse questions, peppered wherever they could get a word in. After an hour and a half, what they got was that Sherry had been a loner who worked at the local gas-station convenience store called the

Stop Mart, and had been attending Rutgers University in New Jersey.

After a long day of misery, they had little more than they started with, but what little they had would take a lot of legwork to sort out. They had rounded off the characters of the three dead women by putting lives to the names and faces. The thread of each woman had unraveled to expose many strings. One of those strings would eventually lead them to the person they sought. And that bastard's string would be the one that would wind all the others up into a neat little ball of twine.

"Let's recap," Beverly suggested.

Hoover had been driving but hadn't really been concentrating on it. He had had an anatomy and physiology teacher in college who had remarked one time that the act of driving became so natural people didn't even realize they were doing it; driving became a reflex handled by the nervous system in the spine. Then Hoover had thought the teacher crazed from the smell of formaldehyde, but driving away from the Dasher house, he held a new understanding for what the guy had been talking about— Hoover had been physically driving, but his mind had been far away, sifting through the information he and Beverly had gathered.

"Two out of the three dead women's families were religious, which means they too were probably raised into the religion," Hoover said, speaking rhetorically.

"They're different religions, though. The Dashers were Protestant, and they didn't say exactly, but I think the Kasays were Catholic. Where are you going with this?"

"Nowhere, just rambling."

"Ramble on then."

"Both of the girls with religion were from good homes. Hustead's mother left, ditching the family. How do we know it wasn't a good home before she left?"

"If it was such a good home, then why'd she ditch?"

"Good point. But what if her mother was the religious one, and the old man couldn't take it and drove her away? He wasn't exactly Saint George, you know."

"That might explain why Andrea turned bad. She might blame God for her mother's disappearing act, and the hooking and the drugs were her way of rebelling against him."

"That would sound plausible to me . . ."

"Except?"

"Except," he continued, "the Kasays said they thought their daughter was involved in extracurricular activities too."

"So what? It's a coincidence."

"I don't think so. Two out of three are excellent odds. I'm willing to bet that the loner, Sherry Dasher, was up to something the good reverend and his wife didn't know about." Hoover was staring straight ahead out the windshield, the look in his eyes vacant— staring blankly outward, he was looking within. "Think of it; it makes sense. Three beautiful young women, all of them brutally slain over sex, sex with a religious undertone or background or whatever."

"You don't know that, John. You're jumping to conclusions."

"Sure it's conjecture, but it feels right. Can't you feel it, Bev? Down deep, where the instincts harbor, you think I'm right. I know you do, because I know you."

"You don't know me, Hoover," she said quietly, but with an edge, her brown eyes ominously darker than usual.

He went on talking as if reciting a soliloquy, as if he hadn't heard her.

"What kind of world is it where a man treats women like this? Slicing them up like pieces of meat, only there for his own twisted satisfaction. Not for a second did he stop to think of the life that woman had, or what he was doing to it. Not one. Fucking. *Second*. Not once did he acknowledge that she was someone's daughter, sister, friend. You know what this guy thinks women are? Pussies. That's all, just a place to stick his dick and shoot his load. They're a tube, a vessel, not a person with a soul. Bastards like this never think of their victim's souls."

"Hoover, relax. You're getting carried away."

"*I AM NOT GETTING CARRIED AWAY*," he shouted, pointing his finger toward her but not turning to look at her. For that, she was grateful. She didn't know if she could handle that vacant, dead stare looking directly at her, looking at her own soul.

"I heard a man call his daughter a whore today. A whore! That was his little girl at one time. I'm sure the day she was born he had a glint in his eye. Right there," he said, turning his pointing finger toward his own eye. "I'm sure he was a proud father, thought he'd move the world for his girl if she needed it. But today, the day he hears she's dead, today he calls her a whore. Old man Kasay realized he dropped the ball, but not this guy. This guy threw it away like it was trash. Why? Are men that evil that they have to treat women this way, treat them like trash? We're supposed to be the stronger sex, supposed to be gentle with them, take care of them, not hang them upside down and cut them so many times that they bleed to death."

"Fuck, Hoover. You're letting it get to you. Stop it. You can't take this stuff personally."

Amazingly, Hoover went silent.

"Look, it's late. It's been a long and trying day for both of us. Let it go for tonight; we'll start fresh in the morning. We're close to the Roundhouse now; just drop me off, and go home to your wife." The last word dripped out of her mouth like poison.

Hoover remained quiet for a minute, then, "Am I that evil, Bev? Am I like him, the guy who killed those women?"

Beverly put her hand to her forehead and closed her eyes, feeling as if she were Sisyphus with his rock—weary of trying to put an end to an endless task. She sighed and turned to him. Reaching out, she rested a hand on his shoulder. "It's history, in our past. Don't do this to yourself," she said, soothing.

"I didn't do it to myself; I did it to you. You might pretend you've gotten over it, pushed past it, but I can tell you haven't. I heard it in your voice just then, when you told me to go home to my wife."

She had tried to go easy with him, but it hadn't worked. It made her angry that he had to keep bringing it up after she warned him more than once not to. Irritated, she said, "No, I haven't been able to get past it. I thought I had, but when I got assigned to this case with you, I felt butterflies fluttering around in my stomach. I knew then that I hadn't gotten past it, had only partitioned it off. This morning Korzenowski tore that partition down, and now I'm trying to put it back up. And you know what else, frankly, I'm not the one dwelling on it; you are!"

"I'm not dwelling—"

"Yes you are, John!"

"Damn it, I said I'm not dwelling. Just trying to talk about it, that's all."

"I don't want to talk about it."

"Why not?"

"It's history. It happened, and now it's over. That's the way it is and that's the way I want it to stay," she told him. They had arrived at Eighth and Race, the Roundhouse. Hoover pulled the department car into the lot from Cherry Street and parked.

"I'm sorry," he said. "I thought talking about it would help us get over it."

"You're not listening to me. I don't want to 'get over it'; I want to forget it."

"Fine. Don't get mad at me."

"Why shouldn't I?"

"I don't know. Look, I'll let it go, like you want. I'll forget about it. I'm just trying to do the right thing by you."

"That wasn't what you were trying to do a couple of years ago." She had bitten him, and now it was time to go. She opened her door and began to get out.

"I hurt you that bad?" he asked her back.

She turned, bent down, and leaned back into the car. She gave him a long, deep look. He could see that her eyes were wet, welling.

"Yes, you did," she said and slammed the door.

* * *

Hoover took a swallow from the glass of bourbon as he mulled over what Beverly had said.

From the bedroom, where the weak light shone, came a voice. Sweet and tender, loving and feminine, it was the good voice of a good woman, the voice of his woman.

"Do you want to tell me?" she asked.

"Tell you what?"

Emerging from the depths of the bedroom, she stopped and leaned against the doorway. She appraised him, and he her. He knew that he looked a mess, she the exact opposite—she looked divine, had the clean smell of a fresh bath.

She wore only a white cotton T-shirt that came down to just below her groin, behind her the single light that weakly shone into the room where Hoover sat His night vision was impaired from having unconsciously been staring at the soft pool of light as he replayed the day's events in his head. Because his vision hadn't adjusted back, the woman before him stood in silhouette.

The glow from the backlight made the thin fabric of her shirt translucent, illuminating the shape of her curves through the material. He could see the hourglass of her body—a shape men lusted after, a shape that belonged to him, the dark sloping heft of her breasts, the rounded arcs of her hips, in between them the flat plane of her belly. Looking at her like this, he could see God's master plan. Women were the procreators of the species. It only seemed right that the oval shape of childbearing hips at one end and the similar oval shape of nurturing breasts at the other were pinched together where they met in the middle of the body, where the uterus could distend, forming an hourglass—the shape of the symbol for infinity, the unending loop of two ovals connected in the middle.

Interesting, if only for a moment.

Hoover was distracted from his theory of life by his maleness. More specifically, by the way his maleness hungered for her femininity. He looked at her standing there and noticed the casual way she leaned her shoulder against the jamb. He enjoyed the confidence she exuded in herself by letting her arms dangle freely at her sides instead of hugging them over her breasts in protective defense. He was excited by the way she crossed her bare legs, the lamplight from the bedroom scantily kissing across her feet and painted toes, the color of which he was too far away to see.

Although he couldn't see her clearly, he could smell her perfectly. It was the sinfully intoxicating scents of mild perfume and the overlaying pheromones of sex.

Her name was Fiona, and he loved to look at her.

When he realized she hadn't clarified her question, he repeated his own. "Tell you what?"

"Tell me where you are," she said.

"What do you mean? I'm right here."

Fiona uncrossed her ankles and walked toward him. He watched her legs scissor open and close as she approached. "You come here in the wee small hours of the morning," she said. "You pour yourself a drink and sit in that chair, languishing and ignoring me. I wouldn't even know you were here if I couldn't see you. You don't move; you don't talk; you just sit. You're here physically, but your mind is somewhere else. So I ask again, where are you?"

She now stood directly in front of him. He looked up at her and noticed for the first time that her black hair and dark eyes were very similar to Beverly's.

"I'm sorry. I've got something on my mind," he confessed.

"So let's talk about it," she said, sinking to her knees beside his chair. Now she was the one looking up, stroking the hair on his arm.

"It's not something I want to talk about. You know I don't like to bring the office home."

"You usually don't, but tonight you did. That's not like you, which leads me to believe whatever's bothering you is pretty heavy."

He smiled. "Think you know me pretty well, huh?"

"After all this time, how could I not?"

"You're a good woman."

She shook her head. "No, I'm the *best* woman."

He let that one lie, remaining silent.

Her slight playfulness/slight seriousness went undeterred by his silence. "We have ways of making you talk," Fiona said in a silly German accent, taking the hand that was stroking his arm and placing it in the fork of his crotch.

"How do you suppose imitating Sergeant Schultz is going to arouse me?" he asked.

"I'm not trying to arouse you I'm trying to lighten you up. Is it working?"

"Not much," he said. She squeezed her stroking hand, causing him to lift out of the seat slightly. "Hey, now. Those guys down there don't enjoy such a firm grip."

She let go, resting her hand on his leg. "Then talk, Detective."

"I'm sorry, Fee. But what I've got on my mind I wouldn't feel comfortable talking about with you. It has to do with some things I saw today. Unspeakable things. It amazes me the level of meanness man is capable of, saddens me and horrifies me at the same time. It's eating me up inside, but I would rather not talk about it, especially not in the middle of the night. I just need to think it over." He swallowed a belt of the drink. Fiona took the glass from his hand, drinking the last of the hard liquor that'd only been slightly cut with soda. She grimaced and sat the glass on the floor, then lowered her head and laid it on top of the hand resting on his leg.

"I've heard tales of murder and mayhem before, you know" she said.

"No doubt, I'm sure you have. But this one's different."

"How? What makes this one so special?"

"Because it's not only about the bad guys out there; it's also about the one inside me," he said, pointing to his chest.

After a slight pause, she asked, "Did you kill anyone?"

"You know I've shot and killed in the line of duty before, twice."

"Anyone today?"

"No."

"Then why are you beating yourself up?"

"Because sometimes I do things I know are wrong, but I do them anyway. A couple of people reminded me of that shortcoming today."

"Who?"

"One of them was a man I don't know, who hurt a lot of women; the other was a woman I did know, who was hurt before."

"What do they have to do with you?"

"Nothing, everything."

"I'm sorry, John. I don't understand."

"I know, forget it. I shouldn't be telling you this. I shouldn't even be here; I should be out working."

"Good mood or bad, happy or hurting, it's never wrong for you to come here, John," she said, her brown eyes looking lovingly into his. "I'll show you."

She put her head fully in his lap. In a second, he was in her mouth. While she worked, he whispered, "Yes, it is. It's wrong for me to come here."

12

As he did first thing every day, he went to the website to scroll through the newspapers.

A telephone line and a modem could bring you the world. It could deliver products, services, or information. One of the many things that it brought Michael Dedaker was the news. At the start of every new day, whether that start was morning or night, the first thing he did after finishing his ablutions was read the newspapers. He usually scanned the *Washington Post* and the *New York Times* for world events, then checked the two local newspapers, the *Philadelphia News Daily* and the *Philadelphia Inquisitor*, to see if he himself—or at least his work—had made either paper. Both Philadelphia newspapers utilized the same website, being jointly owned and operated by the same conglomerate that lorded over multiple newspapers and magazines nationwide.

Today, Dedaker did not have to leaf through the electronic pages one by one, scanning every article on the monitor, because his was the lead story on the cover of both papers. The banners were printed in thirty-point bold black lettering proclaiming, "Nine Bodies Found" as the lead in the *Inquisitor*—the more sophisticated of the two papers—and "Mass Grave" as the headline of the *News Daily*.

Michael Dedaker jumped up from his keyboard, overturning the chair he had been sitting in as if he'd been shocked, which in fact he was. He was shocked at the news of the police discovery, his face flush, his body tense. He didn't know how to contain himself. He paced—stalked—around in a circle, not knowing what to do, not knowing how to act, or more precisely, react. He knew that he had to calm himself and could feel the heat of the blood in his face and chest, his stalking circle getting larger with each revolution around the overturned chair. Finally, he ran out of space and found himself standing up against a wall in the living room of the upper duplex apartment.

He put his hands flat against the wall and bowed his head, leaning it against the thin coating of paint covering the drywall beneath. Eyes closed, he breathed deeply, trying to gather himself but couldn't.

Michael Dedaker was euphoric.

He had broken the lights at the airport hoping that it would lead them to the discovery. It had worked. It was all in motion now, and out of his hands. He had planned for so long, and now it felt as if everything were moving too fast. He had to slow himself down, had to regain control.

"You have to calm down, Michael," he told himself. "You knew they would find out eventually. They *needed* to find out; the whole thing depends on it. You know that the word of God cannot be spread if no one's there to hear it. You have their ear now. You have the ear of the infidel; use it to your advantage. Spread the word, do the work of God."

That quickly, he was back within himself, the serenity of his makeshift prayer calming him.

He took a couple more deep breaths and, after righting the chair, sat back down at the computer and began to read. There was an abundance of material about the find. Dedaker counted twenty-seven pages in total from both newspapers dedicated to the women. The articles had varied slants to them, but they all said the same things. There were articles about the nature of the kills (which the small-minded people of the press would only write of as "murders," not salvations) and articles about the police investigations. There were articles wrongly comparing his work with murders committed by others in the past: Edward Gein, Jeffrey Dahmer, and Philly's own claim to infamy, Gary Heidnik. Most of it was only filler, which illustrated that the police had no concrete evidence as of yet, the articles mainly written to glorify the violent nature of his work. They had to be, because that's what the bloodthirsty public wanted to read. The ink may be black, but the words dripped crimson—no doubt about it, blood sold newspapers.

When Dedaker finished reading all the articles, he read them again. Finally satisfied that he had gained all the knowledge from them he could, he clicked the icon to print then sat back to think about what it all meant, while the printer hummed its soft music.

He was proud of what he had accomplished. He had risked his own existence to save the lost souls of those women. He had made sure that their names would be spoken aloud—proclaimed—by leaving their identifications with the carcasses, so that the newly forgiven could receive their due atonement. This he did selflessly, and did the bastards recognize it? Not yet, but they would, they would. Even though the infidels did not recognize the results of his work for what they were, it had still been a task worthy of undertaking—God would still grant his forgiveness to the women Michael had released from their sinful, bodily prisons, even if the infidels never did.

His, Dedaker's, was a complex, thankless situation, one in which the infidels were both the problem and the solution.

The problem was that it was theoretically possible the infidels could deduce such a line of reasoning that would enable them to untimely reach out and find him, Michael, before he could finish his work.

The infidels were close, but not that close, at least as far as the papers indicated. At this juncture, Michael thought that, if they could reach out for him, they would have. He was still free to complete the job, but it would get tougher from here. The longer he continued to do God's work, the closer they would get to him. But that was then and this was not. He would have to remain one step ahead of them, until Purser Street, then it would be finished.

The world must know why those women had died.

The articles called the deaths mindless, but they were anything but mindless; they were pointed. The slanted views of the news media made it sound as if they were killed without care, but they weren't. It was care that killed them.

Without care *was how they had lived their lives. I came along and cared enough about those women—whom society would cast aside—to save them. I saved them.*

Now that they were aware, he would have to present to the infidels the beauty of these deaths and how they were in accordance with God's will. He now had to step from the shadows, with the burden of that will on his shoulders. It was time to take it to the next level, the last level.

It was time to take it to Purser Street.

And he knew just how to begin the end stage because as he understood, the infidels were also the solution.

13

"Daddy! Daddy!" came a duo of high-pitched voices.

Hoover bent down and scooped up his daughters, one in each arm. "Good morning," he said. It was just after seven o'clock when they rained their kisses and hugs on him. "And how are my ladies doing today?"

"Fine" was the response from Jane, the elder of the two.

"Good" was from his little one, Pamela.

Both of the girls, six and five respectively, tall for their ages, had blond hair and blue eyes—features which represented their mother.

Janey was in first grade, and Pammy had just started her formal schooling in a parent-teacher cooperative Nursery school.

Holding both of his daughters in his arms, Hoover remembered Pammy's first days in the PTCN, and he remembered his wife's pleasure at having been able to experience something like that with their baby, by attending class with her. Hoover himself had even been looking forward to working a few days at the school, thinking that it would be a nice bond to have shared with his daughter, but his job always seemed to get in the way. Attending Pammy's preschool was just one of the many things that all the hours spent trudging through the lives of dead strangers had cost him.

He was a good father in the providential sense, but he was lacking when it came to quality time.

And he thought it showed.

His girls doted over him, couldn't wait until they saw him, always asking their mother when Daddy was coming home. But then, when he finally did get home, he was too tired to do anything with them. How was he supposed to explain to a six—and a five-year-old that he was out cleaning up other people's lives, while he was willing to let his dismantle a millimeter at a time? His children's youths were passing him by, and for what? Justice? He didn't think so. One only had to take a look at the Sullivan debacle to come to that conclusion. No, it definitely wasn't justice. Satisfaction of a job well done? Maybe. But was that a good-enough reason? It's said that in order to be happy in life, you should be happy in your work, and for the most part he was. What he was not happy with was himself, and that left him unhappy in life. Unhappy in life and unlucky in love . . . with the wrong person.

He smiled as best he could while his daughters hugged him, but he couldn't hide the sadness in his eyes.

"Hi, John," his wife said.

He looked up at the sound of her voice coming from the kitchen. The vibrant spring sunlight shone strongly into the house; the morning sun was always brightest in the kitchen, which had been built facing the east His wife stood in the doorway, looking at the three of them, at her little family. Hoover could not see his wife's face, the sunlight behind her so intense, but he knew she was smiling—she always smiled when she saw the three people she loved most all together. Some women want education, occupation, independence; Lauren Hoover only ever wanted to be a mother and a wife.

She stood silhouetted in the kitchen doorway. With the loving embrace of his daughters' small, fragile arms wrapped around his neck, he stared at his wife's form and was reminded of the night before, in another doorway, in another house, with another woman.

"Good morning, babe," Hoover said. To the girls, who were still hugging and kissing, he said, "All right, let's go see your mommy."

Carrying the children, Hoover entered the kitchen. Lauren had been cooking breakfast for the girls, one of their favorites, banana pancakes. The smell of home cooking, after a long day of greasy spoon that started early *yesterday* morning, was tantalizing. His mouth began to water instantly as he looked at the woman who had prepared the food for his babies.

Lauren Marks Hoover was a very beautiful woman. She was what some would consider a trophy wife, if Hoover had been a rich, old bastard. But he wasn't rich and she wasn't a trophy. What she had been was his high school sweetheart, before he took her hand in marriage, and the only reason that a woman like Lauren was with a guy like Hoover was because she loved him. If love were true, everything else in life would take care of itself. Lauren's unparalleled beauty was only surpassed by her sincerity.

Lauren Hoover was, at thirty-three years old, four years younger than John. She stood five foot-seven and had the same strawberry blond hair and powder blue eyes that her daughters shared. As thin as a runway model, her hips were slender, her cheekbones high, and her face unlined by age or worry. Her breasts were on the small side, but it worked for her—they gave off the appearance that it was not quantity, but rather quality, that counted.

"Family hug," screamed Pammy, right into Hoover's ear, dissolving his appreciation of his wife's form. Since he was also holding Janey, the scream pierced her ear too.

Janey gave the younger girl a large, windmilling left hook directly into her shoulder muscle. "That's my ear, you big dumb dork," she added to the punch.

"Hey," said Hoover in a fatherly tone, then immediately looked at Pammy to see what the retaliation would be.

The five-year-old's face was a twisted mask of pain as she rubbed the area Janey had targeted. "You're the dork" was the comeback.

"You are," said the elder.

"You are," said the baby.

"You are," repeated Janey.

"You are," said Pammy.

From experience, Hoover knew this would continue until the older one got mad enough to cuff the little one again, this time much harder and in a more strategic place than the shoulder, so it was his duty to put an end to it here and now. "You're both dorks," he said.

They stopped squirming in his arms and turned to look at him. The look of surprise on their faces, that their dad—who only spoke adult-speak—knew the word "dork," was priceless. To the younger one, he said, "You know, if you use your indoor voice, you might get what you want."

"Can we have a family hug?" Pammy asked in an exaggerated voice that would've been appropriate for a monk who had taken a vow of silence.

The "family hug" was self-explanatory—a hug shared simultaneously with every member of the family. Hoover played dumb. "A family hug? What's that?" He gazed dopily from girl to girl to wife. They were all smiling at him.

"You know, Dad," said Pammy in her cutest, loving coo.

"Yeah, I know," he said to her, then spread his arms as wide as he could with two human child-weights in each to let Lauren into the circle. She fit perfectly. The four of them stood in a tight pack, hugging each other, both of the girls alternately kissing their parents.

"Okay, that's enough," said Lauren. "Your pancakes are getting cold, and we all know that neither of you will eat cold pancakes." The thing about children was that they were susceptible to mind tricks. If you inadvertently placed an adverse idea in their heads, they'd run with it, and it was almost impossible to remove such an idea, once fused with their intelligence. Naturally, the mention of cold pancakes was enough to negate any desire for eating that the children had.

"Yuck," said Jane.

"I don't want any," said Pam, shaking her head, a queasy look coming over her.

"You're both going to sit down and eat some of them. Your mother worked hard for you to have a nice breakfast."

"Aww, Dad, do we have to?" Janey pleaded.

"I'm not eating them," Pammy said, putting her foot down, still shaking her head.

"Of course you're going to eat them. We can't let all of those soft, wet, mushy, cold banana chunks go to waste, can we?"

"Gross! Let me out of here!" Jane used her weight to push off Hoover's chest. She dropped to the floor and scampered out of the kitchen. As for Pam, she covered her mouth and made a choking noise that sounded like she was going to throw up. For real. Apparently, mind tricks worked strongly with this one; after all, she was the one with the weaker constitution of the two. Hoover chuckled and started to make gagging sounds of his own.

Adamantly, Lauren said, "If she pukes on the floor I just mopped yesterday, you're going to *wax* it, John." She was serious; he could tell because her emphasis finger was pointing at him.

He gently lowered Pammy to the floor and swatted her on the butt. She ran off to join her sister as quickly as her little legs could pump.

Alone, Lauren playfully slapped him on the chest. "You're rotten. Why'd you do that? What am I going to do with all that food now?"

"I did it on purpose. I wanted the pancakes for myself. There's a method to the madness."

"Yeah, but now they didn't have anything to eat before school."

"I'll hand them an apple and a juice box on their way out the door."

"You better," she warned, but there was laughter in her eyes. "Come here, you big lug."

Hoover walked over to her and they shared a hug that was strictly *not* a family hug.

Encircled in his arms, Lauren laid her head on his chest. She said, "I saw the news last night. Did you hook the big one?" She was referring to the bodies in the woods.

"Yeah, sure did." He sounded tired, as if the whole idea of plodding along, trying to find the answer to the riddle of why someone would want to butcher such beautiful young women, wore him out.

"Think you'll be able to reel him in?"

"Hope so. It's early yet, but Korzenowski put a pretty good team together—six homicide dicks with me as the lead. We pounded the beat pretty hard yesterday. Nine bodies; each one of them a twentyish female with multiple cuts and her throat slit, then dropped in the woods where we got them."

"Oh, those poor people."

"Tell me about it. I had to break the news to three of their parents today . . . yesterday . . . whenever. I'm emotionally drained."

"How'd they take it?"

"Exactly as you'd expect them to take it. Imagine if it was—"

"Don't say it, John! Don't even *think* it!" Hoover could feel Lauren's body tense up at the thought, unable to take her own advice. He hugged her tighter, and she shivered a little. "You're home now," she said after banishing the evil image. "After I get the kids off to school, I'll give you a nice warm bath. I'll wash *all* the places you like, and then we'll crawl into bed naked, without even drying ourselves so the covers stick to our bodies."

"That sounds like fun . . ."

"But what?"

"But I can't. Korzenowski called for meetings first thing in the morning for the duration of the investigation."

"You just got here. Can't you stay for a while?"

"No. The meeting's at nine; I've just enough time to eat and shower before I have to run."

"That's not right. You never even came home last night. You must be exhausted."

"I caught a couple of hours on a couch around three," he said, lying.

"How can they expect you to get anything done on two hours' sleep?"

"Nature of the beast."

Lauren looked up at him. At six foot-three, Hoover stood half a foot taller than his wife, the height difference acutely noticeable when she wasn't wearing any shoes, as she wasn't now. He held onto her and looked down into her upturned face. He could feel the love radiating back up at him. It was a trusting, depending love. It was an unquestioning love. It was her love.

Hoover didn't know how to categorize his own feelings for her. He had fallen in love with her while in high school. Had fallen pretty hard too. There were days when he couldn't think about anything except being with Lauren Marks, times when he couldn't concentrate on the rest of the world spinning around him. Being with Lauren was like looking into the corona of the sun—if you looked directly at it, you'd be glare blinded, unable to see anything else except the afterimage. Stare too long and you could go blind permanently. Hoover had stared too long, and the result had been marriage.

For a while, Hoover thought himself happy in marriage, blind and blissful, then along came a miracle worker who restored his sight. Or maybe she was an enchanting witch. One way or the other, he had been too close to the epicenter to judge. He thought he had known right from wrong, learning it at a young age. But after having met this bewitching woman, he began to wonder if there could be a center position, a median, a place where things equaled each other out.

It was a mere four years into his marriage (which was about to enter its fifteenth year this September) that this miracle worker/enchantress came into his life. She had been a college coed; she had been fun. She had been on fire.

He met her while working out of South Detectives. He had been investigating the robbery of a nightclub on Delaware Avenue for which she had been an employee working the night of the incident. Her name was Kelly Connelly, Irish to the bone, and it showed in her coppery red hair—hair that gave him the impression of her being "on fire," the same hair that restored his sun-glared vision. Restored it in vivid color. Her hair had been the first thing to strike Hoover, and it struck him like a shot to the groin. His eyes followed the flow of it as it cascaded over her shoulders like a river of molten lava, her long strands curly but controlled. Its waves caught the light and shimmered, giving off sparks. As soon as he saw its splendor—and the beauty of the woman beneath—he understood what it meant to want, to yearn. "Yearning" was one of those words you thought you knew but never really comprehended the true meaning of until something like this came along.

On the morning he met Kelly Connelly, Hoover knew what it was to yearn.

He looked at her and, in one second, knew that he had to have her. In the next second, he remembered his wife, and that angered him. He had the audacity to be angry at being held back by a woman he supposedly thought he loved. He began to doubt himself and his relationship with Lauren. Had he jumped the gun too soon, marrying the first woman who would have him?

His wife was a very beautiful woman indeed, but she could not compare to the beauty possessed by this redheaded vixen. Kelly was young and vibrant; she flew by the seat of her pants. His wife was more mature and rationalizing. The two of them were like oil and water. One was smooth and slick and made things shine, the other the bland, colorless, building block of life. Two elements that certainly would not mix.

Or would they?

Their separate properties were too different from each other for them to blend on their own, but what if there was a catalyst to change their base? What if he could be that catalyst, and their mixture—while impossible to join with each other alone—could be united within *him*? He could take as much as he wanted from each without them ever having to collide with each other. They could each unknowingly collude with him without ever being told of the other, their infusion forming solidly within him, within his heart.

He had contemplated this devilish idea when he first saw Kelly. The pact was sealed when he talked to her.

When they were introduced, she had been working behind the smaller of the two bars in the building. The club was one of many along the Delaware River that changed hands often. Under the current management, it had been called Caliente—a Spanish word that meant "hot." When Hoover first noticed the name on the responding officer's report, he had imagined it would be a bar frequented by Hispanics. He had been wrong. Caliente was a club full of young Caucasians who thought themselves socialites but in actuality were Pavlovian dogs—the only difference being that they were programmed by their uppity parents rather than by Ivan Petrovich Pavlov.

Walking into the club, Hoover had expected to see members of the Hispanic and Puerto Rican communities alike. Instead, he had seen yuppies. He had been surprised, to say the least, but once introduced to Kelly of the coppery red hair, he thought the name of the club an appropriate one—*ella es muy caliente.*

He was led to her by a huge, burly man with graying hair. Hoover put him at around forty and thought it pathetic for a man his age to be trying to recapture his youth by working as a bouncer at a club that catered to twentyteens. Not to mention that the man was bulging all over with steroid-induced muscles so asininely large that he couldn't lower his arms all the way to the sides of his body properly.

Then he met Kelly and forgot all about how pathetic recapturing lost youth was.

"Kelly, this here is Detective Smoother," said the hulking bulk. With her back to them, the woman he addressed held up one index finger to indicate that she was busy and would be right with them. Having accomplished his one-step goal, the bouncer walked back to the door where Hoover had met him to stand sentry.

Standing behind a bar lined with liquor bottles and a large mirrored backdrop, she was positioned to the left so that Hoover was unable to see her face. Changing a roll of receipt tape in the cash register, Hoover watched as she finished.

Her shirt was black, and her red hair hung halfway down it. Printed to either side of the spill of hair were yellow letters; to the left, a capital letter S" to the right an F. Hoover guessed that the rest of the letters would spell out the word "staff." Completing her ensemble, she wore a pair of black shorts cut so high he could see the roundness of her cheeks peeking out beneath the hem.

The cash register stood high in the air for some reason Hoover couldn't figure. He guessed it was some kind of art deco thing that made it cool for the employees to have the register's keypad at eye level. What the hell did a bar need a register that printed out receipts for anyway? Never once in his entire existence over legal drinking age had he asked for a receipt with his shot and beer. Regardless of why the register was as high as it was—or what the Caliente did with its receipts—Hoover liked the way Kelly had to stand on the tips of her toes to reach the spool reservoir. She had long, shapely legs unrestrained by pantyhose. When she stood on her toes, he could see the muscles in her calves flex and harden, and he enjoyed the fluid way she moved her body as she bounced from side to side on the balls of her feet.

At last, flipping the reservoir shut with a snap and a click, she turned from the register and smiled at him, her green eyes shining like emeralds. She wiped her hand on the miniscule apron around her waist and stuck it out for him to shake. "Smoother, huh? Is that a name or a reputation?"

"It's Hoover, actually, but I wasn't going to correct *that* guy. He might've beat me up," he said with a smile.

"Easily intimidated, are you?" she asked.

There was no tactful way he could tell her that he hadn't been intimidated by the muscle-bound side of beef, but that a certain redhead was making his knees feel watery.

He said, "Nope, nothing fazes me. I'm a cop."

"Detective Hoover, eh? Any relation to J. Edgar?"

"No, Herbert."

"Really? How close?"

"Distant."

"How distant?"

"Very."

"Died before you were born?"

"I was born in '67, four years after he passed."

"You a Republican?"

"Yep."

"You think the Depression was his fault?"

"Who knows? Probably. He was the leader at the time, and look where he led." He was impressed with her on-the-spot knowledge of the thirty-first president. "Inquisitive, aren't you?"

"I like to know a little something about any man about to delve into my personal life."

"You should've been a cop."

"Nah, I'm no good with the whole paramilitary thing."

"Then what's your big plan?"

"What makes you think I have a big plan? How do you know tending bar isn't what I aspire to?" she said, grabbing a fistful of red hair and flipping it back over her shoulder. When she did, he noticed a smattering of freckles along the back of her neck. Looking closer at her face, she had another dash of them running across the bridge of her nose. The slight pigmentation of the tiny freckles gently offset the beauty of her pale complexion. Hoover wondered if love at first sight were possible.

"You're better than this. You're too intelligent to be a barmaid."

"Insulting now, are we?"

"No. I just think you look like the type of person that likes a challenge," he tapped his finger on the bar. "And this is not challenging."

"No, it's not much of a challenge. But the pay is good. Real good."

"But not good enough for you, is it?"

She laughed, and it was cute. "I tell you," she said, "men never cease to amaze me. You've known me for all of two minutes and you already think you know my whole life story."

"Your words, not mine. I'm not pretending to know what your life is about. All I said was you're better than this."

"All right, Detective, you're so intuitive, wooing the young maiden with your deductive skills."

Hoover tried to brush it away gently. "I don't want to do that. You misunderstood me. I wasn't trying to bait you. I was trying to compliment you, in my own clumsy way."

"I know you were, but you've started this game, so now let's finish it. I can already tell that you're not as good a detective as you think you are. If you were, you would've known I was going to make you finish what you started. You missed the most obvious clue imaginable."

"Oh yeah, what was that?"

"I'm a redhead, and that means I'm stubborn. If you couldn't see that, then I've won already."

"Don't you have customers to take care of?"

"This is official police business, which I'm undertaking on behalf of the ownership," she said with a smirk, both of them aware that no actual police business had been discussed so far. Hoover didn't care; he'd get to that in due time. The longer it took to get around to talking about the robbery, the longer he'd be in the company of Miss Connelly. Hoover figured it would take a while to get down to the real reason he was here—this one liked to talk to men. "And besides, it's quarter of eleven on Monday morning," she continued. "Look around you, not many people drinking at the moment. The lunch crowd won't be here for a while; till then the rest of the staff can handle the dregs." She shook her head. "Detective, *shesh*. You get those badges mail order?"

"No, there's a test."

"Some test that must be."

Hoover was grinning from ear to ear. "Fine, what do you want me to do?" he asked, giving in to her play.

"Hmm, let's see. I want you to guess . . . no, *deduce* . . . three things about me, using only what you've seen and heard so far."

"How many tries do I get?"

"I'll play fair. You get four guesses."

"What happens if I lose?"

"Since we're talking personal like, you'll have to tell me something you consider very personal to you. Something no one else could guess without you telling them."

"And if I win?"

"The same. I'll tell you something about me that no one else here knows."

"Deal," he said, finding it remarkable that she had him wrapped around her finger so quickly. She had, in mere minutes, reduced him to the equivalent of a dog in heat. And now she was making him jump through hoops by playing truth-or-dare games.

She propped her chin in her left hand and said, "Begin."

"Observation number one: you do not want to be a bartender by profession."

"Vague. Back up your guess with information, and turn it into a theory; otherwise, I won't say yea or nay, and the point goes to me."

"There are textbooks behind the bar where you're standing. One is entitled *The Theory of Logic* and the other *Bio-Med*. From those two titles I'm going to say that you are in the latter half of a college degree. I can back that up because I've taken logic and know that it's a philosophy course offered to upperclassmen. The bio-med book indicates that you're going for a bachelor's in science, rather than arts. You don't strike me as being a science teacher or as a person who'd want to be in a "hands-on field," so that rules out nursing, occupational therapy, and a job working in a research lab. Furthermore, I think you like mind-fucking people, so I am going to guess what you really aspire to become is a psychologist—a career that'd present a suitable challenge to a woman like you."

Kelly shifted her gaze to the mirror behind the bar. In the reflection she could see the textbooks he mentioned sitting on a shelf by her knee. She could not deny that these books were hers because her car keys were resting on top of them—attached to the ring, a fob with her laminated high school graduation picture on it. The cheeky image with high-poofed hair in the photo could be clearly seen in the mirror's reflection.

Hoover looked at the reflection also but this time wasn't taking notice of the textbooks. This time he noticed the way she cocked her hip, leaning forward with her chin cupped in her hand.

Kelly looked up at him, eyes of jade impressed. "Psych major is correct, Detective Hoover. One-love," she said, tallying the score.

"Observation number two: you only work this job because you get a kick out of it. It amuses you. In more ways than one, I'll add."

"I can't wait to hear the explanation for this one."

"Lying directly on top of the aforementioned textbooks is a set of keys, your high school graduation picture attached to the ring.

On that ring there is a very distinct key in the shape of a cylinder rather than the flat of a normal key. A cylinder-shaped key is only used by one type of car that I know—a Jaguar. A very expensive car, of which the convertible XK8 model I saw out front probably runs around seventy Gs. Although you say this job pays well, I don't think it pays well enough for you to afford tuition, a Jaguar, *and* the astronomical premium of the insurance to cover such a car within the city limits. My bet is that the car belongs to daddy—who's probably a doctor himself—and it's at his expense that you get half of your kicks out of being a barmaid. It's not about money; it's about fucking with people. If my guess is correct, this job is your rebellion—you don't have to work to support yourself; you're only here to screw with your parents' heads. You've got them all freaked out that their little girl is working in the big, bad city."

After a pause, she said, "Point, Hoover. Two-love. But this is where it gets more difficult, now that you've run out of things that belong to me under the bar."

"I've got one more point on the last observation that will tie in with my third one."

"Please, do tell."

"The other half of the kick you get out of working here is that you can continually stuff it in your fiancé's face. I'll bet that he probably can't stand you working here—in a club filled with men with only two things on their mind, alcohol and pussy—and it gives you a rise that it pisses him off. The engagement is my third observation."

Kelly snapped to attention, her mouth hanging open. She was flabbergasted. "How . . . How . . . ," she stammered.

Hoover reached over the bar, picking up her left hand from where it now hung limp at her side. He held it in both of his. As he did, he felt a tightness crawl across his stomach from the physical contact with her. He pointed to her ring finger, where there was no ring.

"It's the middle of summer, and while your light skin doesn't tan deeply, it does tan a little. See this mark at the base of your finger? Notice how this area of skin is lighter than the rest of the skin around it? Because of the lighter discoloration on your ring finger, I would deduce that you have an engagement ring somewhere, one you don't wear while working because it distracts the men who regularly lavish their attention on you. It distracts them from that fiery red hair and those beautiful green eyes and cuts into your flirting, not to mention the unneeded tips you receive."

She quickly retracted her hand from his, unconsciously rubbing the empty spot where the engagement ring would be. Snapping her mouth shut, she began to chew her bottom lip while she sized him up. He imagined that she was thinking she had underestimated him, those precious green eyes dancing with the heat of anger. Redheads were notorious for having a quick temper, and he thought Kelly Connelly had just gone a long way to prove it. Were they also sore losers?

Almost as quick as it flared up, the anger drained from her eyes. Whether it went on its own or she had to force it down, he didn't know. Putting her hands on her hips (and damn if that wasn't sexy), she smiled at Hoover in an impish way, suggesting she had only been toying with him, and now that she had him where she wanted him, she was going in for the kill.

Hoover returned her smile. "I won," he said.

"Yes, you did, Detective Hoover. Good show. I'm impressed."

Hoover leaned in toward the bar in the reverse fashion of the way she'd been standing during their game of wits. "So what personal thing are you going to tell me that everyone else here doesn't already know?" he asked.

She leaned down to him, their faces inches from each other. From this distance, Hoover could smell the fresh cleanliness of her. One look at Kelly and anyone would know that she wasn't the kind of woman who would have a need for perfume. Without the heavy cloying smell of perfume, and over the odors of flat beer, spilled whisky, and never-to-dissipate cigarette smoke, Hoover could smell her. She smelled like shampoo and powder. It was a feminine smell, that of lilacs. Hoover inhaled deeply but slowly, as to be inconspicuous.

Kelly's eyes met his, locking there as she said, "I am a natural redhead."

"That's my reward?"

"Yeah, that's your reward."

"I think I was cheated. By looking at your hair and the fairness of your skin, it would've been easier to guess that than the things I guessed."

"But you didn't. The agreement we had was that if you won, I'd tell you something personal that no one else here knows about me. That's what I told you—I'm a natural redhead. Debt paid in full."

"You mean to tell me no one else here knows you're a natural redhead?"

"That's what I'm saying. You're privileged to be the only one here to have restricted information about my body."

"I find it hard to believe that no one in the club Caliente has seen *all* of you."

"I didn't say that."

"But you—"

She took the back of her hand and put it over his mouth to still his speech. For the first time, he noticed that her fingernails were long but unpainted. "My exact words," she purred, "were that no one here knows I'm a natural redhead. They don't, only you know. And that's not because no one has seen me naked; it's because I shave myself. Completely."

She dropped a wink at him, her eyes positively sparking with satisfaction as she took her hand away from his face. This time it was his mouth hanging agape.

Standing in his kitchen, holding his wife in his arms, Hoover could still smell Kelly's powder and the lilacs of her shampoo. Eventually, he pried the information about the robbery out of her, but he couldn't remember too much about that. He knew it had been a strong-armed robbery—meaning the perp had brandished a firearm—and he knew Kelly had given him a description of the individual. Other than those sketchy bits of information, he couldn't remember much more about the case, though what he could remember clearly was every word they had exchanged that *hadn't* involved the robbery. Was that wrong, or something extraordinary? He didn't know. She had been an individual he had formed a sexual relationship with, which was something he supposed should stick in a man's mind. Kelly Connelly had been the first woman he had ever enjoyed carnal knowledge of other than his wife. The robbery suspect was just another faceless drone among the hordes the cops hadn't caught.

The perp had gotten away with it, and so had Hoover. At least, he had thought so.

His wife had never found out about Kelly during the six months he had seen her on and off. He hadn't meant anything to her, and that was just the way he had wanted it. She was an engaged woman, and he, a married man sowing some wild oats; that was all. What they had done together was but a trivial act that happened a million times a day across the country.

Lauren hadn't found out about Kelly (or any of the women that had followed), but he knew. He had always thought he was okay with it, harboring no guilt, but in the past twenty-four hours, he wasn't so sure.

"What's wrong, John?" his wife asked.

"Huh? Nothing, why?"

"You looked a little confused there for a minute. You sure everything's all right?"

"Yeah, I'm fine. It's the stress of this case, knocked me for a loop." That was no lie.

"See, I told you. It's because you didn't get enough sleep."

"Probably, but what am I supposed to do?"

"I wish I knew."

"Don't worry about it, I'll be fine. But thank you."

"Maybe, when this case is over, you can take a vacation. The girls would love that."

"Sure, that sounds like a good idea."

"Then sit down and eat those pancakes before they really do get cold."

"Yuck, gross, cold pancakes."

Pushing out of his embrace, she poked a finger into his chest. "Don't you friggin' start. Sit down and eat."

"Okay, okay," he said, sitting down at the table. He watched as Lauren walked around the table, mocking a glare at him, and out of the kitchen. From where he sat he could see her walk toward the stairs leading to the second floor and the bedrooms and to where the girls were. The house was big enough for the four of them, but it wasn't that big that he couldn't hear her bare feet as they whisked through the rug, followed by the small hollow thumps of her weight as she climbed the steps.

When she was out of sight, and he could no longer hear her walking up the steps, Hoover glanced around the room. He admired the decorative touch that his wife displayed in her kitchen. And it was *her* kitchen, make no mistake. Hoover and his daughters were allowed to use it, but they were only guests in this room. From the simple pattern the appliances and utensils were set in for her to find with ease to the perfectly squared-off dishtowels and the way the childish artwork Pammy had made at the PTCN hung by magnets on the refrigerator door in symmetrical lines rather than the hodgepodge more common in a less meticulous kitchen, it was clearly Lauren's room.

He admired her for the order and structure she had in her life. Order and structure, two things he felt he was lacking; he could even feel the shallowness of the empty spaces left behind by the missing virtues. And those were but two of his many flaws. Thinking about such flaws made him feel dull, a knife without an edge, like he didn't belong anywhere. In a house he owned, in a room full of shining chrome appliances, almond-colored walls, and tasteful oak-finished cabinets, sitting at a table with home-cooked food and a centerpiece of wildflowers, listening to the pitter-patter of three separate sets of feet belonging to the women that loved him the most as they hurried along on their own busy schedules, he felt alone.

He took a forkful of pancakes and ate.

It was a cold meal.

14

Over the course of a lifetime, a person makes thousands upon thousands of choices: yes or no, right or left, in or out. Most of them get lost in the hum of the normal, mundane routine of everyday living, going unnoticed even as they dictate the next turn of events, and ultimately, the next choices. But every so often, people come upon a crossroads in their existence. Standing at that crossroads, trying to decide whether to take the beaten path or the road less traveled, a person will make a decision that will affect the total outcome of the rest of a person's life. Sometimes the crossroads can be seen far off, on the horizon, leaving ample time to prepare for it, but usually they rush at you from out of nowhere in the blink of an eye. Whether you are prepared or not, the repercussions of decisions made at the crossroads run deep.

Much like Sherry Dasher, John Hoover came upon his crossroads in a parking lot.

* * *

Behind the Roundhouse, Hoover parked three spaces from where he dropped Beverly off the night before, in a narrow gap formed by two other cars in a lot reserved for official vehicles only. The space was so small that he could only open the door a few inches, barely enough to squeeze his body out. By the time he had worked his way free of the automobile, he had been recognized. Hearing the confusion behind him, he knew what was going on. He turned around and saw a group of people standing alongside of and behind his car. The reporters were on the scent.

"Detective Hoover, I'm from Fox News," screamed a voice close to Hoover, over the heads of the others. "What progress has there been in finding a suspect in the recent rash of murders?"

Hoover followed the sound of the question to a chiseled young man with gelled hair and a bottled tan. The man thrust a microphone with the television station's trademark insignia and its call numbers prominently displayed on it beneath Hoover's mouth. Directly behind this man was another—this one overweight with drooping pants—who balanced a video camera on his shoulder. The man with the camera had his left eye open, looking right at Hoover but not seeing him, not seeing anything. This man's view of the world was seen through the tiny cube of the camera's viewfinder.

Hoover scanned the rest of the gathered, counting four more talking heads and their cameramen along with three others who were recording with microcassettes. Hoover assumed that these three were from the *Inquisitor*, the *News Daily*, and probably the once-a-week, freely circulated local paper called the *Glancer*. The name of that last one always bemused him because as far as he knew, "glancer" wasn't even an actual word. What kind of journalistic integrity could a newspaper have if its own title was grammatically incorrect?

At least, the ones with the tape recorders looked like real people, and not like cookie-cutter movie stars.

Hoover didn't even have a chance to answer the first question before the next ones were flying. The questions were many and varied, running the gamut from the intelligent to the absurd. As the questions were hurled at him, he began to weave his way through the parking lot to the entrance of the PHQ building. The small herd of reporters followed behind him like a pack of hyenas on the scent of a weaker animal. This was a tired ritual, but the hyenas kept at it because every now and then they'd be able to pick off a weaker-minded person and get a sound bite for the evening telecast or the morning ink.

This tried and true method wasn't going to work on Hoover because he invariably gave the same answer to every question.

"Detective, were the bodies bound?"

"No comment," he replied in monotone.

"Detective, were there any unusual mutilations?"

"No comment." The department rules stated that whenever encountering the media, whether on duty or off, your only response was "No comment." Repeat as often as necessary.

"Detective Hoover, was there any indications of the dead women being lesbians or transsexuals?"

The "repeat-as-often-as-necessary" instruction had seemed a bit redundant during lecture at the Academy. But apparently, it wasn't as redundant when put to use in the real world—if the edited-to-specification descriptions of life seen through the media could be considered the real world. "No comment," said Hoover, toward the area of the pack closest to where the schmuck who had asked the last question was.

"Why did he leave them at the airport?" asked one of the guys wielding a cassette recorder.

Hoover had thought about that one himself. As far as he could see, there wasn't any tie between any of the dead women and the airport itself; it had only been a dumpsite.

Maybe it had to do with the privacy? The airport provided decent seclusion for an urban setting—with the darkness of the woods surrounded by the vast open and unattended space of the airfield, it was pretty safe to say that someone could carry a body around in the middle of the night without being observed. It was also convenient because of the availability of the industrial park access road. A person could simply drive up and park in one of the warehouses' lots then do whatever he felt like doing.

But then, why take all the precautions only to break the lights? The only sense that made was that the guy *wanted* them to find the bodies—which wasn't unheard of—but again, why the precautions?

What had he been waiting for? The right number, time, date, season, what? The only discernable answer Hoover had up to this point was that the airport was as good a place as any.

No matter what he thought the reason for using the airport, he still repeated the same answer: "No comment."

"Detective, were the bodies piled in the same position, facing the same way, or had they been piled head to toe?"

That was an interesting one. They had all been facing the same way—up, staring right into the eyes of their abductor, their murderer—but Hoover couldn't see any relevance there'd be in that information making the news.

Reporters were generally slugs, bottom-feeders, one-step up the evolutionary scale from lawyers, a step they tenaciously clung to only because they couldn't charge by the hour while sucking the life out of the ordinary joe for their own financial gain. The absence of fee-charging abilities made them slugs rather than sharks. But Hoover listened to all of their questions no matter what kind of invertebrate they were. Who knew, one day their persistent questioning might give a different slant in his mind to stale information he thought he had seen from every angle.

"Were all the bodies naked, Detective?"

No, he was wrong. They were only useless slugs.

Hoover didn't even bother to give the toss-off response to that one. He knew they already had the answer to that question and that they were just trying to circle around him, catch him off guard so that they could bait him into saying something, anything. No matter what he said—even if it was only to confirm information that had already appeared in print or been broadcasted on television—they would still be able to quote his name as a source of information. If that happened, the brass would not be happy.

"Were *you* naked, Detective Hoover?"

Even with a well-armed psyche against their questioning, that last *did* succeed in catching him off guard. Whether it was out of the sheer moronity of the question or because of his recent unease with how his mind drew a likeness between his casual regard to sleeping with women and then dumping them and the killer's brutal treatment of women, Hoover stopped in his tracks. Turning to look for the individual who asked the question, he already knew whom he would see because he knew the voice.

Seated on the bumper of a patrol car was the man that voice belonged to.

Hoover became agitated at the very sight of him. "Agbalaya, you son of a bitch. What're you doing here?" he demanded, his eyes red with hatred.

"I'm a reporter; there's news happening here," he said. Still seated on the bumper, smoking a stub of a cigar that stank, Agbalaya spread his arms wide, "I only go where the news leads me."

"Fuck you. You're not here for the news You're here on a witch hunt."

Agbalaya had been the investigative reporter for the *Inquisitor* who had "uncovered" the information on the phantom suspect in the Sullivan case.

With a name like Nicos (shortened to Nick, when necessary), Agbalaya on his byline, Hoover would've guessed that he was probably Greek, or Slavic, or something like that. But in actuality he was as American as apple pie. Or at least, crabapple pie. Hoover didn't like reporters in general, but he distinctly didn't like Agbalaya because of the mess he made of the Sullivan case with the bullshit lies he had printed, lies that had caused a lot of fervor and could result in a murderer walking free. Never minding those reasons, the reporter just struck Hoover as a person whom he'd dislike on sight anyway, for the general principal of it.

Agbalaya was a short man, about five-four, who wore wire-frame glasses and had brownish hair, a narrow, birdlike chest, and a smug-looking smile. He projected an air about himself as if he shit gold bricks rather than turds. Agbalaya was one of those chest-thumping people who felt the Constitution was written specifically for them—an opinionated bastard who spoke loudly, the kind who would tell you that it was not only his responsibility to report the news, it was his God-given right. If he were wearing a fedora with the word PRESS printed on a card and stuffed in the band, he would be the absolute caricature of personification of his profession.

Maybe it was *his democratic right, but damn*, thought Hoover, *get out of* my *ass.*

"A witch hunt? I take offense to that," said Agbalaya. "A witch hunt is when someone makes up his own version of the truth in order to wrongly persecute someone else. I have never done such a thing, and you know it. The reports I've made on your investigative techniques and abilities have all been factual."

"Do you really think anybody in that building," Hoover cocked his thumb toward the Roundhouse, whose shadow they all—Hoover, Agbalaya, and the rest of the vultures—stood in, "is going to answer any question *you* ask?"

"I don't care if they answer 'em or not, I'm going to ask anyway. Do you think I haven't had anybody tell me to fuck off before? Do you think I'm scared of you lower-class pukes who think you're better than the rest of society because you carry a badge?"

The rest of the reporters remained ominously quiet. One of their brethren had found a crack, and they were all soaking it up—on audio and video.

Hoover thought about it for a second and realized that Agbalaya's goading him was just another trap, a trap using his own anger for bait. He turned away from Agbalaya before he could trip the wire and snare himself, and began walking toward the safety of the building.

"What's the matter, Detective?" Agbalaya had pushed off the patrol car and began trailing Hoover. Striding behind the six-foot-plus cop, Agbalaya's diminutive height looked even shorter than it was. The rest of the pack followed right behind the squat reporter. They say that history repeats itself; if true, then Hoover leading the reporters was definitely one of those overlapping moments in the space-time continuum in which St. Patrick fronted the parade of snakes.

"You know what I think? I think you're afraid. Deep down inside, you're afraid."

Hoover stopped short again, his mouth tightening, crow's feet appearing at the corners of his narrowed eyes. "Afraid of what?" he asked without turning around, already knowing the answer.

"Afraid that you'll blow this one like you did with the Sullivans."

Hoover wheeled, thrusting a finger in Agbalaya's face. "We didn't blow that case! We caught the perp with the weapon, and we have his fingerprints in the house. End of story."

"How about that eyewitness, Detective Hoover? Young black kid, about the same age as the perp you caught. You know, the one who says he saw *two* gunmen exiting the Sullivan house."

"Funny how he didn't surface until *after* the suspect got nabbed in the pawnshop, isn't it?" Hoover said.

Agbalaya ignored Hoover's insight. Preaching to the rest of the flack over his shoulder so that they could catch everything on tape, he said, "At first, it must've looked like a godsend; an eyewitness who says he can finger the guy you caught, what a break. Things couldn't have been any better, wrapped any tighter; the wheels of justice never turned so smoothly. Oh, but wait a minute. Suddenly, a new wrinkle appears when the witness states that a *second* perp had been in the house. Not only was there a second crook—a white kid—but the witness also says that it was this mysterious second gunman who actually shot poor old man Sullivan and his wife."

The day after the perp—one Clifton Reginald—was found trying to pawn Mrs. Sullivan's necklace, a man by the name of Dallas Hopkins went on the record stating that he had been innocently walking by the Sullivan house when Mr. Reginald burst out the front door holding a gun and a pillowcase filled with misappropriated goods. Hopkins's attention had been drawn by the actions of Mr. Reginald, and that's how it came to be that he had been looking directly at the Sullivans' residence when he heard the shots fired. A minute later, a *white* gunman emerged to join Reginald. Together they ran north toward a subway entrance where they descended and disappeared. When asked why he had waited so long to come to the police, Hopkins said that he had been minding his own business and hadn't known what was going on in that house on the day of the robbery. It was only after he saw on TV the cops take a brother down at gunpoint in a pawnshop that he remembered the face that went with the crime.

"The witness is a setup," Hoover said. "He's working with Reginald to get him off the hook by placing blame on an imaginary figure, trying to incite a hung jury. You idiots in the press fell for it."

"Where's the connection? Hopkins says he doesn't know Reginald, and Reginald says the same thing."

"He might *not* know him. It might've been set up by a third party, someone close to Reginald, someone looking out for his interests. Or Reginald might know him *real* well. Hopkins might even have been the fucking getaway driver."

"You're grasping at straws, making up unsubstantiated facts, looking for a conspiracy! I'm not a detective, Hoover, but in my profession I investigate the same stuff you do, and I wasn't able to uncover any conspiracy."

"There's no evidence to back up a second perp being at the scene—Reginald shot and killed the Sullivans."

"Regardless of who pulled the trigger, I believe there were two men in the Sullivan house and that they should *both* be doing time for it. But they won't, because as you say, the cops are being played, and your perp—along with the unfounded suspect—is going to walk. However you look at it, it's one botched investigation; Hoover and I only wish that I had the proof to back up what we both know is true so that I could run it all over the press, but I don't. Eventually I'll get that crumb of evidence I need, and your cookie will fall to pieces. It's a Pulitzer waiting to happen."

"It's all bullshit, everything you said," Hoover said, without much conviction. He turned toward the other reporters. "You all hear me? What this man has just said is bullshit. Do not report any of it, or your company will be sued by the city," he told them, not knowing if such a thing were true.

It was Agbalaya's turn to directly address the crowd of his peers. The cameras whirred and the cassettes recorded. "You know why Detective Hoover is scared of this homicide case? It's because he knows he's a fuckup. And if he fucks up this time, more people are going to die. Up till now, in every homicide he's pulled, the victims had already been dead before he got a hold of the case; that's a fact, I checked it. If he fucked up those cases, the dead would rest uneasy, but they would still be just as dead as if he did his job properly. Not this time. This time, for every fuckup, another young woman will pay for it. Pay for it with her life.

"And that would make you a murderer," Agbalaya said, pointing at Hoover as if proclaiming a heretic, "because *you're no better than he is.*" The reporter smiled at him with tobacco stained teeth. "Ain't that right, Detective?" Agbalaya asked Hoover from the crossroads.

Agbalaya thrust the stub of cigar in the corner of his victor's grin and had just turned to his right to flash the victory smile to the cameras when Hoover rung his bell. Hoover's right hook—combined with the forward inertia of Agbalaya's head—caused a sound like that of a pair of hands coming together to form one solitary, forceful clap.

Hoover's fist struck true, hitting Agbalaya on the bridge of his nose. The short reporter's eyes rolled up to the whites and his knees unhinged. He collapsed to the ground like a tent that had its center pole pulled out from under it. Agbalaya's cigar popped out of his mouth when he hit the asphalt. The cigar, which had started it's journey at a sweatshop in Costa Rica (rolled by a fourteen-year-old girl who earned barely enough money to feed herself and her son for the week) and had then been transported to the humidified atmosphere of a glass display case at Holt's Cigar Company on Walnut Street, continued to roll until it hit the lip of a sewer and plunged into a darkness as repugnant smelling as the smoke the cigar had been emanating moments ago.

Hoover had been accused of some things in his life before, but this prick had finally crossed the line; there was no way he was going to let Agbalaya blame murder on him.

But as he stood over the writhing form of the man who stated he was a lousy detective, had labeled him as lazy and inept, and had accused him of murder in an aphoristic way, Hoover knew he was in a lot of trouble. He had created a personal catastrophe at a time when the department could ill afford it. Korzenowski had stressed they handle this case with special aplomb, and he, Hoover, had just tossed a gallon of fuel on the fire.

Hoover looked up and directly into the many convex eyes of television-news cameras that had documented the incident. Every newscast throughout the City of Brotherly Love would run, at the top of its broadcast, the clip of a cop assaulting a civilian, a member of the media who had a First Amendment right to be where he was, reporting on a felony crime committed against the city, state, and humanity.

The film spools recorded as Hoover, his fists clinched tightly in front of him, stood over the bleeding man. Not once did any of them stop gawking to help their fallen comrade. There would be all the time in the world to help later, after the violence ended and was immortalized on videotape. After all, no one watching the evening newscast wanted to see people being kind to one another, they wanted to see ass-kickings. The ratings demanded it, and by golly they would get their full tonight.

Hoover looked down at Agbalaya and noticed that with his eyes squinted in pain, the reporter's smart-ass mouth had nothing to say.

Unconsciously, Hoover drew his legs together, relaxing from the boxer's stance he had taken before striking his opponent. He could almost hear the anticipation of the gathering, leaning forward as they mistook his movement.

They probably think I'm going to kick him while he's down.

Hoover had no intentions of causing any further hurt to Agbalaya. He let his fists unclench, shaking them out, and straightened his suit jacket while glaring at the rest of the reporters one last time.

When he turned around, he noticed that there was a small gathering of cops, dressed in their blue-on-blue street uniforms, standing behind him among a smattering of civilians. It was just after nine in the morning on Friday, and the business day in the city had begun.

Hoover stalked toward the building without checking to see if anyone followed him this time. The civilian and the cop onlookers who were in front of him now parted as if he wielded the wrath of God before him.

You're no better than he is, Agbalaya had said.

Hoover pulled open the door on Cherry Street and took solace in the cool, confining darkness of the Roundhouse.

15

$\mathcal{B}$y the time Hoover reached the second floor, Korzenowski had already heard about the fight. The captain stood outside the door to room 104, waiting for John to get off the elevator. When he saw Hoover, he didn't say anything. Tight lipped, he raised one index finger and used it to beckon Hoover to follow him. Hoover also didn't say anything as Korzenowski led him into his office.

The door to the captain's office had a pneumatic elbow which had been broken for some time. After Hoover stepped into the office, Korzenowski slammed the door so hard the pane of frosted glass with his name stenciled on it in black letters threatened to shatter.

Hoover and Korzenowski were inside the office for the next forty-five minutes, every ear in the homicide division straining to hear through the walls. The only clear words audible were the occasional expletives Korzenowski interjected, the rest of the conversation but murmurs to the others who were all busy trying to look busy.

At ten of ten, the door opened and the two men emerged into the general population of the other detectives. Every eye was on them, and yet no one was looking in their direction.

Korzenowski was carrying his folders when he addressed the room. His voice sounded harsh when he said, "Those of you who were supposed to be in the meeting with me about the airport, get your asses into the interrogation room. The rest of you, get the fuck out of here and solve some crimes."

A few minutes later, they were all seated around the conference table, Whaat, Meltzer, Holmes, Sako, Farrell, and Hoover. Korzenowski leaned up against the wall, hands deep in his pockets, looking at the floor. No one said anything to disturb his respite; no one dared to look into the eye of the storm.

Cold as a curator of a funeral parlor, he announced, "Hoover is no longer the lead dick on this one. I'm turning the reins over to Beverly. It's hers because she was working with Hoover from the beginning, and because she was at the scene."

Korzenowski pushed off the wall and opened one of his manila folders. Donning a set of half glasses, he started to hand out more papers. "The pathologists at the morgue were working overtime last night while you people were getting your beauty sleep. The brass have been pushing this one hard, as evident by the quickness with which the protocol has been filed."

"Protocol" was the official term for the coroner's report.

"What I'm handing you now are the reports on *all* nine victims You already know the how of it, death by loss of blood from multiple incisions. The protocol continues by stating that there were no internal injuries or abnormalities in the blood or kidneys, as concluded by the toxicology screens. One of the women— Hustead—had a good amount of heroin in her, but it is the coroner's opinion, based on other signs within her system, that she was a habitual user, and that the drug is not related to our guy."

Korzenowski looked up from the paper he paraphrased, removing the half glasses from the edge of his nose. "None of that is terribly new information. But what you don't know yet is that each victim was raped. Raped just like the Philadelphia Police Department will be when the news airs tonight, thanks to Mr. Hoover."

Just as they were taught at the Academy whenever the press was mentioned, the cops in the room had no comment.

"Our boy is a necrophiliac," Korzenowski continued after the grouse. "The ME has determined from the pathology and the location of friction marks on the immediate adjoining cadavers that the women were all raped where they were found, in the woods, the latest victim done directly on top of the previous one. This sick asshole wasn't bothered by the nauseating stink of rotting flesh or disgusted by the eyeless sockets staring up at him as he got off. He didn't mind the constant buzzing of the circling flies, was undisturbed by the way the maggots fell off the bodies and onto the soil only to die themselves from lack of nutrients as they struggled to get back to their feeding ground on the corpses."

"Goddamn, that's nasty," interrupted Holmes.

"Yes, it is nasty, but it's helpful to us. The ladies' vaginal canals were perforated, due to lack of moisture in the membranes of their flesh. Because of the rigidity of death, this joker used KY jelly to lube up so that he could glide in and out smoothly and later insert the IDs. After he shot his load, it mixed with the jelly, giving his sperm a longer half-life than normal. It sat in the jelly as if on a petri dish.

"The lab took the sperm and has given us a framework for this guy, a virtual description, minus the personality." Putting the glasses back on, Korzenowski consulted a paper. "The guy we're looking for is a Caucasian male, approximately thirty-five to forty years old, blood type O. From pubic hair samples left behind, the color of our guy's hair is brown. That's all we've got, a description that fits nine million John Does in the city, but it'll be substantiated evidence when we get him to court. That's everything on the doer at this point.

"As for the ladies, a second missing person's report had been filed for Sherry Dasher. Who has Dasher?"

"We do, sir," Beverly said. Korzenowski handed her a paper.

"It wasn't matched yesterday because it had been drafted under the name Desiree Sheer. The report had been filed by a guy named Victor Preak, owner of a titty bar called the Hippy Hippy Shake. It had been filed three days after the one her parents filed. In the report, he describes a woman who meets the exact physical description of Sherry Dasher. Four o'clock this morning, Preak opened his newspaper and saw Dasher's picture. He recognized her as Desiree Sheer, her stage name, and preformed his civic duty by coming here to inform us. Sheer was a dancer at the Hippy, and she had been last seen on Tuesday night, the eleventh. It seems as if Miss Dasher had an alter ego." The glasses came back off. "That's what I've got. Now show me yours."

"Our girls had alter egos too," said Meltzer. "Three for three, all of them were prostitutes. Considered themselves 'escorts,' rather than 'streetwalkers'. Each one of them had a regular job but hooked on the side. One worked at a supermarket, one a hairdresser, and one over at the New Jersey State Aquarium. We already checked the supermarket. It was a dead end—no new, usable information to further the investigation. Sako and I are betting that the other two, the salon and the aquarium, are both going to be busts as well. Our money's on the escort services. Three dead women, all hustling on the side, isn't a coincidence."

"You got the names of the businesses that pimped them?" asked Holmes.

"Yeah, we got them."

"How'd you do it? We couldn't get anything on our girls' night jobs."

"The Griffin girl lived at home with her widowed mother. The mother knew about the hooking job, and readily gave up the information. The Goldberg girl had pay stubs in her bedroom with the name of the place on it. Leta Hursch roomed with a coworker from her club."

"Looks like you got the easy ones. We had to pull tooth and nail, and we still don't have anything concrete, just a glimmer."

"Wait a minute; back up, Holmes. The three women you investigated, they were prostitutes too?" asked Korzenowski.

"No, but they were on the fringe. One worked in a booth at Pepper Johnson's." Pepper Johnson's was an establishment that sold all types of pornography—movies, magazines, and paraphernalia. In the basement of the store, down a flight of dark stairs lit indirectly by red neon tubing, were peep show booths. A person, a surprising ratio of which were women, checked in with a bouncer working the door—so to speak, because what he really worked were the *stairs*, seated at a diminutive desk stationed at the foot of the flight. The bouncer would point out an unoccupied private booth painted jet-black, inside of which there was a stool, a trash can, a box of tissues, and a machine that collected money. Peep shows used to cost a quarter, the machine that handled the transactions resembling a parking meter. In the twenty-first century, the machines became scanners that accepted ones, fives, tens, and twenties. The cost of living is steep, ask anyone.

The customer deposited the cash, each denomination of which bought time in minute increments. When the transaction was complete, the wall panel in front of the customer slid upward, revealing a woman in lingerie. The woman was in her version of the same booth that the customer was in, only hers was a little larger and painted a yellowish orange. The caged woman, having heard the cattle call of the panel sliding upward, began to strut her stuff for the viewer—batting her eyes, tossing the trusses of her wig, making scratching motions with her long, painted, fake nails. These women were professionals, and they knew how to work the clock, of which there was one fastened to the wall directly above the viewer's window so that it could only be seen by the working gal. It'd cost the customer a good amount of cash before he or she or both (couples have been known to enter these booths with their spouse—or their john—and one or both will get off while enjoying the show, hence the tissues) see any of the good stuff. If the person entering the peep booth was goal oriented, he or she better have enough money, for the panel had the tendency to drop down unannounced in the middle of the action with a loud bang of finality.

The late Tammy Allensworth, third of the nine victims, worked in one of the several peep show booths in the basement of Pepper Johnson's Adult Entertainment Superstore.

"A thousand anonymous people, from stockbrokers to derelicts, go through the doors of Pepper Johnson's," Holmes said. "We talked to Pepper himself, and he gave us Tammy's employment history, but it's impossible to comb the clientele of that joint. Pepper's is a dead end; the best we can do is pass out our boy's description and hope for a nibble.

"The next one had her own business, complete with license and tax number. She was what they call a "sex demonstrator," which means she went from home to home, like the Avon lady, performing demonstrations about sex toys. From what Wh—. Wh, Whaat—. Sorry about that, it's quite a tongue twister," he said, stumbling on his partner's surname. He wasn't joking either, not with the mood Korzenowski was in. In order to get it out, he had to break the sentence down. "From what. Whaat. And I could gather the demonstrations didn't include any hands-on stuff—no touchy-feely. It was strictly demonstrations where she showed off the latest model of sex toys and the like, after which you placed an order for what you wanted. The ordering was said to be done very discreetly. It's like a Tupperware party with plastic dildos instead of plastic containers. An anonymous, guilt-free way for white middle-class suburbanites to get their toys, that's all."

"What about the third girl?" Korzenowski asked.

"The third girl, Ms. Kristin Fiorella, was a genuine masseuse at an up-and-up massage parlor. Take that however you want to, but it was a hands-on profession."

"Did they all have straight jobs?"

"Allensworth was a secretary at a uniform company. The demonstrator was a social worker, of all things. The masseuse was a masseuse. I think her job was for real."

"All right, there's a pattern starting to form here. What do you have, Farrell?" The way Korzenowski deliberately dismissed the work Hoover had done by immediately referring to Beverly was like a public shaming in the ilk of a scarlet letter.

Beverly turned to look at Hoover before she answered Korzenowski.

Hoover gave no indication of what he was thinking, seated slouched down in the hard plastic chair, one arm draped over the back. The papers containing the coroner's protocol were lying in front of him, unread. He was paying attention to what was being said, but an air of sulking densely enshrouded him.

He saw Beverly look at him before she gave her dissertation of their legwork and was grateful for it.

"Our findings parallel what Holmes just reported. We found that the latest victim, Sherry Dasher, had been a dancer at the Hippy Hippy Shake, which has been corroborated by the Desiree Sheer missing person's report." They hadn't known this, but no one in the room would be the wiser. Besides, what they did have was weak compared to what the others brought to the table. Making it seem as if they knew about the titty bar before Korzenowski told them might cast them in a better light. It was cheap, but they could use all the help they could get at the moment.

Beverly continued, "Andrea Hustead, according to her father, was heavily involved in narcotics. She sometimes whored herself to get fixes. It's not a structured form of prostitution, but it fits the pattern. The last girl, Judith Kasay, who was actually the first victim, told her parents that she worked in a shoe store at an outlet mall. Nothing's definite, but her parents seem to think the shoe store job was a front for other activities."

"Why?" Korzenowski asked.

"Late hours, strange behavior when asked about her work, things like that."

"Do they have any idea what else she was up to?"

"No. They respected her privacy, and now they're kicking themselves for it. They feel that they're partially responsible for her death."

She stopped and Korzenowski waited, looking at her. Finally, he said, "That it?"

"Yes, sir" came out meekly.

Korzenowski looked over at Hoover. The assessment on his face was clear. *Lead detective and that's the best you could come up with in twenty-four hours? A dead woman whose occupation was already known from a missing person's report, a discovery of narcotics involvement that was also reported in the protocol, and a solid "maybe" on the most important victim, the first one—the one most likely connected with the killer.*

"Okay, fine. Despite the three-ring circus that happened today, it's business as usual. Hit the streets and dig up more on these women. They all led upstanding lives, and they all had a darker side, which was probably what got them killed. Delve, delve, delve. I want to know everything. I want names, I want photographs. I also want two copies of everything that each of you has done so far. Put one in the file and one on my desk. I have to take it all upstairs to the commissioner's office myself. He invited me up for lunch, which means I'll be eating crow for assigning Hoover to a high-profile case when I had full knowledge of the Sullivan situation. He, in turn, will be chewing on my ass.

"Does anybody have anything else? No? Then get busy." Korzenowski gathered his paperwork and headed for the door.

"Hey, Captain," Whaat said before his boss could exit the room.

"Yeah?" he answered with his hand on the door, waiting for it.

"Bon Appetite."

There it was.

16

They didn't talk much throughout the day, even though it was an industrious one—Farrell and Hoover had visited the workplaces for both of their dead that'd held employment.

Unlike novels and movies about police work, there was usually little action and a lot of questioning. Interviewing techniques were the backbone of a decent detective's career.

Victor Preak, the owner and operator of the Hippy Hippy Shake, was very forthcoming with everything he knew about Sherry Dasher, stage name Desiree Sheer. Unfortunately, what he knew was very little, and it was already on record with the missing persons report from the previous week. Most of the information they obtained from the Hippy Hippy about Sherry was names, places, and dates. They had her work schedule for the last six months and got names of regulars who attended the club and names of patrons who concentrated exclusively on Sherry's work, and also got names and addresses of employees, past and present, who had worked with the deceased. The coworkers on site were interviewed and asked to please give statements about any unusual mood swings Sherry had or any weird requests made by patrons and the like. There were some that would be looked into, but Hoover didn't think they'd bear fruit.

On to the next one.

Judith Kasay did indeed work at the shoe store she claimed to be employed by. And she was in control of the store's inventory, just like she had told her parents. The thing though was she only worked two days a week at Walking on Air. The rest of her time was anybody's guess, until Hoover asked Judith's manager, one Rena Potts, if she had had a boyfriend.

"A boyfriend? No," said Rena. "Or, at least, not one she talked about." She was a very tall woman, so thin she looked emaciated. Without one ounce of body fat on her, her features were gaunt and skeletal. To accentuate the look, she wore clothes so tight they molded to her body. Rena was well over six foot, but because she was so thin and without a noticeable curve anywhere, she looked even taller. Hoover stood eye to eye with her but still felt as if she towered over him when she talked. The short of it was that Rena Potts was one long lady.

And bitter.

Her nose was in a constant wrinkle, her mouth a perpetually small, tight line, her face etched to prove it all. The eyes behind her glasses were small and fierce looking. Hoover tried to notice the color but couldn't quite see them behind the lenses and through the squint. No matter what they were, he supposed there wasn't any color vibrant enough to warm them up.

For all that, she was very straightforward with the detectives, answering every question they asked in a clear and concise, if clipped, tone which both Hoover and Farrell were thankful for. Cryptic answers were annoying and misleading. Rena Potts, no matter what her personal feelings about other people or her own self-image, was an excellent character witness.

"Did Judy—," began Hoover.

"Judith. She wasn't the type to go by a slang name."

Her parents didn't seem to think she minded being called Judy. It was from Ed Kasay himself that Hoover had picked up the shortened version of her name. *Maybe the use of her full name was a way to separate her identities—keeping the mainstream job uppity and pristine by using Judith, while going by Judy at the other job, whatever that might turn out to be.*

The three of them were stuffed in a tiny office at the rear of the store. It was filled with shoes, catalogs, and green-bar printouts. From what could be seen of the carpet (it was covered with shreds of paper and thousands of hole-puncher waste dots), it looked as though a vacuum hadn't been run there since the current owner opened up shop. Ventilation was poor, and the room smelled like shoe leather.

"Did Judith ever mention any friends?" Hoover started again.

"No."

"Never?"

"Never."

"How closely did you work together?"

"Very close. She was my purchasing agent, in charge of the inventory for the store. She'd go through the receipts and pick out certain patterns the shoppers tended to have. From those patterns you got a feel for what you needed to stock on your shelves. The location of a store begets a certain type of clientele. Race, sex, income, they're all factors that have to go into deciding what to purchase from our venders—you have to know what will sell in order to sell it. That was what Judith did here, she generated the inventory. She decided what to purchase and what not to, based on sales figures. But no matter what she decided on, she'd have to pass it by me before she filled the orders," she added, letting them know who was still boss.

"She did all of that in a sixteen-hour week?"

"Twelve. She only worked six hours a day, Tuesday afternoons and Saturday mornings."

"So you worked hand in hand?"

"Yes."

"How about you? Did she *like* you, you know, as a friend?" Intentionally pushing a slight accusation of lesbianism, Hoover didn't know how the question would go over. He specifically asked it to see if he could shake Rena's tree a little. Catching people off guard was a good way to get them to slip and reveal something they didn't want to—something trying to be concealed was always the foremost thing in a person's mind; give a little push and it might fall.

"Yes, she liked me. You might say we were friends." It didn't work, no acorns fell; Rena hadn't even flinched. Hoover contemplated shaking a little harder, but then decided not to. Maybe later, if the need arose.

"I assume that in your working relationship together, some casual banter was passed back and forth."

"Of course."

"And never once did she mention any other friends?"

Rena thought about it. "Only once can I remember her mentioning anybody's name. It was Marty or Martin or something like that."

"I thought you said she didn't have a boyfriend?"

"I did. As far as I know, they weren't a couple."

"What did she say about him?"

"It was last winter and it had been snowing very hard all day. She offhandedly mentioned that she was grateful this Marty or Martin was working tonight, so that she could get a ride home. Her car had been in the shop for a week, and you know how public transportation runs in the snow."

Hoover hadn't ridden a bus in over twenty years, since the day he got his driver's license. Beverly, who lived on a street where she had to jockey for a parking spot, occasionally rode the subway, but never in the snow.

"This guy work here in the mall?"

"Yes, at the sporting goods store. It's two doors up on the right."

"Did she mention his last name?"

"No. That was all she said about him," she said, before adding, "ever."

"Did she ever mention working any other jobs?"

"No."

"Did she ever talk about anything in her life outside of this store?"

"No, sorry."

"That's all right. You've been very helpful, Ms. Potts. I can't think of anything else at the moment, but if we have any more questions, either Detective Farrell or I will be in touch."

The detectives left Rena and Walking on Air, made a right, and headed toward the sporting goods store without even discussing the next move.

Hoover always held a theory that an unlucky person could not be a good detective. If a person had no luck, and nothing ever broke his way, then he was going to constantly be walking in circles, treading the same ground without any forward advancement. The business of deduction hinged on stringing together many seemingly unrelated thoughts and connecting them in such a way that they made sense. Sometimes the answers could be sitting right in front of you, but you still couldn't see them because the facts were out of sequence. Until that one stroke of luck put everything in order, the picture would remain a blur.

If he could have recognized it immediately for what it was, the entire aftermath could've been avoided, since that stroke of luck was about to be handed to him by Judy Kasay's ex-boyfriend, Markus.

They entered the sporting goods store, which was exactly where Rena Potts said it would be, and approached a clerk working one of the four checkout windows cut into a long counter much like at a bank. There were only two clerks—one male and one female—working the late afternoon shift before the evening rush. There wasn't anyone in line at the moment, so Hoover chose to approach the male clerk. He chose him because his window was closest to the entrance of the store.

"Good afternoon," Hoover said.

The male looked up from the magazine he was reading. "Yeah," he said. Not a question, not a comment, just an acknowledgement.

In his early twenties, the clerk had a good physique, not so much a bodybuilder, but rather a person whose gene pool had tapped the right code to effortlessly produce a nice sculpt. *This kid could probably eat bacon and eggs for breakfast every day, and steak sandwiches with fries for dinner every night, and never gain an ounce,* Hoover decided.

He wore a navy blue golf shirt with the insignia of the store over his left breast, which probably served as the store's uniform. The shirt was two sizes too big for him, and yet the end of his white undershirt still stuck out beneath the hem, above a pair of khakis. He had two earrings, one hoop and one stone, in the same ear; there were no visible tattoos. Completing the rest of his style was a bracelet on his right wrist that looked like it was a remnant of a thin piece of rope and an oversized diver's watch on the left, the watch so large Hoover wouldn't be surprised to see a miniature hunchback come out to ring off the hourly chime. He had a chiseled chin, minus cleft, gray eyes, and hair dyed beyond blond, the result so white that it gave off a shiny, silvery reflection beneath the stark luminescence of the store's fluorescent tubing. The color of his hair would look unnatural anywhere in the world, except maybe on the streets of New York or Hollywood, but damn if it didn't look right on him. Women would swoon over this one. And from the way his female counterpart (who also wore the overlarge navy shirt) looked at him with large, doe eyes, they did.

Hoover, an average-looking thirty-seven-year-old, instantly envied the male his youth and looks. "Does a guy by the name of Marty or Martin work here?" he asked.

The male clerk looked Hoover up and down then glanced over his shoulder to give Beverly a good looking. The kid smelled cop.

"I'm Markus Eaton. People sometimes call me Marky."

"Hi, how are you doing, Markus. I'm Detective Hoover and this is Detective Farrell. We would like to ask you a few questions."

"I was wondering when you would get to me," he said.

"What do you mean?"

"I read in the paper about what happened to Judy. I figured that sooner or later, someone would tie her to me." He unfolded his arms from his chest and gestured to the two cops. He smiled at them and said, "Here you are."

"If you knew something, why didn't you come forward on your own?"

"That's just it; I don't know anything that'll help you. That's why I didn't go to the police myself."

"You'd be surprise what you know. Every miniscule detail helps."

"Maybe. We'll see."

Hoover pointed at the counter. "Do you have to stay here? Can we go somewhere to talk privately?"

Markus looked over at the female clerk, a mousy-looking girl with straight hair and acne. Hoover thought that with some work, she could turn out to be a beauty. A little acne medicine, a hairstyle and some confidence added to the high cheekbones and blue eyes, and she would be the one getting flirted with at the counter instead of Markus.

"Are you okay with that, Helen?"

Helen? Well, the name would have to fend for itself.

She nodded her head and flashed a smile that wouldn't necessarily weaken the knees but could make you feel good about yourself. "Sure. I'll be fine."

Hoover got the feel that she was new to the sporting goods industry and that Markus had just given her a tiny bit of the confidence she lacked by turning over the reins without having to add something stupidly cocky like "It's dead in here anyway" or

"I'll be right over there, if you need me." Instead of saying anything of the nature, he rapped a knuckle on the top of his counter and walked over to the two steps that led down from the raised dais the counter stood on so that the employees could symbolically look down upon the customers.

Helen triumphantly stepped up to Markus's cubed window and smiled out at the empty store. Yeah, Helen was going to do just fine in the world.

"Come on in the back; there's a canteen room."

Canteen room?

What it turned out to be was the exact same room that Rena Potts used as her office. Only this time, instead of a cluttered desk, there was a Pepsi machine, a change machine, a junk food vending machine, and a goodwill box. The goodwill box was made of cardboard and filled with various junk foods just like the machine, only it was left right out in the open and unguarded. It was up to your own goodwill to pay for what you took. This particular box was completely empty except for one balled-up Butterfinger wrapper. There was a handwritten sign taped to the top of the box. It read, *This box is short $37.75! The man won't leave any more until he gets the money. If you ate—PAY! This means you, Denny!* The note was signed MANAGEMENT in big, bold letters.

Markus pointed with his chin at the sign. "When word gets around that the cops were here, I'm going to stick it to Denny, let him think it was because someone's been stealing from the box."

"You sure he did it?" Beverly asked.

"Positive. I've seen him tip over the change machine there, then turn around and drop the money he looted back into the soda machine."

That got a laugh out of both Beverly and Hoover.

Markus suddenly turned serious. "What do you want to know about Judy?"

Since Hoover had been the one to initiate contact with Markus, he continued with the questioning.

"What was your involvement with her?"

"My involvement? I don't understand what you mean. Do you think I had anything—" The kid's hackles were up, but Hoover didn't think it was because of any accusations; he thought it was out of compassion.

"Whoa, whoa," said Hoover. "We're not making any accusations, Markus. You misunderstood me. All I wanted to know was if Judy and you had any romantic attachment. Were you boyfriend and girlfriend, or was it platonic?"

Markus looked down at his hands and began to pick at one of his cuticles. "I'm sorry. I guess involvement *is* the right way to put it. I was involved, that's for sure." He looked up at the detectives. "I loved her."

"Tell us about it."

"I only knew her for about six months. We met at the food court one night while she was working and I was picking up my paycheck. I had a friend with me, a girl." At this he looked at Beverly. "I was kind of seeing this friend. She sat down to hold a table for us while I got the food. When I was standing in line, I met Judy." This time it was Hoover he looked at. "She was the most beautiful woman I'd ever seen. I thought I'd seen some beauties, thought I'd been around the block, done everything there was to do. I was wrong. When I met Judy, she made me realize how small my existence really was."

This time when he looked back down at his hands, it was the rope bracelet he toyed with instead of the cuticle. He spun the ivory-colored string around and around his wrist, first examining the pattern woven into the front, then pulling at the loose strands of the knot in the back. He continued speaking while he fiddled with the bracelet.

"She was twenty when I met her. At least, that's how old her body was. On the inside she was much older, much more mature. She was so sure of herself and it showed, but not in an arrogant way. It was like she knew the meaning of life but didn't want to bore you with the details. She had been extremely intelligent without being smug. When she would describe or explain something, she would simply tell you, not to impress you with what she knew, but so that you would know more, so that *you* could be a better person. I loved to talk to that woman.

"But apparently, I wasn't the only one."

"What do you mean by that?" asked Hoover.

"Hang on. Let me work around to it. I want to tell you the good things about Judy before I tell you about the other stuff. I want you to see the pretty picture before I taint it. She was beautiful and pure and . . . what I want you to know before . . ." For a minute, Markus was at a loss for words. He didn't want to breach into the area the detectives needed him to until he was ready. They would wait.

Without giving any more reasons for holding back, he continued to memorialize Judith Kasay.

"The day I met her, she was standing in a line, reading a book, when I literally ran into her. I had gotten the food for my date and had sat a stack of napkins on top of the tray. As I walked back to the table, the napkins caught air and fluttered off. Trying to balance the food in one hand while trying to catch as many napkins as I could with the other, I kept walking. Judy must've seen me coming. Instead of leaping out of the way of the runaway locomotive, she opened her arms to catch me. I crashed into her at walking speed. Somehow, she had managed to get her free hand up under the tray and supported it enough that none of the food fell off, while her other hand, the one with the book in it, wrapped around me and held tight, balancing my body so that *I* wouldn't fall.

"When I stopped dead in my tracks, I didn't know what had happened. I wheeled my head around. With a tray full of chicken sandwiches in one hand and a fist full of napkins in the other, I gazed right into her eyes. They were the deepest blue eyes I'd ever seen, blue like the ocean is blue around Florida, light at first, then as the depths mount, it gets darker. Her eyes were like that, layered light and deep. Looking into that ocean of blue depths, I felt like I was drowning.

"She looked at me and said, 'Hey, big boy.'"

Hoover, an avid novel reader and movie watcher, was captivated by the way Markus wove his tale of budding young love. Beverly on the other hand thought Markus's story was fluff. She wanted to skip over the bullshit and get right to the facts. Time was short, and her patients was thin with Hoover and how the day had started and had since proceeded. She wanted to get through with their work as quickly as she could, because the real questions she had to ask were for Hoover. Beverly Farrell quietly sighed, rubbed the back of her neck, and waited.

The Markus kid had reeled off the whole story of how he had come to know Judy Kasay and how he had finally found the courage to ask her out. When he did, she accepted. Their schedules conflicted a lot since the retail hours he worked tended to be haphazardly strewn throughout the week rather than a straight forty. They worked around it, and their relationship blossomed. Markus talked of sex and love, passion and lust.

"Everything was going great. I mean, it was a peach. Then, six months to the day I met her, I broke it off."

"Suddenly? Just like that? Why?" Hoover hadn't seen that one coming, but in retrospect, should've.

"She told me about her other job."

Beverly leaned forward. *Finally*, she thought.

"What was her other job, Markus?" Hoover asked.

Markus looked both the detectives in the eye before a tear spilled out of his, one single tear that rolled wetly down his cheek. "She was a phone sex operator."

Now they were getting somewhere.

They pumped Markus for the next twenty minutes. He ran down a story that played out exactly the way it probably should have. Markus, who had loved Judith, couldn't stand her working as a phone sex girl. He was extremely jealous of the other men, even though she tried to explain to him that it was only a job. A job of lies. She didn't really have sex with those men, just used their own imagination to get them off. She was trained to ask a couple of specific questions, the answers to which were jumping-off points into their fantasies. They supplied the material, and she verbalized it back to them. No harm, no foul.

Markus couldn't stand it and demanded that she quit. She refused. He asked her why she hadn't told him this before She said she thought he would take it the wrong way and get upset. She'd been right. He asked her why she'd ever think of doing such a thing. Her answer was that the money was there. She earned sixty thousand last year, working thirty hours a week. Four-ninety-nine a minute adds up in a hurry.

Markus demanded she quit yet again. She refused yet again. Then, in a fit of anger, he did the unthinkable.

"I called her a slut." There was a sour croak in his throat when he told them this. "I didn't know what else to do. I was at my wit's end. It'd been two weeks since she told me, and I'd been trying to cope with it. It was a fact, there the whole time I knew her, and I loved her then, but I couldn't after. They say what you don't know won't hurt you; how right they are."

"What happened?" Hoover could guess the rest but thought the kid needed to get it off his chest.

"It was our sixth-month anniversary. I bought her flowers and some earrings and took her to a romantic little restaurant out on Buck Road. We talked about it . . . her second job . . . a little, and then, over chocolate mousse, I called her a slut. Can you imagine that?"

Hoover thought George Hustead would be able to.

"Naturally, she got pissed off. We left in a hurry and fought the whole way back to her house. Right before she got out of the car, I laid down the ultimatum—quit or we're through. She said, 'we're through,' and got out of the car. I never heard another word from her. I tried to push her out of my mind, but couldn't. I think about her every day. This morning, I read that she was dead. I cried and blamed myself."

"Why would you blame yourself?" This was from Beverly.

A shoulder went up, then down. "I don't know. Maybe she wouldn't have been wherever she was if I was still with her. Maybe she would've been with me instead of with the bastard who killed her, if only I hadn't been so shallow."

"Hey, you can't shoulder responsibility like that." Beverly reached out a hand and touched Markus on the forearm, Hoover experiencing a pang of the jealousy that Markus had described. "She was a grown woman who made her own decisions and chose to get involved in a dangerous profession. You were trying to help her, not hurt her. Don't blame yourself for what happened," Beverly finished. Her support visibly lifted Markus's spirit.

"Did she ever mention the name of the company she worked for?" Hoover asked, as Lady Luck turned her eyes his way.

"The Grapple Company," was the answer. "It's located in an office complex up on the boulevard."

"Roosevelt Boulevard?"

"Yeah." Markus reached into his hip pocket and pulled out a battered blue-and-red trifold wallet with Velcro clasp. He opened the wallet and removed a clipping from the local newspaper. It was an advertisement usually found buried in the sports pages of the *News Daily*. It read LIVE PHONE SEX. IT WILL BE OUR *PLEASURE* TO TALK TO YOU. CALL US, NOW There was a 900 number listed on the ad; no company name, no address.

"She came right out and told you whom she worked for?"

"No. She'd only give vague details about the company itself, hiding it like the dirty secret it was."

"Then how do you know this was the one?"

"I followed her one night. I'm ashamed to admit it, but I was obsessed; what can I say? When she went into the building, I asked the cleaning guy which office the business was in. It was a chance, but how many phone sex companies could there be in one office complex? He knew and told me. I then checked the directory listed on the foyer wall and found the name. The Grapple Company."

"Can I keep this?" Hoover asked.

"Yeah. I kept meaning to throw it out, but couldn't bring myself to do it, you know."

"What did her parents think of this job?" Ed Kasay had said they didn't know for sure if she had been working any type of demoralizing job but assumed. But then, Mrs. Kasay had also said that they'd never met any of Judith's boyfriends other than David Stanton, but Markus had just said he had dropped Judith off at her house the night of the breakup.

"I don't think they knew about it," Markus said.

"Then they never mentioned anything about the Grapple Company or anyone who worked there to you?"

"I never met them. Whenever I arranged to pick Judy up, she'd come outside to meet me. I was never invited in," he said, shooting down Hoover's theory that the Kasays were lying to hide something.

"Did you find it strange that they never invited you in?"

"No. I've dated a lot of girls who were ashamed of their parents or where they lived."

Hoover hoped that when his girls got of dating age, they wouldn't be so ashamed of him that they felt they couldn't bring someone home. He would try to make sure they weren't. "Ever hear of a guy by the name of David Stanton?"

"Yeah, he was Judy's high school sweetheart. They broke up not long after. As far as I know, she never saw him again."

"Why'd she mention him to you?"

"I asked about the tattoo . . . um, do you guys know about the tattoo?"

"Yeah, we know. Did she talk badly about him?"

"No, just the facts. We only talked about him that one time. Do you think he had anything to do with it?"

"We haven't even met him yet. Thank you, Markus. I think that about does it. If you think of anything else, call." Hoover handed him a card. "I'm serious; call us, even if it's something you think inconsequential."

"I will, I promise."

Hoover and Beverly left the outlet mall.

It was just after seven on Friday night when they got in the car. Hoover immediately turned on his cell phone, noticing the little icon indicating missed calls and ignoring it. He punched the numbers for information, stroking his lucky break without realizing he did so. When the operator answered, he asked for the number to the Grapple Company, located on Roosevelt Boulevard. The number listed had a 215 area code. He wrote it down on the scrap of newspaper Markus Eaton had given him then dialed it into his phone. Voice mail picked up the other end, the canned speech spoken by a woman with a sweet-sounding southern drawl. Hoover had never in his life had phone sex and couldn't see what people would get out of it. A nameless, faceless woman whose job was conjuring up images of sexuality in your mind sounded sterile and boring, if you asked him. Maybe he was too analytical, didn't have the imagination for such a thing. Either way, the sexy-sounding, prerecorded voice informed him that the office for the Grapple Company was now closed for the weekend and would reopen at nine on Monday morning.

Damn, that was a long time to wait.

Without knowing it, Hoover had just crapped out on his luck.

If the start of the day had not been delayed by the fight, if Hoover and Farrell had gone to Walking on Air before the Hippy Hippy Shake, if Markus had been forthcoming with his information instead of circumlocutory, they might've caught someone still in the Grapple office before the last employee locked the doors at 6:30. If they had been able to get access to Grapple's records, they may have been able to prevent the tragedies that were to come and may have been able to save so many lives.

"It's closed for the weekend," Hoover told Beverly, who was driving. "We can try to get a judge to sign off on a warrant, get them to open it back up."

"Who you going to serve it to? We don't even know who runs the place, let alone where to find them when they're not there. Besides, what're you going to say we need the warrant for?"

"Subpoena the phone records."

"For what? What are you looking for?"

"Repeat callers."

"The perverse people who use services like that are *all* going to be repeat callers. Needle in a haystack."

"I know; I was only going to target the locals to start. How many repeaters can there be from this area?"

"The advertisement was in our newspaper I'm sure there'd be plenty of repeaters from in and around the city. More than we'd be able to handle ourselves."

"You're right," Hoover said sullenly.

"If you take that to a judge on a Friday night, you're going to piss him off. And he'll tell you to wait until Monday for a warrant, if he even grants one at all for such a flimsy supposition."

"Right again."

Silence for a while.

"What next?" Beverly asked.

"The phone records are the best we've got. But as you've said, our hands are tied on that at this juncture." Hoover shrugged. "After that, it drops off severely. We could beat the bushes for some of Kasay's friends, see what they know. Try to locate David Stanton."

"That won't be easy this late on a Friday, either."

"I know it."

"Are you tapped?"

"Yeah, I am."

"Me too. Let's knock off for the night."

"Fine."

"Want to get a drink with me?" she asked, hoping for a little time to talk about things other than work.

He was shocked, but not very. He had expected something like this. She had respected his privacy with the Agbalaya thing all day when others would have jumped on him the minute they were alone. Asking him for a drink was her way of offering the olive branch.

Hoover looked at her, radiant in her beauty. She had worn her brunette hair pulled up in a ponytail, exposing one of her finest features, her neck. Of the female anatomy, the neck had always been one of Hoover's favorite parts. Beverly Farrell's was no exception. It was long and graceful, the flesh delicately fair. There was a single tiny mole where her neck met her shoulder. Hoover wanted to nuzzle that spot.

There were few things in the world Hoover would like to do more than have a drink with the woman he was in love with. But it would be costly if he did.

First, there would be the inquisition about the morning's events with the reporter. He would answer her questions honestly; after all, everything she'd want to know would be public knowledge after the board of review ruled anyway.

Secondly, there were the final shreds of professionalism he still held for his work—saying yes to her might put his job at further risk. There had already been a previous request made by Detective Beverly Farrell that she not be assigned to work with Hoover, due to preexisting conditions. Nothing had been written up formally, but it was still there, understood, if unwritten. If he agreed to the drink, it might topple that shaky foundation, causing a skeleton door to spring open. Mixing business with pleasure was not a good idea, he knew, having already tried it once and almost getting burned. *How many times could a man reach into the flames and come away unscathed?*

Third, there was his wife. And if he went with Beverly, his wife might not be there afterward. He was already going to face a lot of heat from her over his actions this morning. Undoubtedly, she had heard about it by now, on the news or from one of the other detectives' nosy wives. Hoover had turned his cell phone off after the meeting with Korzenowski without having called home.

Finally, there were the children to think about. Janey and Pammy. No matter what he did for a living, no matter whom he chose as a lover, they would always be his children, even if Lauren left. They would be judgmental of his actions, of course, but he thought them chips off his block, rather than Lauren's, and thought they'd want whatever was best for him. That was a supremely selfish way to think, and he knew it, but selfishness was part of the issue here, wasn't it? Part of what was eating at his soul?

Those were some heavy issues to weigh, and Hoover found that he didn't know what to do. He already felt like a man without purpose lately. He had goals (chief among which right now was finding the monster who killed nine women and dumped them in the woods) but no purpose. He didn't know what he wanted from life, what he wanted to do. He needed something to streamline his thinking, something outside himself to push him in the right direction.

To drink or not to drink with Beverly, that was *a* question. But was he at the crossroads again? That was *the* question. He had already come upon one intersection this morning; was it possible that he could come upon a second in the very same day?

He didn't know. What he did know was that he was a man who stood behind his decisions as a man should, come what may. Hoover was not one to make a life-changing decision—whether in the heat of anger or passion—and then hide from it.

Fuck it, he thought, *let's roll the dice and see what happens.*

"A drink sounds good," Hoover told her, choosing his path—a path that would probably lead to another intersection on a horizon not too distant from this one.

"I know a place a couple of blocks from my apartment. Medium sized, not too many kids, not too many old farts. Nice décor; you'll like it."

"If it's got bourbon, I like it already."

17

7:20 p.m.

Michael Dedaker waited for her in the place where he knew she would come.

Tonight's work had to be exact. Flaws happened, as they usually did whenever more than one person was involved in something, but especially when the other person (in this case, a woman whose soul would be returned to God) was unsuspecting and unwilling. Tonight, flaws were unacceptable. This particular woman was a special case, and had to be treated as such.

A methodical planner, Michael had this specific woman chosen late last summer, shortly after Tammy Allensworth was accepted back into the Creator's loving embrace in July due to Michael's diligent, hard work. This one had not been chosen at random, as the others had, based solely on their sins. She had been *discovered* at random—like the women previous—but upon further conjecture, Michael had held off from her deliverance until the timing was right, costing him the whole month of August's servitude to the Father. Other than the holy months of December (his son's birth) and January (when the wise men—the first of the human souls drawn to the Christ child for salvation—had their epiphany and found the infant in the manger), Michael had furthered his work at the pace of one soul a month. The two voluntarily missed months were for retreat, a time of solitude and prayer.

However, the empty month of August—when Michael had found quarry but had chosen not to act upon it—was always a thorn in his side. He had found a woman among the horde, but he had not released her soul from its purgatory, because of his own selfishness, instead having left her toiling in her sins for what he knew would ultimately be the greater good of all in the end. But was letting her soul disintegrate and rot with its unrighteous cancer of sin in order to save his own the right thing to do? Or was it an even greater sin than anything the woman herself had done? Knowing she'd char in eternal damnation if she happened to die before he delivered her to the Lord, was taking that risk for the greater good acceptable, or would such a thing cost him his own salvation?

The questions within were many, the answers varied and gray. Dedaker had wrestled with them for some time, only allayed by the fact that the sins marring her soul were *her* sins, not his. To ease his burden, that understanding would have to do. This woman had been chosen for sins that were far from venial, but she was not just another redemption—she was the first step in *his* redemption.

Up until the moment Michael had discovered her iniquities, he was uncertain how his work would end, what the finishing touch would be. But after ascertaining all of the components in this particular woman's lifestyle, Michael had been able to glimpse his final act of personal sanctification, and how glorious it would be.

But all of his fears and worries regarding the timing of her redemption would not matter if he didn't perform his work like a well-oiled machine tonight. Part of the usual routine before he ventured out to do God's work was to rest during the day, to sleep. But this day, sleep eluded him. He had been too nervous for his body to cycle down to a restive state and had lain in bed as tense as a piano wire. He tried everything from counting sheep (which had never worked for him) to drinking warm milk (which had also never worked, causing him nausea). A large quantity of alcohol would have done the trick, and quickly, but then would have been counterproductive to what he was trying to achieve—a rested, clear mind.

Finally, he lay as still as a snake in the highland grass and tried to think of nothing—a feat harder to do than most people would believe. Imagine being able to completely empty your mind of thought while in a wakeful, conscious state. Michael couldn't do it. The more he tried to do it, the more he *thought* about trying to do it. He was finally able to achieve a state of almost complete thoughtlessness when he focused his mind to concentrate solely on the color black. Nothing but blackness; blackness surrounding him, swirling, floating; blackness within him, swallowing him. He couldn't comprehend what it was like to be fully in that void, because he couldn't allow his mind to think about it, else he would lose the state he was trying to reach. But he *felt* that he liked it, liked being there, liked just being.

He was Michael Dedaker, and he was. That's all, nothing more. Just was. Had he been able to think about it, he would have found the sensation exhilarating, would've been like seeing oneself but not seeing anything. Like standing in front of two mirrors, one in front and one behind, both reflecting your image into each other, causing a lack of depth perception. It would've been like being alive within another living being. Would life with a complete lack of perception be like existing within the womb, being in utero?

He slept without knowing he slept.

Now, standing next to a tree in the deepening dusk, waiting for a woman, Michael thought that achieving a state of nothingness—of blackness—would be what it would feel like if the soul could be freed of its husk and still remain mortal here on earth, floating and drifting, swaying in the gently blowing breeze like the new, green leaves on the tree above him. Michael closed his eyes and breathed deeply of the vernal air. It was sweet and smooth and fresh. To be a soul unencumbered, sailing free on the wind, would be the ultimate mortal achievement, the pinnacle zenith. It would be the feeling of dwelling in God's grace in heaven while still being alive. A state of conscious nothingness would literally be like heaven on earth. But the conflicting fact, the paradox, was that one could not achieve an absolute zero level of knowing and still know it.

Michael's ruminations were interrupted by the sound of a door slamming.

Looking toward the sound, he saw it was her, the woman he had been waiting for. He had looked just in time to see her reach to retrieve the screen door. The wind—which had gusted up and was blowing harder than he had first thought—had caught it and, having forcefully pulled the retaining spring off the top of the door, banged it against the house's white siding. A rite of spring was to remove the energy-efficient windowpane from the screen door and replace it with an actual screen. Had the window still been in place on this door, it would've shattered, fragments of glass strewn over the stoop and flower bed.

It took a little effort on the woman's part to pull the door back to a position in which she could reattach the spring to the arm overhead. She was almost six feet tall and the door seven. Dedaker watched as she stood on her tiptoes to rehitch the spring to the top of the door. While she did, the soft-pleated skirt she wore, perilously short to begin with, rose up enough for him to see that she also wore white cotton panties. The flash of whiteness beneath the burgundy of the skirt gave Dedaker a tingling sensation in his scrotum. It was but a quick flash, brief, and Dedaker wanted more, craved more.

Having fixed the spring and shut the screen door, the woman bounced down the three brick steps that led to the entrance of her residence. Assisted by the billowing wind, her bounces caused the burgundy skirt to flutter once, twice. With each happy leap downward the woman took, Dedaker stared intently at her thighs, hoping to catch another glimpse of the forbidden whiteness that complemented the flesh tones of her legs so perfectly. By the third and final step, she had modestly placed a hand against her thigh so as to keep the offending fabric from revealing her womanhood.

The woman's discretion saddened Dedaker. He was eager to glimpse her panties again, maybe even desperate to. But wasn't that the nature of man? Always wanting more than he could have? Man had a car; he wanted a nicer one. Man had a house; he wanted a bigger one. Man had a woman; he wanted another. Man wants; it's his nature to always strive for that which is out of reach. It was how he aspired to be godlike, by always wanting to ascend to a higher status. More than anything, what Michael Dedaker wanted right now was another glimpse of the woman's panties.

But he had also been angered by her sudden chastity and inhibition. Who the fuck did she think she was that she could blithely expose every facet of her life to the entire world and yet *not* show something to him? Soon enough, she would learn her lesson.

Dedaker closed his eyes for a second to regain his composure, but there wasn't enough time for total placidity. He only had but a brief moment to regain his poise. He knew that he would again get to see this woman's underwear—as well as the rest of her naked form—under his own power. But that wouldn't be the same, would it? No it wouldn't, not by a long stretch. First, because the true thrill of seeing that peek of white cotton was in the fact that she didn't know he had seen. While releasing her soul, she would be well aware of what he saw, canceling out the voyeuristic principle. Second, he would be doing God's work then, and there was no place for his own perverse thrills while doing his work. Dedaker would have to be satisfied with the brief, spasmodic glance that he had been granted.

A shrill chirping sounded, which acted like an alarm clock for Dedaker. With a dash of serenity back within him, he shook his head briskly, reopening his eyes. The interior light and the fog lamps were illuminated on the car. The chirping sound had been the woman deactivating the car's alarm. The car was now unlocked, and she was walking toward it.

This was it; the entire of his work would hinge on the next couple of minutes. If he botched it, it was over. There would only be one chance. If he failed to subdue the woman, the rest of the plan would collapse like a house of cards. Dedaker had watched the six o'clock news tonight and was acutely aware that a timeline had been placed upon the completion of his work. The music was cued, and God had picked a partner with whom Dedaker would dance. God had picked a man named Hoover, Detective John Hoover. And as always in his perfection, God chose wisely, for this Hoover was truly an infidel, a rogue who used his fists on innocents and bent the law to satisfy his own version of justice. Just ask the battered reporter Agbalaya, or the old, dead Sullivans.

She was ten feet from the car.

Dedaker had to time it exactly right for it to work, had to act as soon as she was in the car, but before she drove away. That might not have been as hard as it needed to be, if the people weren't as hasty as they were. Everything had to be done immediately, if not more quickly. One of the many things that suffered from this impetuousness was the life expectancy of cars. Most people simply did not take the few moments necessary to let it warm up before dropping it in gear and zipping on with the rest of the busy lives.

Although not a mechanic, Dedaker was wise enough to know that letting enough time after ignition for the previously stationary liquids to circulate within the engine probably added years to a car's life.

Of the many things he did know about this woman, he didn't know how rash she would be while warming up her car, so he had to act as soon as she got into the automobile. He could not take her before that because it was still early in the evening, and if she screamed, someone might hear and come to investigate. He also could not take her before she got in the car because the car was imperative to the evening's agenda as well. Along with her, Dedaker needed her car—it was part of the plan.

Five feet.

The tree Dedaker leaned against (hiding would look suspicious if seen, loitering not as much) was half a dozen yards or so from where she parked her car. Dedaker knew he could span that gap in three seconds flat, having made trail runs before this night which had always gone smoothly. But the dry runs had been done alone. The more people involved, the more variables involved. More than anything else, Dedaker wanted to keep this to just the two of them, wanted it to go unseen. Any other people—as in witnesses—and the variables would stratosphere.

The woman pulled up the handle and the car door opened. That was his cue it was time to spring into action. Dedaker used the tree to push himself forward with a burst of momentum. With a jarring first foot, he stepped and leapt off the curb and into the street. He moved at a trot—not quite running but certainly not walking—keeping his eyes focused on the interior of the car, which was a sandy shade of brown. If that tan color were to disappear from his sight, then she had closed the car door, and all was probably lost.

The woman, who had not noticed Dedaker leaning against the tree, did not see him coming up behind her, either. She had removed the small black clutch bag she'd been carrying over her shoulder and tossed it onto the passenger seat. Again modestly holding her skirt close so as not to give anybody a peek at the goods, she put her right leg into the car and lowered her rump to the seat. Just as she was about to pull her left leg to shut the door, Dedaker was upon her.

"Hey!" he said, calling her attention. It worked; she was startled, her face looking like a deer caught in headlights.

"What—," she began.

Dedaker grabbed the door and, tendons standing out in his neck, used all of his strength to slam it as hard as he could. Still outside the car, the woman's left leg was struck by the door across the hard bone of her shin.

Car designers specifically round the bottom edges of the doors so that they can seal tightly to the frame, keeping the snow, slush, and rain from getting in. Because of this, the woman was struck by the thin edge of steel hiding inside the rubberized material that acted as a gasket. The force behind the thrust caused the steel to pierce her skin so deeply it scrapped bone. The tibia itself, strong enough in concert with the fibula and the femur to support her whole frame and propel her while walking, did not break from the impact but only sustained a hairline fracture.

Dedaker didn't care what happened to the woman's shin, only needing the car door to distract her, not to cripple her. It did not matter to him if she could walk or not, as long as he had control.

The woman reacted to the injury exactly as scripted. With one hand, she reached down to comfort the wound; with the other, she pushed open the door to free her leg from the snare. Dedaker did not resist, letting her push as hard as she wanted. As soon as the space was wide enough, the woman drew her injured leg up to her body, cradling it.

Dedaker reached in and roughly shoved her across to the passenger seat. In her contracted posture, she rolled like a ball. Dedaker plopped himself into the driver's seat and slammed the door shut.

"What—," the woman began to ask again. Dedaker turned toward her and let fly a roundhouse haymaker. It struck her right between the eyes, her head helicoptering and striking her forehead on the rolled-up window.

Dazed, she slumped against the passenger door still cradling her cut and bleeding leg. Dedaker looked at the wound he had inflicted on her shin. If this had been any other time, she might've needed two or three stitches to close the gap. His gaze lazily ascended up her body, appreciating as he went. When he got to her slack face, he noticed that a large black-and-blue egg was quickly forming beneath the lines of her brow. He judged that she would not put up a fuss until he got them back to the duplex.

Only one more thing, then we're out of here.

The keys.

Dedaker reached around the steering wheel to the column and felt the ignition switch. It felt fuzzy. He bent to look. A green rabbit's foot was attached to the ring. The keys were in the ignition.

Dedaker smiled. *Luck be a lady tonight.*

He looked up at the house sitting a tasteful distance back from the curb. It was one of twenty on the long block, ten to a side. He didn't see anybody watching what was happening on the street. While he looked, a light came on in an upstairs room.

Deciding that luck would only smile but so much, he drove away before it ran out.

18

Ten minutes later, Beverly pulled over to the curb and parked next to a playground complete with swings, slides, and a baseball diamond. They were at Bustleton and Rhawn, about six or seven blocks west of Roosevelt Boulevard. Getting out of the car, she pointed across the street. "There it is," she announced.

A large yellow sign with green letters proclaimed the bar to be called the Tabard Inn. It was the last building in a string of stores before a Mobil station capped the corner.

"You like corned beef?"

"I like anything with the word beef in it," he told her.

"Good. This place has the best Ruben sandwich in town."

She was on his side of the car now. They looked both ways and waited for a break in traffic before jogging across the busy street.

The doublewide front doors of the Tabard Inn were propped open with a trash can on one side and a cinder block on the other. The window was draped with emerald green curtains that matched the lettering of the sign. Behind the steamy glass was a chalkboard informing incoming customers that every Thursday was ladies' nite, and that the specials for happy hour were dollar drinks and ten-cent wings. The closer they got to the door, the louder the music could be heard spilling out into the temperate, if a bit windy, night. The music wasn't too noisy, and it wasn't honky-tonk, so it was okay with Hoover. A few steps farther and they descended from the deepening twilight into the darkness of the Tabard Inn.

When his eyes adjusted to the dimness, Hoover stuffed his hands in his pockets and took a look around.

He could see booths lined up along the wall on either side of the triangular-shaped bar. At the rear, beyond the base of the triangle, there was a small alcove with the prerequisite pool tables and that strange bowling game played with a sliding metal hockey puck, whatever that was called. On the far wall there was a dartboard and a chalkboard (the twin of the one in the front window) to keep score for cricket. Four men currently held beers and darts there.

In the few empty patches along the walls that weren't covered with college basketball memorabilia, he could see that the place was colored with coats of dark brown paint that matched the tiles on the floor. On this particular Friday night, the bar was half full of twentysomethings, which seemed like a respectable crowd for a neighborhood-type of establishment. The patrons were middle-class citizens, and Hoover guessed the rowdiness was kept to the occasional loud argument. Fighting was probably sparse at the Tabard.

All in all, it was the kind of place he could hang out in.

"Hoover, over here," Beverly beckoned, causing him to reminisce that those exact words were the ones Korzenowski had first used yesterday morning, in the woods. Those words were essentially what led him to Beverly Farrell yesterday and would now lead him to her tonight.

Standing next to the only empty booth on the right-hand side of the bar, she waved him over, then sat down facing the back of the room. Hoover strolled to the booth. There were hooks screwed into the wooden sides of the seats to hang coats on. Hoover removed his sport jacket and hung it up. His .38 was in a holster on his belt. He removed the firearm and stuffed it in a pocket of the sport jacket, within easy reach of his hand but out of eyesight of the drinkers. Rolling up his sleeves, he took a seat across from Beverly on the booth's padded bench.

Beverly, who was also wearing a sport coat (albeit one shorter than his, the middle tailored to her waist and hips), chose to keep hers on.

Before either of them could initiate conversation, a waiter appeared at the edge of their table. Beverly ordered for both of them.

"We'll have two Coors Lights and two Rubens."

"You want the deluxe?"

"What's with the deluxe?"

"Fries, slaw, pickle."

"And without?"

"Bag of chips."

"We'll have the deluxe." He disappeared.

"I've never had a Ruben," Hoover confessed.

"You'll like it, trust me," she said.

"What is it?"

"Corned beef on rye, Swiss cheese, and sauerkraut."

"Hot or cold?"

"Hot."

"Sounds good."

"I know it does."

The waiter returned, carrying a tray with two bottles of beer and two mugs. He pulled a couple of napkins from his apron and laid them in front of each detective. As he set a beer atop the napkins, he said, "First round's on me."

"Really? Why?" Hoover asked, surprised. He wasn't one to look the gift horse in the mouth, but was still wise enough to know that in this world, nothing was ever free.

"The owner considers this place to be a 'sports bar.' It's really only a speakeasy with televisions bolted to the ceiling so that people interested can keep up with the scores. He's got satellite dishes on the roof and keeps all seven sets running continuously." He paused and pointed out four televisions. "Those four are tuned to the local affiliates. ABC, NBC, CBS, and FOX," he said, indicating each individually. "Throughout the day, on all four of them, I saw you kick the shit out of that annoying midget reporter. I like your style— hit first, ask questions later—so this one's on me." He sat a stack of napkins for the food on the table and added before walking away again, "It's not often you get to meet a celebrity who's actually in the spotlight of the moment."

Hoover glanced at Beverly, knowing what he was going to see when he did. Yep, just as he suspected, her face was the questioning whiteness of a blank sheet of paper waiting for the author to fill it up with a good story. Hoover was ready to talk but decided to let her sweat it a few more minutes, content to let her suffer until she asked the first question. Her respect of his privacy went up against his wall of silence—a game of wills, if you will.

After eight hours of following Hoover's lead while he questioned people connected to the dead girls, Beverly was ready to ask her own questions, practically jumping out of her skin with it. And barely a few seconds later, just as he figured, she cracked first. "Why haven't you said anything to me?" she accused, tinted with a hint of anger.

He decided not to insult her intelligence by playing dumb, but he did let her hang a moment more, just a moment more—it was the mean streak in him. "What do you want me to say?"

"Why don't you start with what Korzenowski had to say about your antics this morning?"

"He said that I've created a nice, big, throbbing headache for me, him, and the department collectively."

"No kidding. Did he mention any ramifications?"

"Yeah, he did. He said that if Agbalaya lodged a complaint, he, Agbalaya, would have to do so with Central Detectives. Because the complaint concerns a police officer, me, it would get turned over to Internal Affairs. IA would then have to investigate the complaint, which won't be too difficult seeing as it's the lead story on the news and will probably make the headlines of tomorrow's papers. Once the complaint is verified, the whole thing gets bumped to the commissioner's office. The commissioner then sets up a preliminary hearing so that assault and battery charges can be brought against me. Once the charges are levied, I should receive a thirty-day suspension with intent to discharge."

The sandwiches arrived with the cynically starstruck waiter. He put one down in front of each of them then went to the bar for refills on the beers.

Hoover looked at his plate, impressed. The sandwich was overly packed with stacked slices of corned beef, the fries so plentiful that the plate couldn't contain them, and the scoop of coleslaw was in a paper holder that kept it from running. It was a king's feast, garnished with half a Jewish dill pickle. He glanced at Beverly's plate, noting that hers was just as full as his.

"This is huge," he commented.

"I know," she said, muffled around bites of Ruben. "Isn't it great?"

Having taken a big chomp of his own sandwich, Hoover had to agree that it was. He found himself nodding his head at the sandwich as he ate—a quirk he had while enjoying a really satisfying meal. With good company.

As he entertained that last thought, he spied Beverly sneaking the pickle off his plate, hers having already been eaten. Caught like a thief in the night, she pleaded with large brown eyes. He acquiesced with a grin. While he grinned, he remembered that in all the time he had been partnered with Beverly Farrell, he had never gotten to eat his pickle. God, how he ached to be close to her.

After they were done eating, their plates cleared and their beers refilled for a third time, Beverly prodded again.

"When will your thirty days begin?"

"Korzenowski says I have about three days for the paperwork round-robin to go between the sixth district—where the Roundhouse is located—Central, Internal Affairs, and the commissioner's office, then another ten until the preliminary hearing. All in all, I could have approximately another two weeks left of active duty on the force. After that, I cool my heels on suspension, waiting for a trial to be scheduled, where I'll show up in court for the verdict."

"What did Korzenowski say about the trial?"

Hoover smirked. "He told me to buy some new suits."

"Teddy sure is getting droll in his old age. I can hear those exact words coming from his mouth."

"Actually, that was the good part."

"What's the bad part?"

"He said that one way or the other, the commissioner's going to have my balls."

"What does that mean?"

"It means that even if I win by proving I was provoked into taking the actions I did, I'll still be discharged."

That angered her. "How the hell can he say that? He doesn't know what the commissioner's thinking."

"He said that in the rare cases when a cop wins a verdict like this, the commissioner still has an escape clause to wash his hands of the whole thing. If I win, he'll slap me with a conduct unbecoming rap and still be able to discharge me under that blanket."

"That's bullshit."

"Bullshit or not, it's fact. I have a total of about twelve days to finish out this case and catch the twisted son of a bitch who did that to those girls."

"We will; we'll catch him. After that, maybe the commissioner will show a little mercy."

"Don't get your hopes up," he said, but wondered that himself.

"Told your wife yet?"

The little laugh he produced sounded weary. "Not yet," he said, pointing to the table. "Figured I'd have one last supper before she crucifies me."

Beverly stared right at him. He looked at her and noticed the way she chewed her bottom lip. The lip chewing was part worry—worry for him professionally, as well as worry for him personally—and part something else, some deeper feeling. He knew what she wanted now.

"Go ahead, Bev, ask."

She chewed once or twice more, then, "Why'd you do it?"
You're no better than he is.

"That guy's been pushing my buttons since DiSilva and I caught the squeal on the kid they busted in the pawnshop. That was almost two months ago. He finally pushed the right one, and I punched his ticket for him."

"That's bullshit," she said again, meaning what Hoover had done.

"Sorry. That's the God's honest truth."

"You've been on the force for what, twenty years?"

"Eighteen."

"Thick skin like yours; how could you let him get your goat?"

He sighed. *You were untruthful the last time you were on conversational terms with her, and look at the disastrous outcome. If you've learned anything, it's that she would want you to be truthful—even if it hurts her.*

"Because of you," he said, and it was the truth.

"What's that supposed to mean, because of me? What could I have to do with it? Please don't tell me you were defending my honor or something, because chivalry doesn't—"

"I wasn't being chivalrous. He didn't say anything *about* you. He said it about *me* But what he said made me think of you. And how I've treated you in the past." He took a long drink from the mug.

Beverly sat back against the padding. It was stiff and bulbous, not very comfortable. "I don't understand."

"Remember last night, when I asked you if I were evil?"

"Yeah, so?"

"Well, it's been a long time since you and I have, well, been together. Since you and I have even had a conversation. Yesterday, when I saw you in the woods, with all those poor dead women lying on the ground, in my mind I connected the way I treated you with the actions of the bastard who did that to those women."

"Hoover—"

He raised his palms. "Hold on. You've started this, now let me finish it. I don't mean to insinuate I'm a murderer. I'm not. What I mean is that he took any woman he wanted and did whatever he wanted to with her. Now that *is* a crime I'm guilty of, and one you yourself have chastised me for, I might add. I've used women for my own personal needs, my own pleasures, only to leave them behind in my wake like so many carcasses.

"Seeing you standing among the cadavers of those women made me understand how I must've made you feel dead inside, how I must've killed your spirit."

"Hoover, that's a silly correlation. And I—"

"Is it really?"

"Of course it is."

"Then you're saying that when I treated you as I did, it didn't kill your spirit or make you feel dead inside?"

"No, I'm not saying that. You hurt me. You hurt me bad. But you're comparing what you did to murder, the worst crime imaginable against humanity."

Hoover rubbed the heels of his hands against his eyes. "You're not getting me. This doesn't have anything to do with killing, with murder. It has to do with spirit. I broke your spirit. If my wife knew, her spirit would be broken too. I've broken many other women's spirits, whether they knew it or not, sucked the souls right out of them."

"It's only sex, Hoover. Every male in the world—animal, reptile, mammal, human—they all want sex. They need it. It's programmed inside the chromosomes. What you did was what every male in the world does—look for a way to procreate. The whole reason we're in the world at all is for pronatalism. You responded to the call of nature, simply put."

"You're trying to sugarcoat it; I can see it in the way your jaw's set. You don't believe what you just said any more than I do."

"All right, what do you want me to say? That you hurt me? I've already said it, but I'll say it again. You did, you hurt me. What else do you want to hear? That I hate you? I did. I hated you for what you did to me, but I'm a big girl; the scars have healed. There, are you happy now? Will that make you stop with the self-destructive attitude?"

"No, hearing you say that doesn't make me happy. I'm not trying to win points."

"Then what *are* you trying to do?"

"I'm trying to say that I'm sorry. I'm sorry for hurting you."

There was a pause. The heat of her anger could be felt arcing above the booth.

In a small voice, she said again, "You did hurt me."

"I know."

"I fell in love with you."

"I know. I was in love with you too."

"Ha," she leaned forward, blurting it in his face.

He looked down into the mug and swirled the amber-colored liquid.

"I was green when I met you," she said. "I wasn't a rookie, but I'd just been promoted to a gold badge when we got partnered. In uniform, I'd never had a steady partner before, didn't know what it was like to work hand in hand with someone. Then suddenly I was spending every waking minute with you. I become attached to people too quickly; it's a flaw in my character. Especially when they're handsome men with cocksure attitudes who listen to me. Everything I said, you paid attention to. Do you know how rare that is in men? What I said a minute ago about the call of nature? It's true, but I thought you were better than that."

That was meant to hurt him, to cause him some penance, and it did.

"Not only did you respect my intelligence, you were a shoulder to cry on. You were a confessional when I needed it. That's why I fell in love with you—you were interested in my mind, not just my body. Something like that means everything to a woman, or so I thought." He could see tears welling up. "The funny thing is that I don't blame you," she said. "I blame myself. I'm a woman working a man's job in a man's world. There are exactly three of us in homicide. One's a dyke, one's pregnant, and the other's me. I knew that going in, and I still choose to do the job. Naively, I thought that my sex wouldn't matter."

"I didn't mean to hurt you," he said, and it sounded weak to his own ears.

Suddenly, she slapped her hand down on the table, rattling the metal rack that held the salt and pepper shakers. "Then why'd you do it? Why'd you lead me on? Tell me that! Tell me why you didn't let me know you were married until *after* you fucked me."

He frowned and shook his head. He couldn't raise his eyes to look at her. "I can't tell you why, exactly, can't explain actions I knew were wrong. I knew they were wrong then, and I know they're wrong now. I can't tell you why; I can only explain how . . . how I was feeling."

She crossed her arms over her chest. "Go ahead, Hoover. Explain to me how *you* were feeling," her voice brittle with scorn.

"All right, goddamn it, I will!" Hoover found he had raised his voice to match hers. She wasn't the only one involved in the situation between them, a situation that had festered from the initial copulation until now, ending up as sour feelings spilled like skunked beer in this dim, dank bar.

"At first, I didn't know what had come over me," he confessed. "I was in love with my wife, and then I wasn't. I can't explain it any more than that. There was no reason for the vast change in my heart. One day I loved her, and the next I didn't. As simplistic as that sounds, it's been the hardest thing in the world for me to deal with.

"And I've been dealing with it for almost thirteen years.

"We were going along just fine, no problems in the relationship. She was happy; I was happy. Money was tight, but whose isn't? We'd always bicker over money, just like anybody else. I could see the things that were needed around the house, but what could I do if there was no money to take care of them? She complained, but she understood. Money wasn't what drove the wedge between us. There were no kids when the cracks started to form, so I can't point to them. And in fact, since Janey and Pammy were born, they have been nothing but a delight. So Lauren and I were cool on two of the major topics domestic disputes are based on: money and children.

"That leaves sex.

"Sex was where the problem was, and it's all one-sided. Near as I can tell, Lauren has never strayed from the marital bed. But I have. Often. I've used women—

You're no better than he is.

"—and then thrown them away."

Beverly's face was tight with emotion. It was a bitter pill for her to swallow, knowing that she wasn't special, that she was only one among many. Hot tears were glistening, but she was damned if they were going to fall.

"I know how that sounds. I know you must feel—"

"Cheap is how I feel. Fuck, Hoover, why'd you do it?"

"That's what I'm trying to tell you—why I did it. Why I continue to do it." He cleared his throat. "At first, I wasn't sure. I was angry with myself and felt dirty for doing it, for cheating. I would look at Lauren and be ashamed. But shame didn't stop me. Nope, I kept right on going. Do you know how easy it is to get laid as a cop in this city? They throw it at you. The long hours on swing shifts only lends itself to perfect opportunities. *Opportunities that I took.* And after I took them, I would kick myself for it. But it didn't stop me. I kept right on fucking, without understanding why.

"Then I met you."

She had to laugh at that. When she did, one betraying tear slid down her cheek. To cover it up, she drank some of her beer, wiping the foam—and tear—away with the back of her hand.

"I met you and understood what was missing from my marriage. I'm not sure if I can explain it exactly, so bear with me. Between my wife and I, there was no heat, no passion. We weren't simpatico. We were—and are—only together because we're used to each other. I know what she likes; she knows what I like. It's easy that way. There're no games to play. We stay out of each other's way. Basically, we coexist.

"I had come to the point when I thought that cohabiting was all life was really about Then I realized that that was all I was doing, just existing, not living. There was a person who woke me up to that realization and made me reevaluate the motions I had been going through with Lauren. That person's name was Kelly Connelly.

"She was the first one I cheated on Lauren with. When I met her, I thought the reason I didn't love my wife was because I had married the wrong woman, married the first woman I had a relationship with. Not only was she the only woman I ever had sex with, she was the only woman I had ever dated. I never sowed any oats. That's what was missing from my life, I thought. I gave myself some breathing room by coming up with an excuse about exercising demons, after which I'd be able to be a good husband; I'd be able to love my wife again because now that I had something to compare her with, I wouldn't take Lauren for granted.

"Didn't work; I still whored around. I was disgusted with myself, even went so far as to look into the causes of sexual addictions, shopped the bookstores for a cure, looked on-line, and had even scheduled an appointment to go see a shrink.

"Then you came along.

"At first, I didn't think much of you. You were beautiful—stunningly so—but I thought of you in a nonsexual way, as a coworker. You know, my partner. Then, over time, I began to think of you more and more. I found that I'd be spending as much time on the job as I could, and it had nothing to do with hoarding overtime. I was doing it because I wanted to be with you as much as I could, no other reason. I was smitten. I loved the way you looked, the way you thought, the way you walked, acted, smelled, smiled. Everything. I found myself being jealous of other men whenever you paid any attention to them. I still do."

"Is that supposed to make me feel better, handing me some romantic bullshit?"

"No. I'm not trying to make you feel better, not trying to make myself feel better, just trying to clear the air. My career in the police department is over, and I want to let you continue yours with an understanding of what happened between us—no, of what I caused between us."

"You still lied to me. What difference does it make if you thought you were in love?"

"I don't think, I *know*. And the difference is huge to me. It's life changing. You're everything that my wife isn't. Within you is everything I dream of having."

Beverly was fully crying now, and she didn't care who saw. "Then why did you hurt me?"

"I didn't mean to hurt you. And I didn't do it all by myself. If you don't have feelings for me—feelings as strong as I do—then it wouldn't hurt so much."

"Damn it, Hoover, I *do* love you. But we're not in high school. We're adults with responsibilities. We can't afford to harbor some romance-novel, unrequited love for each other."

Hoover pointed at her as if he were going to say something. When nothing came out, he opened both his hands, showing her the palms, and sat back. "You're right."

She looked him in the eye. "I don't want to be right. I want to be kissed."

19

They were in the bottom apartment of Dedaker's duplex.

Everything was going exactly as planned. The woman had been surprisingly easy to succumb. After Dedaker hit her in the car, she had not regained consciousness, having been hazy and woozy throughout the drive back to the duplex. When he brought her into the house, and then dropped her down the hole, she had not put up a fight.

Now she was stripped and prepped.

As was Dedaker.

Standing naked on the tarp and looking at the woman as she hung upside down, listing a bit, he could see that her eyes had rolled back into to her head, leaving only the whites showing through half-lidded openings. Blissfully unconscious, she snored.

Dedaker had only hit her once, and he hadn't hit her all that hard. Having no experience with narcotics, he wondered if there was drugs involved, something that would induce an overly relaxed state. Unfortunately, the only reference points he could draw on to determine if she was under the influence came from those asinine hour-long cop shows on television—the ones where life and death were neatly wrapped up in the allotted forty-six minutes, packed tightly between commercials for beer, underarm deodorants, and pizza deliveries—which were useless.

The extra-large industrial tub (which was stainless steel and had originally been used to catch the cider and pomace of pressed apples) was in place to capture the spilled blood. Dedaker liked to use the apple tub because it had a spigot on its side, which previously functioned to fill bottles, probably gallon milk jugs, with apple cider. For Dedaker's needs, he screwed a garden hose onto the threads and ran it outside the rear door to the mesh-covered drain located at the bottom of the sloped driveway. The weight of so many pints of blood was too heavy and cumbersome to carry all at once, and Dedaker didn't want to have to bucket it out in separate containers. Besides, blood coagulated after it cooled and therefore needed to be disposed of quickly before it hardened. While the blood drained, the rear door must be kept open an inch so that the tip of the black and yellow striped hose could reach the drain. The three sliding-chain safety locks were used during the draining period.

But all of that came later. First the blood had to be spilled.

Dedaker reached into the podium, pushed aside a box of charcoal, and picked out a scalpel. He preferred this tool to the others because it had a perfectly balanced heft to it that felt right seated in his palm, and he was enamored with the fluidity with which it cut—flesh parted behind it like an eel swam through water.

Looking at the scalpel, he could understand why surgeons enjoyed their craft. The blade was nary an eighth of an inch thick, and yet it held the ultimate power—the power over life.

As he looked at the scalpel, he saw his reflection distorted on the matte of the blade, while even farther out of focus in the background the woman hung waiting. It was moments like these that made him appreciate the beauty of God's perfection.

Dedaker went to her.

He stepped into the cider tub and immediately felt the chill of the stainless steel on the bottoms of his bare feet. Other than having the blessing of God's grace, Dedaker's favorite part of doing his work was when the warmth of the blood of the sinner splashed over his feet. The most beautifully written sonnets could never describe the ecstasy of that feeling—the feeling of his feet being canonized in the crimson river of life.

Dedaker's interest was piqued (as evident by his erection) by how fast the woman's blood would pour from her body. Usually, his modus operandi was to make twelve incisions (six in front, six in back, each representing one of the apostles) throughout the body so that the woman's impurities could leak out before she died, and her soul, cleansed through her pain and suffering, could be released free of sin when he cut her throat. Tonight, though, time was a factor; he needed to release her soul as soon as he could so that he could get her back into the car. He did not have enough time to let the woman slowly bleed out her impurities. He would still make the ventilating incisions for the impurities, but then, rather than wait for them to slowly escape her body, he would have to immediately slit her throat to exacerbate her soul. God would understand.

Dedaker held the scalpel up again and went to work.

20

*H*aving already had three beers at the Tabard—and little sleep the night before—Hoover felt slightly buzzed.

He hadn't noticed the warm feeling spreading over his body until Beverly said she wanted him to kiss her. Now, it was all he could feel. From the top of his head all the way down to his farthest extremities he felt flush. Feeling the blood pumping in his toes was actually quite unique, like he had immersed them in a sun-warmed creek or freshly drawn bath water.

But here he was. Beverly had made a statement of her feelings that had brought him to the crossroads again. It was time to decide.

"Bev, I don't think—"

"I don't care what you think. Frankly, I'm tired of hearing about what you think. I want you, and I want you now. I want to do this for once and for all. Let's put paid to what we started a long time ago."

"Are you sure?"

"Do I sound sure?"

"Yeah, but—"

"No buts! Do it or don't."

"What about your boyfriend? Won't he—"

"Don't have one."

"How come?"

"Who has the time? Working this job with the swing shifts, you only get to meet people who are suspects and cops. And you know how I feel about cops," she said with an amused sneer. "Are you done stalling now, or would you like to ask me some other irrelevant questions?" she asked, seeing right through him.

There was a brief pause as Hoover looked down both roads before him. He knew what the right choice was, but with the way his luck was running lately, the right choice had ultimately proved to be wrong. This time he was choosing the lady. Let the tiger bite him on the ass, if it could catch him.

"It's now or never, what's it going to be?" she asked.

Hoover leaned forward, bent over the table, and kissed her fully on the mouth.

It was rapture. Her lips were warm and soft, a touch of moisture on them. He kissed her long and deep, wrapping a hand into the thickness of her ponytail as he pulled her even closer.

While they kissed, all the senses of his body came alive—he could hear the life of the bar around him, feel the hard wood of the table beneath one hand and the silkiness of her hair in the other, and the sweet, sweet taste of her mouth.

She had no fragrance to speak of, but he could smell her personal scent. The type of essence that could only belong to the person it emanated from and could only be found in the place that someone lived or the clothes they wore. It was her incense.

Breathing deeply of Beverly's aroma reminded him of when he was a small boy and had spilled cherry water ice down the front of his shirt. He and his mother had been visiting one of her friends when the accident occurred, and he had to borrow a shirt from the woman's daughter. He and the girl had both been eight years old and of the same stature, which enabled him to fit into her clothes. Since the incident had happened almost thirty years ago, Hoover wouldn't be able to remember the girl's name if his life depended on it, but the T-shirt, he could remember clearly, white with a dolphin on it. Moreover, Hoover could remember the scent his nose had detected as he slipped it over his head, standing among the frills of her bedroom. It smelled like the girl. It was her personal smell, and it was pleasurable. Young John Hoover inhaled deeply of the girl's essence. Breathing her personal aroma had been the first sexual experience of his life. Many hours later, and home in his own bed, Hoover could still smell her person on his body. It was a beautiful smell, a passionate smell.

That was what he smelled on Beverly right now.

He smelled her person.

And he smelled her passion.

Hoover breathed her in deeply, as his mouth parted and her tongue slipped over his teeth, sensually probing.

After long, they parted. Staring into each other's eyes, Beverly said, "Let's get out of here." Grabbing his suit jacket, Hoover threw two twenties down on the table, and they left.

* * *

Beverly had been driving when they arrived at the Tabard Inn, so she went to the driver's side when they got outside. Hoover walked up behind her.

Throughout his life he considered himself a man of action, and this was one action he had always dreamed of doing again. Now was his chance. Hoover wrapped his arms around Beverly's midsection and kissed her on her neck from behind. Moving his lips up and down the incline behind her ear, pushing her shirt aside on the shoulder, he kissed her again and again. He used his tongue and his teeth on her nape and could taste the sweet tartness of her sweat, the fear, anticipation, and anxiety of what was to come.

It tasted as sinful as it felt, and she responded in like to his prurient desire.

Beverly moaned so deep in her throat that Hoover felt the vibrations on her skin—vibrations that made him quicken his lustful kisses. She swayed her hips, rubbing her buttocks against his groin, as he pushed her up against the car. One of his hands slid up the tight fabric of her shirt to her breasts while his other found the fork of her crotch. She could feel his hardness through his pants and arched her back into a position of acceptance. Hoover thrust his hips in time with her gyrations, dry humping her in the middle of the darkened street.

Beverly reached up and, grabbing a handful of his hair, turned to face him over her shoulder. She pulled his face close to hers, knocking her ponytail loose and spilling her hair down to her shoulders, covering the sensuousness of her neck. With the cool pressure of the car's steel on her front and the heat of the man behind, she kissed him again.

Hoover spun her around and started to kiss her from the front. Beverly pushed him off and held him at an arm's length as she wiped her lips with the front of her hand.

* * *

The car ride to her apartment had been exciting and exasperating. These feelings had been built up inside both of them for so long that they couldn't keep their hands off each other. Every chance they had—red lights and stop signs—they groped uncontrollably, the anticipation of promise stimulating them.

Fumbling the key into the lock of her third-floor apartment, Beverly opened the door and strode in, Hoover in tow. By the time he closed the door behind himself, Beverly had already stripped off her feminine sport coat, beneath which she wore only a body-forming black tank top. Her back to him, she raised her arms above her head and stretched. In the moonlight shining through her living-room window, Hoover could see the weight of one breast as it pressed against the clingy material of her shirt.

Hoover went to her. From behind, he undid the button of her pants and, hooking his thumbs inside the elastic of her panties, pushed them both to the floor. He knelt. The same kissing and licking and nibbling that he had done to her neck he now did to her hips and rear. With her eyes closed and her hands resting atop her head, she let him do as he pleased.

With his physical arousal so intense, he couldn't wait any longer. He reached up and pulled her to the floor in front of him. Still wearing her tank top, her pants in a bunch around her ankles, she was down on all fours and open to him. She lowered her head, her hair hiding her face behind a dark curtain as she waited for him to take her.

Looking at Beverly from this perspective, Hoover knew he was not going to last long, that he had to have her and be done with it quickly, or he would burst from the buildup. He didn't say it out loud, but he vowed to himself that the first one was going to be all his. After, he would take care of her.

Removing his pants, Hoover went to her.

* * *

Three hours later, Hoover was gone.

After the initial beastly fuck, he had made love to Beverly twice more, a not-unimpressive feat for a man of his age. When it was all over, he knew he shouldn't stay the night in her apartment. What they had done had been their final act as a couple. From here on, they were two people living lives separately from each other. They both knew it. And as soon as their heat was expelled with their fluids, they both felt it, and it felt awkward.

Hoover dressed. Beverly, in fuzzy pink bathrobe and sweat socks, walked him to the door.

"Is there anything to say?" he asked in a soft, caring tone.

"No," she replied, surprised by the way she was able to hold eye contact with him. She had thought that when they were through, she would revert to the place she had been after she'd found out about Lauren, his wife. She had been scared then, and withdrawn—almost as if she were hiding from him. She didn't feel that way now. The only things she hid at the moment were her hands, because they were buried deeply inside the bulky robe's warm pockets.

"Thank you," he whispered, bending down to her.

"You are welcome." With one foot flat on the floor and the other bent behind the first, her toes pressed to the hardwood, she accepted his kiss. It was short, sweet, and on the cheek.

He left.

Now he was outside in the chill night air, standing on the top riser of the stairs that led to the entrance of Beverly's building, an entrance that actually opened on to the second floor. From the foyer, you had to go down one flight to reach apartment number one and up one to reach number three, Beverly's.

Because of the wind that had kicked up earlier, the air was sharp, almost biting. He breathed it in, feeling the warmth of her domain leaving him from the inside out. For the first time in a while, his head was clear.

On that top step, Hoover looked around. He noticed that he stood within a pool of light being thrown by an outdoor fixture bolted into the red brick of the building. The light was pure white, shining on a man who had experienced a resurgence. Hoover liked that and thought it symbolic.

Yet standing in that light, he was a man without a country. He could not go home yet, because he didn't want to wake Lauren up in the middle of the night and have to start explaining about Agbalaya and the approaching doom Internal Affairs and the commissioner had in store. Neither of them would get any sleep that way, and he was dog tired.

Besides, Lauren deserved more. The next time he saw Lauren he would be at his best, would be refreshed and renewed. What had happened tonight—down the road he had taken—was that he had become a man. Lexicon has it that a shot of pussy will turn a boy into a man. Whoever coined the theory had neglected to say *which* shot would be the one to do the turning. Hoover thought he knew now which one it was.

Lauren had waited patiently without knowing it all these years; she would wait one more night. There was something he had to take care of first. Someone, actually. And creeping into her house at quarter of one in the morning would not seem abnormal at all. It would seem routine.

He had to go to Fiona's.

Tomorrow was a day for new beginnings, tonight a night for endings.

He had ended one relationship already this evening. Starting tomorrow, Beverly Farrell and John Hoover would be only coworkers. Friends—even close friends—but lovers nevermore. The strange thing was that both Bev and he had known it without having to say it. It was over because they had finished it. What had started with love ended with love.

Now he needed to end another relationship. But the next one would not end with love, he knew; it would just end.

As far as he was concerned, he had never felt anything for Fiona. Hoover had come to realize in the past two days that with her dark hair and features, she had only been a substitute for Beverly. He had risked everything by spending countless nights with a woman that hadn't meant anything to him. How stupid he was.

But no more. Tonight he had become a man, and he would spend the rest of his life devoting himself to the lovely—and up till now, lonely—mother of his children. All of his concentration, all of his desire, all of his love would be dedicated to her. On the horizon, there was renewed love for his wife—and an eventual new career, it seemed. Together those two things would lead to a new life.

He took the first step on his new path, which happened to be the first of twelve that led from Beverly's apartment entrance to the curb, with a clearer consciousness than when he had climbed up them hours before. He took that first step and left the round pool of light he had been standing in.

Tomorrow would be a day of new beginnings; it would dawn clear and bright.

Little did he know how darkly it would end.

21

*D*edaker was elated and ready.

His elation was caused by how smoothly the night had passed. Everything had gone exactly as planned with the woman. She was dead and had been bled as much as possible with the time restraint. Afterward, he had taken her out to the exact spot in the woods where he had brought all the rest, not to dump her, but to . . . well, you know. He knew it extremely brazen to return to the scene with a fresh corpse, but the thrill of it was just too great to pass up. The thought of sticking it up the cops' asses was too amusing to refuse. Besides, if there were one place in the whole city that the numbfucks would never think to look, it would be there, in the woods. There he placed her body on the ground, directly on the bald spot (new grass had yet to grow, but he could tell that it was on the precipice) that had been created by the weight of the previous women he had dumped. Then he took his pleasure with the remains. When he finished, he inserted her driver's license into her cavity.

For just a second, Dedaker considered that there might be something wrong with what he was doing, that there might be a flaw in the synapses of his thoughts. *Why, if I'm supposedly doing God's work, would I risk walking the distance into the woods, carrying the husk to sexually pleasure myself, when I know I have to take her body somewhere else, that her journey isn't yet finished this night?*

Originally, he had come to the woods to retrieve something that he needed to accomplish the rest of the night's task, something that he could've gotten anywhere, but he thought that getting it here would be a lark. *Should any aspect of the Lord's work be construed a lark?*

Dedaker was shocked. He felt as though someone had thrown a splash of icy-cold water in his face.

And then suddenly, the thought was gone. Forgotten. Disappeared like something glimpsed but not fully seen. He had cognized a rational that had disturbed him and then had erased it—it had been a negative criticism, and there was no place for negativity in God's work.

In the twists of a mind like Michael's, things were never as they were in reality, but only as they seemed to him. With casual disregard for the thoughts that could've been so dangerous to him (and he was consciously aware of the danger that had been lurking behind those not-so-random thoughts), he lifted the woman he had killed—and had now soiled with his semen—and walked her all the way back through the woods, to where her own car waited.

With her stowed safely in the car, he went back and got what he had come for before being sidetracked. He stowed it in the trunk, got in the car, and continued on to the next phase of the evening's outing.

Driving away from the silence of the woods—where he had almost been able to end his own reign of terror himself before so many others would die horribly—he did not remember that for the briefest instant, he had seen himself for what he was.

* * *

Now, here at the end stage of the night's work that had gone off without a hitch, without one single flaw, Dedaker actually had a smile on his face, as he got out of the woman's car. The flashers blinked, and he had double parked in the street. At this time of the morning, no one would take specific notice of a man tending to an automobile with the flashers on.

Leaving the driver's side door open, keys in the ignition, Dedaker walked around to the trunk. As he passed the rear window, he looked in on the woman. She was lying on the back seat, completely naked and completely bloodless. Death, as well as the lack of blood and clothing, had turned her skin a pale shade of white, her body color so light it held an alabaster glow. Lying dead in the car, she looked like an apparition. A shiver ran up

Dedaker's spine, and he was grateful that the woman's eyes were closed.

With a conscious effort, he stole his stare away from the backseat and continued to the trunk. He had already popped the release before he got out of the car by using the tiny lever on the floor alongside the driver's seat. When he got to the trunk, he could see the darkness within through the inch of space between the car and the open lid. He stuck his hand into the crack, into the darkness, and pulled the lid the rest of the way up. As soon as it sprung wide, the interior convenience light illuminated to life. Using the tender edge of his fist opposite the thumb, Dedaker smashed the bulb. He didn't fear drawing the attention of any onlookers, but a spotlight shining directly onto his facial features was out of the question.

He peered around the side of the trunk lid at the building across the street from where he parked. Even at this late hour, many of the lights shone in the building. He knew for a fact that there were numerous people—adversaries—walking the halls and sitting in the offices within. Dedaker looked but didn't see anybody looking back. He had gotten lucky; no one had noticed the trunk's light.

That's what happens when you start counting your chickens before they're hatched.

He had just been thinking about how smoothly tonight's exercise was going, and then—whack—a fuckup. A major fuckup, for measure. Dedaker had been in this woman's trunk barely a half hour ago. He had noticed the convenience light, but hadn't thought twice about it. Such an oversight could've cost him the rest of the project, and so close to the end. If the conclusion had come right here, on a city street, his work would still be recognized, sure, but it would be on their terms, not his. He found that unacceptable.

The proud smile that had been on Dedaker's face had left without a trace. Keep your mind in the game, he scolded himself.

He reached into the once-again dark trunk and picked up an object. As he eased down the lid to close it, he held a tree limb approximately two and a half feet in length. He didn't know the exact length because he had used his arm to take the measurement. He had placed the palm of his hand against the gas pedal and pressed down. Then he had checked to see where the edge of the seat was along his arm. He then took this eyeball measurement and sized up a thick limb from a tree out at the Northern Philadelphia Airport, his dumpsite. The limb he chose was almost two inches in diameter, and he had needed a hacksaw blade—one he usually kept under the podium but had never used previously—to sever it from the tree.

The limb had been the real reason he had gone back to the woods. He needed it, or something of its stature and strength, to depress the accelerator of the car so that it would have motion without him being in it. Whatever he chose to do the job, it had to have been able to be adjusted in length on the fly, as he couldn't predict what size he would need since it wasn't his car to start with and there was no way to prepare ahead of time.

So he decided to go with natural wood, the limb of a tree. And as soon as he arrived at the woods, he spied the exact limb he would take. He recognized it immediately because it had a yellow ribbon tied around it.

Dedaker, once again cheery as well as amused at his own dry humor, carried the limb around the side of the car. He got in and began his final mental checklist.

He had left the car on when he went to the trunk, so it was still running.

In case the car sustained a major amount of damage, he checked that all of the car's doors were unlocked, wanting to make sure that they could gain entrance from any of the four doors in case one of them should become blocked in the accident. It was a redundant precaution, but he had already used up his mulligan for the night with the trunk light.

Finally, he took one more look over the seat at the dead woman in the rear. The note he had written was still attached to her chest. It looked as if it were secure enough and would not fall off during the accident. Standing on the podium beneath the access hole, he had wrenched a long old nail free from one of the support beams between the two duplexes using the claw of a hammer. He then took the note (which he had written on the back of a piece of wallpaper torn right from the wall next to where he pulled the nail, the glue old and dried and easy to rip off) with a black felt-tip marker. Once the note had been written, Dedaker pushed the nail through the center of it and then used the hammer to drive the nail into the pulpy meat of the woman's breast. It went in so easy that there was a moment when he feared the woman had a silicon implant and he had burst it. She didn't; her breasts were real, and the note was as tightly adhered as he could get it, considering. He had used all of the prudence he could have, having written it on thick paper and placing it as securely as he could. There would be nothing he could do if it did fall off; he just has to cross his fingers and hope for the best.

Everything was ready.

Shifting so that he was half in and half out of the car, he laid the limb with its yellow ribbon still attached on the floorboard next to the gas pedal. Using his right foot, he held the brake while he moved the column gearshift from park to drive. Still keeping his foot firmly on the brake, he depressed the accelerator as far down as it would go with the limb. With the car's engine revving loudly, and the orange flashers still blinking, he wedged the limb beneath the edge of the seat to hold it in position.

All in one motion, Michael Dedaker released the brake pedal and jumped out of the car. He hit the concrete pavement rolling and watched as the car streaked its way across the street, carrying its horrendous cargo. There was no traffic on Race Street this early in the morning, and the car traveled unimpeded toward its destination.

Dedaker sat on his rump where he had landed. When he had parked the car, he had aimed its nose perfectly along the trajectory. With his arms wrapped around his knees, the chilled pavement quickly sucked the warmth from his body as he watched the car go up the first tier and then the second, until it struck the building dead on. He guessed it had been going somewhere around sixty miles an hour when it hit. There was a massive bang—intermingled with the more high-pitched sounds of shattering glass and crumpling metal—as the dead woman's car struck one of the main-entrance revolving doors of the Roundhouse.

With a bitter resentment at being unable to hang around and watch the repercussions of the madness he had just unleashed, Dedaker fled into the night.

22

Clattering.

Through the semidaze of the complete darkness, Hoover could hear it.

Clattering.

Again the noise came. This time, he was slightly more awake—although he still had his eyes closed, his ears were wide open and listening.

Clattering.

He knew this noise. What was—?

At recognition, a surge of adrenaline ran through his veins, bringing him to the surface. He groaned and reached for the nightstand just as the noise started again.

Clatt—

Hoover pushed the button on the side of the small flip phone and stopped his cell from vibrating against the glossy top of the nightstand. After the incident with Agbalaya yesterday, he had shut the phone off, doing so to avoid the frantic calls from his wife. He hadn't been worried about the department looking for him because he had been with Beverly, and if a problem arose, they would've called her too. After he left Beverly's apartment (and knowing that his wife would've been asleep so late at night), he turned it back on, in case there was an emergency in the middle of the night. He had set it to the vibrate mode, as was his habit at night, so as not to wake anyone else up if it went off.

Not wanting to awaken anyone else reminded him. He looked to his left and groaned again.

Pushing down the covers, he swung his legs off his side of Fiona's bed. He pushed the button that activated the incandescent light on the cell phone and squinted. He still couldn't read the number, the light too weak, the room too dark. Fiona liked to sleep in absolute darkness. For this purpose, she kept her blinds closed at all times and had draped two thick comforters over both the windows.

Groping through the darkness, he made his way toward the bathroom from memory. Halfway there, he stubbed the pinky toe of his right foot, muttered a curse, and limped the rest of the way. He shut the door before flicking the switch, the bright illumination knifing into his pupils. When he could see, he closed the lid and sat down on the toilet to check the injured toe. It was sore, the nail having the bluish black telltale sign of a laceration forming underneath. He would probably lose the nail, but he didn't think the toe broken.

There were *two* phone numbers listed on the phone's LCD.

The first one was for the desk officer at homicide, the second for Beverly's apartment. The whole time Hoover had known her, she had lived at the same address. He had called her number a thousand times, whether work related or not, over the course of their history, but he had never gotten a call from her this late at night. *Why is she calling me at this hour? What hour is it?* Hoover looked at his wrist at the exact moment he remembered taking his watch off before lying down—the watch was still on the nightstand where the phone had been.

He had to call in immediately. Without checking the phone's internal clock for the time, he hit the TALK button to automatically dial homicide.

It was answered on the second ring. "Homicide," said a voice with an upbeat lit.

"Hey, Garret, it's Hoover." Garret was on Three Squad, and must've drawn desk duty off the wheel tonight. "You guys calling me?"

Six city-miles away, the cop on the other end chuckled. "Yeah, man. You better get your ass down here."

"Why, what's wrong?"

"Hard to explain, has to be seen to believe."

"Is it my guy?" Each department on the force is a clique in and of itself. When a high-profile case like the one found in the woods came in, every other member of the department was made aware of it at roll call, even if he or she was not directly involved. Police work was done as a team, not as an individual.

"Oh yeah," Garret confirmed.

"Has there been another one?"

"Oh yeah," Garret repeated.

"Where?"

"Here."

"*There?* What do you mean there?"

"Get here as quick as you can, Hoover." The phone went dead in his hand. He looked at the display again, and again noticed Beverly's number on the display. This time, he understood why she had called. And the miniscule seven digits made him fully comprehend the situation he was in, the situation he had created for himself. Beverly had called him because Garret would've notified her about the homicide first. She was the lead detective listed on the case, and naturally, the desk would've called her first. She had then called him to let him know that there had been another murder. He was second in line. Fuck, that made him bitter.

Back in the bedroom, he turned on the light.

Fiona sat up groggily, her black hair corkscrewed. She wore pink-flowered pajama pants and a T-shirt with paint stains and the West Chester University insignia on it. It was his shirt that he had left here sometime in the past, the paint stains from when he and Lauren had redone their living room.

Fiona rubbed her eyes. In a voice nasally from her stuffy nose, she asked, "John, what's wrong?"

"Nothing, I have to go to work. There's been another murder."

Hoover had come to Fiona's apartment tonight to tell her it was over. But he hadn't gotten a chance.

When he arrived, he found every light in the apartment off. That was unlike Fiona. She was a night person, always was, always would be, hence the comforters draped over the windows to block out the sun during her natural sleeping hours—daytime. A big reason for the nocturnal life she led was her job. But then, she had been drawn to the profession because of the late hours it required. Fiona was a manager for an office cleaning company. Her day didn't start until the nine-to-fivers went home for the night.

For a living, Fiona managed thirty-two employees for a company called Corporate Cleaning Corporation. The company—more commonly referred to as C-Cubed—had contracts with a good many office buildings in the heart of the city, as well as in many other metropolises across the country. From four to twelve-thirty, Fiona oversaw five separate clusters of C-Cubed employees as they cleaned the offices, bathrooms, and lobbies of the twelve buildings under her purview.

When Hoover arrived here late last night, she should've been just getting home from work. One of her favorite sayings was "1 a.m. is like five o'clock for me—it's dinnertime." When he strolled in late at night, he usually found her eating a big meal before sitting down to watch a two o'clock movie and knocking off around dawn.

But not tonight. Tonight, he found her huddled tightly in her covers, sound asleep. He looked at her and knew right away that she was sick. He could hear the rattling of her respiration, could see the growing pile of used tissues beside the bed, and could feel the death-room closeness of her apartment.

Not one to kick a person while she was down, Hoover undressed and climbed into bed with her, where she was lying in a fetal position, shivering beneath three blankets. Hoover snuggled up against her and fell asleep from the exhaustion of the day's events, as well as the night's. Two hours later, he awoke to the clattering of the cell phone. Now wide awake, he sat in a rocking chair positioned on the side of the bed he normally slept on. Fiona watched him through red, leaky eyes.

"Will you be back?" she asked.

He was going to be back all right, but she might not like him as much then as she did now. "I don't know when I'll be able to make it back, but it definitely won't be tonight. This is going to take a while. The crime scene investigation has to be very thorough, which makes it lengthy. Then there's the follow-ups with the victim's family, and finally a ton of paperwork."

"Do you know how sexy I think you are right now?"

He didn't feel very sexy.

"It turns me on to hear you talk shop." Her voice had a scratchy, deep timbre from her cold that he found appealing. That was not the way he wanted his mind to turn, so he shut it off and steered the conversation to another topic.

"How do you feel?"

"I feel like I'm getting better I can hold my head up at least. Woke up yesterday and couldn't breathe. I called out sick, drank half a bottle of Robitussin, then crawled back into bed and have been sleeping ever since. I think I'll be fine by later today though."

"The twenty-four hour flu, huh?"

"Yeah." She pulled a tissue from the box and blew. Dropping the crumpled wad on the floor, she asked, "What's wrong, Hoover?"

"What do you mean?"

"I can hear something in your voice. You sound different. Is something wrong?"

You're no better than he is.

There's a lot wrong with me, and I don't know where—or how—to start telling you about it. "Nothing's wrong. I'm tired, that's all. Ran into a little trouble at work yesterday morning, and with this case, I'm burning the candle at both ends. I'll be fine."

She looked him in the eye and he could tell that she knew. But this wasn't the time to do it. It would be unfair to tell her as he ran out the door. He lowered his eyes and concentrated on tying his shoes.

"You want to talk about it?" she asked, and he knew what she meant.

"I think we need to, but not tonight. We'll talk about it the next time I come over. Tomorrow night, maybe."

"Okay."

He stood up and grabbed his watch off the nightstand.

She lay back down and pulled the covers up to her head. "Turn the light off when you leave."

He did, leaving her in the quiet darkness.

*   *   *

Race Street at Tenth expanded from three lanes to five to accommodate for the on-ramp to the Ben Franklin Bridge. Directly across from the Roundhouse was a stretch of actual green grass

within the city called Franklin Square. Hoover drove the Crown
Vic with municipal tags over the curb and parked it on the expanse
of grass. He had to; there was no other parking available—every
inch of the street was occupied, along with the PHQ's lot. Lining
the street were patrol cars with red and blue roof lights flashing,
news vans with their spotlights shining, and tow trucks with their
yellow caution lights spinning. The red lights on top of the fire
truck were the closest to the front of the building.

Hoover got out of his car, and the news media swarmed down
on him. This time he didn't just ignore their questions, he didn't
even hear them. Not looking at the vultures (and not caring if
Agbalaya was among them), he said, "No fucking comment," as
he ran across the street to the Roundhouse. There he got his first
view of Dedaker's handiwork.

Hoover was astounded.

When the Roundhouse was built in the early sixties, it had
been constructed with a two-tiered patio that led up to two large
revolving doors, which were the official entrances to the building,
but were always kept locked. Currently, a car was wedged into
one of the revolving doors, half in and half out of the building and
surrounded by broken glass and twisted metal. The car itself was
an older four-door Chevy from the look of it, but Hoover couldn't
tell what model it was; in fact, he wasn't even sure what color it
was. Sometime after the car struck the building, it had caught fire.
Either the car had been black, or it had burned so long that the
flames had consumed every inch of paint.

Hoover trotted through a puddle, noticing that the entire area
was wet from fire hose discharge. He glanced over at the truck,
witnessing two firemen replacing the flaccid ivory hose they had
used. Hoover scanned the rest of the crowd gathered around the
accident, looking for Beverly but not seeing her. It gave him a
cursory spark of pleasure at having arrived before she did. Finally,
he noticed Korzenowski, standing about ten feet from the wreck,
talking to Meltzer.

"Captain, what happened?" Hoover asked, winded.

"Hoover, what we've got here is one antagonistic motherfucker.
This," he pointed at the wreck, and Hoover could see that the
color of the Chevy had indeed been black, "is a homicide. Can you
believe that?"

"What'd he do, hit somebody with the car?"

"No, the body's in the back seat, cut up like the rest, same patterns. What he did here was deliver her to us. Can't believe he didn't hit the fucking statue." In the middle of the upper tier, there was a twelve-foot-high statue of an officer holding a child.

He's taunting us, just like I told Beverly after we left the Dasher girl's house. Jesus, was that only two days ago?

"There an ID in her?" Hoover asked.

"Don't know; the ME hasn't had his way with her yet. He didn't feel like having his marshmallows toasted, so he waited for the fire guys to douse the flames," Korzenowski said, pointing out an average-sized man wearing an overcoat and a dress shirt, sans tie. He was using both hands to hold the large satchel containing the tools of his trade and waited patiently at the edge of the crowd for his turn. "What I do know," Korzenowski said, "is that he sent us a deadgram this time."

"What's a deadgram?"

"A deadgram is a note nailed to a corpse's tit."

"Un-fucking-believable, this guy," Meltzer said. Hoover wasn't that surprised to hear of this development—he knew their boy would be in contact eventually. People who did this sort of thing had agendas they wanted you to know about.

"Where's it at?"

"Still in the car. Nobody's been able to get inside because of the fire, but you can see the note through the rear window."

"What does it say?"

"Go read it."

Hoover approached the car on the driver's side. Cupping his hands to block out the flashing lights, he looked into the car without leaning against it—first the front, then the back, feeling the heat still radiating from the metal.

In the front, the only thing of interest was a tree limb wedged between the gas pedal and the driver's seat, a scrap of yellow caution tape tied around it.

Hoover looked at the backseat.

There she was, just like Korzenowski said, dead and naked. Somehow, being naked made her seem even deader. There were six cuts that Hoover could see on the front of her body—one across each breast, two on the belly under the ribs, one on each thigh—as well as the killing stroke drawn across her neck. He knew from the other bodies (or more accurately, the coroner's protocol) that there would be six more cuts on her back. Her eyes were closed. She had medium-length honey-colored hair. Her skin—other than the cuts that had been made during the assault—looked flawless. She was thin but still had an hourglass shape. She had been young and, in life, would've been very pretty.

The note was nailed to her left breast.

From his vantage point, Hoover couldn't read what was written on the coarse paper. The impact against the building must have caused the note to shift, and it was now reversed. Hoover walked around to the other side of the car and, again without touching the window, read the note.

It said, "III. Holy the Sabbath. Purser."

What the hell does that mean?

"Thank you for not touching the glass." Hoover turned and saw the coroner standing behind him. He was not a tall man, and his hair was mussed up, which gave him a disheveled look. "Would you believe I saw four cops touch that window within the last twenty minutes?" the man said in a nasal voice.

Cops were notorious for contaminating crime scenes before the ME and the CSU got a chance to investigate. Valuable information was lost by simply doing things that would ordinarily go unnoticed such as walking, smoking, opening doors, using a faucet. "Yes, I would," said Hoover. He sidestepped so that the man could get on with his job, and he went back over to Korzenowski.

"Hey, Captain, who's that ME?"

Korzenowski looked at the man again, a little harder this time. "Never saw him before." Whaat had now joined Meltzer beside the captain.

"There's a piece of caution tape tied to the branch he used to floor the accelerator, did you see it?" Hoover asked.

"Hadn't noticed. Why?"

"Wondering why he tied it there."

"I don't know. We'll have the lab take a look at it. What do you make of the note?"

"It says, 'Holy the Sabbath. Purser,' preceded by the roman numeral three. If there's a religious angle, I'm not the guy to ask.

But what I can tell you is that 'Holy the Sabbath' refers to the Ten Commandments."

"You sure?" Korzenowski asked. At this point, the heat from the Commissioner's Office was so hot he couldn't risk guesses.

Hoover shrugged.

"He's right," said Meltzer. "In Exodus 20, God gave Moses the commandments up on Mount Sinai. 'Remember to keep holy the Sabbath' was the third."

The other three cops—his peers—where looking at him dumbfounded. Emil Meltzer shrugged, "Twelve years of Bible school, my mom was a stickler for it. Every friggin' Monday night at seven that short yellow bus would pull up in front of our house, and I had to get on it."

"Well, that explains the roman numeral three—it stands for the third commandment," said Whaat for those in the cheap seats who couldn't put that together for themselves. "Why do you think he wants with the third commandment?"

"He's a religious nut," said Korzenowski. "I hate that shit. Sometimes my wife will go off on a tangent about it until I feel like going upside her head."

"'Sabbath' stands for Saturday," said Meltzer. "Today's Saturday. He thinks he's a funny guy, that's all. Probably killed the woman after midnight tonight, and he's rubbing our noses in it. He's fucking with us, sticking his tongue out at us."

"That's a possibility, Emil, but we can't be sure of anything without the rest of the information from that car," Hoover said. "For all we know, the reference to Moses could mean the corpse was a Jewish Rabbi."

"Rabbis can only be men," Meltzer corrected him.

"Whatever. What I'm getting at is we don't have any information about *her* yet. It's too soon to try to grasp the meaning of a scrap of sentence without knowing all the details. Haven't you ever done a crossword puzzle? Every scrap of sentence is a tiny puzzle in itself. Nothing is ever as it seems, and your first knee-jerk guess usually ends up wrong."

"If she's a religious woman, what's the connection going to be with the sexual side jobs the others were involved in?" Whaat asked Hoover. Everyone knew he'd been yanked as the lead, but they still deferred to him anyway. Some men were born leaders, people others were magnetically attracted to for answers.

"That's the point I was trying to make. We don't know yet. If she had a dark side, we'll find it. If she didn't, we won't," was Hoover's only answer.

"Maybe he's changing his pattern," Meltzer offered as another angle.

"I don't think so. It's too late in the game, and he hasn't made his statement yet," replied Hoover, still acting like their leader.

Meltzer indicated the car parked halfway in the lobby of the Roundhouse. "He's never delivered us one before."

"That was before we found his hiding spot," Whaat said.

"True. So you think every time he offs one, he's going to drive it through the front door?"

"No," Hoover broke in. "He tipped us to the drop zone by breaking the lights. He wanted us to find the bodies. And he drove that car through the door for a reason too. My bet is it has to do with the note. It's the only variant from the previous murders that I can see so far."

"You don't suppose that 'Purser' could be this clown's name, do you?" Korzenowski asked rhetorically.

"Could be. It's a handwritten note, and 'Purser' *is* where the signature would traditionally be," Hoover agreed.

"Guys like this love to leave their signatures. That's why they always use the same patterns—it's another signature. I wouldn't be surprised if Purser was his name," Whaat said, putting both of his cents in, one at a time.

Hoover had his hands stuffed into his pockets, staring at the car. The coroner was now inside the vehicle with the body. "What is a 'purser'? Isn't it someone that has something to do with money? Like a school treasurer or something?"

"No. That's a 'bursar,'" Whaat corrected.

"*What?*" yelled Meltzer.

"Come on, man. Don't fuck around with my name. That shit ain't funny anymore."

"I'm not fucking around. Did you say 'bursar'?"

"Yeah, 'bursar.' Why?"

"Because in Latin, 'bursa' is a case made out of cloth used to carry around the linens for celebrating the Eucharist—you know,

Communion. In fact, now that I think about it, Communion is also the *third* sacrament in the Christian religion," Meltzer, all of a sudden an impressive wealth of information, told them. Again they all stared at him. Even Hoover turned around in wonder. "Don't ask. I know I'm a Jew; just trust me. I know what I'm talking about."

"What are you getting at? What would a dead woman have to do with Communion?" Korzenowski asked.

"That's simple. The Eucharist is the representation of the body of Christ, which they originally ate at the Last Supper. The apostles were supposed to be physically eating his human body, which he knew he would soon be shedding in death. Our boy's note was attached to a *body*. *Nailed* to a body, I might add, which could be some crucifixion symbolism. That sounds significant to me."

"You think he's going cannibal?" Whaat asked.

"No, I think it has something to do with Christ. Third commandment, third sacrament, Christ is one of three in the Holy Trinity. It's all too neatly wrapped together to be a coincidence."

"Sunday *is* Easter. Could be that's why he tipped us to the bodies now instead of before," Whaat said. "He's some kind of Jesus freak."

"The two-week period immediately preceding Easter is sometimes referred to as Passiontide. It was the period in which Christ went through his trials and tribulations before they killed him," Meltzer informed them. "Maybe our boy considers the murders to be his passion, his trials."

"Wait, wait, wait. Stop it. You guys are snowballing a piece of ice," Hoover voiced over the din of the crime scene. "You're heading down the wrong path. The note doesn't say 'bursar'; it says 'purser.' And as far as we know, that doesn't have anything to do with Jesus or any other religion."

"The two words are only one letter apart, a letter that almost looks the same. What if he made a mistake when he wrote it?" Meltzer theorized.

"Why would anybody go through all this trouble to deliver a message and then spell it wrong? The answer is that he didn't spell 'bursar' wrong; he spelled 'purser' right. It doesn't matter if the words are only one letter apart; it's not a mistake."

"Actually, there are two letters separating 'purser' from 'bursar.' 'Purser' has an *e* and 'bursar' has an *a*," said a woman's voice from behind Hoover. He knew without looking that Beverly had arrived. "Hi, guys. Hi, John."

She stepped into the center of the group of detectives, forcing them to form a ring around her. "A bursar is a treasurer in a school or an institution. A purser is an officer that runs the treasury onboard a ship. The year after my dad died, I went on a cruise with my mom. Any monetary transactions onboard the ship had to be done in the purser's office. Now tell me why we're arguing semantics this early in the morning while there is a car parked illegally in the lobby of a city building?"

As they informed her of the story as far as they knew it, Hoover stared at her.

She wore black slacks with a matching pair of flats, her shirt a violet-colored button-down, the sleeves rolled to her elbows. Her hair was in a twist and pinned at the top of her head with something that resembled a crocheting needle in a hue that matched her shirt. Very faintly, at the base of her neck, Hoover could see a red mark. He had left that mark on her.

All in all, she looked very put together, while Hoover felt like a crinkled shirt that had spent a whole day at the bottom of the hamper before being pulled out and put back on without being washed.

"Okay, all we're sure of is that we don't know what the word 'purser' signifies," she started. "The commandment stuff is good, Meltzer, but the 'bursa' bit is a little convoluted for me. We'll work on it and try to figure out what the final word of the note means when we have more information about the young lady in the car. For now, spread out and work the crowd, see if there were any witnesses. Whaat, have a couple of blues shut down Race Street before the morning rush hour hits."

They were all beginning to stir at her directions, including Captain Korzenowski.

"Anybody know who that medical examiner is?" she asked.
Nobody knew.

23

*H*er name had been Michelle Laplin.

And she had lived at 1278 Purser Street, according to the Pennsylvania state driver's license found inside her, giving definite clarification to at least one part of the note. None of the detectives on the investigative team had ever heard of Purser Street, so Sako pulled a tattered copy of McNally's Road Atlas—the word "Homicide" written in permanent marker across the front—from a desk drawer and perused it. Purser Street was north and east of the city.

"What's the jurisdiction?" Beverly asked Sako. "Is it in the city?"

"Yeah, it's in bounds. Zip code 19154."

"So it's close to the airport, where his original dumpsite was found?"

"Ten miles, maybe twelve."

"Think it's a coinkydink?" Holmes asked. He had arrived about ten minutes after they had started to canvass the sparse crowd. No one had seen anything.

"What's a 'coinkydink,' Holmes?" Beverly asked with a smile.

"That's how my three-year-old pronounces 'coincidence.'"

"Both places are a little too close for me to think it's just coincidence. We'll have to see if there's any connection."

Leaving Meltzer and Sako with the paperwork, Whaat and Holmes were sent back to the airport to see if there were any possible connections to Purser Street, while Beverly and Hoover went out to Purser Street itself to inform the parents of their daughter's untimely death.

What they found when they got to 1278 was unexpected, to say the least.

*   *   *

The address on Michelle Laplin's driver's license was indeed her
residence, but she did not live with her parents; she lived with
three other women, all of whom were approximately the same
age as Michelle, twenty years old. In itself, it wasn't unheard of for
several people just starting out in the world to share the expensive
costs of living. What was unusual about 1278 Purser was that it
was wired with digital cameras in every room of the house—
including both bathrooms.

Laplin's residence was a community house that had been
hardwired for visual display over the Internet. The rules of a
community house were that if you were picked to move in, you
could live there free of expenses. Everything was paid for by the
company that hired the resident (read: actress) as long as said
person signed an agreement to live completely on display, twenty-
four hours a day. Along with the bathrooms, there were cameras
in the bedrooms, hallways, living room, kitchen, and basement. A
community house resident had no privacy; she was a voyeuristic
matinee idol for the horny and curious. If one of the four females
that lived in the house were to pick her nose, shave her legs, change
her tampon, or orally pleasure someone, the whole world could
watch. For $19.95 a month. Free enterprise was a remarkable
privilege.

Beverly and Hoover had just found Michelle Laplin's dark side.

Tragically ironic, Michelle's community display house was
owned and operated by the Grapple Company—the same company
that ran the phone sex operation Judith Kasay had worked for.
The same company that they were unable to reach yesterday
evening. The same company that, unless someone could unearth
the owner, would take another forty-eight hours before they were
able to make contact with at 9 a.m. on Monday.

On Saturday afternoon, Hoover and Beverly spent three hours
going over the house that Michelle lived in and questioning the
other three residents. What it all amounted to was that no one
knew anything about the disappearance of Ms. Laplin. She was
last seen at around seven the night before, as she left the residence
to go to her boyfriend's more private house. It was widely known

across the country to anyone with a subscription to BarbeesDollHouse.com (for that was the name of the website) that Michelle's boyfriend worked in New York during the week, and that they only saw each other when he came home on the weekends. Michelle left the community house to meet him every Friday evening like clockwork, and was usually gone until Sunday morning. No one in the house knew that she was missing, until the cops turned up on the doorstep. What her boyfriend thought about her not showing up at his residence was uncertain at this point because the detectives hadn't heard back from Meltzer and Sako who were taken off the paperwork when Beverly called and dispatched to his residence across town.

Other than an illegal stash of Valium, Michelle Laplin's case was a shallow one—it wouldn't provide many new leads to investigate. Originally hailing from Oregon, where her parents still lived, she had been at the house for eleven months, but the other three residents said that she hadn't made any friends in the vicinity, just them and her boyfriend.

The boyfriend was a thread that needed to be tied off, but Hoover thought it would prove to be yet another dead end. The guy that they were after hadn't known Michelle Laplin personally but knew her as a member of BarbeesDollHouse. After speaking with the other three residents—Amber, Natalie, and Gwen, respectively—and determining that they had all remained in the house last night, the detectives suspected that Michelle was probably chosen among them simply because she was the most accessible. The killer knew her Friday night routine and used the information to pick her off That's it; nothing astounding. Because every facet of Michelle Laplin's life had been on display, the man who took her life knew when she would leave the safety of the house and get into the car he later drove through the glass entrance of the Roundhouse.

After gathering all the information they could, Beverly and Hoover went back to the office to wait and see what the other two teams would bring back from the airport and Michelle's boyfriend's house.

24

*N*ightfall found Hoover sitting in his own house.

He sat on the couch, the television on in front of him, but not watching it. In his mind, he was still standing in front of the chalkboard that had all of the information he and his . . . no, Beverly's . . . team had gathered. It was a wealth of information and, at the same time, none. There were dates, times, pictures, places. Collectively, it told a story, but the story it told was in the past tense—all of the events had already happened before they were related to the cops. Going over it and over it, there was not one thing he could project into the future, not one fact he could look deeper into and pre-guess what the killer's next move was going to be. This Dandelion was a sly one—he knew exactly how much information the cops were going to be able to gather and what they would be able to do with it.

How did he know so much?

Because he's a cop.

No. It was a possibility, but it was grasping at straws at this point. The city of Philadelphia employed almost six thousand police officers—any one of which could be a suspect, if Hoover were to pursue that path—and that number didn't include any of the civilian employees who worked hand in hand with the men in blue, such as the 911 dispatchers stationed two floors above the homicide department in the Roundhouse, any of whom could work an agenda from the inside out if so desired. More straws to grasp.

Hoover's mind was fried.

Since he had caught the squeal—around eight on Thursday morning—he had only been able to snatch two hours of sleep a night. He had amassed a combined total of four hours of sleep in the past sixty. He was so tired; he was almost delirious.

He wanted a drink, but didn't think that would be such a good idea, based on the frosty reception he had received when he finally came home this evening. He and Lauren hadn't talked about it yet, but he knew it was coming. Tonight. Although it wasn't a school night, she had put the girls to bed early. That could only mean one thing—there was going to be an argument. And it was probably going to get loud.

The thing about it was she had a right to be angry.

You're no better than he is.

His career was in shambles, and although she didn't know it, his adherence to his wedding vows was laughable.

That drink sure sounds good.

When he and Beverly had gotten back to the station, Korzenowski had called him into his office. It had been the middle of the afternoon when they arrived. The late Michelle Laplin's car had been removed, and the city maintenance workers had boarded up the smashed entrance. Race Street was open for traffic, but caution tape still cordoned off the sidewalk and half the patio that led to the doors. The news media types still swarmed like the carrion birds they were.

To make matters that much worse, it had gotten awkward with Beverly. If it wasn't about the case, they didn't talk about it. Even then, their questions between each other were limited to "yes, no, maybe." They did not talk about last night—that was the past; this was the present. What they had done last night had closed the door. But had it locked it? What happened over the next couple of days would determine how tightly the door had been secured. Hoover intended to deadbolt it.

Bourbon over ice; that smooth, soothing amber liquid swirling in the glass, that's what I need.

In Korzenowski office, the captain handed him a copy of a legal document. It was a restraining order against him issued by a judge Friday afternoon, stating that he must remain at least a hundred feet away from one Nicos Agbalaya.

"Word came down from on high that you're to be strapped to a desk, pending the outcome of the investigation into police brutality," Korzenowski said in the voice of someone reading from a cue card. It was a rehearsed statement; Korzenowski was beginning to separate himself from Hoover. After all, who wanted to go down with a sinking ship? That type of valiance was scripted Hollywood bullshit.

"If I'm chained to a desk, who's going to take my place?"

"DiSilva. Late yesterday afternoon, the case against the punk in the pawnshop was decided."

"That quick?"

"Jury came back in forty minutes."

"How'd we do?"

"We lost; he walked. Jury hung itself, couldn't be proved beyond a reasonable doubt with the phantom suspect involved. It was all over the papers before they did a reprint to include the mess out front. Once that hit the headlines, the Sullivan case dropped below the crease."

Hoover could only nod his head.

Tennessee sipping whisky, goes down like acid and lands like a rock.

He went back to the bullpen, as the area with the desks where the detectives worked was known, and stood staring at the chalkboard. With the same abandon that Korzenowski had shown, none of the other detectives talked to him. They walked around him as if he weren't there, standing in the middle of the room, staring at a wall of papers concerning all ten of the murders. They walked around him, making sure not to touch him, afraid of catching the disease he had, as he looked for answers that wouldn't come—pushing and hoping to make a connection they had all missed previously. He knew that come tomorrow, he wouldn't have another chance at his Dandelion. In his new capacity, he would answer phones and file paperwork from a desk. The death knell for his career had begun.

He wanted—needed—so badly to make that connection right then.

But nothing came. The board had held only bare facts, no insights. He went over it again and again and again, beginning with the airport woods and ending with the note III. Holy the Sabbath. Purser. The note that had only been another bare fact that posed questions ad infinitum. Was it a gibe meant to mock and jeer them, or the final piece of the puzzle? Only time would tell.

Although it had been a busy day for the Dandelion case, there was little to gain from it.

Michelle Laplin's car yielded friction ridges—fingerprints— inside, on the steering wheel, as well as on the piece of tree branch. The prints were ran and the results negative. The yellow caution tape tied around the branch also produced prints, which were traced as belonging to Joseph Boland, the responding officer to the initial call made after Art Fleuridor's discovery at the airport. It was the police department's own crime scene caution tape—the Dandelion had been back to the location. Yet again, Sako and Meltzer made the trip to the NPHIA, this time to search through the woods. They found nothing.

Michelle's boyfriend's name was Frank Bell. He was visited by Whaat and Holmes on Saturday afternoon at his place in Philly. While he did confess to being the one who supplied Michelle with the nonprescribed Valium (purchased from an unnamed source in Manhattan for three dollars per ten milligrams), his alibi remained sound. He had left word for Michelle on her cell phone's answering service (Sprint's records logged the incoming call at 1905 hours, Friday evening), stating he wouldn't be able to meet her for their normal rendezvous. His mother had been admitted to Frankford Hospital with appendicitis, and he spent the whole night there with his father and three brothers. The appendix was removed, and his mother was doing fine. More players for the stage with no denouement in sight.

When Hoover finally looked away from the board, Two Squad was already on duty. His shift had finished and everybody had gone home. No one had bothered to nudge him out of his fugue. No matter, his squad's regular days off this coming week were Monday and Tuesday. After the RDOs, the rest of One Squad would rotate to the four-to-twelve shift, and Hoover would rotate with them, leaving behind the three teams investigating the find in the woods. How quickly friends could become associates.

A drunken stupor, followed by a complete lack of thought and sense in the blackness of sleep, was what he needed. But he couldn't go there yet because his day was not over. It wouldn't be over until he heard the lecture that awaited him. And it was sure to be a lengthy one.

"John," his wife called into the gloom that was broken only by the flashing blue-and-white glow of the television screen.

He got up and walked into the kitchen where she waited.

* * *

Two yellow Easter baskets, filled with candy and plastic grass, sat on the table. One was Jane's and one was Pam's. They were identical in content, down to the exact amount of jellybeans, to avoid arguments. The Hoovers weren't religious, but Easter—like Christmas—had gotten away from the original intent and gone commercial. Lauren had assembled the baskets of candy; she was a good mother. If Whaat hadn't mentioned early this morning that tomorrow was Easter Sunday, it would've passed Hoover by without even a thought.

"John, I love you," was how she started. There was a pause, and then, "What happened?"

Oh, where to begin?

He had been wrong. She wasn't yelling; she was concerned. He decided that he would tell her everything about the recent events . . . with the exception of what happened at Beverly's last night. He began with the capture of the punk in the pawnshop and had talked for a full half hour when he got to the note and the house on Purser Street.

"Such horrible things. How do you live with it all in your mind?" Lauren asked when he was done.

"It seems like I won't have to anymore. They're going to drop the hammer on me."

"What will we do then?"

"I'm not sure yet. I haven't thought that far into the future. The good thing is I'm still young enough to start over. Still young enough to begin building Social Security, because they're probably going to strip me of the pension, except maybe for what I added myself." In the Philadelphia Police Department, cops pay into a city pension plan for their retirement; they do not contribute to the government Social Security fund. In order for an ex-cop to collect

Social Security upon reaching the age requirement, he has to have put in enough quarters to be eligible. The eligibility level for an ex-police officer is the same as it is for any civilian—forty quarters, or the equivalent of ten year's work.

"What kind of job will you get? You never finished college."

"I know. As I said, I haven't thought about it yet." *Honey, I'm sorry that you and your daughter's futures are in jeopardy because of my stupid actions, but I can't think about that at the moment. Right now, I can't get this case out of my head.*

Ten dead. How many more to come?

You're no better than he is.

"I'm going to stick it out as long as I can on the force. After that, I'll get another job. I promise that we'll never do without."

"Okay, John. I trust you."

"Thank you."

"Maybe they won't fire you. Maybe you'll get suspended or demoted or something," she said hopefully.

Hoover shook his head. "I think I've worn out my welcome with the commissioner."

"I'm sorry, John," she conceded. "I feel so . . . I don't know . . . ungrateful or something, worrying about your job, while those women are being killed so brutally."

"I know what you mean. I can't seem to shake it, either."

"Is there anything you can do?"

"I'm afraid not. It looks like I'm out of the loop for good. I'm going to be chained to a desk, probably working the wheel, until the ax falls."

"What about tomorrow? What's he going to do tomorrow?"

"Who?"

"The killer."

Tomorrow? What's she talking about?

"What do you mean? What about tomorrow?" he asked.

"The note. Tomorrow's Sunday, the day Christians celebrate the Sabbath."

The cogs in Hoover's mind spun at warp speed.

The note: III. Holy the Sabbath. Purser.

Why a note this time? Because he's telling us something. What's he telling us? Break it down—who, what, when, where, why, how.

Where? *Easy enough. The note said Purser Street, the location where the dead woman was from.*

What? *Also a no-brainer, murder and desecration, the only things this bastard was good for.*

How? *His MO has always been the same. He bleeds them dry then rapes them and leaves them to be found by us—nothing new there.*

Why? *Why not? It's what people like him do. People with hatred, people missing something, people who don't function in society— dandelions in the grass. Still nothing.*

When? *The Sabbath. Did he mean the traditional Jewish Sabbath on Saturday, today? Or did he mean the reestablished Christian Sabbath, Sunday, tomorrow? Who knows?*

Who? *The dead woman, Michelle Laplin? Apparently. That could go either way—maybe so, maybe no.*

Hoover was still drawing a blank. And yet, at the back of his mind, he felt a tickle. It felt like a fly buzzing around the base of his skull. If so, then he was the spider spinning the web to entrap it. And if he didn't catch this particular fly, it would cost him his life—his life as a cop. If he could stop this madness, then there might be a glimmer on the horizon of his future. The sun might not sink on his career yet, if he could put this devil behind bars.

If, if, if.

Think, Hoover, think.

There *was* something to that note, and he could almost see it. Almost.

Break down the note from a new perspective—word for word.

Purser. *The location. Obvious.*

The Sabbath. *The date, for sure. Whether it was today or tomorrow was the question.*

Holy. *Why is it holy? Obviously, the Sabbath is considered holy by any religion that acknowledges the creation story and is considered the day God rested. Wait a minute, God rested—that's what's holy about it!*

The Sabbath was when God kicked back and had himself a beer. God rested on the Sabbath because his work was done. The killer will rest on the Sabbath because his work will be done.

That's what the significance of tomorrow is: his work will be done.

But that was tomorrow, this was today. He had worked today. He had murdered Michelle Laplin and delivered her to the cops. *And now he was done? Just like that? Convenient how the third commandment lent itself to his bent vision, wasn't it? He had . . .*

Hold it a second! The third commandment? The number at the beginning of the note wasn't the numeral 3. It was a roman numeral. Or more specifically, it was three separate capital letter Is.

What is an I? It's the singular letter of the alphabet that represents a person. I equals me equals you equals her.

The three capital letter Is represents three people.

There are still three people living in the house on Purser Street. Three women—Amber, Natalie, and Gwen.

He is going to kill them and then *his work will be done.*

He's going to kill them tonight.

And then he's going to rest on the Sabbath, tomorrow.

III, period. Holy the Sabbath, period. Purser, period. Who, what, when, where, and how—all the answers were right there. Revelation had dawned.

Hoover jumped up from the kitchen chair so fast it flew across the room with a clangor.

"John, what's wrong?" Lauren, frightened by the unexpected movement, nearly screamed at him.

He had blanked out for a good thirty seconds and had completely forgotten that his wife sat across from him. When she called out his name, he was confused. *What's Lauren doing here?*

He had forgotten that they had been discussing the future—a future that suddenly might be within his grasp, if he acted quickly.

Hoover picked up the almond-colored phone from where it hung on the wall, near the basket for the incoming mail. He punched in numbers on the receiver from memory then put the handset to his ear. The phone on the other end rang once.

"John, what's wrong?" Lauren asked for a second time. He did not answer her.

It rang again. *Come on, please be home.*

A third time. *Where the hell could she be?*

After the fourth ring, he was about to give up and go it alone when she picked up. "Hello," the voice on the other end answered.

"Bev, it's John. What took you so long to answer the phone?"

"I was taking a bath. I'm dripping wet. What's the matter?"

"Bev, listen to me, this is important. I need your help. I'm out of the loop in the department; you're the only one I can go to."

"Hoover, I can't do anything—"

"Listen! This isn't about me; it's about the case. I think I've figured out the note he sent us. I think he's going to do the other three women at Purser Street tonight."

"Okay, you've got my attention."

He told her everything he thought the note meant. When he finished, he asked, "What do you think?"

"I think it's a possibility you could be onto something. If nothing else, the girls will have to be checked on."

"Good. Will you meet me out there?"

"Sure. After I call it in, I'll be out of here five minutes later."

"You can't call it in."

"Why not?"

"Because it's only a hunch," he said. In the Hoovers' kitchen, John put his arm up against the wall and leaned his head into the crook. What he had just told her was only partially true. It *was* a hunch, but Hoover was ninety percent sure he was right. He didn't say so to Beverly because he was drawing cards with his career, hoping to pull a flush from the deck.

If he was wrong about the hunch, he could be brought up on charges for interfering in an investigation. In that case, the worst that would happen to Beverly would be that after pleading she was unaware of what Detective Hoover's status was at the time of the incident, some of his negative stigma could rub off on her.

If he was right, and they saved those three women from the horrendous death that possibly stalked them, then his career might be set back on track.

It was a gamble, but one he had to take. Unfortunately, lives were the ante. Hoover drew from the top of the deck and hoped not to bust. "You can't call it in because if I'm wrong, I could drag you down with me."

It was a line, and she could probably see through it. There was a pause on the other end while she pondered. When she replied, Hoover didn't know whether to be glad or mad at what she said. "I think not calling it in is the wrong move. But I'll do it your way, only because it could help you." The one thing he did know about her statement was that he had underestimated her. Big time.

"Thank you, Bev. As soon as we get out there and determine what's going on, we'll call it in I promise."

"Fine. I'll get dressed and head out."

"Whoever gets there first, wait for the other one. I don't want either one of us to get hurt," he said.

"Deal," she replied, and the line went dead.

25

The 1200 block of Purser Street was residential. There were ten larger-than-normal houses on each side. Number1278 was the middle house on the right-hand side of the one-way street.

Hoover parked his car alongside the curb, one house above the Internet-televised house, next to a tree. He had arrived before Beverly, got out of the car, and looked up at the house. It was almost completely dark, except for a single light in an upstairs room. Hoover found the darkness suspicious, even though it was ten after ten at night. He found it suspicious because it was ten after ten on a *Saturday* night, and based on the nature of their business, the young actresses living in the house should be at the peak of their performances after sundown on weekends.

Hoover had told Beverly he wouldn't approach the house without her and physically had to restrain himself from breaking his word. While he waited, he leaned up against the tree and observed the neighborhood. It was evident that this was a higher-priced residential area, not only from the sizes of the houses, but also from the way they were constructed. Every house looked vastly different from its neighbor, each having been built from different blueprints. In true-middle, middle-class neighborhoods—as well as in lower-class ones—all the houses were built off the same blueprint, to keep costs low so that the intended buyers could afford to purchase. In more upscale areas, this was not an issue; thus, each had its own individual design. This was one of those latter environs.

He looked back at 1278, squinting, hoping to see some movement. While he strained, a strong gust of wind dusted up and blew something into one of his half-lidded eyes. It began to water as he rubbed to force the irritant out. Blinking rapidly, he got it. With red-rimmed eyes, he gazed up at the night sky. It was overly dark with the absence of the moon and stars hiding behind nimbostratus clouds. It would rain before the night was over; he could smell it on the air.

Beverly pulled her car up directly behind his. She got out and walked around to him. Her dark hair was still damp from the bath, and it hung freely about her face, its ebony shimmer complementing the deep chestnut of her eyes and making the creamy whiteness of her skin resemble porcelain. The rest was a white T-shirt over blue jeans. She was participating in this excursion on her own time, and her apparel showed it. Hoover's dress reflected hers, the only difference being that his T-shirt was black.

"Please excuse the way I look, I rushed here as quick as I could," she said, always the consummate professional. He had misjudged her again. "How long have you been waiting?"

"Couple of minutes."

"The house looks kind of dark."

"It does," he agreed, his back to it.

"You seen anybody up there?"

"No one."

"Any movement at all?"

"None."

"How do you want to do it?" she asked.

"I'm not sure. If we knock on the door and he's in there, we could scare him off and lose our chance at this. If we go creeping and he's not inside, we could end up spooking the women. How would I explain to Korzenowski why I was creeping around their garden in the middle of the night on a case I know he took me off of earlier in the day?"

"The Hoover I used to know was a man of action. When'd you become so indecisive?"

She meant it good-naturedly, but it stung nonetheless because she was right. "Who knows?" he said. "Guess I'm getting old."

"I think—"

She never got a chance to tell him what she thought because out of the corner of her eye, she caught a glimpse of white streak by. The image originated from the rear of the house and was now hurtling down the hillock of lawn. Beverly couldn't ascertain exactly what it was she saw because it had not been in the foreground of her vision, and it moved with a speed that had made it blur in her depth perception. After noticing it, she tried to adjust her eyes to take it in, but Hoover was standing in her line of sight. She took a step to her right and fully saw what it was.

There, running down the lawn toward the two cops standing beneath the tree, was a woman. Beverly had initially perceived the woman as a streak of white because she was dressed in a frilly body-length nightgown. It was sleeveless and went from the woman's shoulders all the way down to her ankles where it ended above bare feet. A nightgown of such a length should cover all of a person's body, but this one didn't. This one exposed more than it covered because something—or someone—had shred it.

Through the slits in the satin, the detective could see the woman's breasts heaving up and down from her motion and exertion; she could see her bare, thin midriff and the soft, curly triangle of her pudendum. What Beverly had mistaken for frills were the cut shreds of fabric trailing behind the running woman.

She made no noise as she came down the hill, her mouth held securely by a thick band of silver duct tape, her honey-colored hair twisted in knots as if someone had been forcefully holding her by it. Instead of cutting through the air in scissoring motions, the woman's arms were held out directly in front of her—reaching— like Frankenstein's monster. Reaching for the detectives, reaching for help, reaching for freedom.

"Oh my God, Hoover," Beverly said in a cracked, frightened voice.

John Hoover spun around to see what had scared her. When he did, he caught a split-second image of what was behind him. What his overtaxed mind caught was one single glimpse of the fleeing woman—a picture, one frame of a movie. What he had actually seen had only been a fragment of the woman with her arms spread out, her hair a mess, her eyes crazed with fear, her white nightgown strips floating. What he thought he had seen was a ghost.

Hoover began to scream, but before anything could come out, she was on top of him, her inertia casting her directly into the solid mass that was John Hoover. Together they went down in a heap.

Beverly was there almost instantly, trying to pull them apart. When she rolled the woman off, Hoover scurried out from under in a backward crab crawl. There was blood on Hoover's arm.

Beverly flipped the woman onto her back and immediately recognized her from this morning. The woman that had run down the lawn, nude except for the scraps of nightgown, was Gwen, one of the three women who lived in the house.

Gwen was hyperventilating against the duct tape.

Beverly grasped a corner and pulled. A searing pain flashed across Gwen's face but was gone quickly, leaving behind only the raw red mark where the tape had been. Gwen sucked in a deep lungful of the crisp air.

Beverly grabbed a handful of what was left of the nightgown in her fist. When she did, Gwen's breasts flopped all the way out, the chill night causing the brown areolas to harden. "Gwen, what happened?" Beverly shouted at her.

"There's someone in the house. H-h-he did this to me," she sobbed, and began crying now that she was out of harm's way. Beverly looked her over but didn't see any slices in the woman's skin, only in the nightgown. The wind from the coming storm was swirling the scraps, making them dance.

If there are no cuts on the woman, then why is there blood on Hoover?

She looked over at him for an answer and found one. Hoover had received an unsuspecting impact that caused him to take the brunt of the fall. When the two of them hit the pavement, Hoover had sustained a long, burning scrape along his ulna, the bone on the pinky side bottom of the arm. It was gritty and bleeding, as was the new gash on the left side of his forehead. Hoover was sitting up, but in a daze. As she watched, he shook his head once, twice, trying to clear it from the impact.

"Please help us," Gwen begged. "The guy's got Amber and Nat. I think he's going to hurt them."

I think he's going to kill them, Beverly inwardly corrected, but said, "Okay. You stay here." She rose up off her knee, leaving the woman lying half on the grass and half on the pebbly pavement. "John? *John?*"

"Yeah," groggily

"He's in the house. I'm going in. Call for backup. Tell them to send an army; the guy inside means serious business."

"No, Bev, we go together."

"No, we don't. I'm lead on this case, not you. I hate to pull rank on you like that, but you leave me no choice. You took a hit and are in no condition to be running up against this guy." Reaching around to the rear of her waistband, Beverly pulled out her gun, which was the same make and model as Hoover's, a 38-caliber Smith & Wesson Detective's Special. "You stay here with her and call for backup." She turned and ran up the hillock that Gwen had run down minutes before. Hoover watched her until she reached the house and disappeared into the shadows.

Gwen was sitting up now, clutching the remnants of her nightgown closed against her chest. Hoover stood too quickly and felt a dizzy spell wash over him from the head rush. He steadied himself and waited for it to pass. He had to get into that house and help Beverly. He hastily grabbed the scared woman by the arms and picked her up off the ground. He hustled her to the car, opened the front door and dropped her onto the seat. Reaching past the shivering woman, he grabbed the mike for the police radio bolted under the dash.

"D-Dan 28 to radio," he said, depressing the transmit button.

"Go ahead, D-Dan 28," came the disembodied response from a speaker inside the car.

"D-Dan 28 needs an officer assist, detective inside house with suspect. 1278 Purser Street. Repeat 1278 Purser." Each district had its own individual wave band it transmitted over. Hoover's homicide radio was on J-band, which transmitted over all police radio frequencies throughout the city.

"Copy, D-Dan 28. All units, officer needs assist, 1278 Purser Street. Officer by radio." The last part was so that the responding officers knew who called the job in. "Officer by radio" meant that the call was for real—it was founded, not suspected.

As the call went out over J-band, Hoover dropped the microphone, the coiled wire retracting it back into the car. By heeding Beverly's advice to call it in, Hoover probably saved himself from any indictments later. Once again, the killer had changed the game.

He looked at the woman. "Stay here, I'm going into the house." He had his gun drawn and turned to leave. He ran off two or three steps then came back to the car as a plan of attack began to form in his head.

"Gwen, how'd you get out? Can I go in that way?"

"The back door. But you can't get in that way."

"Why not?"

"It's locked."

"Why would you lock it?"

"I didn't. He did."

"He locked the door after you escaped? How do you know that?"

"Because I didn't escape. He opened the door and let me out. He told me to run down here, to where you were, as fast as I could, or he would kill me."

Hoover didn't get it.

What was this guy thinking? What was his game? Why would he let her out to warn us? To taunt us? No, that doesn't make sense. Why would he let her go if she's the third on the note?

Because she's not the third.

"Beverly," he said, and took off running.

*   *   *

The house loomed in front of him; the closer he got, the larger it seemed. He tried to recall walking around the interior this morning while they were looking into Michelle Laplin's background. All he remembered exactly was that the interior was a maze. There were four bedrooms, two bathrooms, a living room, a kitchen, a Jacuzzi room, a billiards room, and the basement. Three floors of interconnecting halls, and the Dandelion could be holed up in a closet in any one of them.

Shit, things couldn't be worse.

Then it started raining.

Just as Hoover reached the closest corner of the house, a streak of blue-white lightning flashed across the western sky, and the rain-heavy clouds he had noticed earlier opened up and spilled down on him. The heat lightning was unusual for this time of year, but the precipitation was typical of spring rain—cold and dampening.

With his back against the siding of the house, Hoover peered into a first-floor window. The combination of gray mesh screening and the absence of light in the room beyond made it impossible to see anything within.

Keeping his body away from exposure to the window, Hoover pushed the screen up and tried the window. It was locked from the inside. He tried the one next to it with the same result.

Next was the front door.

Locked tight.

Beverly was inside of the house, he knew that. What he didn't know was how she had gotten in, because he had been dealing with Gwen instead of watching his partner's progress.

Maybe he let her in then locked the door behind her.

Hoover didn't think so. This guy liked to play the game. If he locked Hoover out, then the game was over. No, there was a way in, but it would be as difficult to find as possible so that it would stall his pursuit.

*   *   *

Beverly was walking around in pitch black.

She had never before been in darkness so complete that she had to use the walls as guides to go from one room to another. The cloud cover, along with the new rainfall that had just started drumming on the siding of the house, cut down the visibility within to near nothing. The only breaks in the darkness were from the occasional stroke of lightning.

Damn, I wish I'd taken a second to get the flashlight out of the trunk.

She knew that that hadn't really been an option. Somewhere in here, two women's lives were on the line, and every second counted.

But how many seconds would I have saved without having to feel around in the dark like Jodie Foster at the end of that creepy film?

Woulda, shoulda, coulda, get on with it, she thought, feeling along the wall with the tips of her fingers. *Just as long as no cats jump out like the cheap theatrics they use in all those shitty horror movies and give me a heart attack. Funny what your mind thinks of when you're scared to death, isn't it?*

A change in the pattern as her fingers bumped over ridges after the smoothness of the painted wall. Molding followed by a recess. A doorway.

She was on the second floor and didn't know what was behind the door—a bedroom or bathroom. She had chosen to go upstairs, rather than to the basement, simply because she had come upon the stairs going up before she found those leading down. Time was a factor, and she had to take the first opportunity that presented itself, even though she felt it was most likely he was in the basement with the women, rather than upstairs. She thought so only because it was where she would go because it would be easier to escape from if deterred. From the second floor there was no way to get out of the house except to jump, while the basement might have its own door.

She groped farther until she encountered the cold, cut glass of a knob. Holding her breath, she turned it and pushed the door in.

Just as the door swung wide, she heard the sound of a breaking window from the floor below her. It frightened her, and she felt the cool wind of her indrawn breath pass over her teeth. On instinct, she automatically turned toward the tinkling sound of the falling glass.

It could be anything, her mind told her. *It could be a tree branch broke a pane or the strengthening wind shattered it.*

Or it could be him.

Stop it, Bevy. Self-doubt will get you killed here. Stick to the original plan. You're halfway finished the upstairs, and then you can check out the broken glass.

She turned back to the open doorway. Beyond was more unending blackness. But straining to see directly ahead of her, she could tell that it was a bedroom, rather than a bathroom, by how spacious it was. Projecting her senses into the area, she couldn't feel any movement inside the room. She was just about to begin feeling her way around the bedroom, in search of the next doorway, when she heard her name called aloud.

"Beverly?"

It was Hoover.

Damn it, he knows better than to give away his position like that.

"Beverly?" Again, louder this time. Against her better judgment, she would have to answer him. Otherwise he would keep screaming his fool head off until the perp snuck up behind him and slit his throat.

"Beverly, where are you?"

She turned to head back out of the room, to quietly yell down to tell him that she was upstairs, when she saw something. There, a shadow stood up against the wall where the light switch would be. If she had started to inch her way along the wall, as she had been planning to do when Hoover started to call out, her hand would've touched the shadowy thing. In a house full of shadows, this one was somehow different than the others—it was blacker. Instead of the scant lighting from the world outside reflecting off the object, giving it size and shape and depth, this shadow seemed to suck in what little lighting there was. It was a black hole standing up against the wall.

A flare of incandescent lightning bedazzled the room for an instant. In the brief strobe of illumination, Beverly saw what was in the shadow. Her heart leapt, for the shadow was a man. The shadow was evil.

The shadow was *him.*

His face was still shrouded by darkness, hidden above the flash of lightning, but his eyes were not. They were the black, empty eyes of a madman, a murderer. In those eyes she saw her fate.

Then the lightning was gone, and the room was once again consumed by the nebulous murk, her fate's shadow entombed among the rest, unseen but known. Beverly felt her bowels contract in her abdomen and the large muscles in her legs quiver. Throughout her life she had been scared and frightened time and again, but never had she known true terror. Standing next to her was an incubus of terror.

With quick ferocity, the shadowy fate swung its arm at the woman gone frozen with fear. Its fist impacted against her nose and mouth with bone-crushing authority. Beverly Farrell dropped to the floor without resistance.

Another flash of lightning and the storm was stronger, as a rumble of thunder could be heard above the thrumming rain.

* * *

Halfway down the side of the house, toward the rear, he could hear the noise.

Bang!

At first, he thought it was the muffled sound of a gun being fired through the denseness of the thunderstorm, and he dropped to the muddy earth for protection. There was another bang, and then another. Lying in a puddle of thickening mud, he realized his mistake. With a slurp, he pushed himself up out of the muck and continued to slink along the side of the house.

At the corner, he peeked around, and just as another bang sounded into the night, he saw the rear screen door of the house—the source of the sound—slam shut. He rushed over to the door just as the wind caught it to blow it wide again. Holding the wooden side of the door, Hoover examined the lock. The screen door swung freely because the hasp was broken. Forced broken.

He broke the lock and gained entry through this door, Hoover's racing mind spat at him.

Looking at the inner door, his suspicions were confirmed. The interior lock had the same jimmied markings as the screen door. He grasped the knob and turned. The door did not open. It was locked from inside with a deadbolt.

"Fuck, what else could go wrong?" he said out loud through angry, gritted teeth. *I need to get in there.*

He looked at the solid wood of the inner door and noticed that the upper half of it contained four muntins—rectangular squares of colored decorative glass. Not thick stained glass, but thin tinted sheet-glass. Each pane had a different color: blue, green, red, and yellow. The green was closest to the knob.

Fuck it, he already knows I'm here with Beverly, and he knows that I'll come inside for her, Hoover thought, as he broke the green pane with the butt of his revolver, not caring who noticed the sound of shattering glass inside.

Now came the hard part. Hoover didn't know what—or who—was on the other side of the door because of the impenetrable darkness beyond, and he had to blindly stick his hand inside in order to turn the tumbler on the deadbolt. It would only take about ten seconds, but that was ten seconds of vulnerability, in which time someone hiding on the other side could take aim and lop his hand off at the wrist. It would be like sticking his hand into a nest of scorpions and hoping one didn't sting him.

But he had to do it. He hadn't found any other way in, and time was short—Beverly's life might be depending on him.

Hopefully, the dark will be working for me, as it's working for him, he thought, and stuck his hand through the ad hoc opening he had made in the door.

Hoover concentrated on his hand while it swiveled around searching for the lock. The cold rain pelted down into his upturned face as he imagined the white-hot searing pain of a knife cutting through his wrist.

When his forefinger struck the raised metal of the locking mechanism, he wrongly envisioned that it was the tip of the inevitable knife and almost let out a scream. Realizing his mistake, he grabbed hold of the brass lever between his thumb and index finger and turned. As the tumblers fell, Hoover could feel the vibration through the wood of the door as the deadbolt retracted from the jamb.

Satisfied that he had achieved entry into the tenebrous house of horrors he was sure awaited him within, he swiftly retracted his arm back from the window rectangle. Naturally, he cut his hand on a green shard of glass still wedged into the tiny wooden slot—angry at having its life shattered, it exacted retribution on the pulp of Hoover's soft, vulnerable flesh.

The devil's luck, but at least I've still got the hand.

Pissed off, John Hoover flung open the rear door of 1278 Purser Street. As far as he could tell, there was no one standing behind it in what looked like a laundry room.

"Beverly?" he yelled into the gloom. He knew that by yelling into the dwelling he was giving away his position. But right now, his position was to make sure that Beverly was safe. There was no answer, so he called again. "Beverly?"

Still nothing.

"Beverly, where are you?" Lightning sparked to the west and was followed by a booming roll of thunder. He cocked his head and listened for her to call out to him. There was still no response, but he did hear a thump and some shuffling. Standing outside in the din of splashing rain, he couldn't tell what that thump had been or where it had come from. It could've been a rat scurrying around inside, under the cover of darkness, and he had startled it with the noise he was making.

Using the same hand that he feared losing when he stuck it in the broken window (and was now bleeding freely from the palm), Hoover reached for the light switch. If a light switch were installed correctly, it'd be in the up position when the lights were turned on. This switch was in the up position already, but the lights were definitely not on.

Hoover flicked it down and then back up. Nothing, it was dead. The storm was too young to have had an effect on the electricity, based on the absence of lightning activity up till now since he had first arrived on Purser Street and noticed that there were hardly any lights on in the house. The bastard had cut the electricity down here after he set up for his game.

Maybe the son of a bitch had touched the wrong circuit, and I'll find him lying next to the fuse box fried to a crisp.

Hoover was scared of electricity. It's one of those things that people think they have under control, but it can get away from you if you turn your back on it, just like an open fire, or a big dog, or a gun.

Another flash of lightning, followed by an even closer clash of thunder, and the storm had fully arrived.

John Hoover stepped into the Cimmerian house, intent on coming face to face with the Dandelion.

He would.

And it would cost him.

* * *

She was being dragged along the floor, groggy and unsure of what had happened. She had heard Hoover calling her name, and then had seen the guy they were here for. She had seen him swing at her, followed by a double bolt of pain in her face and neck. After that, it was all a blur. What she felt now was a dull, aching throb and a sensation in her head that felt like the cranial fluid had been replaced with sand.

How bad her situation really was could be judged by the fact that she was bound hand, foot and mouth.

God, Hoover, hurry up! She concentrated all her thoughts on him, in the futile hope that the unexplored areas of the human mind truly were capable of extraordinary abilities, such as telepathy. It was not an ideal that she normally subscribed to, but she would hope for anything (and become an instant believer if it managed to save her) while staring into the maw of hell. *Isn't that a quote from somewhere, something out of Herman Melville?* She giggled behind the gag as fright turned into giddiness. *And I thought I wouldn't use English Lit out in the real world; how silly was I? Here I am on my way to the afterlife, and I'm thinking about books written in the 1800s. Talk about a lasting impact.*

They veered to the left, her outstretched arms trailing behind her, slinging in an arc and striking the opposite side of the doorframe as they entered another room. She winced, tears streaming from her eyes as the pinky finger on her right hand broke. Her fractured finger effectively put an end to the hysterical giggle fit. *Hoover, please help me!*

Suddenly, they stopped, her feet dropped to the floor so that she was lying flat. They had arrived at her destiny's destination.

That was too much for her stressed mind to bear, and she immediately tried to flip over onto her belly. He must have noticed what she was trying to do or—God help us—he had had enough experience that he knew what she would try, as he put a large booted foot down on her shins locking her in position. The boot hurt as the treads dug into her skin through the denim of her jeans.

She looked down the length of her body to see if she could visualize her assailant. She couldn't; his back was to her, and he wore dark clothing in the dark room—black on black.

Damn him for putting the gag over my mouth. If I could talk to him, I could try to plead for my life. Beg, cry, whatever. Or I could call out to Hoover so that he would know where I am. But that was the reason for the gag, wasn't it? Hoover, please come!

There was a metallic click. Immediately thereafter, he was lifting her feet again.

And lifting.

And lifting.

As her shoulders were about to rise off of the floor, she realized that whatever that clicking noise was, he must have attached her to something—he wasn't lifting her; he was hoisting her. Her neck bent at an odd, ninety-degree angle, and then she was up in the air, dangling freely.

One, two, three more pulls, signified by a jerking sensation on what could only be a rope, and then she stopped again. She was lightly listing to the left when she saw his legs and boots come into visual range. Her bound arms were hanging down, and she could probably swing her body in such a way to strike him on the kneecap—the groin was too high and out of the question—but she didn't want to irritate him further with a measly, one-play offensive. She wanted him calm, wanted him to slow down, so that Hoover could have enough time to find her. If she injured him, he might quickly kill her in retribution. If he stuck to the MO he used on the previous women he had assaulted (her mind refused to use the word "killed"), then there would be some extra time while he made the incisions in her body through which she would bleed out before dealing the final death cut. She was sure Hoover would be able to find her before she could bleed out. She hoped.

She saw movement. He had something in his hand, something that seemed to be long and slender. There was not enough light for a glint, but she knew what it was he held.

Oh my God, oh my God, it's a knife! John, I need you NOW!

The knife rose up and up until she couldn't see it anymore. Her chest contracted in quick gasps, unable to suck in enough breath through her nostrils to fill her lungs. Her throat was dry, and there was a tickle at the rear of her tongue where it plunged into her chest cavity. Her fright mixing with the tickle and the lack of enough fresh air made her esophagus contract, drawing up bile from her stomach. The bile was bitter and it sickened her enough to make her vomit. It wasn't much because she hadn't eaten since lunch over ten hours earlier, a hot dog from a vending cart on Eighth Street, but any vomit restrained behind a gag was too much. Under her tongue and in the space between her teeth and gums, it filled her mouth. She thought she was going to choke to death on her own vomit, which would be the irony of ironies if she died before he could kill her.

Trusting that Hoover would make it on time, and envisioning the oily, congealed water that vending cart hot dogs swam in until fished out for the bun, she swallowed the vomit back down. She had a will to live, and she knew that Hoover would kill this motherfucker for the audacity of doing this to her.

There was a tug at the end of her jeans' leg, and then the knife was working its way down. His weapon must've been sharp, because there wasn't any resistance from the thick blue denim as the instrument cut all the way up to and through her waistband. Then it started on the other leg.

Her jeans fell to the floor.

He was behind her now as he grabbed her shirt around the collar, sticking the knife between her clavicle and the cotton. A forward pull and that shoulder was exposed. The process was repeated just as quickly for the other side. He grasped the collar from the back, and a slit parted down—*up?*—her shirt. One more for the bra strap and it all fell away from her like the shed skin of a reptile. Of her clothing, all that were left on were her panties and her plain white Nike sneakers. It was impossible to ever feel more naked than she did, as she hung upside down from a ceiling of a second-floor room in a house she didn't know. With her eyes closed, she waited to feel the cold harshness of the blade against her skin.

But it didn't come.

With her sight useless, she had to depend on her ears for information. She listened.

He was doing something behind her. For a moment, she heard the sound of a jingling tune, like that of a musical box.

We must be in one of the girl's bedrooms, and he probably opened up a jewelry box for some reason.

Then the musical jingle was gone—stilled—and she suddenly sensed hastiness about her abductor. He was moving much quicker, much more hurried than before, the calmness gone.

What is he doing?

There was some shuffling, and then it sounded as if he were rummaging through her clothes looking for something. *What?* She had been holding her gun when he hit her, so it couldn't be that. He must've either picked it up or left it in the other room, unneeded.

She was already bound, so he wouldn't need her handcuffs. *What else could he possibly want from my pants? My wallet?*

Then she knew.

He was looking for her driver's license so he could dog tag her body.

And she knew where that would go.

In her right hip pocket there was a black bifold leather wallet specially designed for cops with a flap of soft chamois to cover the stiff metal of a badge Inside the wallet was the badge, some cash and credit cards, her police department photo ID, and her driver's license.

Behind her, she heard a sound she had heard a million times before, every time she paid for something—the sound of leather slapping against leather as her wallet was opened. Slightly after the leather, there was another sound, one of metal tinkling against metal, like that of two utensils brushed against each other at the dinner table. *Metal?*

The badge. The tinkling was the badge being unpinned from the wallet.

Oh, no. Please let him use the license, not the badge.

The badge of a homicide detective in the city of Philadelphia was gold in color and shaped like a shield, on the top an eagle perched with its wings splayed, about to take flight. It was smaller (roughly twenty centimeters through the middle) than an officer's badge, and its numbers were etched into the back rather than the front.

The wallet dropped onto the pile of clothes lying beneath her as the elastic leg band of her underwear was pulled aside. She could feel the cotton bunching up, exposing her. A pubic hair was caught and yanked out unintentionally. Then he was probing and spreading—rough fingers doing what should be a delicate job. She felt the cold chill of metal as the badge pressed against her, taking her breath as a stethoscope does a patient's.

Then it was in her.

On its side, it was pushed downward as she opened up around it. As it slid along the canal, she thought about contracting her muscles and trying to squirt it back out, but any resistance would only make him push harder. She was positive that he would push as hard as necessary, even if it tore her. She had never given birth but was fully aware of what an episiotomy was, and it was not something she needed right now. She relaxed and let it slide. Her badge traveled another inch then stopped as she enveloped it.

There was a harsh tug as her panties were ripped from her body. With nothing left, she was prepped. And now the first cut would come.

Hoover, if ever . . . now.

Approaching sirens could be faintly heard over the pitter-pat of the rain against the window as he cut her.

*   *   *

Sopping wet and streaked with mud and blood, Hoover stepped into the laundry room. The first things he noticed were the steady red lights on the digital cameras placed in the upper corners of the room. The Internet cameras for BarbeesDollHouse were still operating even though the electricity had been cut. Whatever was happening inside of the house was going out live over the net.

It made sense that the electrician who installed the cameras had attached them to some sort of auxiliary power in case of a utility failure. The whole idea behind a reality-based project like this was for the viewers to share in the life experiences of the residents. Four young women trapped in the dark would probably be something the people who subscribed to sites like this would find very interesting. Not to mention a serial killer stalking the women. Somewhere inside this house, Beverly was hunting for their Dandelion live on the Internet to the delight of perverts all across the country. It was his job to make sure that that didn't get turned around the other way—if it wasn't already too late.

Using the red indicator lights on the cameras to show him where the corners were (and thus to guide him to the doorways), Hoover inched deeper into the house.

He had been throughout most of it earlier in the day—when he and Beverly had come with questions about Michelle Laplin's life—but because they had entered through the front door, and focused on Michelle's person, he hadn't paid that much attention to the surroundings at the time. Now he wished he had, as he came upon a closed door that he had no idea what was behind. Standing to the far side, he opened it. No one came out, and no one shot at him, so he risked poking his head into the opening. The darkness within was so complete it was almost a void. Using his other senses since his sight had been castrated, he cocked his head and listened. Nothing, not a sound came from the open room. He reached his hand in and to the left. He hadn't reached far when he hit a wall. The wall was too close, marking the room as small or narrow. He reached to the right and quickly encountered another wall. As he guessed, the room was very narrow. It was a hallway, he decided.

Before proceeding, he looked for a red light on a camera to guide him. There wasn't one. Either there was no camera, or it was broken. He opted for the former—why spend the money to operate a camera in a hallway?

Hoover stepped forward and fell.

His instinctive thought was that the floor had disappeared out from under him, and he was right. He banged a knee and slid the rest of the way down a flight of stairs. Hoover had found the basement.

"Shit," he said, pushing himself up to a standing position.

Down here it was like being in a coffin. It was blacker than possible, and since he was underground, the silence was perfect. He couldn't even hear the rain anymore. What he did have, though, were three red dots on cameras. With them to guide him, he quickly made a search of the entire basement. Other than sustaining a bruise to his thigh from striking it against a billiards table, he came up empty handed.

He mounted the stairs, recrossed through the laundry room, and found himself in the kitchen. He knew it for the kitchen because the first thing he touched was the cool slab of the refrigerator. From the kitchen, he could remember the layout of the ground level. Still using the red indicators (and the slight incandescent of sodium arc lighting from the streetlight that managed to cut through the gloom of the rain), he searched the first floor as fast as he could. It was painstakingly slower than he wished it could be, as he went from room to room, fearful of what was behind every door. But he got it done—in record time, under the circumstances.

And he had nothing to show for it. It was time to go upstairs.

Holding on to the banister as well as his breath, he listened up the stairs. There it was, a creak. He heard it. Someone was standing on the floor above him. He was almost comforted by the familiarity of the sound of old wood being trod upon.

Two at a time, he raced to the second floor.

When he reached the top, he stopped and spun in a tight circle in case someone was lying in wait for him. Nothing happened, and he assumed that the area was clear. He desperately wanted to call out to Beverly, but this close to the danger he was fearful of tipping his hand. He took a step and the floor creaked beneath him. He realized that he was standing on a hardwood floor. This afternoon, he had thought it odd that the carpet stopped on the final step below the landing, but modern décor was an odd thing. *The whole house is carpeted except this fucking ten-foot-square area,* his mind recalled with bitter cynicism. He would have to cross the creaky hardwood to get to the carpeted bedrooms; there was no other way; it had to be done.

Treading as lightly as he could, he made his way to the first room. Open the door; wait for the gunshots to erupt. When nothing came, proceed with an interior search of the room. People not found, continue to the next one.

Second room—empty.

He entered the third room, and something brushed against his face, a musical jingle exploding in his left ear. His skin crawled in fear as he brought his gun up and swung it around haphazardly. In the darkness, he didn't know what he was aiming at or where to point the weapon. He had never been so scared in his life. After a period when nothing else happened, he reached up and stilled the dwindling musical notes. His head had struck a wind chime, causing the suspended ceramic pieces to dance musically.

Who would hang a friggin' wind chime inside *a house?*

Someone who lived out her life on display in the menagerie of a computer screen, that's who.

Back on the second-floor landing and only one door remaining. He had been in all the rest and now knew what was behind the last door. *How come what you're looking for is always in the last place you look?* he wondered.

He could hear approaching sirens in the distance as he reached for the doorknob.

* * *

It was like the fabled light at the end of the tunnel.

Hoover had been walking in the dark for so long, and staring at tiny red indicator lights, that the sudden burst of light blinded him much like he thought the gates of heaven would after the trek through the tunnel. The similarity between the tunnel and the white light was so compelling that he actually thought: *Have I been shot dead and am I now standing before St. Peter?*

Then he heard the voice of a man speak from inside the room, and he knew that he was still corporal. "That's far enough," the voice said.

When the burst of light flared in front of him, Hoover had covered his face with his injured and bleeding arm. With that same arm shading his eyes, he squinted into the room, trying to see who addressed him. Try as he might, he couldn't see anything through the glare-blindness.

"Who are you?" he attempted.

"You know who I am," was all the answer he was going to get.

"Where are the women?"

"One is here with me. The other two are gone."

"Gone where?"

"Just gone." Hoover could tell by the man's syntax that any further questions in that direction were going to get him nowhere.

Gotta keep him talking; the cavalry is on the way.

What he wasn't aware of was that Calvary had already arrived

Hoover didn't know what to ask, so he tried another approach to the same question. "Are they dead?"

"Aren't we all dying?"

"Philosophically, metaphorically, but I'm talking about now—actually, mortally. Are they dead now?"

"'Actually,' they were dead before I met them. Now they're 'saved.'"

The afterimages that had been imprinted on his retinas when he opened the door were fading, and his vision was slowly returning—he was starting to be able to see the room in front of him. The light source was from a portable spotlight that ran off of a large square battery pack. Hoover had seen that type of spotlight before, but it was an older model. Since the turn of the millennium, they now made handheld spotlights. Hoover had one of these newer types at home in his basement. It was about the size of a normal flashlight, but it shone like a supernova. It was made by a company called Stinger, and he had bought it for about eighty bucks from one of those mail-order catalogues that cater to wannabe law enforcement people and EMT nuts who wore their company jackets with the pens in the sleeves even when they were off duty. The older-model spotlight inside of the Purser Street room was sitting to the right (Hoover's left) of a single shadow that seemed to stretch from ceiling to floor like a column. He couldn't discern what that column was yet, but as his eyes adjusted, he was able to make out more and more of his surroundings.

"Why are you doing this?"

"That's an irrelevant question right now. But in the near future, you will have your answer. Why don't you ask the question you really want to?"

Hoover knew what he was talking about. He also knew that the man in the room was an intelligent individual—a sadistic piece of shit, but probably an educated one. Further, he also knew the answer to the question as soon as the man proposed it. The answer was in the column he hadn't quite been able make to out. Now he knew what it was. The column of shadows was *two* people—one standing and one hanging—together in the middle of the room. The one standing was the Dandelion, the one hanging Beverly.

Questions hammered at Hoover's mind like the falling rain. They were erratic and rambling and overlapping all at the same time.

What does he want from me? What did he do to Beverly? Is she alive? If she's alive, how do I get her out of this room? Where are the other two women? Are they alive? How can I talk him out of this? And so on.

As proof that the sadistic piece of shit was intelligent, he guessed what Hoover had already figured out and kicked the light with his foot, changing the direction in which the beam shone. The beam now illuminated Beverly and the man standing behind her. It lit them as if they were actors in a play or a statue in a gallery.

Hoover had expected what he finally saw when the light was moved, but there was nothing that could've prepared him for actually seeing it. And it infuriated him.

Beverly hung upside down from a pulley that had been driven into the ceiling and tied off beside the window behind the two of them. She was bound and gagged and stripped. The pallor of her face and neck were livid with the flow of blood being pulled into her head by gravity. In contrast, her legs were deathly pale from their lack of circulation.

And she was cut—three times, once across both thighs and once laterally across her belly. Each wound was narrow and freshly weeping a red-black flow of blood.

But what captivated him the most was the relief and reassurance he saw in her eyes now that he had arrived. Those eyes saw him as a knight in shining armor, even though Hoover believed his armor to be tarnished. *Oh God, how do I fix this? What is the answer to the riddle?*

Outside, the sirens were closer, almost on top of them, but not yet here.

With his anger at Beverly's condition occluding his mind, he hadn't yet taken a look at his Dandelion. Now he did.

The man hid behind Beverly's body, using it as a shield. Because he was partially hidden, Hoover couldn't measure his physical attributes precisely. What he could judge, because it was in plain view and lit by the spotlight, was the man's face. The only thing remarkable about it was how unremarkable it was. Over the past three days, Hoover had built this man up in his mind to be the devil himself, a man whose nature was worse than any incarnate evil that has ever lived throughout history. Worse than Hitler. Worse than Genghis Kahn. Worse than Manson, Bundy, Dahmer, and Heidnik combined. Hoover didn't know what he expected, but what he saw was not it. The man hiding behind Beverly's naked, bleeding body was so goddamn *typical* looking. The Dandelion had brown hair parted to the right, a perfectly sized nose, and a shapely mouth to go along with a fair complexion devoid of facial hair, a smooth forehead over thin eyebrows, and very brown eyes behind a pair of glasses. There were neither any worry lines nor laugh lines. No moles, no scars. Nothing anyone would notice. Nobody would pick him out of a crowd. He would be but a face on the street.

But what couldn't be seen from the façade was the decaying, rotting madness that harbored within his mind. That mind was the lair of the beast. No matter what kind of sheep's clothing it wore, the wolf was still a carnivorous creature. It was time to engage the animal and try not get bit.

"What do you want from me?" Hoover asked the Dandelion.

"Ah, now we're at it, aren't we? It's simple really. I want what you want. You tell me what you want, and I'll bet we'll find I want the same thing."

"I want her to live."

"Of course you want her to live. That's a shallow answer. Delve deeper. Swim in the pit of your heart, where the hatred is. I want you to tell me what you want more than for this woman to live."

"There is nothing I want more than for her to live."

"Wrong," the Dandelion hissed, and then in the time it took to blink, he sliced Beverly across her breast. Through the gag, Beverly whimpered. Her body thrashed against the restraints like a drowning fish pulled from the water. Fresh tears were born and ran into her hair to dampen it with their salty sorrow.

The incision had been made on the breast furthest from the man's position. Because she hung inverted, the slash he had drawn was on the exposed underbelly of her breast and ran from side to side a scant inch from her nipple. The gash parted rapidly, blood welling in the wound.

"*NO!*" Hoover screamed. Shocked by the abused condition Beverly was in, and the commonplace appearance of the killer, Hoover realized that he hadn't brandished his weapon directly at the assailant. He did now and he burned to use it.

The Dandelion's slim, small-bladed knife now dimpled the soft flesh of Beverly's other breast. The gun and the knife, stalemate.

"Now, Detective, I ask again, what is it you want more than anything else in the world?" the man asked as patiently as a kindergarten teacher asking a small child what he wanted for Christmas.

His bottom jaw shivering and his own fresh tears streaking through the filth on his face, Hoover said without hesitation, "I want to fucking kill you! I want to tear your balls off! I want you to suffer and die! I want to kill you dead!"

"And I want the same thing, Detective Hoover," the monster in sheep's clothing said. "See, I told you we think alike."

You're no better than he is.

In the confusion of his mind, Hoover wasn't sure he heard him correctly.

Just as quick as the knife had appeared to do its dirty work, it was gone. In its place, on Beverly's uninjured breast, there was a sinister red line—a line of blood. Hoover could not be certain if that line was testament to the sharpness of the blade—that it had pierced the skin merely by touching it—or if it was residual blood from her other breast.

Still pointing his gun at him, Hoover confessed his ignorance. "I don't understand what you're talking about. Don't hurt her again. I'll do whatever you want."

"That's good, because if you do what I want, then I *won't* hurt her. I won't be *able* to hurt her. If you don't do what I want, she dies. And then, after I kill her, I'm willing to bet my *life* that you'll do precisely what I want."

"Okay, fine. Explain to me exactly what it is you want."

In a surprising motion, the Dandelion slipped out from behind Beverly and sank to his knees beside her. The knife was back. It had switched hands and was now being pressed against her neck, beneath her chin.

"Detective Hoover, I want you to kill me."

"What? Why?" Hoover asked, not exactly surprised. There was a documented psychological syndrome called "suicide by cop," in which the goal of the criminally insane was to purposely get caught in order to die at the hands of a law enforcement officer. It was a way of committing suicide while being absolved of the sin.

"I want to be martyred," the kneeling man said. "I want to die for God's cause. I want you, an infidel, to release my soul and deliver me into his grace, broadcast live around the world." He pointed to the video camera mounted within the three-dimensional triangle formed by the meeting of both walls and the ceiling. The telltale red power-indicator light blazed accusingly, and Hoover thought that he could actually hear the whirring of the tiny working mechanisms within the camera. "I want the world to witness my sacrifice—and your heinous malevolence."

Oh shit, I'm fucked. I can't kill him in cold blood. Think, Hoover, how can you get out of this? The easiest way is to keep him talking until the SWAT team gets here. SWAT was an acronym that stood for Special Weapons and Tactics. Formally called the Stake-Out Unit, they were the cream of the PPD's shooters and negotiators. As soon as some backup arrived, he could pass the baton to SWAT and they—professionals specifically trained in this type of warfare—would get Beverly out of this mess.

The guy on his knees with the knife to Beverly's throat nixed that idea by saying, "I'll bet you're thinking you'll just stand there, with your all-talk-no-action gun pointed at me, and wait it out until someone who's trained in this sort of thing shows up and offers me a jet bound for anywhere in the world I want to go. Wrong again, Detective. There's nowhere I'd rather be than right here, right now. I do not want to flee the country and go live with radicals in Saudi Arabia or Afghanistan. I have a message I want the world to hear, and I want you to help me say it. So if that was your plan, I'd like to inform you that there is a time limit for your decision."

Hoover could smell the dampness of the rainwater and his own sweat steaming off his body. This was too much of a burden to have to suffer. The nut wanted him, Hoover, to give up his life (not only his career, but possible jail time could depend on his next decision) and in turn give up the lives of his wife and daughters, so that he could get his rocks off by being killed on an Internet feed. If Hoover chose to save his own hide, then it was Beverly's that got skinned. Literally.

"As you can hear," the head-case continued, "the sirens have ceased gaining in amplification; their drone is now that of one monotonous, level reverberation. That means the cars with the sirens have arrived. At this emphatic minute, cops are probably walking around the lawn of this very house.

"It's time to choose your path, Detective."

The crossroads, revisited again and again.

"Will you satisfy both me and yourself by giving in to what I want, and what you've said you crave more than anything in the world at this moment, by shooting me? Or will you let me take the life of this woman, spill her blood, and free her soul so that it can haunt you for the rest of your days?

"Here I am, a penitent on my knees, ready to see the Lord. Choose your fate, Detective Hoover. Either way, the trials and judgments of your soul are just beginning."

The rain was being driven against the windowpane. In the darkness of the house below them, the front door was kicked in. The three of them could hear a man's voice call out, "Police. Is anybody in here?"

"Stay focused, Detective Hoover," the man on his knees growled at him, his eyes glaring, never wavering. "If you call out to them, she dies just as quickly, and I will be arrested, leaving you without the scant satisfaction of retribution. This is between the three of us, this game of hearts."

Yes, it is a game of hearts. It's the last meld of the game, and it's my trick that has yet to be played. I've seen every card thrown in this game, and I know that I hold the highest, strongest heart left—the gun. He is holding the queen of spades, the highest point valued card in the game, Beverly. I must make a play, and he will have to throw the queen. I will win the trick and take the points.

Unfortunately, in the game of hearts, the player with the least amount of points against him wins.

The final meld is mine and all the points are stacked against me; there is no way to win.

"A game of hearts, indeed," the Dandelion told him, as if reading his mind. "It's your turn, and you must look into your own heart and decide if your hatred for me is deeper than your respect and feelings for this woman."

Does he know about the relationship between Beverly and me? No, there's no way he could know. Man, don't bring any more angles into an already-fucked situation.

From downstairs and roaming, "Hello, this is the police. Is anybody in the house?"

Maybe I can tip them off, make the floor creak. No, the knife is right against her jugular; they wouldn't make it in time to save her.

"Do you know that a heart beats approximately eighty times a minute?" the kneeling man asked, the knife pressing even tighter against Bev's throat. "Since we're playing a game of hearts, I'll time your final move by the beating of _my_ heart. You have twenty until endgame—when one of the three hearts in this room will be sacrificed. Make your decision, Detective Hoover. My heart _races_ to see what it will be."

Fifteen seconds at most; what to do, what to do, what to do? Hoover could feel his own blood pulsing throughout his body. There was no time; he had to decide now.

He looked at Beverly's wide, pleading eyes and realized that there was no decision; her life was worth more than any disgrace he could ever suffer. He would kill this man in public view and try to explain it later.

Hoover mopped sweat off his face as he raised the gun to aim at the Dandelion's head. The man was kneeling in a kind of trance, listening to his own inner clock tick, waiting for the final decision to come. Hoover gritted his teeth and started to squeeze the trigger.

His shoulders slumped; he couldn't do it, murder someone outright.

You have to, his mind chided him. _How many heartbeats can be left?_

Beverly was still looking at him. She had witnessed his inner turmoil and his subsequent defeat. He couldn't stand the look of despair he saw in her eyes. He would not let her go.

He sighted down the barrel and—

Halfway up the stairs, the police officer that had come to investigate the assist call Hoover had radioed in asked, "Hello? Is anyone up here?"

Christ, that guy sounded like he was right on top of us, Hoover thought, startled. He made a slight, unconscious motion to look over his shoulder toward the questioning patrol officer. It was a motion he made without thinking, a motion that people make every day of their lives when they hear the call of their name or the honk of a car's horn; it was instinctive. The motion was almost imperceptible, but it had been enough to distract him so that when the killer on his knees played his queen by saying, "Time, Detective," he was unprepared for it.

As quickly as he had drawn the knife and cut Beverly's breast, he sliced her throat.

A torrent of blood erupted from her neck as her body began to thrash about. Her eyes rolled up white, and her bound hands began to pound on the carpeted floor.

Hoover, who had never fully turned away from the Dandelion, but just enough, just enough, finally pulled the trigger of his gun. The crash of the gunshot boomed in the small bedroom as if lightning from the raging storm outside had struck the room itself. The bullet flew, but Hoover knew immediately that it did not fly true. It did not hit the man who had slit Beverly Farrell's throat because just as Hoover asserted enough pressure on the trigger to revolve the gun's cylinder, firing the action, the murderer nudged the spotlight, turning it back in the direction of the doorway where Hoover stood. The spotlight shone directly into his eyes, glare-blinding him again as he pulled the trigger to kill.

Hoover covered his eyes to ward off the fifteen thousand CPs of light (of which one CP equaled the amount of light given off by the flame of a candle) and fired in the direction he thought the man would have veered. He partially chose that direction so as to not shoot toward Beverly, and also because a door leading to another room was that way—the logical route for escape.

Hoover stepped all the way into the room just as he heard the cop who'd been searching the premises use his handheld radio to call in the shots fired. Hardly had Hoover moved more than two steps before the light blinding him was gone and the window broken. Immediately, rain began pouring into the room, pelting the carpet.

Shit, he's going out the window.

Above the staccato tattooing of the rain, Hoover heard what sounded like two thumps, the second louder than the first. He madly dashed the yard to the windowsill. Thrusting his head out into the rain, he looked toward the ground. The large spotlight, which was still working and shining on the house next door, lay on the muddy lawn. Right next to the light's square orange battery container was a deep indentation. An indentation that was as big as a man.

The Dandelion had jumped from the second floor.

Hoover, who was in no condition to jump fifteen feet to the slippery ground, scanned the area with eyes that were slowly regaining their sight. The guy was gone; he had disappeared.

Then, from the corner of his eye, Hoover saw a pair of red taillights flash on then off, the way they would if the driver had put his foot on the brake pedal while he shifted the gears. Hoover looked at the car whose taillights had just winked at him. It seemed to be a black station wagon parked behind the house next door. *That's him. He's in that station wagon.*

There was a crack of thunder as lightning peeled across the sky, bathing everything in the silvery shimmer of a nightclub strobe light. In the illumination, the rain seemed to be falling in slow motion, the trees swaying in choreograph. In that flash, Hoover saw into the car. The lightning had outlined the driver hunched over the wheel and two moving shapes lying in the flat cargo area. It was Natalie and Amber; they were alive—for now.

As he watched, the car sped off into the night.

Beverly.

John Hoover spun around and cast his way back into the darkness. With his hands out in front of him, he searched for Beverly hanging. In an instant, he encountered her inverted form, her naked flesh slick with blood and cold to the touch—too cold, very cold, deadly cold.

Intending to untie the rope holding her suspended, he slid his hand up her leg to her foot. He found the knot in the rope and was trying to untie it when the metal pulley it was looped through ripped out of the ceiling under the stress of the dead weight.

Beverly's body fell to the floor. Hoover knelt down next to her and pawed around until he found the spill of her hair. He sat flat on the floor and cradled her head in his lap. Reaching for her wrist, he felt for a pulse, but knew he wouldn't find one—he had let too many heartbeats pass, and now they were gone altogether.

He thought about the last thing she would ever see. He thought about how she had watched his shoulders slump in defeat, and how she must've thought that he had let her die.

You're no better than he is, the reporter's words echoed in the hollows of his mind.

He knew that he should call out to the officer who was probably crouching in the hallway or hiding on the stairs, trying to avoid any shots being fired. He knew that he should call out that there was an officer down, but he didn't. They would find out soon enough.

Until then, he would hold her head in his lap and cry. He would kiss her face and cry. He would stroke her beautiful long hair, keeping it out of the blood that was still draining from the wound, and he would cry.

He would spend his last final minutes by himself in the dark with a woman that he had loved.

He said it out loud, "I love you, Beverly."

And the infrared camera hooked up to the Internet watched it all.

Meting

1

The rain had stopped, and he could hear a bird singing its early-morning tune through the open window. The trees were fully in bloom and heavy with the lush thickness of green new life. The litany of the bird perched high up in one of those trees painted the picture serene.

He reached over to the passenger seat, and picking up first one and then the other, he stuffed both parts of the newspaper into a plastic bag and threw them out the car's window. The bag landed on the lawn, sliding on the rain-slicked grass until it came to a stop on the walkway exactly where he wanted it to. He was satisfied with the throw and smiled to himself, gloating. He had been doing this for a long time now, and he knew how to play the field.

He reached over to the passenger seat and picked up two more sections of the newspaper, stuffed them in a bag, and tossed them out the window. The throw landed perfectly.

Darren Roberts considered himself to be an excellent thrower. Personal opinion: nine and a half out of ten, and would probably rank within the top ten in the country, if there were such a ranking. Still, he had had his miscues. In the five years he had been delivering the *Inquisitor*, Roberts had roofed a dozen papers, broken two windows, ripped one screen, cracked ten or fifteen potted plants, took out flowers in garden beds, and hit one skunk that had been quietly skulking around a yard. And man that was one pissed-off skunk. His toss struck the poor, unsuspecting creature squarely in the ass. When the paper hit the animal, it sprayed. Darren, who had never before seen a real live skunk in his life, did not know that when a skunk sprayed, the mist could be seen rising from the tail. The skunk had shot its stink right onto the newspaper. Roberts thought it an honest criticism of the writing committed to print on the pages of the *Inquisitor*. Darren, who wasn't going to get out of his car to retrieve that paper under any circumstances, hoped that the people who lived in the house hadn't taken the rag inside without first sniffing it. It had been almost two weeks before the odor had entirely dissipated from the yard; he could only imagine what the stink would have been like inside a confined area like a kitchen or living room.

Darren Roberts smiled his self-satisfied, gloating grin and drove his car forward at five miles an hour, headed for the next mark.

Roberts was an experienced home delivery carrier for the *Philadelphia Inquisitor*. He would rate himself at nine and a half out of ten and would place himself among the top ten in the country. Darren Roberts was a man happy in his work.

Darren Roberts was also a Peeping Tom.

Up ahead the road curved, and Darren took the bend around to his left. He was approximately halfway through his route for the morning (he had already thrown about three hundred of the six hundred and twenty-odd papers he delivered every Sunday) when he saw a light on in a window up ahead.

He crept slowly down the street, throwing his papers to the left and the right. He was distracted by the lighted window, and his actions showed it. He knew the route by heart, true, and he didn't have to keep rapt attention on which houses he threw the papers to, but the attitude he displayed at the moment was one of disinterest. And that was definitely not Darren Roberts. Not at all. No one took their job more serious than Darren. He took his work so seriously because it was the one job he found he could handle. It was the one job he felt in synchronization with—it understood him, and he it.

As a carrier, he worked alone. There was no one to bother or distract him. He had a manager that he saw every day at the warehouse where he picked up his papers, but neither rarely had anything to say to the other. The manager's position was to field the complaints of the customers and to keep the slackers among the carriers in line. Darren did his job perfectly, almost religiously. He hardly ever had any complaints, was always on time, and had never *ever* taken a day off in all five years. Darren was a manager's dream, so there was nothing to discuss. At the warehouse, the manager said good morning to him, and he returned it then left with his bundles of papers.

Out on the street, he set his own pace, did a thorough job, then went home to his mother's house, where he has lived with since birth. He was satisfied to work alone and unhurried. The job was a no-brainer. It was monotonous and tedious, and an unskilled chimpanzee could be taught to do the work. Those were facts Darren was aware of, and he liked them that way.

The lonely, independent nature of the job was perfect for a guy like Darren, who did not enjoy interaction with people. Not antisocial or agoraphobic—and no bigot—he was a person who thrived in solitude. He lived his life that way because it was the way he had been programmed by an overbearing, ignorant mother. He did not have an Oedipus complex, as the professional shrinks might diagnose. In fact, he didn't feel one way or the other about his mother—he neither loved nor hated her. She was his mother, his provider, his lawgiver, and his structure, as all mothers should be to their children.

But back to the lighted window.

Roberts, eyes glazed, mouth slightly agape, halfheartedly lobbed papers out of the car. They landed where they would, and he didn't bother to make any adjustments, all because of the lighted window that was still five doors down from where he was. He was not disinterested in his job; he was distracted by the window and its light that beckoned him. It called to him like Juliet to Romeo.

The light that he saw was only a sliver wide. It peeked out from between the widow frame and a maladjusted curtain. Narrow and yellowish, it was enough to cut through the dim, gray-blue color of the approaching dawn of another rain-soaked spring morning.

He was aware of the quickly lightening sky above him, and he knew that he had to move quickly if he wanted to catch a glimpse of what was behind the curtain. If it had been any other day, this wouldn't even have been a question—he would sneak up to the window and take a gander at what was going on inside without pause. But today the papers had been late arriving from the manufacturing plant, and since he had gotten out of the warehouse later than usual, it would be risky to be peeping around with the quickly advancing dawn. He was two hours behind his routine schedule. Normally he would be finished delivering by now, but there had been a late breaking-news story last night which had held the paper up from being put to bed on time. Over Sunday morning bacon and eggs, people would read about the murders of a female police officer and a woman named Michelle Something-or-other, along with the abduction of two other females. Believe it or not, the incident had taken place not fifteen miles from where Darren Roberts was now delivering his newspapers—and eyeing up a prospect. He pulled over and parked the car.

Due to the lateness of his working day and the coming of daylight, Darren was nervous about peeping in the window. He worried about early risers looking out *their* windows and spying him in the act. His usual method was to get out of the car (while it was still very dark, mind you) under the guise of delivering a newspaper by walking it up to the house he wanted to take a closer look at. This way, if anybody saw him, he would drop the paper at the doorstep then continue on to the next stop, thus giving the impression that he was just doing his job, the same as he did every day.

But the hour worried him. It *was* getting late (was there such a thing as getting *early*?) and people *would* be getting up. On the other hand, it was Sunday, the day most people were off from work and would likely sleep in. And he did have the overcast working in his favor. Pros and cons, checks and balances, the teeter-totter of the scale.

He sat in his car, undecided on whether to proceed or not. He raised the binoculars that hung about his neck from a chain made up of tiny linked ball bearings that would break away if the chain were tugged hard enough. The binoculars were a tool he used to watch people. He much more preferred to get as up close and personal as he could, the naked eye being the choicest way to watch people do what they do. But for those occasions when that wasn't a possibility (a lot of the best action took place on second floors, where people tended to leave their windows uncovered, wrongly believing that no one could see up there), he had the glasses.

Another positive of the binoculars was that they could be used over great distances. He could sit unnoticed in his car (actually Momma Roberts's car) and watch people conduct whatever business they were involved in. He liked to watch people when they didn't know they were being watched. If a person knew he or she were being supervised, he or she will always act civilized. If they didn't know, then millions of years of evolution got thrown out the window like so much back story in a newspaper, and they reverted to the mammals they were. Civilization is a spectator sport. Without the judgment of public and peers, watching human beings' actions were a lot like watching those on the Discovery Channel—wild, untamed, and ferocious.

Life viewed through the glasses was fun, but the same fête seen up close and personal from behind a bush or shrub was exhilarating, if you could get it. Sometimes the preferred was out of reach, so the binoculars were the standby, and the one thing Darren never left the house without. While he delivered newspapers, they hung around his neck. During the rest of the day, they were folded in his pocket, ready at his disposal. They say a dog is a boy's best friend. Roberts preferred the fourteen-ounce, fifteen-by-twenty-five power-zoom Bushnell binoculars. A dog provided company; binoculars provided entertainment. The uses for a dog were limited to that of a companion, while the uses for binoculars were manifold.

This was one of those times when the binoculars came in use in a different way than the primary intention—a way that would pave the path to the up-close-and-personal shrub, the locale for peerless peering. This time Darren needed the glasses for reconnaissance.

He brought the binoculars to his eyes and scanned the neighborhood, looking for any signs of life—or at least awake life. There was a small rounded button on the top of the binocular housing that activated the night vision. He depressed the button, and the world turned lime green inside the glasses. Through the viridity of his vision, he did not see anything moving in the area.

Low-level lighting, no witnesses, and a house with a history of a payoff—it was decided; he would risk exposure and go for it.

The knowledge of that previous payoff was what sealed the deal for him.

Roberts had an above-average memory capacity, but he only used it for things he chose to use it for. In other words, he had a selective-perceptive memory. One of the things that he held strongly in the bank of his brain's filing system was a categorized system of all the windows he had peeped in over the years. He could cross-reference them by year, season, date, day of week, activity, genders, and nudity.

The house with the light peeking out from the side of the maladjusted curtain had a history to it. As soon as he had seen the light on, his mind had retrieved the information on this particular residence from his filing system. It hadn't taken a fraction of a second, a fraction of a thought, to retrieve the information he requested, because the house in question was the one that had given him the best peep show he had ever seen. It had been hot and sexual and demoralizing and violent. For the players, it had been beastly. For Roberts, it had been ecstasy.

It was the sex of the previous tenants (ironically, the same tenants that Michael Dedaker hadn't wanted to hassle to vacate the bottom unit of his duplex because he hadn't wanted to do anything that could draw undue attention to himself and could later be remembered) that made Darren Roberts risk exposure—and ultimately his job—so that he could take a peek into the duplex. That past payoff had been huge enough to risk anything to see it again—even the loss of another job, followed by the wrath of Momma.

It was Darren Roberts's lust for another payoff like the previous one that sealed the fate of the deserving Michael Dedaker.

And of the innocent Emma Anderson.

Leaving the binoculars on the dashboard, Darren readily assembled a newspaper, put it in the bag, and got out of the car. Taking slow, purposeful strides, he approached the concrete steps that lead up the short but steep hill the duplex had been built upon to accommodate for the sloping decline of the street. The sound of a cricket could be heard coming from somewhere deep in the ankle-high grass.

He climbed the six steps (a habit that Darren found annoyed him but couldn't shake was counting risers every time he walked up them, even those in the house where he lived) and headed toward the line of small shrubs that grew directly in front of the window. There, a valley had been created between the stacked bricks of the house and the foliage—nature's own hideaway. It was about two feet wide and provided the perfect viewing spot, hidden from the public and the resident at the same time. As he approached the point of no return, he put on an air of being confident, as if he were just dropping off a newspaper to a feisty customer who demanded his paper be exactly at the door. Darren felt the display of confidence would help cover up his true intention if a chance witness happened to see him. Maybe it would or maybe it wouldn't, but the one thing that could be said about Darren's confidence was that it was some fine acting, possibly even Oscar worthy. Beneath the phony laissez-faire attitude and the bored-to-tears-of-the-same-old-same-old loping walk was a man who would shit his pants if an ant sneezed. The only giveaway of his apprehension was his nervous, fluttering eyes. He darted them left and then right, checking every inch of the visible neighborhood, all the while restraining his head from glancing back over his shoulder.

Darren Roberts's rule number 1 for the peeping hobbyist: confidence is protection.

With his bogus confidence pinned to his sleeve and a newspaper dangling from his hand, Darren ducked behind the bushes. He went in fast and low. The need for alacrity was obvious, but the reason he had to crouch low was so that whoever was in the lighted room wouldn't see his head as he sneaked by the part in the curtains. The sound of the cricket's song was gone, frightened off.

Safely behind the bushes, he spun in a tight circle so that he faced the front door, the walking path, and the escape route. One could never be too safe.

Crouched down in the mud created by the heavy rains during the night and the sparse grass that grew in the shade of the shrubs, Darren reminisced about the last time he had been in this exact spot.

He had been hiding behind these very bushes, about to spy on the wildest sex he had ever seen in his quarter century of living. He remembered it clearly. He'd been hunkered down just as he was now, and about to peek into the window, which at that time had white frilly—nearly transparent—curtains, not the heavy dark ones that hung there now. The smell of eucalyptus had been strong in his nostrils, as it was now too. Remembering that fateful day, Darren glanced down at the front page of the paper that he delivered every day but never read.

On the cover of today's *Inquisitor* were two photographs of two women. They had been abducted, and it was their story that had caused the paper to go to bed late, thus causing Darren's trepidation over peeping because of the lateness of the hour.

A simple-minded person, Darren easily dismissed the headline, the photos, and the abductions, letting his memory drift back to that previous morning behind this bush.

At first, when he looked in the window on that early morning, he thought he had struck out. He watched for a minute or two, but there was nothing happening. The only thing he saw was a woman sitting in the corner of the couch. Her blond hair had been pulled up and twisted into a style that sat atop her head. She had been wearing a black dress, black nylons, and a pair of black high heels. Darren assumed she had been out for the evening, had come home late, and had not gotten a shower yet. She hadn't been doing anything but sitting there with her legs tucked up underneath her—after the kneecaps, all he could see were the soles of her shoes and the slim shafts of stilettos sticking out from under her hip. The couch she sat on was not against the wall directly across from the window but rather along the wall to his left. She had positioned herself so that she was looking into the house instead of out the window. He looked for a TV that she might've been watching, but there wasn't one in the room.

The woman hadn't been doing anything, just sitting there bouncing one foot up and down beneath her. Darren waited, staring at her staring at the wall. He crossed his fingers—actually, physically crossed them—in the hopes that sooner or later she would stand up and at least shimmy out of the dress that hugged her body so tight. She didn't. She continued to sit there with her head tilted to the side and her chin high in the air. It stretched on like this for minutes until Darren was about to give up and finish the rest of his route out of sheer boredom. Just as he was about to slide out from behind the hedges, he saw the woman's head tilt down as she covered her eyes with her hand. Her bouncing foot had stopped moving, and her chest began to heave. She was crying—lightly at first, then heavier until she was sobbing. Darren looked on rapt. He had never seen a grown woman cry before, other than on TV, not even his mother.

The woman cried so hard that her cheeks were wet with tears that glistened in the lamplight. Darren (who had no idea of what it was like to raise a child or be in debt up to his eyeballs) wondered what could make a woman cry like that. And then he knew. As if in answer to his thought, he heard a bellowing shout come from somewhere offstage. A man's shout. It was muffled and unclear, but Darren was sure that whatever had been yelled was not an endearment of love. He looked in the direction he thought the shout had originated, waiting for the man to enter the room. With his attention drawn elsewhere, he was surprised to hear a softer and higher—but no less hostile—reply. The woman had stood up and was shouting back at the as yet unseen man.

Darren was hypnotized by the back and forth yelling, the drama playing out this way for a spell, until the woman sat back down with a smirk on her face. Even with the streaks of mascara running down her wet cheeks, she had the air of someone who had just gotten off a good one. Darren wished he could've heard what it was she said. Apparently, it had been biting enough—or mean enough—to bring the unseen man storming into the room.

And it looked as if he were none too happy about it.

The man stomped over to the couch where the woman had retaken her previous seated position. Instead of her foot bouncing, her head moved from side to side as she continued to spout quips at him.

Darren was worried for the woman. Worried that she would go too far and incur the wrath of the man towering over her. He was a big, husky man wearing a black suit to complete the out-too-late-just-got-in motif. His tie was gone and his shirt unbuttoned almost to his waist, but he still looked dapper. Having no fashion experience at all, Darren at least thought the mean man's clothing looked quality made and expensive. Darren wondered if it was hard for a man that size to find clothes that fit properly.

Darren found himself jealous of this man with his fine clothing and his beautiful, but sad, woman. He hated this man for the way he was treating the lady, glowering over her and yelling in her face until his mouth frothed with spittle, but she held her own. They were trading verbal parries with such scorn that the window glass vibrated with it. No matter what he said, she had an answer; and boy, if her answers weren't raising his ire. The extra-large man's eyes were glowing red with rage, and Darren knew it was coming before it came—the man hit her.

It was an openhanded slap that cracked right across her tear-wet and makeup-stained face. The slap had been so hard and unexpected that Darren heard the woman's gasp through the partition of the window.

Darren—who hadn't been quite as surprised as the woman had been because he could see the steam building inside the man and knew that sooner or later, the steam would fill up the kettle, and it would whistle—stood up. He had been so mesmerized by the actions of the two people inside that he had forgotten where he was. When he heard the slap and then the gasp, he had leapt to his feet, a primal urge inside him triggered to go to her. In the herd of society, the strong had to protect the weak so that they were not eaten. That's what went through Darren's mind when he saw the titan inside the house slap the woman across her face.

Whatever the notion he had entertained, it had been fleeting, because as soon as he realized that he had stood up, he unlocked his knees, dropping back down to the ground. He lay beneath the windowsill and out of eyesight, waiting and listening to see if the shouting would resume and be redirected at the interloper peeping in on the domestic dispute. The shouting did in fact resume, but it hadn't been redirected toward him. He could tell because it was now accompanied by the sound of blows.

Nimbly, Darren propped himself up again to look in the window, fearful of seeing the mammoth pounding the woman into the couch. What he saw was the reverse—the woman was repeatedly striking her husband, slapping and punching the man in his thick torso. She was the one shouting now, he the one backing away.

Okay, you did it, Darren thought. *You've made your point; now let it end for your sake.* But she didn't. She kept hitting and slapping, slapping and hitting. She felt she had the upper hand because he had struck first (and might've been appalled at his own actions), and now she was going to show him that she was woman, hear her roar.

Stop it, lady. Can't you see his pressure's building again?

And it was too. The man's fuse was like that of a Revolutionary War musket—it fired off only one shot, then took a bit of time to reload. The next shot had been placed in the barrel with the powder, and now she was unknowingly packing it tight so it could be fired again. The gun cocked and, with a loud crack, fired as the man slapped the woman across the face a second time. This time the striking of his large hand knocked the woman to the floor. She had the nerve to reach up to cradle her cheek, red with the heat of embarrassment and pain.

They had yelled, cursed, and hit each other. And then it really got ugly.

The woman on the floor was now lying in a position so that she rested on her hip and supported her weight with her arm. Her legs were together and trailing out like the tail of a snake.

The woman turned her head, gazing down her legs. Darren did likewise. They were nicely shaped and ended in feet wearing black high, high heels.

Suddenly, the woman whipped off one of her shoes and sprung up. Her legs, which had resembled the tail of a snake a moment ago, were now spread wide, like a gunfighter's. With the quickness of an asp, she swung the stiletto-heeled shoe, and it bit into the man like a sharp, poisonous fang. In the melee, his unbuttoned shirt had fallen open. The woman had aimed for flesh and hit him in the meaty part of his shoulder. The stiletto of the shoe, which she had on all night and had probably worn on many other occasions, must have been worn-sharpened from supporting her standing, walking, and dancing weight time and again. The spike of the stiletto sunk into the man's shoulder muscle. The woman let go of the shoe, and it remained protruding straight up from where it had penetrated him.

The man bellowed in rage at the pain. He yelled one long, loud word that even through the windowpane Roberts could hear clearly. "Motherfucker," the man screamed, blue veins standing out at his temples. With a speed that matched hers, the man brought his arm across his chest, reaching for the heel embedded in his skin, while his free hand reached to grab her. There was no way he had telegraphed his movement, so the woman must have known that she had finally gone too far, and that it was time to get out of Dodge stat.

The woman feigned to the right just as his huge claw reached for her. She went one way and he went the other, reversing their positions like pirouetting dancing partners. She was now facing toward the door—and might have made it out of the room, if the other heel hadn't picked that exact moment in time to snap off. She had already been off-balanced from having only one shoe on, and when the second heel popped, she stumbled. If she hadn't stumbled, she might've gotten away. Or at least have been able to keep her dress on.

As she was trying to regain her footing, her husband's reaching hand caught the collar of her black, silky dress. The heaviness of his grope threw off any equilibrium that she had been able to establish, and she fell to her knees. When she fell, he did not let go of her neckline. The result of his strength and her inertia was a rending of the thin silk, an article of clothing that was in all likelihood purchased for the sheerness of its textile. The zipper's teeth held tight, but the stitching holding the zipper's apparatus onto the dress parted as easily as one could tear a tissue.

Knowing that her situation was worsening by the second, the woman made an attempt to crawl out of the room. The man, who still had a stiletto heel driven into his shoulder, stepped on the hem of her dress, pinning her to the floor. Acting more like the snake of the simile, the woman began to slither out of the party dress that had become her restraint. Off the shoulders, as she was pulling her arms out, the dress slid down her back until what remained of the zipper got snagged in her pantyhose.

She flipped over onto her back, and Darren saw that she had not been wearing a bra. He had not noticed that her breasts weren't supported under the dress until it was around her waist. Once they were in sight, he could see how she could get away with it— her breasts were tiny, perky little things. Darren, feeling fulfilled by the nudity, did not know cup sizes, but he would guess that the breasts of the half-naked woman on the floor would be whatever the smallest size was. She had probably never used a training bra because there had been nothing to train; her breasts were barely more than a nipple apiece, and she had no cleavage.

By now the woman had flipped onto her back so that she could hook her thumbs into the elastic waistband of the hose and, lifting her rump at the same time, slide them off.

The man, sure that she would not be able to escape from him, was busy with the shoe in his shoulder. Grimacing against the pain that was going to come and wincing with resolve, he wound his hand under the high arch of the shoe and pulled. "Aaaaarrrrrgh," he moaned like a dejected Charlie Brown, but the shoe had come free. He tossed it to the floor before turning his attention back to the woman.

She had slid out of the combination of dress and pantyhose so far that they were tangled around her knees. Throwing Darren into a tizzy, like the bra, the woman had not been wearing any underwear beneath her dress, preferring to go *au natural*. The woman's conflicting dress—proper evening wear covering up the dirty secret of no undergarments—a fact that only she (and possibly the man she had once been trying to entice, but was now trying to flee from) knew, had little Darren straining the front of big Darren's navy blue work trousers.

Darren stared at the woman's naked beauty: her small breasts heaving with exertion and fear, her too-thin stomach beneath the outline of her ribs, the two points of her hipbones poking through the skin of her pelvis, and the soft curly hair of her pubis that was much darker than the pinned-up blond hair of her head. Darren looked at her with lust; the man poised above her looked at her with hate, two four-letter words from opposite ends of the same emotion.

Her clothes were now all the way down to her ankles where they clung to the same high-heeled shoe that had broken and caused her to fall in the first place. She tried to kick the shoe off with her other foot, but couldn't get any purchase through the silk and nylon.

She had bent at the waist to reach down and try to free herself by hand as her husband unbuckled his belt and slipped the leather through the loops. She saw what he was doing and tried to hurry up her own release. He watched her while he took his time wrapping the buckle end of the belt around his hand. Realizing that she was out of time, she gave up and pointed at him. Her head thrashed from side to side as she said "No" and other variations of things warning him that he would not dare do that to her; she had drawn her line in the sand.

He crossed her line as the belt whistled through the air and lashed her across her naked thighs.

The woman's head flung back, and she let out a wail as Darren once again responsively rose from his hiding spot. This time he had no intention of stopping the woman's punishment. He had never seen anything as erotic in his life as a naked woman being strapped with a belt.

The belt flew through the air again and stung the white smoothness of her tense muscles with a whack. As the sound reverberated off the glass, Darren remembered that he could be seen standing in front of the window as he was. He dropped back down to a crouch, like a duck in a carnival shooting gallery, but did not sink low enough that he couldn't see what was happening inside. There was no way he was going to miss even a second of this, and it didn't matter because the people inside were too engrossed to have noticed his face at the window for the instant it had appeared.

The woman was now screaming anything she could think of, almost jabbering at the man above her, as the belt came again. It whipped across her thighs, leaving an angry red mark in its wake. The fist holding the belt rose back up and came down with rapidity. She saw it coming and, digging the heels of her palms into the carpet, tried to pull her stripped thighs away from the blow. She pushed so hard that her foot slipped out of the shoe and she was freed. The incoming blow landed across her instep, but she didn't notice as she pushed herself up onto her feet and turned to run.

She wasn't fast enough. The man gave chase and caught a fistful of hair. Tossing her like a rag doll, the man flung her against the wall directly across from Darren's vantage point. The mirror hung from it shook as her weight slammed up against the drywall. Darren looked at the mirror, waiting to see if it would topple down onto the couch below. It must've been fastened securely because it did not lose purchase.

As he slid his eyes from the mirror to look at the naked and strapped woman standing in front of him, he caught a glimpse of his own reflection. He was perplexed by the sight of his own eyes looking into his own eyes in such an unfamiliar place. Then he saw the naked woman and forgot all about it.

Her hair had spilled down around her shoulders, and the disarray of her makeup made her look exotically radiant. Her nudity was an afterthought in light of the perfection of her anguished face. She huddled between the end of the couch and the wall, holding her arms across her breasts and trying to make herself as small as she could. She hadn't started crying again because it had all happened so fast, but the tears were soon approaching. As was her husband with the belt still looped over his hand.

When he was about a foot away from her, standing in her

personal space, she made one final request. Darren watched her mouth the word "please."

Her husband, clearly one who believed in the adage that "if you spare the rod, you spoil the child" slowly shook his head no. To Darren's astonishment, the woman dropped her protective arms and turned around of her own accord. Facing away from her husband, she bent over the arm of the couch. Propped up by her elbows on the upholstery, she pulled her legs together. He applied the belt to her buttocks.

Again and again and again.

Holding her head up so that her golden hair tickled the skin between her shoulder blades, she made no movement to avoid the lashes. With her eyes closed, she endured the torment of her lover's fury. When he felt that she was done, that she had had enough, that she was expertly chastened, he let go of his grip on the leather, and the belt uncoiled to fall harmlessly to the floor.

She remained in position while he looked at her flayed nates. They were red with the heat of punishment and embarrassment. Satisfied with the thoroughness of his work, the man unhooked his pants and let gravity pull them down. Naked from the waist down and protruding out at length, the man saddled up closely to his girl's self-held prone position. She made no protest as he began to copulate with her.

After a number of dominating thrusts, the man pulled back and, once again grabbing a fistful of hair, turned her around to face him. They began kissing, alternately hard and soft, blood from the hole in the man's chest smearing over their bodies like paint.

Then *she* took control.

The rest of their intercourse was a varied display of malicious passion. There was pinching, biting, slapping, and kissing, but there also seemed to be love and understanding. The two performers, each sustaining the other's sexual torment, knew their mate's limits as much as they knew each other's bodies.

Darren had looked on, unable to comprehend what he had just witnessed and the conundrum of affections after such a display of brutality. The humbled woman, who not ten minutes ago had been crying on the couch, was hugging and kissing and caressing the man who had stripped her down and thrashed her for stabbing him with the spike of her shoe.

Darren, who had never seen anything like this before in his life, couldn't figure out what the hell was going on. *Why was she all lovey-dovey with someone who had abused her in what this paperboy would consider a sexual way? He was the one on the floor now; why didn't she kick him in the nuts and take off?* Darren kept waiting to see if the amour had only been a decoy, a setup so that she could take the man down hard. But the woman seemed to be enjoying what she was doing, enjoying it so much that the cheeks on her face were as flush as her recently spanked ones. *Is it possible that she had enjoyed the beating? Was this the way some people made love, by using fists and leather? Can there be pleasure in pain?* Darren wondered.

Darren, whose only experiences with the forbidden fruits came from prostitutes, had been unsure. Up until that night, he had never heard of such a thing, much less experienced it. Before watching the man and woman from the shrubs of their front lawn, his version of lovemaking involved an exchange of cash. He would pay the required sum, usually to a rather mangy and unsightly woman, and then sit back while she pleasured him to the sound of faux moaning.

After the night at the window, things changed. He found that it cost more (sometimes a lot more), but there *was* pleasure to be found in pain. Once that door had been opened for Darren, he discovered that there were endless combinations of feelings that could hurt so good, combinations that could nauseate the pit of your stomach while your testicles pulsated and quivered.

He was beginning to feel that familiar tightening of his testicles now as he sat hunched beneath the same window that had offered him such a recherché experience. Recalling all the glorious details, he wouldn't even consider not risking everything to watch those two again—the man, domineering in size and overbearing in surety, and the woman, petite and timid, uninhibited and frolicsome.

From her lonely, crying solitude, through the whipping and the fucking, until they turned out the light and walked out of the room naked and abused and spent but content in love with their arms around each other, Darren remembered it all, the drool running from the side of his mouth as he revisited their lust in his mind.

With sweaty palms and a dry mouth, Darren Roberts rose to one knee. His head came above the windowsill to the right of the opening, between the curtain and the wall, and grabbed hold of the windowsill, the dim yellow light from inside painting the knuckles of his hand. Slowly, ever so slowly, he inched his head toward the opening and looked in.

At first, he thought he had hit the jackpot. He thought that what he was seeing was the most twisted act of sexual perversion imaginable (and perhaps it was on some level, but not on the level that Darren had expected).

This time there were *three* naked people in the room, two females and one male. One of the females was lying on the floor, propped against the wall where the couch that had acted as the whipping post had been. That woman was spread-eagled and bruised. The other woman, also bruised, was *hanging* upside down from the ceiling.

Holy Christ, what is going on here? What's he going to do with her hanging upside down like that?

After the initial shock, Darren began to notice the differences in the room between this time and the last time. To start with, all the furniture was gone. The tasteful, modern décor, the leather couches, and the ornate mirror had all been removed and replaced with a metal tub and a podium(?!).

Aside from the changes in the habitat, the people were also different. Neither the man nor either of the women was one of the people that he had watched that long-ago summer. He had never seen any of these people before.

Normally, such changes would've angered Darren, but in a case like this, when the actions were even more interesting than what he had been expecting, who could complain?

Now what were they up to in there? The women had been beat around, that was obvious, but why was the one lying against the wall not moving? Was she unconscious? Come to think of it, why isn't the hanging one moving either? And why does she look so familiar?

Darren looked closer at the upside-down woman. Her features weren't clearly defined because of the bruises she had sustained, but he thought that he had seen her somewhere before. Where, though? Darren didn't know any females personally, so that was out. For any bit of a clue, he looked at the other woman and experienced that same feeling of déjà vu.

What the hell was going on here? What was it about this house?

Darren watched as the unclothed man began to push the metal tub beneath the hanging woman. "Aha," Darren spoke softly aloud as a sudden understanding of what the tub was for came to him. He didn't mean to speak it out loud; it just kind of slipped, and it almost got him killed. The revelation was so sudden that the "aha" was out of his mouth before he even realized he had voiced it, like a light bulb that appeared above a cartoon character to signify the sudden occurrence of an idea. Darren would have comically slapped a hand over his mouth at the analogy, but he was too afraid to move.

The man stopped pushing the tub and stood erect. Strangely, he began looking around the room; looking in the corners, looking at the floor, the ceiling, the curtains. Darren didn't know what the man was looking for; he didn't see anything in the room other then the three naked people.

Then the man started walking toward the window.

Oh, shit, Darren thought, *he's gonna see me. I'm caught.*

Darren wanted to run, but he couldn't. The man had given no warning that he was going to come to the window, and now Darren was frozen in place. If he made a mad dash for it, he could probably outrun the man. Certainly, a man without clothes on wouldn't give chase, would he? But where would Darren run? He delivered newspapers on this street every day of his life, and the man wasn't apt to forget the face of a person that he saw looking in his window. With no time to run and no place to go, Darren stayed where he was, hidden behind the small bushes, hoping that it was predawn-dreary enough out that he wouldn't be seen.

The man grabbed the leading edge of the curtain and moved it slightly farther aside. Darren held his breath only an inch of glass away from the man's bare abdomen. Instead of looking down at the Peeping Tom, the man looked up at the top of the window. Darren didn't know what was up there, and he didn't dare make a move to find out. Seconds spun out into eternities, until the man let go of the curtain and receded back into the room.

Once again alone at the window, Darren lifted his head to see what the man had been investigating. He noticed that the window was one of those types in which the frames could slide up or down for ventilation. The upper half of this particular window was currently slid down and was open, covered only by a screen. That was it; the man had come over to see if the window was open.

Had he heard me, or had he been overheated from exertion and wanted to make sure some air could get in?

Darren couldn't believe his luck. He was not a religious man, and he had never made a desperation pact with any deity for anything before in his life. Straying true to character, he did not attempt to make such a pact to cover the personal foul-up this time, either. He made no vows to repent for his sins or to give up peeping. He didn't believe in spirits in heavens who had the ability to grant wishes like that anyway. Instead, he preferred to believe in luck. Sometimes you had it, and sometimes you didn't. And today, luck was with him. When the man let go of the window, it had drifted closer to the sill, but it had not closed all the way—he could still see into the room.

Although his vantage point was no longer as large as it had been, he could still see the woman hanging over the tub, but he could no longer see the second woman lying against the wall on the floor. He also could not see the man.

Where was he? Darren pressed his eyeball right up to the glass, trying to see as far into the room as he could. It was useless; he could see no farther than the hanging woman. Switching eyes, he tried to look for the doorway that led into the rest of the apartment, but the interior had been constructed in such a way that his view was obstructed.

Where did he go? Had he known I was here and pretended not to notice me so that he could buy some time to get dressed? Was he coming around the back right now? Or would the man's eye suddenly appear on the other side of the curtain's gap to stare directly at me, unblinking as they always do in those made-for-cable, people-from-hell movies on the USA Network?

That image got to Darren's imagination and freaked him out a little. He pulled back from the window to glance over his shoulder. A chill ran up his spine as he noticed the emptiness of the dark, early-morning neighborhood. A neighborhood in which, a few minutes ago, he had been worried about being seen. Now he was worried that no one would notice if this guy grabbed him, took him inside, and killed him.

There was something wrong here, but Darren didn't know

what it was. The thought that had caused his near-miss gasp had been that the tub was a catcher set up for water sports—he thought the guy was into urinating on women, the tub there to catch the runoff so that he wasn't inadvertently pissing on the carpet. But that wasn't really what it was for now, was it? Why *were* those women unconscious?

Darren thought for a second that he should forget the entire endeavor and take off. *Cut the losses and live for another day,* he reasoned. But he couldn't do that—his curiosity was too stoked to walk away from something like this. After all, wasn't it his heightened curiosity what had brought him to all the windows he had visited in the first place? He would feel like a failure, not to mention a hypocrite, if he turned away from this window now.

Steeling himself for the eye that he was sure would pop up and scare his hair gray, he bent down to the gap and peeped into the room.

Even with his taste for sadomasochism, nothing could've prepared him for what he saw the final time he looked in that particular window. The man was back, and the tub was filling up with something that was a far cry from urine. And yet, he watched. He couldn't *not* watch—it was what he did; it was who he was. He watched until the man was done with both of them.

When it was over, an unexpectedly warm sun was high in the sky and turning the remnants of the rain's moisture into early-morning fog. Darren, dazed and sickened by the appalling exhibition he had beheld, stood up from his position behind the bushes for the final time. He brushed at the knees of his pants to no avail—they were brown and wet from the mud.

In no hurry to leave because he feared that any quick motions would make him whoopsie the bagel he had gotten from the Dunkin' Donuts drive-thru somewhere around three o'clock this morning, he bent down and picked up his incognito copy of the *Philadelphia Inquisitor*. As he did, he noticed the pictures of the two abducted women again.

He now understood that feeling of déjà vu.

Darren climbed into his car and went home without delivering another paper that morning.

2

*W*ednesday.

It had been a long week of introspection since the bodies turned up in the airport woods, the kind of week that tested a man's mettle. Hoover's mettle hadn't been broken from the psychological burdens of the investigation, the death of Beverly, his partner and lover, or even the leaving of his wife, Lauren, with the kids. Hoover's mettle hadn't been broken, but it had been dented to hell and back.

Hoover spent most of the week drowning his sorrows in sour mash. He was depressed and disheveled. Beverly had been laid to rest this morning.

After her body had been carted away in the ambulance, Hoover had given a description of the Dandelion and had remained at Purser Street while the cops went over the scene. After the call went out about the slain officer, Korzenowski, who'd been at home in bed with his wife, arrived at the scene. The captain of homicide had the area closed off, and the street, in his words, "lit up like a Christmas tree" even though it was the middle of the night and a pouring rain. He had officers go door-to-door, waking up every household and searching every yard, in the hopes of finding the killer or someone who had seen him. Hoover had watched the perp drive off with the two women in the back of the station wagon and told the captain so, but they still searched the neighborhood—sometimes perps liked to stick around to watch the aftermath. But Hoover knew their guy was gone; he had other fish to fry, and he knew that Hoover would now be able to ID him on sight. The Dandelion was definitely gone.

The crews did what they could but hadn't found anything of remark in the house or yard. Matches of the perp's fingerprints from Michelle Laplin's car were found in the room with Beverly, and also on the orange plastic spotlight he had used. The results of the new prints were rushed through NCIC—the National Crimes Information Center—again, as they had been with the car, and had come back late in the evening with the same negative response—the Dandelion had no previous criminal record. Military records and other noncriminal forms of fingerprinting were still being checked, but there were no nibbles so far. The Dandelion, although known on sight, was still a no one.

Pictures of the missing two women from 1278, Amber Knoble and Natalie Fattore, were rushed to the media for print and broadcast. Partial molds of the tire tracks Hoover indicated as possibly belonging to the black station wagon were made because unique wear on a tire could corroborate information in a court of law as placing a certain vehicle at a specific location and time. The tracks had still been fresh but had filled up with new rainwater at their deepest, and clearest, points. Their use in court would be iffy at best.

Later, in the small hours of the morning, Hoover sat in Korzenowski's office. It would be the last time he would ever speak to Captain Theodore "Teddy" Korzenowski.

The elder man, and his one-time friend, sat behind the desk and stroked his mustache. He still wore his overcoat, which was a light tan but had been rain-wetted to a dark brown that almost looked like leather, as he leaned back in his chair.

Hoover sat across from him, covered in dried mud and blood. His hair was finger combed back, and fresh bandages had been applied by EMTs at the scene to the cut on his forehead and the scrapes on his arm. There was no one in the homicide squad room when they got back to the police headquarters building except for the desk officer, so they left the door to Korzenowski's office open. Hoover already knew what was going to be said.

After the long silence, "John, what the fuck happened out there tonight?"

Hoover recited everything, from the minute he arrived on Purser Street until the guy jumped from the second-floor window.

"Why didn't you call it in?"

"We did call it in."

"Yeah, you did. After you were already out there. Didn't I take you off this case yesterday?"

"You didn't take me off any case," Hoover said vehemently. "You said I was going to be reassigned to a desk. Until then, I was doing the job I had originally been assigned to, which was handling this case."

Korzenowski sat up, slamming an elbow down on his desk and pointing a shaking, accusatory finger at Hoover. "Goddamn it, boy, don't try that semantic bullshit with me. I know I told you DiSilva was going to take your place, *after* you asked me who was going to step in. So I'll ask again, what the fuck were you doing out there?"

"Had a hunch on the note; I was following it up."

Korzenowski leaned back in the chair, tight lipped. "I'm not stupid. And I know you're not stupid, so get off it. We both know what you were doing out there. You wanted to grab some glory to get the whammy off you. Well, that was a bad play, and it cost Beverly her life."

You're no better than he is. Hoover smoldered, but didn't say anything, as he stared burn holes through his superior.

"You fucked up good this time. I'll do what I can for you, but that was your third strike, John. The dropped ball in the pawnshop, the reporter mess, and now, God forgive you, Beverly. You know what that means, don't you?" Hoover knew; it didn't take Abner Doubleday to know what three strikes meant. "I'll be lucky to keep my own head off the chopping block, being your superior officer and the one ultimately responsible for your actions."

Hoover said nothing.

"You've got some vacation time on the books, Hoover. Go home, and don't come back until someone from the department contacts you. Take this," Korzenowski said, and tossed a business card at him. "It's the number of a police shrink. You go see him three times a week until further notice. That is not a request."

Hoover picked up the card from the desk and tucked it in his breast pocket.

"That's it, get out of here," Korzenowski said in dismissal. "Stay away from this case, Hoover. Beverly's dead. There's nothing you can do about that. Let us take care of it from here. Keep your nose clean and ride it out as best as possible."

Hoover pushed himself out of the chair and left Korzenowski's office without looking back. He pushed through the slatted rail and headed for the elevator. He exited the building into the predawn light, taking the business card for the psychiatrist out of his pocket and crumpling it into a ball. He threw the tiny wad toward the ruined entrance of the Roundhouse. He had about as much intentions of seeing a shrink as he had in staying away from this case. He was breaking a cardinal rule and a direct order, but it hadn't been he who made this personal. He vowed to himself that he'd find a way to catch this guy—*You're no better than he is*—if it was the last thing he ever did in life.

But three days of hard drinking later, he still hadn't thought of what to do or how to catch his Dandelion. He didn't even know where to start.

He had come home Sunday morning to find his wife a tearful wreck. She had been crying and up all night worrying. He said he was sorry and went right to the cabinet above the gas range that held the liquor without embellishing.

"That's it, you're sorry?" she shouted at his back.

He pulled an eight-ounce tumbler from a cabinet next to the one that held the liquor. He poured an ounce and knocked it back.

"You ran out of here last night without even saying goodbye. You didn't tell me where you're going, and you stayed out all night. I wake up to an empty bed, and I don't think anything of it because that's how I frequently wake up—by myself. Ah, well, I think, it's just John being John. Then I turn on the goddamn TV."

He glanced at the nine-inch color television mounted under yet another cabinet, its hard plastic shell an almond shade to match the rest of the kitchen. It was on, blaring away some early-morning talk show. He hated that television. He lifted the square bottle and poured himself another drink, filling the tumbler a quarter of the way.

"The news said that a detective was killed last night in connection with the case you're working. They didn't release the name, and I had no way of knowing if it was you or not." She had begun to cry, her voice becoming almost unintelligible. "You don't answer your phone; you never call home. I sat here crying all night. I cried so hard, I woke up the kids. *Why do you always do this to me, John?"*

He drank a swallow of the bourbon. "Where're the girls now?" he asked without turning.

"Upstairs. I gave them their Easter baskets to calm them down. They fell asleep again around six." She waited to see if there was going to be more. The thin red hand swung the width of a half moon around the almond clock decorated with a hand-painted cornucopia and hung above the refrigerator. Through her teeth, Lauren said, "You son of a bitch, don't you have any remorse? Why do you always do this?"

He spun on her. "Do what, huh, do what? What do you want me to say? I already said I was sorry."

"You didn't mean it. You *never* mean it," she said, her face a twisted mask of hate. "You drag your ass in here whenever you want to and think that saying 'I'm sorry' will cover up for everything. Well, it won't anymore. You're going to have to do better than that from now on."

"Lauren, I was out doing my job."

"Your job, ha! It's always the goddamned job."

"Don't feel too bad; you aren't going to have to worry about the job much longer."

She could only shake her head at his last remark. In a way, she did feel sorry for him. She knew the pressure he'd been under lately, and was only venting her frustrations on him out of fear. The life of any law enforcement officer's spouse was a lonely one, always standing vigil, waiting for the doorbell to ring to inform you that it was your husband or your wife who had been lost last night. Feeling a little sorry for him (and a little ashamed of herself), she tried to veer the argument on to a different path. More conversationally she said, "You could've at least had the common decency to call."

"A friend of mine died last night," Hoover erupted at his wife, "and I'm partially responsible for her death. Yeah, that's right; I was right there in that house. Pardon me if I couldn't find the time to call home. 'Excuse me, Mr. Crazed, Psycho, Lunatic, Killer Asshole, but I'll be right back; I've got to go check in with my wife. Don't kill anyone while I'm gone, okay?' I'm sorry, dear, that's not the way it works! I deal with matters of life and death, while you sit here doing dishes and laundry."

Lauren was crying again. "I'm not talking about last night. I'm talking about all the nights, over all the years. All those times when you would be gone for days on end, doing Lord knows what. That's what I'm talking about. All of those years that you haven't been a father to your children, haven't been a husband to me."

"Jesus Christ, you want to do this now? You want to pick a fight, criticize my shortcomings, when I've just gotten my partner killed? While there are two other young women out there somewhere in that bastard's lair, waiting their turn to be led to the slaughter, you want to have a lover's spate? You've got some shitty timing, lady."

"I hate you."

"I hate you too," he said, and threw the glass in the sink. It shattered into a thousand pieces, and the acrid, bitter smell of alcohol permeated the air. Lauren strode out of the room, leaving behind the broken pieces of her marriage, strewn among the slivers of glass.

*   *   *

Although she couldn't stand him at the moment, there must've been some shred of 'them' left inside her, because she hadn't packed up the kids and left. Nope, she didn't do that until the following evening, when all three network news affiliates started airing the video of Beverly's murder.

Some cybergeek had decided to spend his Saturday night checking out the women of BarbeesDollHouse. He had logged on just as the Dandelion was subduing the women. Sniffing something amiss, the kid started to record the action.

There was a short vignette interview with the kid (whose name Hoover couldn't remember, even though he was one of the co-conspirators who brought an end to his marriage). The kid, the archetypal nerd, was skinny, fifteenish, and frail looking, with thick black glasses and severe acne. He sat in a studio greenroom and discussed the physics behind his technological marvel. He said things like "the house was equipped with network cameras. They transmit their information through WAN/LAN connections over the Internet. The cameras have their own individual IP addresses which allow them to generate real-time motion without having to be connected to PCs." And "they have DC-Iris lenses down to one lux, which allows them to function even in extreme low lighting levels." Once it was out on the World Wide Web, the kid was able to "download the video stream onto his motion video capture card at the rate of 3K per second." From there he saved the information as a JPEG (motion) file, transferred it to a writeable CD-ROM, and sold the exclusive rights of the video to ABC for an unspecified amount. It all sounded like gobbledygook to Hoover, but the kid seemed to know what he was talking about. And after fifteen minutes, Andy Warhol would've been proud.

Then they showed the video.

Hoover, who was sitting on one end of the couch (with the ever-present drink in his hand) while Lauren sat on the other, a wall of silence between them, leaned forward when it started to roll. Preceded by a parental advisory about the nature of the grisly footage, the video started with several edited scenes of Beverly's search through the house, then Hoover's. Despite the bragged-about DC-Iris lenses, the images were not sharp enough to make out the exact details of their faces, but Hoover and Beverly were recognizable enough. The video's longest, uninterrupted scene was in the room where Beverly had been killed, when all three actors were present. The infrared cameras had captured everything in a nonglorious, night-gray color. The three of them in the room— Hoover at the door, Beverly hanging (with her nudity blurred out by the television studio), and the Dandelion hiding behind her— seemed to be slow-motion shadow people; they were clear but indistinct. The footage even had sound, which Hoover hadn't thought possible but, on second thought, figured that there would've had to have been sound in order for the exploits of the women who lived in the house to be expressed in moans, hissy fits, and complaints.

In a jumpy imagery like that of the Zapruder film, Hoover got to relive the worst moment of his entire life—and the final moment of Beverly's—along with everybody else in America.

The length of the footage lasted a total of seven minutes—long for today's newscasts—and had been broadcast on every news station in the country. The news media, being the whores they were, bootlegged the footage from ABC's telecast and showed it on their own channels. There would be no lawsuits over copyright infringement because ABC had gotten the scoop (they had been the first to show the lamentation and the brutal slaying on their affiliate stations) and because every bootlegged copy jacked from their telecast had the alphabet network's logo displayed in the bottom right hand corner of the screen each and every time a competitor played it. There was nothing like using distress and death for advertising.

Hoover and his wife watched, stunned. He watched the face of the man standing behind Beverly. She watched her husband and the woman she had met on a few occasions.

There had been two cameras set up in the bedroom, both at opposite corners from each other. The one attached to the wall with the window was behind the action and focused on Hoover in the doorway. The second camera was to the right of Hoover, its lens trained on Beverly. The film alternately switched back and forth between the two views. Hoover didn't think the intersplicing had been done in an editing room since it lacked that seamless quality of a movie or TV show. There was no *flow* to the footage, and the elapsed time spent on each view was too short, even by the standards of the MTV generation. Each view would be shown for a nanosecond and then would flip to the other. In between, there was a slight pause in which a frame of blue screen could be seen. It gave the footage the feel of watching a film on a projector moving at too slow a speed so that the eye caught the change of each passing still. Hoover supposed that the view flipping could be credited to the people who had programmed BarbeesDollHouse website and had given their subscribers the ability to change the views at whim. Capturing unbeknownst, traditional storytelling suspense, the cybergeek who'd recorded the footage had flipped back and forth between views, waiting to see who would break first, the nut or the cop. The kid would probably win an Emmy.

All in all, the film (if information compiled on a CD-ROM in kilobytes of ones and zeros could be called a film) was both gross and engrossing. Beverly was killed on-screen—during which the back and forth flipping had ceased, and the view had been left on the camera that pointed at her. Hoover fired his weapon after the fact, and the man who had caused all the violence threw the handheld spotlight through the window and jumped after it. Hoover thought the footage would end there, but it didn't. It kept rolling as Hoover looked out into the rain after the fleeing murderer. It kept rolling as Hoover went to cut Beverly down. It kept rolling as he cradled her head in his lap. It kept rolling as he told America that he had loved Beverly Farrell.

Hoover kept watching as the talking head came back on the screen with follow-up information. His wife, however, had turned from the screen and was staring at him intently from the other end of the couch. He did not look over at his wife, but he could feel the heat of her glare.

"What you have just seen," said the precision-groomed and tanned male reporter, "was the murder of Philadelphia Police Homicide Detective Beverly Farrell. The other officer present was her partner, and former lover, Detective John Hoover. They had been working together to track down the serial killer who has been terrorizing our city for what has been determined by the coroner's office to be the past ten months. The man who leapt from the second-floor window is presumed to be the suspect in those murders."

A composite drawing of the description Hoover gave of the Dandelion was displayed on the screen. The detective thought it a near likeness.

"Seen here," the television reporter continued, "the vague description of the suspect is given as a six-foot-tall Caucasian male with brown hair and no visible tattoos or scars. He was last seen inside the house at 1278 Purser Street wearing a black T-shirt, black pants, and glasses. He is said to be driving an older-model station wagon, also black in color. If you should see anyone matching this description, please call the number on the screen. This man is considered to be armed and extremely dangerous. If you do see him, do not approach him, contact the police immediately. This man is believed to have abducted the two women seen here, Natalie Fattore and Amber Knoble. They were last seen by Detective Hoover in the rear of the station wagon with the suspect driving as it departed from behind the rear of the house next door to 1278 Purser."

The reporter, who was so perfectly sculpted that he looked fake, shuffled some papers on his desk before continuing. "In related news," he said through pearl white teeth, "this past Friday morning the same Detective John Hoover had struck a member of the media, a reporter for the *Philadelphia Inquisitor* named Nicos Agbalaya. Agbalaya had been the investigating journalist last year on the robbery/homicide case of Mr. and Mrs. Joseph Sullivan, which was handled by Detective Hoover. The outcome of that case—which had sparked racial disparage amongst the citizens of this city—against the young man believed to be one of two who broke into the Sullivans' house, killing the elderly couple, had been decided, coincidentally, on the same afternoon that Hoover struck Mr. Agbalaya. The suspect had been found not guilty by the jury on the grounds of conflicting information, which had been gathered by Detective Hoover and his then partner, Detective Rudy DiSilva. Detective Hoover . . . ."

"Is it true?" Lauren asked.

"Lauren—"

"*Is it true?*" she demanded. They had been watching the news together while the girls played in the yard, enjoying the unseasonably warm spring evening.

Hoover ran his fingers through hair that was well beyond needing a cut. There had been so many lies, and he was so low that he didn't think he'd be able to make it sound convincing even if he tried to spare her feelings. "Yes, it's true," he said in almost a whisper.

Lauren's eyes had been welling up, and now they spilled over. "Why? Why did you do it? Wasn't I good enough for you? Was I not a good wife?"

Hoover didn't like the past tense in her words. "Of course you're a good wife," he said feebly.

"Then why did you make a fool out of me?"

"I didn't make a fool out of you."

"Yes you did, John. I had to find out that you were fucking another woman at the same time that the rest of the *goddamned city did!* How is that not making a fool of me?" The tears fell freely now, and she began to repeatedly strike him about his chest and arm with her fists closed and her elbows at right angles. He balled up in the corner of the couch for protection but didn't try to make her stop or defend himself. "Ah, Christ," she said when she finished hitting him. She pushed herself off the couch with a snap and stood glaring, fists clinched at her sides.

Abruptly, Lauren turned and walked over to the sliding glass door. She heaved it open and yelled into the yard, "Come in here, girls." Leaving the door open for her daughters, she retrieved her pocketbook from the closet and took her key ring off one of the four key holder hooks attached to the bottom of the mail basket in her fucking almond kitchen.

Still sitting on the couch in the living room, Hoover asked through the doorway, "Where are you going?"

"Away," was the simple answer.

"Where? What about the kids? They have school in the morning."

"Don't you worry about them, they'll go to school. I've always managed to get them there every other day, while you were out fucking your bimbo and not caring if they went. They can count on me; I'll take care of them."

"Are you implying that I don't take care of my children?"

"I'm not implying anything; I'm fucking saying it. You were never here long enough to take care of them."

"You're a mean, rotten woman."

"Am I? I wasn't the one caught with my pants down on television. 'I love you, Beverly'—what the fuck!"

"Stop cursing like that—"

"Don't you tell me what to do! I'll curse all I want to, you dick. Fuck," she spat for measure, to prove he no longer ruled her. As of now, she was an independent woman.

"Look, I only told you about it because I didn't want to lie anymore."

"Oh, how *considerate* of you to spare my feelings." She leaned in the doorjamb much as Fiona had only four nights ago, as he sat in the same stagnant position he had then: sitting, looking, drink in hand. This was the second time since this whole mess started that his mind connected his wife with his—let's say it, folks—mistress. Lauren crossed her arms over her breast and said, "Well, take a look around you, John; it's all been a lie." She stalked over to the sliding door to see what was keeping Pammy and Janey—children move at their own speed unless you keep on top of them. She stuck her head out and yelled, "Girls, let's go. Brush off and get in here."

Hoover looked at her as she called for their children. He noticed the way she put her head outside, and how her neck was even with the heavy glass and steel of the door. For the briefest of instants, he thought about how easy it would be to go over there and pull it closed on her neck. Open and close it once or twice with some strength behind it, and it would crush her windpipe, maybe even rupture the jugular.

What's wrong with me? Did I really just imagine killing my wife, the woman I stood before God and all of our friends and families and said I would love and cherish until death did us part?

A dangerous little voice inside head answered, *You've never loved or cherished her. And check me if I'm wrong here, big guy, but the two of you are about to part, so you might as well at least get the death part right.*

Hoover was appalled by that voice, and also scared of it. If a man could entertain thoughts like that, was it not possible that he could commit the acts he imagined?

You're no better than he is.

But the thing is, he was. He was better than the monster that killed Beverly. There's a big difference between planned, precognized murder and the passion of rage Hoover just experienced when he thought about slamming the sliding door against Lauren's neck. The madman who took Beverly's life— and the life of at least ten other women—had wanted to take their lives for the thrill of it, or for whatever reasons his sick mind could justify. Hoover only had a momentary lapse of reason. Killing his wife (more likely his *ex*-wife) would've been a misstep, a hiccup, not a hateful, power-mad craving. It would've been founded in hate and executed in anger, but the difference was that the hate was directed at himself, not Lauren. He hated what he had become, and he hated what he had done to her. If he had control over it—over *himself*—then maybe his life, and that of his wife and children, could've been all it was supposed to be. But he had been unable to maintain control. He wasn't even sure there had been any control from the beginning. And now it was all spinning loose. Every aspect of his life—his career, his friends, his family— was in a whirlwind, with him at the eye of the storm.

Does killing people from the inside out—as I did to Lauren, as I'm still doing to myself—make me better than a man who kills from the outside in?

Lauren stood aside from the opening and the girls came in. They were brushing sand off themselves, heedless of the clean kitchen floor.

"Is it time to come in already?" whined the younger girl, Pam.

"Yes it is," was the motherly reply.

"But it's not even fully dark out yet," said Jane. "Why do we have to get ready for bed already?"

"You're not getting ready for bed. We're going over to your grandmother's for a while."

"Aww, I don't want to go to Grandmom's," complained Jane.

"Neither do I," said Pammy, sitting down on the floor in a protesting huff.

"Life doesn't always happen the way you want it to," Lauren said to the girls, but directed it over their heads at Hoover. "Go get your jackets."

Both blond girls shuffled over to the closet, mockingly kicking up dust with their feet as they went. They reluctantly got their jackets and shrugged them on to protect against the chill that would set in with the downing of the sun. Lauren had crossed the room and now stood at the front door. Hoover still hadn't moved off the couch.

"Give your father a hug and a kiss, you'll see him later," the woman who had kissed and held and comforted him in the past said.

Janey came first. She was almost seven years old and tall for her age; when she hugged him in his seated position, he had to straighten his back and lean upward so that her chin could go over his shoulder. He hugged her tight and could feel the reciprocating press of her small hands around his neck. "I love you, sweetie," he whispered in her ear.

"I love you too, Daddy," Janey said, deep within the safety of his embrace. She was worn out and tired from playing in the warm sun, resting her head on his shoulder.

"I'll miss you so much," he told her.

She pushed back, held him at an arm's length, and looked at him with her cute, acute eyes. "We're only going to Grandmom's, Dad," she said, but it sounded more like a question.

"I know. I'll miss you anyway." He rubbed her back, and she walked over to her mother's side.

Pammy, who hadn't reached her growth spurt yet, was his four-year-old little cherub. She walked over to the couch, climbed up his leg, and plopped herself in his lap. He smiled, but it was hard to keep the quiver from his lip.

"Dad," she said, and held up one chubby fist. He balled his free hand into a fist, and they gently bumped their knuckles together, their version of shaking hands. He kissed the top of her head and then her cheek. "Ouch, your itchies scratched me," she said, and rubbed her own cheek, "itchies" being her word for whiskers.

"I'm sorry, sweetheart. Give me a hug."

She ran her hands across his back as she did. He could smell the odors of dirt and sweat on her skin; it was the smell of a small child hard at play, and it was perfect. When they let go, Pamela Hoover looked over at her mother and sister and, holding her arms wide, said, "Family hug!"

"No, Pam, not tonight. No family hugs," Lauren said as Jane looked up at her with knowledge in her eyes. She was a smart girl, and shrewd. Whatever her apprehensions were about what was happening, she didn't voice them—she would wait until the timing was appropriate.

Pammy shrugged her shoulders at Hoover and said, "No family hug this time. Daddy, why are you crying?"

God, this was too much for him. The people that he loved the most, he had pushed away. It was all his own fault, but he didn't know how much more he could stand. "I'm crying because I love you so much. I love you all so much. And I'm going to miss you, that's all."

"Okay, Dad, I'll see you later," she said, and slid down his leg like it was a fire pole. She scampered over to her mother who now had the front door wide and ready. Janey went out first, followed by Pammy. Lauren left last, closing the door behind her without saying a word.

He drank and cried in the quite house until he was pissy drunk and passed out on the living-room couch. He woke up sometime early Tuesday and started again. He threw up near midmorning and did not go back to sleep for almost twelve hours—all of which he spent downing straight bourbon.

He slept a while on Tuesday night, then got up and, after dry swallowing an entire roll of antacid, got dressed. Today, Wednesday, had been Beverly's funeral, and he had gone. He wore dark glasses and stood alone among people he had known and called friends his entire adult life. Due to the nature of her murder, it had been a closed casket. The last time Hoover—or anyone with a television, for that matter—would see her would be in her final moments of anguish and terror, naked and bleeding to death. Hoover would never get to see her at peace.

At her graveside, he vowed again that he would not rest until the man who did this to her was caught and locked in a cage for a thousand years. Then he got in his car, drove home, and resumed drinking.

In the tempest he created of his life, he imagined himself as its eye. Now his body was so saturated with poisonous alcohol toxins that he could no longer function as a person. He had given birth to this personal, funneling storm and had even lost control of that. He was no longer at the eye of the storm but instead was being tossed around the outer arc, where the ominous gray turned to black. His thoughts were at the same time dire and pacified, a hallucinogenic quality about them.

He was caught in the centrifuge and was going down. He was tired of soul-searching and wished that someone would come along to release his weary soul from its body, so that he could finally be free of this hell of his own making.

And then the priest knocked on the door.

3

*W*hat would you do if you had a really big secret (a secret so big that it has—and might again—cost people their lives), and you had obtained that information in an illegal manner?

Darren Roberts didn't know what to do, either.

It was the second morning after his horrendous discovery, and he was scared on so many levels. Primarily, he was frightened to lose his job. A newspaper delivery job doesn't seem like much, but it's the only job in which he seemed to thrive, the only job that he had ever liked. There was no heavy lifting, no time clock, no forced overtime, no people to have to deal with. Plus, there were his secret studies to consider, conducted through unsolicited windows, one of which had gotten him in the hot water that was now scalding him. What other job could provide all those qualities?

Darren had screwed up big time on the morning he witnessed two women being murdered—he had neglected to deliver 186 Sunday papers. He couldn't even remember not doing his job and didn't realize that he hadn't finished his work until the next morning, when he saw the papers with yesterday's news still sitting in the car. Something had come over him, and he knew exactly what it had been—the black wing of the angle of death. She was a mean old crone, and he had been held under her spell that morning. He still didn't feel a hundred percent. Maybe there was some vestige of her touch left behind, burned on to his soul; maybe it would be there forever. One can't possibly stare into the heart of evil and not be changed.

After he had seen what he had seen, he got back into Momma's car and drove home. He had been confused, dizzy, nauseous, and fatigued even though he hadn't worked a full day. He went home and climbed into bed and, with his thumb in his mouth (something he hadn't done since he was fifteen), slept until the alarm woke him to deliver Monday's papers.

His mother would be infuriated if he lost his job, since it paid the mortgage on the house she owned. The deal was Darren could live with her for as long as he wanted—as long as he maintained a job and paid half the bills. Gloria Roberts thought this as fair a trade as there could be, seeing that he used up half their resources himself. She paid all the utilities and the insurance policies and bought the food from the supermarket; he paid the mortgage. Even-steven. Even Darren would agree. He had no problem keeping up his share, because he made enough money to cover the note and still had enough left over for the things he wanted, like porn movies for his DVD player, top of the line, high-tech binoculars, and black licorice. Yeah, licorice; what could he say, he loved that shit. He got his money from the *Inquisitor* once a month, around the seventh, and the mortgage was due before the fifteenth. It all worked out perfectly.

Until he lost his job. Then the whole system would get fucked, and his mother would be riding his ass every spare minute of every day. That frightened Darren very much—no one could berate like Gloria Roberts could. She was so good at it that when he showed up at the warehouse to pick up his papers yesterday, and his manager who hadn't said more than hello to him in five years had been waiting for him, he had been frightened enough to lapse into a choking fit.

When he saw his manager standing next to the clip with his route number written above it on one of the narrow strips of wood that held all of the carrier's clips onto the cinder block wall, he felt his airways tighten up. He tried to suck fresh oxygen into his lungs in big gulps, but it wasn't able to squeeze through the pinprick opening his esophagus had become two steps back. With no air getting through, he started choking. It did not start out as one or two coughs and progress; it went straight to violent hacking. He doubled over, putting hands on knees for support as his neck and face became scarlet from the bout and the oxygen deprivation. Darren didn't know what an aspirator was because he had never heard of the affliction called asthma, but he sure could've used one right then. All the other people in the warehouse (doing their best zombie impressions in the pre-predawn hour) stopped what they were doing to look at him. He could feel their stares, and it didn't help the situation one bit. He went right on coughing until he was down on one knee and a glob of phlegm with a chaser of blood glistened on the greasy slab floor in front of him.

"Darren? Darren, what's wrong?" a man's voice asked him, the flat of a palm slapping him on the back. The air started to flow, and he could think again. For a minute there, the world had gone black, and white spots burst before his eyes. Still in the position of a knight before his king, Darren took deep breaths that went all the way down into the villi of his lungs. The air tasted of newsprint and moldy paper, and it had never tasted fresher to Darren in his whole life.

Although he was breathing again, the hand was still thumping his back. *Who came up with that one? What was the medical theory behind repeatedly striking someone on the back while they were choking? How's that supposed to help air travel to the lungs?*

"Stop hitting me, I'm okay," Darren said in a hoarse voice. Mercifully, he got his wish. People never noticed things they took for granted until they were taken away from them. Being able to breathe again was about the best thing in the world. For a person who just survived suffocation, there was no other problem that couldn't be solved.

The man who'd been striking him on the back was his manager.

"Darren, what's wrong? Are you sick?" the man asked him, unknowingly providing Darren with the excuse he'd been looking for.

Through a scratchy throat, Darren croaked, "Yes, I am. I'm sick."

"What's wrong with you?" His manager was lanky and tall, at around six and a half feet, and always wore a frown on his face. He was a serious man who had nothing to talk about, much less smile about. He always wore a dress shirt without a tie, even though the other four managers dressed casually. He wore his straight, salt-and-pepper hair parted to the right. He was a chain smoker who was currently blowing the smoke of the perpetual cigarette cocked in the corner of his mouth right in Darren's face, regardless of any breathing problem.

"I have no idea what's wrong with me. I just suddenly started coughing."

"Were you sick yesterday? Is that why you didn't deliver your route?"

"Yes, sir, that's what happened. I delivered half the papers, and then got sick and had to go home. I didn't have enough energy to finish the route."

"Why didn't you call? You should've called me. I would've come out and helped you finish it off."

"I couldn't call. I went home and lay down on the bed and, like, blacked out." That part was all truth.

"That's why nobody answered the phone when *I* called *you*," he told Darren, like he was a third party listening to the story rather than a participant.

"Yes, sir, that's how it happened, I guess. I can't really remember too much. I was so out of it, couldn't think straight." All also true.

"All right, all right. How're you doing today? Are you able to go out?"

"Yeah, I'll be fine."

"Are you sure? Tell me if your not, because if you lose it out there today, and are unable to do your job, I'm going to have to fire you."

"Fire me?" he squeaked. "I've never missed a day in all the years I've worked here."

"I know you haven't, but it's not about what I think about you or your ethics; it's about the numbers. As an independent service contractor working for the *Philadelphia Inquisitor*, you signed a contract in which you agreed that you would not exceed a certain number of complaints from the customers. Don't you remember?" He pulled a pack of smokes from the breast pocket of his dress shirt and lit one off the butt of its predecessor. Once it was rolling, he cocked it in the crook of his mouth and tossed the finished one on the warehouse floor. He used the sole of his maroon (no kidding) plastic penny loafer with tassel to crush it out. He left the flattened remains of the cigarette lying where it dropped. Looking around the warehouse, he wasn't the only one who practiced this habit.

"Yes, sir, I remember." The contract the *Inquisitor* required all of its home delivery carriers to sign stated, among other trite and unfair labor practices, that a carrier could not generate complaints higher than three calls per each one thousand newspapers delivered every month. If a carrier had more complaints than the amount specified in the contract, he or she would be dismissed.

"You were *way* out of the range factor with the complaints yesterday, Darren. Take a look," the manager said, pulling the sheets of papers hanging under his route number from the clasp holding them to the strip of wood. Normally, there was only a single sheet of paper waiting for Darren each morning. One was usually enough to cover the amount of his daily draw of newspapers, and any new starts or subscriptions stopped for vacations or otherwise, as well as the odd complaint here and there. What the manager handed to him this morning was a *sheaf* of papers, the density of which was thick enough to be a decent magazine.

Darren flipped through the pages of NDT (not delivered today) complaints. He had slept for twenty hours, almost a full day, after witnessing the murders and, looking at the papers in his hand, still felt tired. He felt as if he were going to be sick for real. "Oh man," he said.

"'Oh man' is right, Darren." His manager always called him Darren, as if they were friendly enough to be on a first-name basis— or as if Darren's place on the career ladder of the world wasn't worthy of calling him Mr. Roberts. "You sure you're all right to go out there? You look a little green around the gills."

"I'll be fine," he said, but didn't add *until I get home and tell Momma about this.*

"I'm not reassured by looking at you, but I'll trust your track record. This is the only time you've ever screwed up. I don't know what happened to you out there, but remember that you can call me for anything, understand? I mean that—anything at all." He had been pointing at him with the two fingers holding the current cigarette in them. With each movement of his hand, the smoke did a layering, smoldering dance into the air. Darren found the intoxicating plume of smoke hypnotic; for some reason, it reminded him of Zuni Indians dancing around a campfire, chanting.

Darren opened his mouth and almost told the manager (whose name was Gary something) what he had seen yesterday.

What, are you crazy? his mind screamed at him. *You know how upset Momma would be if you lost your job?*

The addendum to the rules of living with his mother had been that if he failed to maintain his half, he would have to leave. The long and short of it is if he dumped the job, he'd be homeless.

And that was just the Gloria issue. What if the cops got involved? If he told Gary (or was it Harry?) why he hadn't delivered those papers, and the guy went to the authorities, he might not only lose his job, he might go to jail for something like invasion of privacy or withholding evidence. Theoretically, he could even be held as an accomplice. Had he not been there while both those women were still alive? Did he not anticipate every cut the killer made? Had he not watched every unbearable second as the blood drained out of them? Yes, yes, and yes, Your Honor. And just like that, three life sentences without black licorice or pornography, and only thieves, rapists, and murderers for company.

Un-uh, no way, not him. He wouldn't tell anyone about this unfortunate incident for the rest of his entire life.

"I'm trusting you, Darren," his manager said, clasping him on the back with one nicotine-stained hand. The manager walked off, and Darren went to a skid to pick up his bundles.

Back out on the road he was moving along fine, resigned that his secret was safe with him, until he had to turn down the street where he'd seen the murders. He hadn't even thought about the gruesome acts a second time since leaving the warehouse until he came upon the bend in the road that would lead right past the house of horrors. As he angled the car around the curve, his body started trembling, his skin cold and clammy. He'd been driving at a crawl which became a complete stop once the house came into view.

It looked like every other house on the block. There was nothing to behold on the exterior that might indicate what had happened on the inside. It was only a brick-faced duplex in the middle of a long row of other brick-faced duplexes. There were no ravens or gargoyles perched on the roof, no blood oozing from the mortar. But for Darren, the stigma was as bright as a neon sign, and it paralyzed him, his fright of driving past that house such that his muscles locked and he couldn't will his body to move.

What if the guy in the house saw me that night? What if he knows who I am and is only waiting until I come back to deliver papers today to get me?

Stop it. You're being paranoid!

But was he? The man had looked out the window barely an inch away from where Darren had been cowering. *What was he looking for? How could he have not known I was there?*

Darren sat in the car two-tenths of a mile away from the house and had a panic attack. He alternately felt as if he was going to suffocate, black out, urinate in his pants, or have a heart attack. His body convulsed, and he became feverish with claustrophobia at being locked tightly in the confines of the car.

Ten minutes later, it had all passed, and he was just a man sitting in a car. Although he was as close to what passed for normal for Darren Roberts, he still wasn't any closer to being able to have his brain command his body to drive down the street. Using the back of his hand to wipe his dry lips, he caught a glint of streetlight reflected off the binoculars, lying unnoticed on the seat beside him where he had left them yesterday as he hightailed it out of this neighborhood.

With the deftness a longtime musician had for the chords of his guitar, he picked up the binoculars and immediately began focusing the lenses for the correct depth perception as he trained them on the structure that frightened him. He thoroughly scanned the entire house—windows, door, roof, bricks—but did not see anything he hadn't been able to see with his naked eye. Despite its interior history, it still only looked like an ordinary house in an ordinary neighborhood.

Frustrated and defeated at not being able to pin his fears to something tangible the whole world could see, he tossed the glasses back onto the seat. *What if I imagined the whole thing? What if I had really been in bed sick, with some kind of malaria or something, and had fever-dreamed the whole thing?*

There were almost two hundred Sunday papers shoved in the trunk that disproved that theory. He had been awake, and he had been at the window of that house. And he had witnessed murder. The certainty of it was inarguable, but that only lent credence to the fact that he was too scared to drive down the street.

He had to calm himself down to think about it rationally. What was he going to do, never deliver newspapers on this street again? He wouldn't have to worry about keeping his job then because he would be fired tomorrow or the next day at the latest. And we all know what that would mean.

No, he had to get over this stage fright, and he had to get over it right now.

He looked around the street, looked at all the dark houses. There wasn't a person in sight. Yesterday at this time, that was precisely the way he wanted it. Today, he wished the whole block teemed with activity. How much difference a day made. To his dismay, there wasn't a soul in sight. At this early-morning hour, the street seemed desolate, dead to the world that spun on around it. To Darren, it was a frightening and lonely place to be.

Holding his breath, he eased his foot off the brake pedal. The car crept down the street with each passing house bringing him closer to the one place in the world he didn't want to be a million miles from. Somehow in his fright he even managed to throw his papers out of the car and to the correct homes awaiting delivery.

When he was only one house up from the house of murder, fear overtook him. His fright was so thick in his mouth that he tasted bile on his tongue. He lost sense of what he was doing, his foot stammering between brake pedal and accelerator. The car had been moving slowly enough that when he briefly touched the brake it came to a complete stop . . . directly in front of the house.

Darren let out a scream and squeezed his eyes shut. He stomped on the gas, causing the car to lurch forward. Gloria's car had a lot of free play in the steering wheel, and Darren was shimming it to the left and to the right, trying to drive in a straight line with his eyes closed.

There was a thump and the sound of metal scraping as the car came to another stop, this time with the passenger side elevated off the ground. Darren opened his eyes, and the first thing he did— even before checking to see what he hit—was look back to see where the house was. Without benefit of sight, he had traveled a total of five houses down the block. In his estimation, he was out of harm's way. By no means safe, but far enough away that he should be able to react to any advances made by the lunatic that had killed those girls. Somehow, just having the physicality of the house behind him— in the past, if only for the rest of the day—relaxed him.

Satisfied with what was behind him, he turned to check on the damage in front. As far as he could tell, there was none. By some miracle, he had piloted the car between two other parked cars and had bumped the front tire up an inclined curb at the base of a driveway. No harm, no foul.

He put the car in reverse and backed up (a foot and no more), put it in drive, and went about delivering the rest of the morning papers.

That had all happened yesterday. Today, the same thing had been repeated with almost comical precision. The only difference had been the outcome—there was now a dent in the fender from where he hit a line of trash cans as he swerved down the street with his eyes closed. The thunderous crash, followed by the now-empty tin trash can warbling down the street, had scared him almost as much as driving past the house had. A dent could be overlooked, but what if he hit a car tomorrow? His mother certainly wouldn't be happy about that.

Things couldn't go on the way they were. What could he do? Ask to change to a different route? No, his manager would want to know why, and he was already under the looking glass; he could ill afford to rock the boat right now.

He had to think of something. And just as he was thinking that he had to think of something, he thought of something. Actually, he drove past something—a building—that he had driven past a thousand times before but hadn't given any thought to, had never even really noticed before. It had always been there, and he kind of knew it on a subconscious level, but it had been in the backdrop, like the trees or the telephone poles, things people see every day and never really see.

The front of the building looked so inviting and comforting and majestic that he knew he would find his answer inside. What better place could there be to find haven?

But it had been too early to go in when he first spied the building, so he finished the morning's papers off, then drove over to Dunkin' Donuts and bought a bagel sandwich. Along with black licorice, he had an undeniable hankering for those damn bagels.

He parked across the street from the building, picking a good vantage point of the door in which to wait. As he ate, he saw a man come out of the building. Darren wondered how the man had gotten past him and inside. Maybe he slept there. The man gave no indication as he stretched his arms wide and took a deep inhale of the morning air. He bent to pull up on the bottom spike holding the second of the two double doors secured then gave a little push to make sure it would swing freely for all those who would cross the threshold seeking solace. Satisfied, he disappeared back inside to start his day.

Darren crumpled the waxy paper the bagel had come in and dropped it out the window. Wiping away a gob of egg on his lip with the sleeve of his spring jacket, he got out of the car and crossed the street. When he stood in front of the building, he stared up at its splendor. It had spires and colored glass and was constructed out of some type of gray stone that looked like marble. Darren couldn't fathom the cost of building an entire edifice from marble. Whatever the stone was it certainly made the building it housed look divine.

There were three very long, but not steep, steps, which led up to a landing. The gait of a normal man could span all three in a single bound, but Darren mounted them one at a time (counting them as he went, naturally), the small, shuffling steps feeling awkward. He didn't know why he touched each step as he did, but it felt right to do so; he was in awe of the place.

The doors did not have knobs but rather long ornate handles that were plated in brass and stretched vertically, the tops and bottoms ending in decorative points resembling acorns being peeled like bananas; the center of each handle had a swirled pattern that was almost worn off by the many hands that had taken hold of it.

Darren reached out and grasped one of the handles himself. He pulled, and the heavy-looking wooden door swung open easier than he thought it would have. An aroma of burning candles and incense wafted out and washed over him. It was the smell of safety. Inside this building was the peace he was intending to find; he was sure of it.

4

The silence was what he loved the most about the dim coolness of the church, a silence only present in the early morning hours, before the first of the congregation started to arrive. It was that silence that drove him to leave the cozy, warm softness of his bed at the unspeakable hour of quarter to four to bask in its unadorned perfection alone. He found the quietness comforting and humbling—nothing could show the humility of man like the empty stillness under the direct eye of God.

Father Thomas O'Malley will have been a priest at St. Tiburtius Church for a full decade one week from tomorrow. Over that time, he'd been the priest who served the 6 a.m. weekday mass more often than not. He did so because that was the way he liked it, and nobody was going to argue over it. There were six priests in all at St. Tiburtius, three others like himself, the pastor—Father Anthony—and an assistant pastor, all six of who were supposed to rotate the duties of the early mass, but over the years, O'Malley had volunteered for it so often that the others just assumed he wanted to keep it that way. The 6 a.m. weekdays slot on the schedule posted on the refrigerator in the sacristy (and also in Mrs. Keener's office at the rectory) was always left blank, in deference to Father O'Malley's preference. The only time a name was penciled in was if Father O'Malley needed some time off, which was hardly ever. The other priests believed him to be an early riser who liked to start his day off in the grace of his religion. They couldn't have been more wrong.

In his forty-four years of living, getting out of bed was the singular hardest thing he ever had to accomplish, and it was a task he had to master every day of his life. For Father O'Malley, nothing in this world understood him more than his bed. And he loved it back just as much. Sleeping for others was a requirement; for him it was a hobby, a passion—lying in bed was like walking in the clouds; in the depths of slumber, every burden of life was lifted off the soul. Dreaming, you were free to be anyone, to do anything, go anywhere; you were weightless. There was no answering or second-guessing; fears were as real as pleasures.

In his single room at the rectory where all six members of the St. Tiburtius staff lived, he had a king-sized bed. His room consisted of one bureau with a television seated on top, one closet, and the enormous bed. It took up an entire side of the room, the bed being the only "possession" he owned in this existence.

Father O'Malley loved to sleep.

No matter what, it was the one thing anybody could look forward to every day. No matter how shitty your day had been, your bed was there, waiting for you when it was over. It didn't pass judgment, didn't care if you smelled; it didn't care if you drank, smoked or swore. Break someone's heart, lie, cheat or steal—it didn't care. It only asked of you to lie down and let go. Your bed accepted you as you were, not as you should be.

For all these reasons, Father O'Malley forced himself to be an early riser.

As a Roman Catholic, he considered sacrifice the one adamant of his faith most vital. Sacrificing was the only thing one could truly give of oneself. The very essence of sacrifice was to give of something you were hard pressed to—or didn't want to—give. Jesus made the ultimate sacrifice when he died for man's sins. And it was through Christ's sacrifice that O'Malley's religion proclaimed any of us were able to obtain eternal salvation. Father O'Malley didn't think himself of the same caliber as Christ, but he made sure he did his part every day, in his own way. Every morning, even before he was fully alive again from the tiny death of sleep, the first thing he did was make a sacrifice for his faith and the church—he got out of bed.

That might not sound like a lot, but for a man who didn't watch TV other than the news, didn't go to movies or read novels, didn't drink alcohol or play bingo, and had abstained from the human crutches of wealth and sex for the greater glory of others, to give of the one pleasure that he's allotted every day was commendable. At least in his own eyes.

Even if the Lenten season had just come to an end this past Sunday, sacrifice wasn't something O'Malley believed should be done at specified times of the year; it was something to be done in every day life. Sacrifice was what it was all about.

Then, too, there was the silence.

It drew him like the moth to the flame to hear the creaking of the timber in the rafters over his head, to hear the clicking of his polished shoes on the waxed tiles of the aisles, to hear the rustling of the mice. Yes, even the house of the Lord was susceptible to vermin.

After he got out of bed, showered, and shaved, he headed directly to the church. He drove one of the rectory cars, parking it in the rear lot usually around four-thirty, depending on the weather. From four-thirty to five-thirty (when he had to unlock the vestibule doors for the public to begin coming in to celebrate daily mass), the church was his. He walked around, taking everything in: the rows and rows of empty brown wooden pews below the sexpartite vaults of the groined ceiling; the comforting purples of the now-ending Easter season; the Stations of the Cross lining the walls between pillars in bas-relief, telling the story of Jesus's sacrifice one still frame at a time; the flickering of the plastic candles with their light-bulb flames lit in prayer for a donation; the way the dimmed lights reflected off the statues of Mary and Joseph standing beneath the larger, central statue of the cruciform Christ, giving the holy family shadowed, unsure faces; the altar standing asea in royal blue carpeting; the tabernacle that—behind velvety drapes— held the wafers representing the body of Christ, a host of unleavened bread made without yeast so that it would *not* rise, the paradoxical symbol for the body of a man who died only to rise again three days later—the centerpiece of the Catholic Church and its mass.

The church itself was resplendent and reverent. It could also be oppressive and suffocating at times. Always, though, it was inviting. The poor in spirit, the sorrowing, the lowly, those who hunger and thirst for holiness, the merciful, the peacemakers, and those persecuted for holiness' sake were all welcomed. As were those who strayed from the light and walked hand in hand with the serpent.

"Hello," a voice rang out, breaking the stillness and finding Father O'Malley halfway down the center aisle of the Church of St. Tiburtius.

A little frightened (and a *lot* perturbed by the distraction from his morning's ritual reprieve), Father O'Malley turned around. Standing before him was a man O'Malley guessed was homeless. Tall and husky, he wore a cheap-looking blue windbreaker that seemed to be made of plastic. Besides the jacket, he had on a black pocket-T that was ripped almost to tatters and so faded it was nearly brown, an old pair of blue jeans worn threadbare along the thighs, and a pair of high-topped sneakers that had started to rot from constantly being wetted. His head of medium-length, stingy, greasy hair was being controlled by a baseball cap that might've been white at one time but was now caked with enough dirt that it was almost black. Stenciled across the front of the cap was the trademark of a local newspaper, the *Philadelphia Inquisitor.*

"May I help you?" Father O'Malley asked. He hadn't gotten to the part of his morning ritual in which he put on his vestments, so he was still dressed in the matching black shirt and pants with accompanying sport coat to keep the predawn chill off. O'Malley pushed back the flaps of his coat and slid his hands in his pockets. He did not approach the man, not out of disrespect or neglect of his duties as a priest for the people, but because of the man's derelict appearance, combined with the fact that the two of them were the only ones in the church. Hallowed ground or not, this *was* a large metropolitan, and crime *was* running rampant.

"Are you the priest here?" the man asked.

"Yes, I am. I'm Father O'Malley. Are you here for the six o'clock mass?"

"Ah, no." There seemed to be more, but the man was hesitant in saying it. With each passing second, the man seemed to be less of a threat and more of a burden that would have to be taken care of before the regular crowd did begin to file in for mass, which would be any minute now.

Father O'Malley took a step toward him, "Is there something I can do for you?"

"I hope so," the derelict-looking man said, glancing over his shoulder. "Is there somewhere we can go to talk? How about in there?" He had indicated one of the three confessionals recessed into the wall on the far side of the door.

"In the confessional?"

The man had no idea what a confessional was, but said, "Yeah, in the confessional."

His suspicion rising again, O'Malley said, "Anything you need to talk about, we can talk about out here."

"I'm afraid I can't, Father. Not in public."

"Why not? Did you do something wrong, son?"

"Ah, no, but kind of."

No, but kind of? Oh boy, what have I just gotten involved in?

The door behind the derelict opened, and the strengthening sunlight shone in behind him. It was Old Man Johnson, as the altar boys referred to him, taking his frail old-man steps into the church as he did every morning.

"Morning, Father," he called as if he didn't see the man in the dirty clothes peeping at him.

"Morning, Mr. Johnson," O'Malley replied.

The elderly man slowly made his way to the side of the pews near the wall, as he was wont to do. He came to a stop under the Station of the Cross depicting Veronica wiping the face of Jesus. He genuflected and slid along the bench made shiny by many years of polyester—and cotton-encased rears, the eyes of the man in the dirty clothes sliding along with him until he was situated in the middle and seated.

"Step over here a minute," Father O'Malley said, and the enigmatic man followed. When they were standing in an apse at the back of the church near the light-bulb prayer candles encased in red glass cylinders, the priest said, "Tell me, what's the matter?"

The man had removed his hat and stood wringing it in his hands. His hair was an uncombed tangle of cowlicks. "I can't tell you out here, Father. I'm worried that someone else will hear it," he said with the tone of a CIA conspirator. As if on cue, the door opened, and a woman whom O'Malley had never seen before entered. She looked right at them and then went to find a seat.

"All right, if it's that important to you, stay for the mass, and we'll go into the confessional afterward." *Why am I patronizing this man who is clearly a nutcase?*

"Thank you, Father," the man said, the flickering of the clear bulbs through the red cylinders along with the pointed tufts of his hair giving him a devilish appearance. The whole idea of a hushed conversation at the rear corner of the church, among the dancing candle "flames," seemed gothic and medieval to the priest. It made him feel like a priest of old, participating in the Crusades or the Inquisition. He shivered.

"Go have a seat. I have to get ready for mass," he told the man, who nodded and immediately sat down at the end of the last pew.

Father O'Malley presided over the mass, but it had been a halfhearted effort—or rather, a half-haunted one. He couldn't keep his eyes or mind off the man who wanted to meet with him alone in a confessional, a man who had done something wrong, but only kind of. O'Malley was hitting all the marks, but he was doing so from memory. Celebrating mass was always something that he enjoyed and, on the rare occasion, relished. Even though he had said thousands of masses over the years since his training at the seminary, he had never found himself bored with it. To him, mass never seemed scripted, even though it was. It had its specific parts in which specific things were said; the same actions were taken and the same words spoken, the only flexible moments coming during the homily. The homily was a chance for the Catholic priest saying the mass to break from typecast and give a personal sermon, in his own words, based on a subject that had been preselected by an advent calendar created at the beginning of the faith and written down in missals.

Father O'Malley usually gave, in his humble opinion, a good homily. He tried to keep his messages upbeat and succinct. Some of his windbag peers have been known to go on tangents, browbeating the congregation. That was something he never did. The God of Christianity was a deity who made you remorseful over your own guilt; he didn't need mortal representatives to do that. That's how he was able to be a forgiving God—guilt was the key. Only through the guilt of the soul could a person be truly sorry for his or her actions. God's grace was the forgiveness of that guilt. O'Malley liked his homilies to be more free-flowing instead of anchoring. He liked it that way because the Catholic God was also a God of choice. It had been so all the way back to Eden, and that was something O'Malley's contemporaries tended to forget.

Today's homily didn't flow at all. It clunked. It fell out of his mouth dead, aborted before it was spoken. It was short, and he struggled to get through it, stringing one word after another in a poetry of gibberish. Even he couldn't follow what he was saying, so he was sure the gathered—all seven of them, including the man waiting to confide in him—didn't have a clue, either. He was distracted, and it was the first time in a long time that he felt he had laid down on the job. He was human and his guilt was heavy.

Father O'Malley hung his head. It was as if the devil himself were smiling on this celebration, but he trudged on, as he was taught.

A few minutes later, he placed the chalice now containing the blood of Christ on the altar and genuflected before it. When he stood up, he was looking directly into the eyes of the odd man who'd requested to see him privately. While everyone else in the church was kneeling in reverence, this man was not. He was seated with his hands in his lap. It was apparent that he didn't put much stock in the service or the flock he was a part of, even if it were only for one mass. Father O'Malley, the only other person not on his knees, couldn't break his gaze away from the man. The priest felt a weird connection with the individual. While the rest of the sheep were bowing in the faith they had been raised into by others (and therefore programmed), O'Malley and this stranger were not.

Who is this man that has been sent before me? Father O'Malley questioned. *What trials does he bring with him that are surely going to be deposited at my feet? And will I be strong enough in faith to weather the coming storm, for that is surely what this man gathers?*

With his curiosity flaring, Father O'Malley rushed through the rest of the mass.

* * *

The silence had returned to the church.

O'Malley had taken off his vestments (purple to match those of the altar) and hung them in the metal locker that acted as his closet here at the church, his mind wandering. He was walking around the sacristy as if in a daze, his thoughts far away and worried. He was conflicted within himself. He wanted to hurry to the impromptu meeting, but he also wanted to drag his feet in the hopes that the man would disappear just as he had appeared—unexpectedly.

Dressed again in the black dress shirt and black trousers, the dry cleaning crease running sharply down the length of his leg, he exited the sacristy through the rear door. He walked in the sunlight along the side of the church before reentering through the main entrance behind the man sitting, waiting in the pew.

"Sir," he said, just as he touched the man on the shoulder. The man gave a start at being snuck up on. It was not without delight to Father O'Malley to cause such an emotion, the priest's actions having been done specifically to make sure the stranger did not think he was going into the forced meeting holding the upper hand. O'Malley preferred the meeting to be approached on even footing. Sneaking up on someone was a small, trite trick, but it had disoriented the man ever so slightly, and was therefore a success. "Are you ready?" the priest asked.

"Um, I think so."

"Do you want a confessional with a partition, or face to face?"

"What's the partition for?"

"Some people don't like the priest to see who they are. Even though he's acting in God's accord, they fear that the priest—through his human nature—will pass judgment on them personally, if he knows who they are. In those cases, we—the priest and the confessor—sit in two separate booths during the confession."

"How can you hear each other through the wall?" the man asked, scratching at the whiskers sprouting on his jaw line.

"There's a little window with a screen in the partition. We converse through that." At the mention of the window, the man started to vehemently shake his head, as if he wanted nothing whatsoever to do with that option.

"No windows. Face to face will be fine," he said, looking over his shoulder to see if anyone was watching them. No one was; they had the church to themselves.

"All right then. Come on over here and we'll go in." The man slid out of the pew, and Father O'Malley ushered him toward a door with a tiny cross-shaped light over it. The cross had been dark, but when the priest opened the door, it lit up red, indicating that this particular confessional was now in use. The light would go out again the next time the door was opened for the priest and the absolved sinner to emerge.

The inside of the confessional was larger than the door indicated. It was a room five feet deep and seven long, carpeted and made cozy by low-level lighting to better put the penitent at ease. There were two large chairs inside. Only the face-to-face confessional had both chairs; the others contained a chair for the priest and a kneeler for the confessor. The chairs were made from a fine, sturdy oak and shellacked with a sealant that gave them a shiny veneer. On the seats were maroon velvet cushions. The backrests had the same shape of the cross cut into them as the one over the door. Other than the cutout, they were simple chairs that a weekend hobbyist could assemble from two-by-fours in his basement shop.

Since there was only one door into and out of the confessional, the priest always sat in the chair farthest in, so that each successive confessor didn't have to climb over him to get to the hot seat. Father O'Malley went in first and took his station in that chair. The man followed behind and sat opposite him, no less than two feet away.

In such close quarters, O'Malley expected to be overcome with the stench emanating from the man, but strangely, there didn't seem to be one. If he were homeless, it was possible that he had taken a shower at one of the shelters before once again donning his only set of clothes. As the minutes wore on, O'Malley wasn't as sure as he had been before about this man's class status. Other than his clothes, he didn't seem to exhibit any of the characteristics of a street person; there were no wild-eyed stares, no blank spots in his actions, no slurring of speech so common in lushes who drank two-dollar bottles of wine by the gallon; none of that, only the oddity of the situation and his clothes.

"How do we start?" the man asked sincerely.

"Is this a confession?"

"I'm not religious. I don't know exactly what a confession is."

"Confessions are very private conversations in which people tell priests of the things they've done wrongly. They confess their sins. They do so in the belief that the priest is acting as a conduit to God, so that their sins may be forgiven by him. It's one of the seven sacraments of the Catholic Church. Another is the Holy Eucharist, which you've just seen me perform when I gave each of the people at the mass a wafer from the ciborium. There are many steps to go through to receive each sacrament. In your case, a nondevotee, we'll waive them at this time as they relate to confessions. Do you understand what I've just said?" *Why do I sound like a cop ready to beat a confession out of someone rather than a compassionate priest?*

"Yeah, I understand."

"Then is this a confession?"

"Uh, yeah."

"Okay, then you begin by saying 'Forgive me Father, for I have sinned.'"

"Forgive me Father, for I have sinned," the man parroted, then stopped. "What comes next?"

"There are a couple more lines that are said, but are of little consequence here. Why don't you tell me what it is that's bothering you?"

"I don't know where to start. I'm scared."

"What's your name, son?" Father O'Malley asked.

"Darren. Darren Roberts."

"All right, Darren, what's with the clothes?"

"Oh, these? I just got off work. I deliver newspapers, and the ink gets all over my clothes, staining them."

"I see. Did what you want to tell me happen while you were delivering your papers?"

"Yes, but not today."

"When?"

"Two days ago."

"Sunday morning?"

"Yeah."

"What happened Sunday morning?"

"I helped kill two women."

All of a sudden, the soft inviting comforts of the confessional felt like the soft inviting comforts of the inner linings of a coffin. Father O'Malley had been slouching as he hand-held Darren through the beginnings of the confessional procedure. Now he sat bolt upright and wondered how he'd be able to get out of the corner he literally backed himself into if this man—a self-proclaimed murderer— went berserk.

"You killed people? You committed murder?"

"I didn't kill them, someone else did. I helped do it."

"Why did you help do something so reprehensible? What'd you do, hold them down?" The accusatory tone was back in his voice, and this time it had merit.

"No, there was no direct involvement, but I didn't stop it, either. They were still alive when I got there, and I knew it. But I didn't do anything about it. I couldn't *not* watch what he was doing to them, Father. I *wanted* to see them die. I couldn't help myself."

"Slow down. Go back to the beginning, Darren. Tell me what it was you saw . . . No, tell me everything you did from the moment you woke up to do the papers on Sunday."

He did. It took an hour, but he told the priest everything. And it changed both their lives forever.

Darren walked out of St. Tiburtius and into the midmorning sun a relieved man. In his twenty-nine years he had never been inside a church before, but he thought there was something to be said for confession. When he left the booth, it was as if he left his problems behind simply by talking about them with the priest. He felt like a weight had been removed from him, allowing him to breath freely again. His spirits were lifted. It was nice to know that there was a higher being out there that was stronger than man and his human weaknesses, a being that would look after you in times of need and times of doubt. On the day that Michael Dedaker's fate was sealed, Darren Roberts found what he had long been missing—a father figure. He had found God.

Once he accepted him into his life, there was no obstacle that Darren could not overcome. The drives down the street where he had witnessed—and maybe participated in—murder were no longer a worry for him. He didn't even give the duplex a passing glance as he went by on a daily basis, and hadn't noticed that the front window of the house—the very window in which he had seen Amber Knoble and Natalie Fattore die—had been shattered outward sometime on Thursday night.

Since that day in St. Tiburtius Church, Darren Roberts slept like a babe. He lost weight, got his GED, and became a Catholic. Along with delivering the *Inquisitor*, he now worked at a church in his neighborhood, attended every mass on Sundays, and had been ordained as a layperson administrator of communion. He still lives with his mother, but their relationship has changed too, become more equal footed.

It wasn't that Darren forgot what he'd been a part of; it was that he accepted it. He knew that he was meant to see what he had seen. God had wanted it that way. By witnessing the butchering (and that was what it was; they had been hung like meat and sliced up) of those two women, he now knew there was a God. Before the incident, he hadn't. Hadn't known that there was a God, hadn't known that there wasn't. Darren had never been taught anything about Him, and hadn't cared to learn. Since then, his eyes have been opened.

He understood that what he had been a part of was wrong to the furthest extreme of the word, that it was despicable. But having God in your heart was like walking with a safety net beneath your every step. Darren truly believed that the forfeiture of those two women's lives had saved his eternal soul.

His rational for being able to find optimism in murder was that he was a better man for it, because he could now prove the existence of God. He believes so because only after you witness the very heart of evil can you obtain the ability to comprehend his existence.

Darren, who had essentially no life before he met death, was now a very busy man. Between working two jobs (the second being with his mother at the diner) and spending all his free time involved in extracurricular activities at the church, as well as the normal maintenance of living such as paying bills, upkeeping the house, and taking care of the cars (there were two of them now, one Momma's and one his), he hardly had time for any of the things he liked to do in the past. There was still his love for black licorice, but his idle time spent in front of the TV had dissipated. Via a drastic event, life had changed drastically. But somehow he still managed—if the right window of opportunity presented itself—to squeeze in a little peeping. You may be able to domesticate a leopard through training, but his spots you will never change. Besides, look at the good that had come from the last time. It had come at a high cost indeed, but it had brought with it a high value. You never knew what the next window might open upon, and there were still only two people in the world that knew about his fetish—himself and Father O'Malley.

As for Father O'Malley, Darren's confessor/mentor, in his work for the church Darren occasionally crossed paths with him. They were cordial, but between each other, have never again spoken of the day that changed both their lives. Darren had risen up from his depths, and Father O'Malley had only just begun his dark journey into his own soul. When O'Malley stepped out of that confessional, he stepped out a changed man. And he stepped into a quagmire that would try to pull him under for the next six years.

5

*H*oover was in no mood, but the knock was insistent.

It was a professional, consistent rapping. Four short, sharp bursts, then a pause. Four short, sharp bursts, then a pause. It must have gone on like that for five full minutes.

Beverly had been put in the ground shortly before noon. It was now late in the evening, and prime time television was about to start. Hoover was three sheets to the wind and had the intention of sinking even deeper into the bottle while zoning out in front of the ABCs and 123s of the sitcom plots, with only the laugh tracks to keep him company.

But the knock was interfering. It seemed as though the person behind it wasn't going to let him have his peace and solitude. He only wanted to be left alone with his sour reveries but, if he wanted the knocking to stop, apparently was going to have to answer the door and tell whoever it was to fuck off first.

Still wearing the black suit he put on to go to the funeral, Hoover hauled himself to his feet. The knot of his tie was down around the middle of his chest, and his shirt—which had been stark white when he took it out of the little box the cleaners returned them in—had brown bourbon stains on it from the times he had missed his increasingly numb bottom lip with the glass.

When he stood up, the blood rushed to his head, giving him a moment of dizziness. He knew he had consumed a lot of alcohol—one only had to look at the high-water mark of the bottle he had opened fresh for lunch—but hadn't felt it, sitting in his stupor. Now that he was standing and trying to walk, he thought that he might've possibly passed his limit. And you know what, he didn't give a fuck. After he answered the door, he planned on heading right back to the couch and finishing the job he had started. Hoover was the type who liked completion, almost obsessed over it. That doggedness was, in his opinion, what had made him real police. When he was on the force, he had taken every case ever assigned to him as close to completion as humanly possible. And now he planned to apply that same gusto to his drinking. Maybe even taking it further than humanly possible. Who would care? His soon-to-be-ex-wife (she was superpissed, irate even, at him, and had already obtained a lawyer in the mere three days she'd been gone) had taken his children, the man had taken his job, and a madman had taken his love. What was left behind was but a shell of a man. And soon, not even that, if he had his way. Lately—no, long before that—he had started making bad decisions. This was one he intended to get right.

But first, the door.

There was an ambient buzzing noise spinning around in his head, and the door seemed to be a thousand uphill-miles away. *Rap, rap, rap, rap*, the knocker tattooed on the door again, sounding like a woodpecker digging its beak into his head.

A couple more agonizingly woozy steps and Hoover reached the door. He tried to open it, but when he turned the knob and pulled, it didn't budge. He must've locked the door behind himself when he arrived home from the funeral, even though he didn't remember doing so. He fumbled first one way and then the other with the inch-long lever of the lock, trying to get the tumblers to fall. It was not an easy task. There had always been a lot of play in this particular lock, and half the time (even when he was sober) he couldn't remember which way he was supposed to turn the lever— clockwise or counterclockwise. If you didn't commit to going far enough in one direction before turning the lever in the other, you might miss the click of the latch being drawn back. At least the insistent knocking had ceased, while whoever was outside waited patiently for him to regain command over the locking mechanism.

An infinity later, the tumblers turned and the lock opened. Subsequently, Hoover pulled on the door, swinging it wide.

Through the storm door—which he hadn't yet changed over from its winter pane of glass to the more seasonal screening—he saw the upper portion of a man. He was tall, with dark, wavy hair that looked like the waves would only show when it was getting close to haircut time. He was a good-looking man with an unlined face and a fair complexion to contrast his hair, his eyes so blue they looked like chips of ice. He did not have a smile for the homeowner, Hoover. What he did have was a firm stature and a stiff collar with a white piece of plastic spanning his throat—a Roman Catholic collar. The insistent knocker was a priest. He was saying something, but Hoover couldn't hear him.

Using the index finger of the hand holding the square bottle of bourbon, he knuckled open the screen door. While doing so, he noticed the amount of brown liquid swimming around near the bottom of the bottle. There might be an alcohol run in the near future if he could get to the state-licensed liquor store before they closed by the mandated time of 9 p.m. He glanced at the green numerals of the digital readout on the VCR to see if he could make it under the wire, but they were blinking twelve noon. Or midnight. Or whatever.

"Yeah?" he said through the crack between the screen door and the wall.

"I asked, 'What are you doing?'" the priest at the door said.

"What? You knocked on my door."

"Do you think the alcohol is a good idea?"

Ignoring the barb, Hoover asked, "What do you want?"

"I'm here to help you."

"I don't need any help, Padre. Get out of here."

Convinced that the man dressed in the starched black shirt was trying to solicit money from him for some holy cause, Hoover was about to slam the door in his face when the priest said, "Then I take it you caught the guy who killed Beverly?"

*   *   *

Five minutes later, Father O'Malley found himself sitting on a couch with a glass of iced tea placed on the coffee table in front of him. He had helped himself to it. His host was still having the bourbon.

When he concocted his plan, he hadn't thought about alcohol being a factor with this particular man—alcohol and depression were not a good combination, especially heading into something as edgy and dangerous as the priest had in mind. The now-infamous Detective Hoover might not be up for the task O'Malley wanted to lay before him. He had expected to find a consummate professional who had suffered a run of bad luck. Instead he found a waste of a human that was being eaten alive by both the outside world and the inner guilt. O'Malley would have to feel him out before he laid himself—and his idea—bare. He would have to alter his original game plan and sniff around the fringe to see how lucid this guy still was, rather than charge right in with such a brazen idea.

"What do you know about Beverly's death?" the cop grunted at him. Along with the priest's statement, Hoover was intrigued by the fact that he called her by her first name, rather than Detective Farrell.

"I know what I saw on TV," he said, even though he knew a lot more. A whole hell of a lot more, thanks to Darren Roberts.

That's why he called her Beverly, because of my statement on the tape. "So does everybody else. How does that help me?"

"It doesn't. It's not supposed to."

"Then you're wasting my time. I'm busy here, so get out."

"Busy doing what? Drinking yourself into a stupor?"

"I plan on going a whole lot further than stupor, Padre; I plan on hitting the sauce until I meet your God. So if you're here to administer Last Rites, then please do so, but do it quietly, huh?" He took a shot straight from the bottle's neck. There was another glass seated on the table beside O'Malley's iced tea. It was filled with some murky-looking water that he supposed was the melted rocks the first three or four drinks had been splashed over before it became too much work to use the glass. Or too slow.

"Last Rites? So then you're Catholic?"

"No, but you could say that I've recently had a crash course in Catholicism."

"Are you thinking about converting?"

"Not at all. I have all the religion I need," he said, and held up the bottle before taking another swig.

"Then what about the sacraments?"

"What sacraments?"

"You mentioned Last Rites, which is one of the seven sacraments, and your crash course in Catholicism. What were you looking to find in the sacraments?"

"It wasn't about sacraments. It was about the commandments. Michelle Laplin, a murder victim, had the third one written on a note pinned to her body when the asshole who killed her drove her through the front door of police headquarters."

"I'm aware of the incident, but I haven't heard of any note like that."

"It wasn't made public."

"Why?"

"For a number of reasons. At first, so that the department could keep an ace up their sleeve in order to weed out any false confessions. Later, after the debacle on Purser Street, it was so we didn't illustrate our own mistakes."

"The third commandment? Keep holy the Sabbath?" the priest asked incredulously. He went over all of the commandments in his head again to see if he had the right one. It didn't take long, and he wasn't wrong; he knew the commandments like he knew his own name. "What's murder got to do with that?"

Hoover didn't acknowledge the question, only sat toying with the wedding band on his ring finger.

Rhetorically, O'Malley said, "The commandments are part of Mosaic law, the guidelines established by Moses in the Old Testament. Indeed, God had been serious about the commandments he laid down in the covenant with Moses. So serious, you might say that he wrote them in stone. But I don't see the connection with that and killing people. It doesn't make sense. What would a commandment have to do with a killing spree?" O'Malley asked.

"Nothing," Hoover informed him. "It was a tip. The note actually read 'III. Holy the Sabbath. Purser.' He was telling us what he was going to do and when he was going to do it."

"Oh. Purser Street was where those two women were abducted, and where your partner . . ."

"Yeah. It's where I let him kill Beverly. She was the third of the three mentioned in the note."

"You can't blame yourself for that."

"Sure I can; you saw the videotape. And besides, I don't have to; everyone else is doing that for me, Father."

"So what are you doing to stop the man who took Beverly's life from killing again?"

"There's nothing I can do. I'm out of the loop, and besides they don't need me anymore."

"Why not?"

"Because they already know how they're going to find out who he is."

"How?"

"The house on Purser Street was wired for real-time viewing over the Internet. You saw the tape, heard the news reports; you know what I'm talking about."

"So?"

"So the company that fronted the money for the wiring of that house is called, you'll like this, Father, the Grapple Company. Over the years, it was shortened down to that name when the owner decided that the original one was too cumbersome—the Garden of Eden Apple Company. Womanly temptation and all, get it?"

"I get it," the priest said drolly. "Very clever."

"Anyway, based here in Philadelphia, the Grapple Company charges a monthly fee for subscribers to watch the young ladies parade around the house in various states of undress via their computers. The guy who killed Beverly knew the lay of the house and exactly how many people would be there on a Saturday night because he was a subscriber to that site himself. He knew exactly how and where to nab Michelle Laplin on Friday because he'd been watching her for a while and knew her weekly patterns. Somewhere, this guy's name is on record as being one of the Grapple Company's subscribers. He might've been using an alias or even set up a whole network of hard drives to bounce the feed around to throw off the track, but sooner or later they'll be able to find out who he was."

"You said you're out of the loop. How do you know all this?"

"Overheard one of the cops at the funeral this morning talking about it."

"Oh."

"It's just a matter of time now before they unearth his identity."

"You keep saying they'll figure out who he is, but you haven't said they'll catch him."

"Because I don't think they will."

"Why not?"

"Because I think Purser Street was his last outing. I think he's ready to run."

That gave O'Malley pause. *What if the rug's pulled out from under me before I even get my feet on the floor?* The priest had a new understanding of the cop's plight. A little shaken, Father O'Malley asked, "What makes you think he'll flee?"

"A feeling mostly. And the part in the note that referred to 'Holy the Sabbath.' I think that that was his way of saying that after he's finished his work—meaning Purser Street—he's going to rest a la God in the creation story; he's going to stop doing what he has been doing. At least around here." Hoover paused to take a sip from the bottle. "But what confirmed it for me was what he wanted me to do in the house."

"What'd he want you to do?"

"Jesus, Father, he said clear as day that he wanted me to kill him! Did you watch the video or not?"

"Yes, but sometimes things are not as apparent to outsiders as they are to those involved."

Hoover nodded his head as far as his slouched position would allow. "Good point, Padre, but it is what it is—he had me in a stalemate, with Beverly as the prize. He obviously knew that the house was wired with cameras, and he wanted me to kill him anyway so that the whole world could see it. Why would he want that?"

"He wanted you to martyr him."

"Yep."

"But why?"

"Who knows? Who knows what people like this think? It could be we were getting too close to him. It could be he reached his limit. It could be he was tired and wanted a vacation. There's a theory that says people like him want to get caught; the thrill of being caught is the whole reason they do it. There's another that says people sick like him want to commit suicide but are too afraid to do it themselves, so they orchestrate the assistance of a cop by committing crimes. Who the hell knows what these people rationalize in their rancid fucking brains?"

Father O'Malley felt his skin crawl, his body shiver.

Hoover, not noticing the priest's reaction, continued. "You know what the saddest thing is about everything that happened at that house? Beverly and I actually knew about the Grapple Company's involvement on Friday—a day *before* the mess out at Purser Street on Saturday night. The whole disaster could've been averted, Beverly and those two other women still alive, if we—if *I*—had acted differently."

"How could that be?" He was shocked at the thought of such a "what-if" possibility. He was beginning to understand the depth to which the cop's soul had sunk.

"We'd been following the back story of one of the girls who'd been murdered earlier, one of the ones found in the woods," Hoover said. "Her name was Judy Kasay."

At the mention of that specific girl's name, the priest stiffened as if a goose had walked across his grave. Hoover gave it no mind, dismissing it as the priest being squeamish because of his inexperience in dealing with such a thing, and also because of the direct affront murder was to his beliefs.

"Judy had been working for Grapple in her spare time as a phone-sex girl. All of the quote-unquote ladies this guy had gone after had extracurricular jobs like that."

That had also been held back from the media's attention, before the aftereffects of the catastrophe at Purser Street. After that, the whole world found out about every little secret skeleton the deceased women had stored in their closets. Although it hadn't been public knowledge, Father O'Malley had known about Judith Kasay's operator job for over two years. Having been her parish priest, she had told him in a confessional. In fact, it was the exact confessional in which he had spoken to Darren.

"We had tracked Judy to her legit job at a shoe store in an outlet mall," Hoover continued. "When we started peppering questions about her personal life, we uncovered a male friend who'd been hooked on her named Markus. We struck lucky with him—even though I hadn't realized it until after Beverly was dead—when he produced the name of the Grapple

Company and its connection to Miss Kasay. The fact that she was involved with a side project such as the kind that company runs was too much for Markus, and he had to go his separate way. True love sacrificed for monetary gain, the American Dream lives on, right, Father?"

"Why didn't you act immediately on the information you had?"

"The main reason was because Grapple, which solicits dark-of-night services, by contrast works banker's hours, and by the time we'd found out about them, they'd already closed for the weekend. Remember, we were only working on filler at the time, so no judge would've given us a warrant to rustle the owner anyway." The cop paused before adding, "The lesser, more costly, reason was because I had other things on my mind at the time."

"Like what?"

"Don't worry about that; it's my sin, Padre."

"Tom."

"What?" Hoover asked, almost shouted.

"Thomas O'Malley, that's my name."

Thomas O'Malley; a nice Irish name that explained the black hair, blue eyes, and pale skin. Hoover laughed mean-spiritedly. "You know there's a cartoon movie about a rogue cat with that same name?"

O'Malley nodded and smiled as though he had heard that one before. "I know. Thomas O'Malley, the Alley Cat. The movie came out when I was sixteen. When my buddies caught wind of it, I was be-knighted the Alley Cat for almost a year."

"A priest known as the Alley Cat; what is the world coming to?"

"Well, I wasn't a priest back then. And I wasn't exactly God-fearing, either. Back then, I'd been known to bend a law or two to satisfy my needs."

"How far did you bend them?" Hoover asked with a laugh, this time lighthearted.

"Only till they broke," O'Malley returned. That got them both laughing.

When the giggling subsided, Hoover turned melancholy. "*The Aristocats*, my kids love that movie," he said.

"You have children?"

"Two girls."

Tom looked around the house and couldn't help but notice that they weren't there. Hoover saw his innocent, if not inconspicuous, glance. "My wife took them when she left me."

"I'm sorry. You're separated?"

"As of this past Sunday, when the networks started airing that videotape. You know, the one in which I declared my love for the dying woman in my arms who just happens to not be my wife."

"Oh," O'Malley said for the third time, finally realizing the scab he'd picked.

"Don't pity me, Father. I've got my friend here to keep me company." Hoover said, showing him the bottle before helping himself to another drink.

"Alcohol is not your friend; it's your enemy. How do you expect to get your kids back, or repair the damage to the relationship with your wife, if you keep drinking this way?"

"I don't. That relationship is beyond repair. There were too many leaks in the foundation for it to hold under the pressure. Unfortunately, but probably justifiably, the kids got washed away from me when the torrent hit."

"Bullshit. Nothing is beyond repair if you have faith," the priest said.

That struck a nerve, causing Hoover to erupt in a drunken spiel, the type of which only made sense to the inebriated. "I'll tell you what's bullshit, Tom," he said, nearly screaming. "Bullshit is the fact that you're sitting there pretending to be my friend. Well, you're not. I don't know you from dick. And now you're going to preach to me from your goodie-goodie holy book about how to raise my family? What do you know about raising a family? You only have to look after yourself, living your life in housing that is provided for you, eating food bought from the coffers of the people you and your kind have brainwashed into contributing a tithe from their hard-earned money for God's greater glory. Now if you don't mind, please peddle your bullshit somewhere else, and get the hell out of my house."

Father O'Malley took a sip of the cold iced tea. He had just been—not politely, but not physically—kicked off the premises. The cop had given him an opening, and this was the moment to go for broke, and he would need his throat to stay moist because there was apt to be either a lot of yelling or a lot of talking. He had to turn this lump of clay of a person into the solid cannonball he needed. The tea went down smooth, and it tasted good. There were few people who made their iced tea the way Tom O'Malley liked his—so sugary you could almost chew it—but this guy did. Or at least his wife did, before she took off.

"You're right, that is a load of bullshit," O'Malley said.

"I'm glad you see it my way."

"Of course I see it your way—the way of a pathetic, drunken slob who's wallowing in his own self-pity because he isn't man enough to do anything about the shit sandwich life served him." O'Malley was trying to stoke the fire, but in a way in which he could control the burn. He wasn't exactly sure how to go about that, and his mother had always warned him that if he played with fire, he was apt to get burned, but he had to try something, or Hoover was going to be lost. And not just for this outing, but maybe in life as well.

John Hoover leapt from the chair to the couch with matching upholstery O'Malley sat on. He grabbed the priest by the front of his shirt and hauled him to his feet, the grip of his big hands causing the priestly piece of white plastic to spring out of its slot and shoot across the living room. Father O'Malley hadn't seen where it landed because he was staring into the hearth of the fire he had stoked.

"Get the fuck out, Father!"

O'Malley held his hands up in surrender. "All right, I'll leave. Don't hurt me."

Hoover let go of the man's shirt with a shove. "Good, get out," he repeated, before turning to fetch the bourbon bottle that had somehow managed to remain upright when he sprung from the chair. He turned his back on O'Malley, giving the priest a chance to size him up. Unaware of what he was going to do, Father O'Malley punched Hoover in the kidney.

With a grunt of pain, Hoover went down on one knee just as he reached his coveted bottle. Pivoting on that knee, he flung the bottle as a weapon aimed at the priest's head.

Tom saw it coming and had just enough reflex time to duck as it sailed by overhead, trailing a stream of acrid-smelling brown liquid, some of which splashed onto his face and shoulders.

With a quickness that belied his lack of sobriety, Hoover swung his fist in a wide arc, catching the off-balanced priest directly on the bony kneecap. The man's leg buckled, and as O'Malley reached down to comfort the knee, Hoover brought his other fist up, smashing it into the priest's cheek. O'Malley went down face-first into the plush seat cushion of the couch.

Hoover was back on his feet quickly, standing over the priest with fists balled tight. The priest didn't move. After a solid minute, sixty full seconds, Hoover asked the prone form: "Hey man, you okay?"

Father O'Malley had never been in a real fight in his whole life, if you discount the time he'd been locked up and the cops had tossed him about a bit while subduing and cuffing him. Even in those hell-raising younger days, when he had stirred up enough shit that he'd been known as the Alley Cat, there never seemed to be a need for an exchange of blows. Truth be told, he never would've guessed that he would've been involved in a fight on this day, either. Proving to him that destiny and fate were overrated concepts of the guilty, Father O'Malley had used his own God-given free will to assault the drunken police officer in his home. There had been no outside help or influence involved; he had wanted to catch the man's attention, and now that he had it, he wanted to see what he would do with it.

Even though he had never been in a fight before, Tom O'Malley had enough sense to know when he was outmatched, as he was going up against this stronger bigger younger (though not that much younger) man who'd been trained by professional law enforcement officials at the police academy rather than the frail, robed old priests of the St. Charles Seminary. So instead of taking up an offensive—or more likely defensive—posture, he played possum and waited for Hoover to get close enough that he could make his move.

"Hey, Tom, I'm serious, you okay?" Hoover nudged the priest's leg with the toe of his foot. Instead of getting the groggy, slow-moving response he expected, O'Malley sprang forward like an Olympic track-and-field runner who had been waiting for the shot to be fired.

O'Malley grabbed Hoover around the midsection as if trying to tackle a ball carrier and drove him backward.

While Hoover was reeling, O'Malley continuously hit him with rabbit punches to the gut. O'Malley had caught him unaware and managed to get a good hold on his midsection. Hoover didn't know how he would've gotten out of the hold if it hadn't been for the chair he'd been sitting in. He had no defense against the furiously moving Catholic, and the priest was hunched in such a position that he was unknowingly protecting all of his vital parts, exposing only his meatless, bony shoulders. Even his head was tucked so that it was safely out of reach in Hoover's armpit.

The priest might've backed Hoover to the wall—and kept wailing on him until he pissed blood—if the chair hadn't been in the way. When the back of Hoover's legs struck the leading edge of the cushion, he let his knees unhinge and plopped down onto the seat, letting his own weight separate him from the priest's hold.

Pushing with his feet at the same time his backward momentum dropped him into a seated position, Hoover toppled the chair over.

The basement did not run the entire length of the house, and since the door that led down to the main area of the basement was in the kitchen, the living room had a concrete slab beneath the carpet and its thin padding. Hoover landed flat on his back, the slap of carpeted slab driving the breath from his lungs. He exhaled so much air that in conjunction with the downward pressing weight of his own body he feared he might have a collapsed lung.

His head was spinning from the fight, his stomach swirling from the alcohol. He turned his face to the side and vomited. He hadn't thought he would've had enough energy—or air—left in his lungs to be able to heave, but he did. Apparently he had a lot more reserves than he imagined because he puked for what seemed like ever. A continuous stream of yellow-brownish water poured from his mouth and nostrils to be soaked up by the rug. When his stomach was empty and the subsequent dry heaves had passed, he opened his tearing eyes to notice that there was not one chunk amid the pool of bile—between all the drinking, he hadn't found time to eat anything all day.

Well at least there's no blood floating in it.

Hoover was hurting and he was tired. He wiped his mouth on the sleeve of his suit coat and closed his eyes to rest a minute before he dealt again with the crazed clergyman.

Father O'Malley watched the cop's eyes slide shut. He had never seen someone throw up that much, not even during the holiday seasons when he helped dish out soup at the homeless shelters to drunks and crackers—people who seem to throw up at any time for no reason other than the long-term abuse of substances.

O'Malley didn't feel one bit of remorse about what he'd done. No matter the way it had come about, Hoover's puking could've been about the best thing for him right now. Judging by the amount of liquid that had come out of the man's stomach, he could have suffered an overdose tonight and died.

Father O'Malley might possibly have saved the man's life—or at least put a momentary hold on the inevitable—but he had lost perspective of why he'd come here this evening. After seeing the computer-generated footage on TV of the Purser house and all of the following exposés that the networks had scrambled to put together concerning Detective John Hoover and his miscues, Father O'Malley would like to have helped him out of this horrid situation the most. He had wanted it so badly that he put on blinders to the condition the cop was in. He should've known how this was going to end as soon as Hoover opened the door. Hell, he should've known by the way he saw him sitting slumped and dazed on the couch, ignoring the knocking, through the half-circle sunburst pattern of the door's jalousie window. But he hadn't. In fact, seeing the cop in that much pain had made him want to help all the more.

As the night wore on, though, he was starting to realize that he had been fooling himself; there was no way this cop was in any shape—mentally or physically—for what he, Father Thomas O'Malley, was planning on doing with the information that had walked into his church in the form of a sleazy voyeur named Darren Roberts.

He was giving up hope in recruiting Hoover, but the event was still going to happen as planned. Even in the early stages of thought yesterday morning, he knew that he wasn't going get a hundred percent participation. For something such as this, to think a hundred percent was possible was ludicrous. That was why he was making these personal visits to the homes of the victim's families—whom he also considered to be victims.

The dead suffered greatly, but quickly, and then were welcomed into the loving embrace of God. For the loved ones left behind, it was a lifelong suffering of missing and second-guessing, never to be vanquished. It was for those people he was making this sacrifice. He so wanted to ease the pain of those families, wanted to give them closure.

On the visits, he was feeling around, trying to measure the psyche of the immediate families of the thirteen women—twelve ladies with their thumbs in dirty pies and the cop, Beverly Farrell—that this maniac had abused and murdered. It was a thin line he walked, trying to decide whether or not to bring the family members into the fold. There were so many variables with each individual person that he was never completely sure whether to tell them or not. He had to rely on gut instinct to get him through each visit. So far, he had not made a mistake; his instincts had proved right each time.

This time his instincts were telling him to pull the plug and give it up. The cop was too far gone to be of any help, and in this condition, would only be a hindrance. Father O'Malley's project could not handle any loose cannons on board. An undertaking of this nature had to be kept in the utmost of secrecy. It had to be guarded with silence to the grave. While he didn't think Hoover might be too far from the grave at the rate he was going, it didn't seem likely that he'd be able to keep this thing a secret if he kept on holding pity parties for himself, sprouting his mouth off to anyone who'd listen.

No, Hoover was a weak link. His gut told him so, his head told him so, and therefore it was so.

Father O'Malley rubbed his jaw as he watched the cop lying flat on the floor, his eyes closed but breathing. He touched the puffiness under his own eye and thought that he'd have a shiner there come morning. He ran his tongue around the inside of his mouth and tasted blood. He sucked his teeth and spat on the floor. It didn't matter; the carpet was going to need to be shampooed, if it was salvageable at all.

He looked around at the mess he had helped make and noticed that there was a bathroom a little way down the hall from where he stood. He walked over to it and turned on the light. The fixture was one of those modern artsy-type things, made up of four bare bulbs running along a mirrored strip, the light it cast bright and harsh. With that much light being thrown on him, O'Malley felt he had entered a hospital emergency room.

He spit again, this time into the sink. It was saliva tainted with blood, not the other way around, which was a good sign; he wasn't bleeding very badly. *Must've bit my cheek when he mashed it against my jaw.*

He looked into the square mirror that doubled as a medicine cabinet behind the sink and began prodding the side of his face where he'd been struck. It didn't look as bad as it felt. It was painful to the touch, but the cop had missed his eye cleanly, and there was no swelling in the surrounding area. Having visibly assessed the injury, he changed his opinion to think that he wouldn't have any bruise whatsoever, which was good because he wanted to avoid drawing extra attention to himself over the next couple of days. He was going to be involved in a lot of nefarious things and didn't need the added questions.

He turned on the faucet, letting the water run. He cupped his hands and bent to splash the water onto his face. When he stood upright, the cop's reflection was looking at him in the mirror.

Hoover charged with a fist raised. O'Malley sidestepped just as the bigger man swung at him. Hoover hit the mirror, and the reflective-backed glass shattered into a thousand fragments, each shining like a diamond under the bright lighting as they fell into the basin of the sink.

O'Malley, who couldn't believe the man had any fight left in him, still knew he was outmatched, only now his predicament had been worsened by the close quarters of the bathroom. He was in for a thumping at the hands of a dangerously drunk man if he didn't act quickly. There was only one move for him to make and he made it.

Slinging his arm around Hoover's chest, O'Malley shoved the odiferous man, who stank of puke and booze, backward into the tub. The shower curtain separated from the round clamps holding it to the rod, one at a time. Miraculously, the rod—which was only held up by the tension of the tightly coiled spring inside it—did not budge from its wedged position between the tiled walls.

Hoover landed in the tub as if he were about to take a bath

fully clothed, the aqua-colored curtain beneath him. His head struck one of the tiles hard, cracking it.

O'Malley reached for the crystal-faceted knob with the blue capital C. He gave it one hard, violent turn, and the showerhead spurted to life.

The stream of icy water stung Hoover, shocking him so that he gasped audibly. He lay there panting under the chilling spray while the tub filled up from the shower curtain blocking the drain.

"All right, I'm done," Hoover said as rivulets of water and cooling sweat ran down his face. "I'm done! Turn it off!"

"Are you sure, big boy?" O'Malley asked, not willing to trust him after he had somehow managed to launch a second offensive after losing the first round by puking his guts out. O'Malley knew that once was luck, and twice coincidence; if there were a third time, he would not come out on top.

"I'm sure," the cop said, and the priest shut off the flow.

Hoover lay stewing in the water as he asked, "What was this all about, Father? I wasn't having a bad-enough week that a *priest* had to come by and hand me an ass-kicking?"

"I came here to help you."

"You have a funny way of helping people, Padre."

"You have no idea," O'Malley said, casting a sarcastic boomerang at himself. He dropped the lid of the toilet and sat down atop the commode. Three buttons were now missing from his black shirt. It hung open, and the pure bleached whiteness of his undershirt beneath showed.

"Please enlighten me on how getting beat down in the privacy of my own home is supposed to help me."

At this point, there was no way he was going to tell the cop what his real agenda had been in coming here. He said, "It was a wake-up call. You've lost sight of yourself. By fighting back, you showed that you might still have something left to live for."

"And you surmised all of this sitting around your church?"

"Something like that," he said, pulling a facecloth from the rack that hung beside the sink. He used it to wipe the blood, sweat, and bourbon from his face, some of the mixture having gotten into his eyes and stinging him. The square of cloth hadn't been washed in a while and smelled like mildew, but he used it anyway.

"I've got news for you, O'Malley," Hoover went on. "I don't know you and you don't know me. I wasn't fighting back because I felt like living to see tomorrow. I don't. I was fighting back because I felt like taking someone with me when I cross over."

That was the final straw; Father O'Malley gave up. *This man is too far gone to help me do anything. He's a lush who's drinking himself to death.* In the end, it wouldn't matter. The cop would just be another statistic added to the killer's total. So be it. Life would go on for some, and end for others, in the next couple of days. Which one it was going to be for Hoover was solely up to him.

Father O'Malley stood up and tossed the soiled facecloth into the half-filled tub where Hoover lay. "Be careful what you wish for, buddy, it just might come true." The priest unzipped the fly of his pants. Hoover watched as he stuck a hand in, adjusting his shirt by tugging downward on the tails. It was an old Catholic-school trick.

When he zipped back up, he said, "One last bit of advice before I show myself out. I know you've been through a lot, but do yourself a favor and go see someone—anyone—who still cares for you, if you can find such a person. Friend, family, loved one, whoever, just go talk to someone; you could use a shoulder to cry on. Regardless of what you say, I still think there's something left inside that you want to fight for; you just need the right person to help you find it and bring it out.

"Otherwise," Father O'Malley said, pointing at the water in the tub, "you're going to keep sinking until you're sunk."

"That's very scholarly of you, Father, but why bother with the likes of me?"

"Because you're a good man, and there aren't too many of those left."

"Ah, you're wrong there, my friend. I used to be one of the good guys; now I'm just bitter. It's unbelievable what a week will do to you."

The priest, having no response, turned and walked out of the bathroom. A few seconds later, Hoover heard the front door open and close.

He was alone again.

Even though it had been a surreal visitation, Hoover felt lost—

dejected—when the priest left. The solitude weighed heavy on him. The fact that a priest he had never seen before came to his house to try to snap him out of his reprieve frightened Hoover. It was like one of those divine interventions he would sometimes see on the "true-fact" shows that were always airing on Fox as he flipped through the channels, or would read about in the headlines of the trash rags while in the checkout aisle of the supermarket. Such unexplained things as people receiving the stigmata, statues of the Virgin Mary bleeding tears, or the voice of God delivering warnings of the future through animals or children who weren't old enough to understand what they were saying. He shuddered, the water in the tub chilling him to the bone.

Had the priest been the voice of God come to warn him of the future? He sincerely doubted it. Hoover was not a religious man, nor did he believe in the occult. Reports of such phenomenon were but fictional stories with hardly a grain of truth to them, sensationalized to separate a fool from his money. They were hoaxes, nothing more, and that was still his belief.

But something had changed. The priest was right. Recent events had proved to be too much; his soul was rotting. If he didn't find a way to get this monkey off his back soon, he was a dead man.

There was only one person left in his life, and she was the only one who could help him now, help pull him out of the funk. It would have to be her.

He would go to Fiona.

6

"Are you drunk?" was the first thing she asked him when she opened the door.

"Not as drunk as I was, but I'm still feeling it," was the truthful response. He had a splitting headache from striking his head on the bath tile, and his body felt bruised and battered from the fight with the mysterious priest. If it weren't for the aches and pains, he would wonder if the priest had really been there at all, or had only been a pink elephant that trampled him.

He had stripped his clothes off and tossed them sopping wet onto the floor of the bathroom, where they remained still. After pulling the ruined shower curtain out from underneath him, he had washed himself off in the icy tub, not wanting to add any hot water to the contents in the hopes that the stimulation from the cold would help clear away some of the grogginess. It had worked to an extent, but he still didn't have complete control over his faculties yet, even though he had driven across town in the city-owned car. Since a suspension was still pending the outcome of the investigation into the assault of one Nicos Agbalaya—and since Lauren had taken the only car they owned—he still felt entitled to drive the department's. Cars were not given to city employees such as police officers; they were issued for use while on duty. Since homicide detectives clocked so much overtime, day and night, they were never really off duty, which made it hard to keep track of when cars were issued. If a question ever arose about the length of a loan on a car, the detective only had to state that he was working on a case while he had possession of the car. More than most likely, he would even put in for the overtime to back up the story.

Since Fiona's apartment was on a street that had little to no parking, Hoover pulled in to an alley behind a Chinese restaurant on the corner across from her place. He flipped the visor down so that the sign proclaiming he was with the police department on official city business, could be read through the window, ensuring that the car wouldn't get towed. He hadn't wanted to park in the alley directly behind her apartment because there was a service entrance that led into the building through the rear. There was no elevator—it had only three floors and a basement—but the residents still used this entrance to bring in parcels and the likes so that they didn't have to stop in front of the building and block traffic while they off-loaded. He had to wait for her to get home from work, and it was just past twelve-thirty. The restaurant had closed for the night, and he wasn't blocking the dumpster if the company came to service it soon. He didn't think he would have a problem. He left the car and went up to Fiona's third-floor apartment.

After she asked about his condition, she frowned but didn't say anything. She turned and walked into the apartment, leaving the door open for him.

He closed the door behind himself and found her in the kitchen. She was still fully dressed in a red, moderately low-cut, form-fitting T-shirt and a pair of jeans. She had only had time to kick off her sneakers before he had gotten there and now stood barefoot at the kitchen sink, her toes painted the same color red as her top. The water was running, and there was soap in the basin with the dishes. The sleeves of her shirt were pushed up and her hands were wet. Something was bothering her.

Without turning, she said, "I saw what happened on TV."

He knew she would have. He didn't have anything to say, so he waited to see where she would take it.

"You said you loved her," she said. From her voice, he could tell she was hot about this.

The woman in question was dead. He had had a part in killing her. And the thing that was bothering Fiona the most was that he had expressed his love for another, just as it had been for Lauren. Leave it to the women to be upset about that part of it. After his thirty-seven years of life, he still didn't have them figured out. He didn't think he ever would.

Not knowing how to defend it, he said, "Fiona, you knew I was married." It was the wrong thing to say.

She spun and pointed an accusatory finger at him. Suds flew everywhere, little clusters of soap bubbles landing around the kitchen. "Of course I knew you were married. What I didn't know was that I was only a sidepiece.

"I'd put up with the fact that you were married to another woman because I didn't believe she was the woman for you. At least, that's how you *let* me believe it. I thought she was somehow lacking in the relationship. I thought that I was better than she was, that I could give you what you wanted, what you were missing. I thought I could outlast the marriage and then you would be mine. But it wasn't like that, was it? You never had any intentions of marrying me, did you?" She put her hands on the hips of her jeans, shaking her head and fuming.

He had never seen her this mad.

"How many other women were there?" she demanded.

"Look, do you know how many fights I've been in this week? I don't want to start another one with you. I came here for some consoling."

She jumped on that. "Is that what I am to you, John, a *consolation* prize?"

He had made a mistake in coming here. He knew he shouldn't have taken the priest's advice; it had come around to bite him on the ass. She was crying now. He had needed her help and had ended up hurting her more, just as he had all the others.

In a tear-filled voice, Fiona asked, "Why didn't you call me? It's almost Thursday morning. That incident happened on Saturday night, you bastard, and this is the first I hear from you?"

"I have a lot of other things going on in my—"

"*Sure you did,*" she said bitingly. "You have all your other bimbos that you had to call first, I understand. I'm farther down the list."

"It's not like that," he said, which sounded weak, even to his own ears.

"No? What's it like then? Is it like you never call me? Is it like you never take me out anywhere? Is it like I just lay around here waiting for you to show up in the middle of the night to stud? Is it like that?"

"I thought things would be different with you," he said softly, drained of all but the energy to breathe.

She wiped tears with the back of her hand. "Well, they're not. I'm just like all the rest of your women—used." Her bottom lip quivered now; she was getting ready to have a full-blown cry. "Is this how you think you should treat women, using them up and throwing them away?"

You're no better than he is.

"I can see that I made a mistake by coming here. I'm sorry, Fiona, I think I should leave."

"I think you should too."

He walked to the door, and she was right behind him. He opened it and stepped out.

"I loved you and you shit on me, John," she said, and slammed the door.

*   *   *

Back out on the street, he fished the car keys from his pocket. He wasn't thinking anything, numb from the experience he just had, but even that was no different from the way any of the other experiences he suffered this week had left him. He had made a clean sweep of hurting everyone that he had known, that he had loved. His wife, his daughters, his mistresses, his colleagues, his friends, there was no one to turn to now. He was ready to go back home and pick up where he left off before the priest interrupted him.

He unlocked the car door and sunk in.

About to put the key in the ignition, he glanced back up at Fiona's apartment for one last look. There was a car parked in the alley behind the building. It hadn't been there when he had arrived, but he felt a little validation for not parking there for just that reason. Somebody had come home with things they needed to bring into the building, and he would've been in their way, even if it were for only the ten minutes he had been inside.

At least he had managed to not piss somebody off, albeit without them knowing it.

The alley behind Fiona's building was a dead end, and the car had been reversed in, parked so that it faced outward. It was a big car, painted a dark color, but in the unlit depths of the alley he couldn't tell what kind of car it was. The driver had pulled it in pretty deep, leaving a long walk between the car and the service entrance. In fact, he had pulled it in so far that he had almost scrapped his roof on the bottom edge of . . .

. . . The fire escape ladder.

With ice running through his veins, Hoover looked up at the third-floor landing of the fire escape, where Fiona's apartment was. Her window was open, the curtain and tail end of the bed sheet she used to block out the sun fluttering in the night breeze.

Oh, shit, he's in there, Hoover thought, and jumped out of the Crown Vic, leaving the door open behind him. He was still holding the keys and trying to stuff them back into his pocket as he ran across the street. He missed, the keys falling to the ground with a jingle where he left them. He drew his gun as he ran for the front door of the apartment building.

Not again, not again, not again, his mind screamed at him, over and over like a needle stuck in a rut.

The perspiration running down his face, he pulled open the entrance door that led to the four stories of the complex. The door was the type through which access could only be gained by being buzzed in, but it was hung slightly out of plumb, the cant preventing it from closing tightly. In order for it to secure, and the buzzer lock to be in effect, the door had to be lifted a little and pushed. Hoover had been the last one out, and he'd just shoved it opened, letting it drift shut behind him. It had stuck on the jamb and was left narrowly ajar. As a conscientious cop, he had told Fiona about this for years and had warned her that she had better inform the superintendent of the problem before someone got hurt. She had said she would. Tonight, he was glad she'd never gotten around to it.

Had he heard us arguing from the window? Or had he been right in the goddamned apartment with us?

With the last vestiges of the hangover dissipating, his headache pushed to the rear of his mind, Hoover entered the complex and mounted the stairs two at a time. He was running as hard as he ever had in his life and was woefully out of shape for it. Too many years of filling out paperwork and sitting in front of the television compounded with too much firewater and a fatty diet made the short run up the stairs from the street an excursion. At 228 pounds, his body was still trim for its frame, if a little spongy, but he was not prepared for this type of exercise. Most in America wouldn't be.

By the time he rounded the second landing and thrust himself over the first two steps of the next series, he was extremely winded and feeling a little dizzy. His equilibrium was off, and his mind felt as if he had been running around in circles. In between two gulping breaths, he burped. It had the acidic taste of vomit. After all he had thrown up at home, he couldn't believe there could be anything more left in his stomach. He thought—hoped—it might be the last bitter fumes of the bourbon, but would have to be careful. He swallowed twice as his hand grasped the newel knob where the railing met the third-floor banister.

At the top, he went to reach for his gun before realizing he had already drawn it and transferred it to his left hand before mounting the stairs. He transferred it back. Hoover glanced down the hall to the entrance of Fiona's apartment. Her residence spanned the whole third floor, and there was only one door in or out. The door was about six walking paces down a short hallway. He closed the distance in two running steps. The third step would take him directly into the door. Still at a run, he raised his right foot while pushing off with his left, and using his forward motion and his weight, he hit the door with the sole of his hiking boot. He had been inside the apartment many, many times and knew that she only had the paltry knob lock and a sliding chain, neither of which would be able to withstand such a blow.

They didn't, and Fiona's door flew inward.

His foot had hit just to the left of the knob and both the locking mechanisms—which she had locked after he left—ripped right out of the jamb in a shower of splinters, the door slamming into the wall behind it, embedding the knob in dry wall.

He heard movement to his right, but couldn't see anything yet.

Since the apartment encompassed the entire floor, it was laid out in a circular pattern with every room having a connecting doorway to the next. Her front door opened onto a dead-end coat closet. This was convenient for the normal, everyday comings and goings of living in a city with a seasonal weather-changing environment, but it was a trap for a hunter trying to get into the living room, as Hoover was. In order for him to enter the apartment, he would have to break cover.

From the perspective of someone who had been there, done that, Hoover hadn't even paused a second before he rounded the final corner into Fiona's apartment. If the guy had a gun, he would shoot Hoover; if he didn't, he wouldn't. Hoover didn't give a fuck either way; he was tired of playing games.

Unfortunately, his adversary was not.

The man for whom he had sought over the past week—and whom he had met once before, last Saturday night—was sitting in the same chair that he, Hoover, had sat in the night after he spent a whole day inspecting the man's handiwork in the woods. The chair had been turned slightly around so that it was no longer faced toward the bedroom, but rather the entranceway where Hoover stood.

Kneeling to the side of that chair, much as she had on the night with Hoover, was Fiona. This time she was completely dressed, except for her feet. And there was no sultry playfulness in her eyes. She was kneeling as straight up as she possibly could and still have her knees on the floor. Her hands were calmly placed on the armrest, but her back was rigid in deference to the knife at her throat. The Dandelion had a full fist of her hair, and she was completely facing him, except for the bare soles of her feet and her irises, which were packed tightly in the corners of her eyes so that she could see Hoover. Except for his right shoulder and a margin of his side, the man was almost completely covered by Fiona, just as he had been with Beverly.

FUUUUUCK! Hoover thought, *not this time*, and raised his gun, aiming it at the man in the chair.

"Now this looks familiar, doesn't it, Detective Hoover?" the killer, who looked more like an accountant or a life insurance salesman, asked him in a precisely annunciated tone.

"How'd you find this apartment?" Hoover demanded, the pit of his stomach churning over what he was sure the man was about to say.

"I find it's imperative to know your pursuer, don't you? Of all idiotic things, your name is in the phone book. Hoover, John, no middle initial. 10030 Tenet Street. Two plus two, I followed you," he taunted, and his taunting was made all the more biting by the fact that yet another of Hoover's indiscretions had put someone's life in jeopardy, this time Fiona's. He should've been more careful, but who would've guessed it would come to this? In almost two decades of police work, he had never seen anything like this outside the local cinema multiplex.

"I'm tired of this game," Hoover told him. "Haven't you taken enough from me?"

"On the contrary, it's *you* who's taken something from *me*, Detective."

Hoover looked at Fiona to make sure she was all right and, for a second, caught an image of Beverly. The two women had similar features—for that was what had unknowingly originally attracted him to Fiona—but it wasn't her appearance that reminded him of Beverly this time; it was her eyes. She had the same look of hope that Beverly had when she saw Hoover enter the room on Purser Street. Desperation had been pushed aside now that the gallant knight had returned.

You're no better than he is, the reporter's prophecy rang in his head.

No matter what, he would not let Fiona down. There was one subtle difference between this time and the last, and it wasn't the absence of the cameras. Hoover was a man on the edge. He had nothing left to lose. If death was coming for him, then it was coming on his terms, not some psycho's. This situation would turn out to be a winner if Fiona walked out of the room alive; his life or that man's death were the only questions. At this point, he was more than willing to sacrifice his own life to shear this Dandelion.

"What did I take from you?" Hoover asked, needing to play along until he could get an opening for a shot.

"You took my crescendo, the final move on the board, the one that would've assured I'd be a mortal winner, as well as an angelic one. By not killing me when I asked you to, you took my chance for incarnate immortality. That night, you ruined the goal I worked so hard to achieve." There was an angry timbre in his voice as he pushed the knife he held against Fiona's neck a little higher. Hoover heard her gasp, and his grip on the gun tightened. Scared of the blade piercing her flesh, Fiona rose up off her knees, using her toes and hands for support.

"Now, because of you, I have to flee and start over in another city; I have to leave this failure behind me and begin anew," the Dandelion said.

Hoover already knew the answer to his next question, but he had to ask it. "If you're ready to run, then why are you here in this apartment, tonight?"

"It's like I said, you took something from me, something I valued more than life—my death. Now I'm here to return the sentiment, to balance the books and make you repay your debt to me. I'm here to take something of value from *you*." He tugged on Fiona's hair, and she whimpered, a trickle of sweat running down her temple.

"But you had it wrong, Detective," the man in the chair continued, "I had no intentions of running before Purser Street. I had intentions of being caught, of being killed. And you ruined that. By not killing me, I must now be born again. Reborn in the blood and death of others."

Like everything else in my life, I only had it half right, Hoover thought. *He was finished killing, but not because he was planning on taking off, because he was planning on being dead, killed. In Mosaic law, there was more to the third commandment than what was written, wasn't there? Wasn't the whole reasoning behind the third rule that when God finished creating the heavens and the earth, he rested on the seventh day? It's spelled out so plainly that I missed it. The Laplin note had said it all. The Dandelion was planning on resting on the Sabbath, but not just because he was done his work, because he was going to be dead, at eternal rest.*

Well, now that the final piece was in place, and he could see the whole picture, Hoover would be more than happy to oblige him.

"You want to die?" Hoover asked. "Let her go, and I'll kill you right now."

The man shook his head, making tsking noises. "No, no, no, no, no. It would be futile to die now, here, where no one would see it, where no one would witness your injustice. If I were to die right now, people wouldn't understand the work I've been doing. I'd be labeled a serial killer when that's not what I am."

"Then what are you?" *Keep him going; sooner or later he'll have to move. Even an inch, and he's mine.*

"I am an exorcist."

"And you think you've exorcised the souls of those women you've killed?"

A grin spread across the Dandelion's face. "Ah, you've finally got it. Yes, I do. I believe that I've saved their souls. You know as well as I do that those women were all involved in, how shall we say, nasty, *dirty* things. They were whores and sluts. But only in life were they thus. Inside, their souls were still pure. By killing them, I freed them—*exorcised* them—of their sins, so that they may be accepted into the paradise of God's heaven."

"Then why did you rape them?"

The one shoulder that was exposed to Hoover shrugged. "Once the soul is freed from the carcass of life, what is left is only but refuse, trash. What do you do with your trash, Detective?"

A momentary vision of walking a bag, heavy with burden in more ways than one, to the curb flashed in Hoover's mind. Pushing the ghost of Tom the cat's final resting place out of his head, he said, "What about Beverly? She wasn't involved in any eroticism; why'd you kill her?"

"Who, the cop?"

It sounded like he really didn't know, and that infuriated Hoover more than anything else the man had said so far. The fact that he'd taken her life and not even known who she was ran right up Hoover's spine . . . to his heart.

"I took her for no reason other than she was the pawn to get *you* to be *my* exorcist. Sadly for her, you weren't man enough to do it. Her blood is on *your* soul, Mr. Hoover," he purred.

The gun was weighing heavy in Hoover's hand, wanting to spit. It wanted to taste blood. Hoover would let it, as soon as the beast reared its head. With his free hand, he made a beckoning motion. "Come on over here; I'm ready to exorcise you," Hoover told him.

The Dandelion slowly shook his head, grinning again. "I don't think so, Hoover. You see, it's not my soul that's to be saved tonight; it's yours. Tonight, we're going to see if you're man enough to save your own soul. The choice is not going to be me or her, it's you or her," he said, pushing higher on the knife again. Fiona, who had rested back down on her knees, shot up so that she almost stood in a crouched-over position, unable to go any farther because of the hand knotted in her hair holding her neck to the blade.

"Save your soul by letting me exorcise it," the Dandelion went on, "and I promise you that she'll live out the rest of her days, and I'll leave your city of Sodom and Gomorrah in God's hands. You must either choose to sacrifice your life for this woman—as well as your own eternal salvation—or take me down and she goes with me, leaving your soul to burn in hell forever."

Motherfucker, there's not going to be a stalemate tonight! Beverly's . . . No, Fiona's womanly wide hips were in the way. *Just give me a clear shot and we'll see whose soul rots in hell.* Keeping his private rages to himself, Hoover asked, "If I die, who'll save your soul?"

"My soul will have to be saved by a different actor other than yourself, in a different state. Tell me, what do you think of Wyoming? I'm kind of partial to that one," he said, tittering a laugh, "I don't think Wyoming gets as much respect as it should from the other forty-nine."

Christ, he's planning on starting the whole cycle over again, Hoover thought. *Beverly's is bad enough; I can't have another fourteen or fifteen innocent deaths added to my burden.*

A bead of sweat trickled into Hoover's eye.

What's worse is what if he fails again in the next state and has to restart the cycle again in Kentucky? In Florida? In Alabama? In New Mexico? How far will it go? How many deaths will be exponentially traced back to that night in the house on Purser Street? How many deaths will be my fault? You're no better than he is. *No, he will not leave this room alive.*

As if echoing Hoover's thoughts, the Dandelion said, "Hopefully, the next man to take your place will be strong enough in his faith that he won't hesitate at the moment of judgment, as you did."

"That's where you're wrong, pal; it wasn't me who made your plan fail, it was you. I have no faith; I'm an atheist," Hoover said.

That was it; that was the key he needed to turn. Through all of this insanity, all of this death, talked about as if it were commonplace, the one thing the Dandelion couldn't fathom was someone *not* believing in God.

Hoover saw it coming an instant before it happened. Not believing was the one unforgivable sin—even in Catholicism, where sins were forgiven as easily as blowing your nose. The Dandelion unconsciously leaned to his right to take in a full view of the atheist. Ever so slightly as he moved, the killer relaxed the tension on the knife.

Hoover had to wait until he was far enough out. There was a saying from one war or another (history was never Hoover's strong suit) in which someone was quoted as saying, "Wait until you see the whites of their eyes." This was precisely what Hoover was waiting for. During the two confrontations with the killer, Hoover had never noticed the man's eyes before. He had seen them and had remembered that they were a deep, dark brown, almost black, but his brain had been too consumed with the surroundings and actions at the time to really *notice* them. When he finally saw them now, he thought they were impossibly large for a human's. They were shielded behind wire-framed glasses and had gone almost completely *white*. Through a combination of the low-level lighting of the room and the man's surprised stupor at Hoover's disclosure, his brown irises had shrunk so that they were seated on an almost entire field of alabaster.

So that's what they mean by wide-eyed wonder, Hoover thought, and then, *Wait for it, wait for it, NOW!*

"Blasphemy," the Dandelion said through clinched teeth, and Hoover shot him.

The gun recoiled in his hand as the blast rang around the living room. Both Fiona and the Dandelion screamed. Then they both fell to the floor.

Most people, before they shot a gun, were afraid of the explosive force about to erupt in their hand. Because of that fear, after they squeezed the trigger, they tended to close their eyes. Even seasoned law enforcement officers and military lifers have been known to do so. Some men and women will deny this fear through their brio, saying the reason they close their eyes was because of the deafening roar the gun made. But it's not true. They do it because on some inner, subconscious level, they were afraid of the deadly power they were wielding.

When Hoover shot the Dandelion, he never blinked.

He watched the entire time as the bullet bore a hole into the man's flesh, slipping into his upper arm and glancing off his humerus before erupting out his triceps. To Hoover, it seemed to happen in the same slow-motion effect filmmakers use to heighten drama. Hoover was amazed by what he saw in that fraction of a second. After he pulled the trigger of the .38, he watched as the bullet's capsule glided out of the gun's barrel in a puff of smoke, saw the rotation of the spin on the slug before it pierced the man's flesh, smelled the bullet singe the newly created edges of skin around the hole, watched as the lead parted the striated tissues of muscle and opened veins, producing a miniscule spark as it ricocheted off the humerus, taking a fragment of bone with it, enjoyed the red spray of blood from the blossom of the exit wound before the bullet emerged (along with the teeny, yellowish white bone fragment) to navigate the rest of its course into the wall behind.

Hoover saw all of this in the flash of exploding gunpowder.

And he relished it.

He had taken the shot before he had wanted to because he had needed to. He had feared waiting too long and possibly losing what little advantage he'd gained over the man.

Hoover won the standoff, and now both Fiona and the Dandelion were lying on the floor of her apartment.

He ran over to check on the woman, knelt down beside her, and gently rolled her onto her back. Her hair covered her face and neck. He used the warm end of the gun to brush it aside. There were three individual red lines running along the valley of her neck where it met the flesh of her jaw, each having been made when the Dandelion applied pressure to her skin with the knife. None of them had drawn blood. Relieved, Hoover looked up into her eyes.

"I'm okay," she whispered. "Go take care of it."

He started to rise when he felt her hand on his forearm.

"Thank you, John," she said. "I love you."

For one aching moment, he wished that there were time for more. There wasn't. He stood and turned. On the floor where the man he had shot should've been was a small puddle of blood. The Dandelion was gone.

"Oh my God, where'd he go?" Fiona asked.

"Stay here, don't move," Hoover said.

"Should I call the cops?"

"Don't call anyone. He's mine."

Hoover leapt over the end of the easy chair the man had been sitting in when he shot him and sprinted into the adjoining room, the kitchen. There was no sign of the Dandelion except for one bloody handprint on the left side of the next doorjamb. It had smeared when he had let go of the wall, the resulting print looking like a question mark.

Hoover sprinted into the next room, the bedroom. It too was empty, the night breeze drafting through the hanging curtains and supplemental bed sheets causing every piece of linen and drapery to flutter in the air from the open window, the whole room seeming to be comprised of ghostly hands reaching out for him.

In one stiff wind, Hoover caught a glimpse of the blackness of the alley beyond. There, sitting on the sill of the open window, was one scarlet drop of blood. For the second time in as many confrontations, the man he sought had escaped through a window.

Either by design or luck, the Dandelion always seemed to leave himself a way out.

Hoover grabbed hold of a handful of sheet and curtain and pulled. They came down, rod and all, to lie at his feet. He poked his head outside the window and looked down. Through the many layers of steel grating that made up the fire escape, he couldn't see anything below.

Slinging his leg over the sill, using his gun hand as a pivot, he went out onto the escape. He bent over the rail. Three stories below sat the same black station wagon he'd seen pull away from Purser Street with the two abducted—and now suspected dead—women in it. It was still sitting under the fire-escape ladder, its engine off. With his eyes, Hoover started at the bottom of the ladder and traced upward. He didn't have to look far; the Dandelion was on the first landing and just about to put his foot on the ladder.

Hoover aimed and fired, the bullet striking the ladder, sparking. The Dandelion drew his body in closer to the brick wall, continuing his flight.

Barely touching the metal rungs that sufficed as steps, Hoover descended to the landing below. He got there just in time to hear the metallic screech of the ladder to the alley being pushed upward into a closed position. Not sparing the time to look down at what the fleeing man was doing, Hoover bent his body so as to not strike his head on the risers above him as he bounded down the next set of steps.

Halfway down the flight and still hunched over, Hoover's hand found some slick wetness on the railing. It was blood from the gunshot wound he had inflicted upon the killer. Hoover's hand slipped in it, causing him to lose his footing and bouncing the rest of the way down the metal steps on his tailbone.

Only one floor above street level, Hoover regained his feet and his composure in just enough time to see the driver's door slam shut. He was in the wagon. Hoover fired three shots into the windshield, shattering the glass into a billion pieces held together by the backing safety tape. The broken glass made it impossible to see inside, and he didn't know if he had hit the man again. When the engine roared to life, he assumed not.

Knowing that there was no time left to do anything else, Hoover grabbed hold of the railing and propelled himself out into space. He landed on the roof of the car with a bone-jarring thud that vibrated up his ankles, the thin metal of the roof denting beneath his weight.

He only had one shot left in the six-round chamber, and not wanting to waste it, put the barrel of his gun directly on the roof of the car, above the driver's seat. As he was about to pull the trigger, the car rocketed out from under him, toppling him over backward. He did not slide down the rear window as he expected to, because the car had accelerated too fast and the wagon had no trunk, only an elongated rear cabin. Instead, he flew through the air slightly, until gravity pulled him down on top of the roof, near the edge. The side of his body struck (and left another indentation) primarily with his hip and shoulder. He then rolled off, dropping the three and a half feet to the oily cobblestones of the alley.

Feeling like he'd been hit by a car, he still managed to hold onto his gun.

In the waft of warm wind stirred by the hastily departing automobile, Hoover inhaled the stench of the alley in his nostrils. It smelled of garbage and decay. It smelled like old moldy food and ancient dreams. It smelled like a woman who needed to douche. Hoover rolled onto his belly on the dank cobblestones. Not wanting to miss his final opportunity, he fired his last shot at the rear of the station wagon. A taillight exploded, showering the alley with bits of red plastic.

Well that's it, he's going to get away again, Hoover thought. Then something unexpected happened. When the man tried to hook a left out of the alley, he cut it too close. With the arm wound and the diminished visibility through the windshield, he must've found it a difficult task to navigate such a long, wide car around so tight a corner. The station wagon struck the building directly behind Fiona's, which split-housed a laundromat and a deli. The wagon had been moving at such a rapid pace when it hit that the wall dented in the side of the car upon impact.

Hoover pushed himself up with his hands, feeling the slimy slickness of the stones under his palms. When he stood, he could feel the toll his Wyatt Earp escapades with the fire escape and car had taken on his body. His back was aching; his muscles were fatigued, and his legs hurt deep in the bones. Supporting his weight on them, his legs felt arthritic, probably sustaining shin splints from the leap.

He was almost all the way upright when he started to stagger toward where the car was hung up against the wall. Suddenly, with a loud ripping screech, the car began to lurch forward. Hoover—still about 150 feet away—tried to pick up his pace. The best he could manage was a loping run as the wagon's engine revved when the man inside pressed down hard on the accelerator. Unable to respond as quickly as the driver demanded, the gunning engine caused the stuck side of the car to lift up off the ground. The higher tilt gave the car enough leeway to free itself.

Hoover stopped in his tracks, watching as the car scraped along the unyielding bricks of the building, spitting sparks. Knowing that he couldn't catch up in time, Hoover stared at the rear of the car, memorizing what he saw. The metal of the car made a high-pitched screaming sound as the side was shredded. At the end, there was a small, burning peel of tires most commonly associated with the slamming on brakes as the car was rudely shoved off the edge of the building. It was almost as if the structure was saying "Get your ass off me." Then the old black station wagon (*It's a hearse,* Hoover realized, *an old Cadillac hearse*) with its one red and its one white taillight turned left and was gone.

Hoover continued his hitching run, his lurching shadow cast in the streetlight looking like a fleeing Quasimodo. Emerging from the alley, he ran and hopped across the street without looking either way—fuck it, he had already been hit by a car once tonight and lived. Behind the Chinese restaurant, he fished in his pocket for his keys. They weren't there. He had dropped them in the street in his haste to get to Fiona.

"Shit," he screamed into the night and slammed both his clinched fists against the roof of the department-owned car. He had been intending on radioing in a description of the Caddy hearse and then giving chase himself. He'd been sure the Crown Victoria's V-8 would've overpowered the older-model wagon. He wasn't even considering trying to pull the hearse over, just slamming the Vic right into it. If one or both died in a fiery ball of flame, so be it. Instead, he was now wasting precious time searching a small side street named after a tree (as all the side streets in the heart of this city were) looking for his keys, while the killer gained distance with each passing second.

There they were, lying in a crenel, up against the curb. He snatched them and loped back to his car before cranking the engine and driving off.

Hoover drove up and down the streets, searching, not for the damaged black hearse—he knew that was already hopeless—but for something else. He drove for five minutes, ten minutes, until he found what he was looking for parked near a curb at the end of a line of other parked cars. It was a police patrol car from the ninth district, sitting under the walkway bridge of the community college, across the street from an apartment complex and a bar.

Hoover thumbed on the hazards and double-parked alongside the squad car, blocking up the nonexistent middle-of-the-night traffic on Seventeenth Street. He opened the door and got out, walked around his car and then the squad car. The eyes of the uniform inside followed him. Hoover reached for his wallet and opened it, tapping on the glass of the passenger-side door with his gold badge.

The officer pushed a button and the window slid down. "Can I help you?" he asked.

"I'm Detective Hoover from homicide."

"The guy in the news," the officer said, and pointed down at the floorboard on Hoover's side. Hoover looked in the car and saw a copy of today's—yesterday's, actually—*News Daily*. the *Philadelphia News Daily* was an afternoon paper, the copy lying on the floor the late edition. There was a picture of a lonely, somber Hoover attending Beverly's funeral on the cover. The headline read, "Beloved Grounded."

"Yeah, that's me," Hoover said drolly.

"Weren't you bounced?"

"Not yet," he said, dryer still. "You busy?"

"Nope. You know, just catching up on some paperwork," which meant he'd been reading the newspaper before Hoover pulled up.

"Look, I need you to do something for me," the homicide cop said.

"What's that?"

Hoover indicated the vacant passenger seat. "Can I get in, Officer?"

"Murphy. Dan Murphy. Sure, get in; my city property's your city property."

Hoover pulled up the handle and, protecting his ailing legs as much as he could, went in butt first. He swiveled around so that he was facing the officer, his foot crinkling up the cover of the *News Daily*.

"What can I do for a fallen comrade?" Murphy asked.

"Fire up your laptop and run a tag."

"That's it?"

"That's it."

Murphy hit a few keys, and the screen on the IBM ThinkPad bolted to the dashboard became a beehive of activity. In the modern age, police squad cars were now directly wired into an information database. They can use this system to instantly retrieve criminal information on suspects, including any reports written regarding their crimes, bring up driving records by swiping the magnetic stripe on the back of a license into a reader, utilize maps and phone books, and even look up tax information on people in arrears. And they can run license plates.

"What's the number?" he asked, fingers poised over the home-row keys.

Hoover gave it to him. It had been a standard Pennsylvania tag, three letters and four digits, separated by a tiny keystone symbol—easy to remember. Murphy typed it in and waited for the search, an hourglass shape replacing the arrow of the computer's mouse, spinning in a circle on the screen to indicate that the machine was thinking.

"Do you smell something?" Murphy asked Hoover.

Hoover sniffed and detected a hint of the alley. "Nah, I don't smell anything."

The laptop made a small beep—it was ready. "There it is," Murphy said. "A black 1969 Cadillac."

"Who's it registered to?" Hoover asked, anticipating.

Officer Murphy read off a name and address. Hoover picked up a ticket citation booklet from atop the dashboard and ripped one off. He flipped it over to the blank side of the last of three carbon copies, the one that goes in the files at city hall. He reached over and pulled Murphy's pen from the slim writing-utensil pocket sewn into all police uniform breast pockets. Murphy didn't protest. *He better not*, Hoover thought, *after all, we're comrades—in arms even, ooh.* He felt as giddy as a child on Christmas morning. He wondered what kind of disorders the department-recommended psychiatrist would diagnose he ailed from in his current state of mind, if he'd ever went to see him, as Korzenowski's last bit of advice suggested he do.

Not wanting to rely on his aging memory, Hoover copied the information down directly off the IBM's display.

He clicked the top of the pen to suck the ballpoint back into the body, then stuffed the pen back in Murphy's shirt pocket. As he did, Hoover noticed the black piece of elastic wrapped around the officer's badge. It was there to honor an officer lost in the line of duty. It was there for Beverly.

"Thanks, Murph," Hoover said, using an apparent nickname that had probably been with the kid since birth.

"No problem. You want me to put out a description on this?" the happy-to-be-of-assistance-Detective-now-won't-you-kindly-be-on-your-way-Murphy wanted to know.

"No, I'll handle it," Hoover said. He got out of the patrol car and stood on the pavement.

If the information from the license plate was real—and the car hadn't been stolen—then it was a simple, stupid, big mistake on the Dandelion's part. Hoover held the citation up so that he could read his own writing. It said that the black '69 Caddy hearse was registered to:

> Michael Dedaker
> 573 Kennard Street, Apt. B
> Philadelphia, PA 19154
> Driver's License No. 222-108-3472

Yeah, it was him.

Hoover believed the information was real. It *felt* real to him somehow, on a sixth-sense level. Michael Dedaker was the Dandelion; the Dandelion was Michael Dedaker.

Now that he finally had what he paid so much for, he would act on it. There were no visions of a return to glory this time, only of retribution. This one was all his. He would shear this Dandelion down right in his own den.

A slightly crazed mirth danced in Hoover's eyes, and for the first time since the night he and Beverly had eaten Ruben sandwiches together at the Tabard Inn and then went back to her apartment, Hoover smiled.

It was a vicious, deadly smile.

7

When he turned onto Kennard Street, Hoover felt like Marlow, the character in Joseph Conrad's book who went up the African river to meet Mr. Kurtz. Just as the jungle of the book had driven Kurtz crazy, maybe this urban one had had the same effect on Dedaker. Or maybe Hoover. Even without the allegory, Hoover was definitely descending into the heart of darkness.

It was after one in the morning, and he was slowly driving down the street, looking at addresses. House 573 was midway down the block on his left. Hoover glanced at it as he drove past. It was dark.

He parked the Crown Victoria at the next intersection, which dead ended in a T, and got out. He casually walked around the side of the last house on the block to see what was in the back—a long throughway with rear driveways on either side. One of them was Dedaker's, but he couldn't be able to be sure without the benefit of the address, so he was forced to go it head on from the front.

He walked back up the one-way street, looking at the neighborhood. It was either a low-middle-class or a high-lower-class burg trying to be a suburban-type community but was losing the struggle, the neighborhood being overran by unkept yards and debris. Most of the houses, which were twin duplexes, looked in need of upgrades the owners couldn't afford. Cars had not yet been parked in front yards, abandoned because the high prices of repairs were not within the budgets of the people who owned them. Not yet, but it was coming, as evident by the ages of the automobiles parked along the curbs. There was not one car on the street younger than five years old, maybe even ten.

This neighborhood was changing. There were neighborhoods like this in every big city all across the country.

It was the perfect place for a guy like Dedaker to hole up and perform his acts. The neighborhood was not wildly out of control by any means, so the police would not have to keep a close eye on it. But in the same respect, no one would really notice any unusual activity, such as a guy with thick black curtains over his windows who only came out in the dead of night; a guy who had no friends, enemies or gripes; or a guy who had nothing of note such as a loud muffler on his car or an overgrown patch of crabgrass for a lawn.

On this street, arguments between abusive spouses or irate neighbors probably happened every single day. One or two more occasional screams would not be noticed among the rest. There were never any block parties here. This neighborhood had no PTA, no Town Watch. What it had was Michael Dedaker. And he had chosen wisely.

Hoover stopped in front of 575, the duplex next door to Dedaker's. The information on the laptop of the ninth district car had said Dedaker lived in apartment B, which meant the upper level, but Hoover was pretty sure he owned both units. One floor would be the living space; one floor would be the dying space. If you're going to commit murder, you might as well do it right.

It was the middle of a weekday night, and there were no residents out and about in their yards, all having been tucked snuggly in their beds, waiting for the morn to come so they could get up and go about their routines. People living in economically tight neighborhoods such as this still had their self-respect; times hadn't gotten hard enough yet that they just said fuck it, and quit their jobs. "Why should I bust my ass working when we're never going to get ahead" had not yet become their mantra. The self-respecting people who live in this neighborhood still had jobs that they got up and went to, more often than not, several jobs.

It was too early in the year for the high schoolers to be hanging on the corners, and the worker bees were all sound asleep and blissfully unaware of what might happen inside of 573 Kennard tonight. And if they did hear anything, they would more than most likely ignore it.

Grim and determined, Hoover mounted the stairs in front of Michael Dedaker's apartment, feeling each step ripple through his injured legs. He thought there could possibly be fractures in the bones, and splints or casts might be in store in the near future. Didn't matter, it would wait; he would endure the pain in order to dole some out. Reloaded, he held his gun patiently in his hand.

There was a line of shrubs in front of the closest window from the path. He walked over to them, past the first-floor entrance, and stood in plain sight to look in the window. He had no intentions of crouching down and hiding. He was planning on shooting at first sight.

He tried to peer in the widow at ground level, not thinking that he'd be able to see anything. The curtains were so black they were . . . blue, the deepest shade of navy Hoover had ever seen. When he angled his head just right, the moonlight shimmered off them, giving them a satiny look. No matter what color they were, they were too thick for him to see through. Even if he could see into the unit, he imagined that there would be nothing to see; it would be empty. He figured that Dedaker would live upstairs, keeping the ground level for his work. That's how he, Hoover, would've done it—easier accessibility, less hassle. Dead weight was heavy lifting for going up and down stairs.

Although this was what he believed the first floor of the duplex to be reserved for, he couldn't be sure. He was going to have to do something that he didn't want to do—he was going to have to try the door and see if it was locked. He had to get into the house one way or another, and a lot of people didn't lock their doors behind them while they were inside. Hoover didn't think Dedaker was one of these. He was sure Dedaker was the type of person who kept his doors locked at all times. Whether he was or wasn't, Hoover was going to have to question the knob for the answer.

Thankful that there was no screen door—whether there had never been one or it had been stolen was anyone's guess; the homeless of the city have been known to abscond such things and redeem them for scrap metal in order to buy their cheap, berry-flavored wines with the paltry sum of money they got for their effort. Hoover reached for the knob. He turned it very slowly so that the latch wouldn't click too loudly. It only turned an eighth of an inch before meeting resistance. The door was locked. That was okay; he was prepared to break in, which he would do from the second floor, the entrance to which was on the side of the building and up a flight of concrete stairs.

Turning, Hoover walked along the short path until it made a ninety-degree angle and headed toward the second-floor stairs. At the edge of the building, a strong breeze gusted and blew right through the cotton shirt he wore. The balmy spring day had turned cold with the setting of the sun. Hoover wished that he'd put on a jacket before leaving the house and remembered that at the time, he'd still been feeling the false warmth of the bourbon.

He stood at the foot of the stairs Michael Dedaker had walked many times, wondering what went on in the mind of a man as he turned his home into a chamber of death.

Hoover's heart froze.

There was a sound—a *clinking* sound—coming from the back of the duplex.

Holding his gun out in front of him, Hoover slunk around the side of the stairs. Behind the stoop, there was a rectangular-shaped recess before the rear edge of the duplex. In the recess were three green plastic trash cans with no lids, each full of bags. Hoover's mind had become so saturated with the evilness of the Dandelion that he had to remind himself that he was but a man, a man who ate and slept and threw away his trash.

What do you do with your trash, Detective? the Dandelion had asked him.

Hoover would show him.

Moving at a glacial pace, Hoover came around the side of the duplex. The driveway was empty, but there was a man standing at the back door. The rear entrance had a screen door, and the figure was holding it open. There was another clink—*key on lock?*—as the man concentrated on what he was doing.

Silently, slowly, Hoover crept forward. The detective's gun was leveled at the back of the man's head. It would be an easy, sure shot, but one Hoover couldn't take for two reasons. First, he wanted the Dandelion to know who it was that killed him. Second, Hoover was planning on using a self-defense plea to protect himself from prosecution of murder in the first, which was premeditated murder.

Shooting someone at point-blank range in the back of the head would not be easy to pass off as self-defense, even if he wasn't already in the shithouse with the department.

He wasn't worried about the Dandelion getting away this time. He was an average man with an average weight; Hoover knew he could take him in a scuffle. The Dandelion's terrible power of abduction had been dependant on deception and surprise. This time, the unexpected was to Hoover's advantage.

It was to be a simple thing. Hoover would grab Mr. Dedaker by the shoulder and spin him around. Once he saw who it was that had found his home, his lair, Hoover would shoot him in the neck, so that Dedaker could think things over while he suffocated and bled and died.

You wanted me to kill you, you son of a bitch; well, here it comes.

Hoover's hand dropped on the man's shoulder and spun him around fiercely. The man had been caught off guard and put his hands up to cover his face in fright, the palms splayed outward.

For a brief second, Hoover thought that the hands of the person in front of him weren't human. The palms were unlined, and there were no breaks where the knuckles would flex; the hands looked alien. Then he realized that the man was wearing tight rubber gloves, the type surgeons wore during operations. Hoover pushed the gun in between the gloved hands and stuffed it in the man's throat, causing a small gurgling sound. That sound made Hoover want to spit. Instead, he pushed harder on the gun, driving it deeper. The man went up against the open screen door, making it yawn even wider.

"I found you, you bastard, and I've brought your death," he hissed.

"No, Hoover, no!" the man hissed back at him, dropping his hands. "Don't shoot; it's me."

Surprise was supposed to be on Hoover's side, but his face went slack-jawed with bewilderment as he was once again astonished by the multifaceted layers this case had taken on. A million ideas ran around in his head, but none of them made any sense. He couldn't believe what he was seeing, but he did not lessen the pressure on the gun. The man swallowed, and Hoover could feel his Adam's apple swell beneath the barrel of the gun.

The neck Hoover held the gun against belonged to Father

Thomas O'Malley, he of the rousing fistfight, Hoover's would-be savior. He was dressed in street clothes instead of the priestly garb, but it was definitely Father O'Malley.

Still keeping pressure on the gun, Hoover leaned in so close to O'Malley's face he could smell the aftershave the priest had used almost twenty hours earlier. "How are you involved in this, Father?" Hoover growled at him through clinched teeth. "Are you his accomplice? Better talk quick or forever hold your peace."

"I'm not his accomplice! I came to *you!*" the priest said, urgency in his hoarse voice.

"You mean you came *for* me?"

"No! I came to help you. I came so that we could help each other," O'Malley said, and Hoover realized that the clergyman's voice wasn't hoarse from the gun being pushed against his throat. It wasn't hoarse at all. It sounded strained because he was trying to whisper, something that was difficult to do after so many years of projecting it over hordes of faithful during countless masses. Hearing the strain in O'Malley's voice made Hoover understand the real purpose behind the priest's strange visit to his house; it was now clear to him. The priest was whispering because he didn't want the man—the Dandelion—inside the house to overhear them talking at his back door. O'Malley had been going for the element of surprise, also.

"You knew who he was. This afternoon, when you came to my house, you knew who he was, didn't you?" Hoover shook O'Malley for emphasis. "I thought you were there to give me the feel-good speech from Mother Church, but you weren't, were you?"

"No, I . . . You're right, I knew who he was," O'Malley said. The gun was still at his throat, and there was a wild look in the cop's eyes.

"Someone else could've died, you cocksucker; why didn't you tell me?" Hoover demanded, thinking about Fiona's close call and his own injuries in the alley, both of which could've been avoided if the priest had given him Dedaker's name when he had the chance.

"Because you were drunk and unstable; with all the melodramatic shit you were saying, I couldn't count on you for this," O'Malley spat angrily back at him.

Hoover lowered the gun. He squinted at O'Malley with one

eye and asked, even though he already thought he knew, "Count on me for what? What *exactly* are you doing here, Father?"

As quickly and concisely as he could, O'Malley told him. He told him everything: from Darren Roberts's sordid tale, through his visitations to the victim's families (those that he had been able to get to in the past forty-three hours; the rest he would try to get to while preparations were being made during the next couple of days), and up until Hoover found him at this door. He told him of the cogitation of the idea and the theorized implementation of the plan. He told him everything.

When he finished, Hoover was looking at him, hard. The cop had guessed right. "Why would you want to do this; you're a priest?"

"I have my reasons," O'Malley said, and Hoover knew it was all he was going to get at this time. But there would be more later, when he asked again. He had one more question before he went along with O'Malley's idea, seeing it was similar to what he had in mind anyway, only better, nastier.

He asked, "I'm a cop; why would you want to get me involved in something like this?"

"Because of Beverly," the priest said in a defrocked way, less like a member of the Roman Catholic clergy, more like an old, sincerely sympathetic friend. "I saw the Internet videotape that kid sold to the news. I knew who you were before that, when the defense attorney made a name for himself with the pawnshop case. I also saw the stress you were under when you punched that reporter. In the past few weeks, you've been through a lot of pain and anguish. The cold-blooded murder of a friend—or lover, as the case may be—done right before your eyes was just too much for one man to have to suffer. I've felt your pain; I've wept for your misery. I wanted to give you a chance to vindicate your soul, to put a satisfying end to something that was wrongly tied around your neck—and has been pulling you under since. I wanted to give this man to you, as well as to the others, the families of the women he has killed."

"I don't know if what you're suggesting is compassionate or savage, Father, but what made you think I wouldn't squeal?"

"Beverly again. I saw the way you held her head as she died. That's what sold me, your tenderness, your affection for her. Any relationship problems that you've had since that day are not because of what you said on that tape; they're because of what you did. Every woman that you've ever known who has seen that footage can only imagine what it was they lost when you walked out of their lives. The way you held her and looked at her and stroked her hair as her life and soul left her body forever, every woman in the world would give up her own life for a true moment of love like that. It was pure. It was chaste. It was a moment of absolute human divination, unknowingly caught on MPEG files and stored on some hard drive to be put up for sale and shown the world over. A bare moment like that, in which the depth of the human heart—the human soul—is so openly and honestly expressed, is magical. It's impossible to ever capture something like that outside of a situation like the one in which Beverly lost her life. That tape *is* reality, the footage worthy of an award; don't be surprised." The cold night was being made even colder by what the priest was saying. With each word, little plumes of vapor floated from his mouth.

"For better or worse," O'Malley went on, "that tape is going to be your legacy. It'll be as infamous as the Zapruder film, or the photos of the Tate house after the Manson Family visited. There was a report in today's paper that it's the most downloaded file in the history of the Internet, even more than the suicide of Bud Dwyer, or the torture murder of some Chinese guy I never heard of, or even Miss Jackson's halftime fiasco. That tape will be studied in psychology classes in every major and minor college around the globe for some time to come, for never has the human condition been so explicitly captured. Beverly's death will haunt you for the rest of your days. It will haunt you from television, from magazines and books, and I wanted to try to lessen some of that pain by giving you this," he jerked his thumb at 573 Kennard. "I wanted to give you *him*."

Some of what was being said Hoover had already figured out on his own, some he couldn't even have begun to imagine. "I shot him tonight, Father, in the arm," Hoover told him. "But he slipped away again, like a ghost through my fingers."

O'Malley acknowledged by nodding his head, but said nothing.

Hoover looked at the house. "I don't think he's here. I can't feel him in there."

"Then we'll wait," O'Malley said, "inside."

"I'm afraid to go in there."

"I am too."

"In all my professional life, I've never come up against something like this. It's too *spiritual* or something. I feel like I have no control over it, no control over him *or* me," Hoover confessed.

"We still have to go in."

"I know."

"Here," O'Malley said, handing him a pair of rubber surgical gloves. Hoover had forgotten that the priest was wearing them. In his hands were an exact replica of the pair O'Malley had on—concealing but formfitting to maintain fine motor skills. Hoover put them on.

"How are we going to get in without him knowing as soon as he gets here?"

"There are three locks on this door—two deadbolts and one on the knob. I have already unlocked the deadbolts, and was just about to run the knob when you showed up. I can get us in."

"Lock picking? They teach that at the seminary?"

"I wasn't always a priest, remember? I was once known as the Alley Cat, and for a reason." O'Malley bent to the door, and Hoover noticed for the first time that there were two slim pieces of metal protruding from the knob's cylinder. Hoover had seen this done before, even though he was untrained at it himself. He understood that the way to open a lock without a key was to insert the tension wrench—one of the slim metal tools—into the lock, turning it slightly so that the tumblers would line up. While doing this, you would use the pick—the other metal piece—to make the tumblers fall, releasing the lock.

It was delicate work, but the priest's skilled fingers moved deftly, fishing the tools around, looking for purchase. One slipped and landed on the driveway with a tiny clink. O'Malley picked it up and reinserted it. While the priest concentrated on his work, he said, as if just remembering, "Oh, there was another reason I wanted you to be a part of this."

"Yeah, what's that?"

"I have no idea what this guy looks like. You've seen him before. I wanted you to ID him for me, you know, to make sure we get the right guy before we . . ." The priest looked up at him with a shy smile on his face. Hoover could see beads of sweat standing out on his brow even in the chill of the night air. "This is not something that can be half done, know what I mean?"

Hoover smiled at O'Malley's candor. "What was your alternate plan after you found me toasted?"

"Well, at first glance, I figured I'd sit in the car and wait for the paperboy to come along, have him point out to me the man in question, and then take it from there. Once you told me your theory that he was going to take to the hills, I panicked, figured that I had to risk it tonight, then try to corroborate his identity with Darren tomorrow. It was a desperation move, but I didn't want this guy to get away. The sorrow that he has caused . . ."

"I know," Hoover said, understandingly.

Just then there was a click, and the priest straightened up. "It's open, we're in," he said, stuffing the locksmith tools in his back pocket. He bent down and picked up a long cylindrical black object which had been leaning against the wall. Hoover had thought it a piece of piping, but it wasn't. It was the largest, longest flashlight he had ever seen. At what Hoover guessed to be over two feet long, it was slick and black and ribbed along its shaft for grip. Printed around the lens casing was the name Maglite.

Christ, there must be half a dozen D-cells in that thing, Hoover thought.

"Let's go," Father O'Malley said, and turned the knob. The door opened only six inches before being stopped short by three sliding-chain locks. Not about to be beaten by such simplicity, O'Malley reached into his other back pocket and pulled out a handheld set of lightweight bolt cutters.

Stalling, Hoover asked, "What did you do, raid the Army-Navy store?"

"Nah, I ordered this," he waved the bolt cutters, "from Loos and Company down in Florida some years back. We had a buildup of rusting bikes chained to the rack out front of the church; I had to get rid of them, so I bought one of these. Before you ask, the picks are from a locksmith shop, and the flashlight is from Kmart, both items of which were purchased especially for this excursion."

Wrapping his fists tightly around the handles, O'Malley inserted the bolt cutters through the opening, and *snip, snip, snip*, all three chains were cut. The door swung gently inward, creaking slightly.

O'Malley stowed the cutters back in the pocket they came from.

Taking a deep breath, he crossed the threshold. Hoover took one final glance around him and followed the priest into the darkness.

The first thing he noticed was the odor. It was slight in the heavy, stale air, as if underlying the rich, peaty smell of offal. Dedaker must've sanitized the apartment as much as possible, but nothing short of a professional airing (or a professional arson) would rid the place of the effluvium smell of death. There was no mistaking it; murder had been committed here.

The next thing to strike Hoover was the *normality* of the place. It was in character with Dedaker's usualness but still seemed to catch Hoover off guard.

In the large halo of O'Malley's flashlight, he could see that the apartment was a typical residence, devoid of furniture and amenities, but everything else seemed to be in place. There were heating ducts and electric sockets, a gas meter and a gas heater, a sink and some out-of-date kitchen cabinets. No phones, no televisions, no skulls or satanic messages scrawled on the walls in dried blood, nothing but empty space.

Hoover was scared shitless, and the commonplace look of the apartment made it worse. He checked the priest and, in the glow of the flashlight, could see tension lining O'Malley's face.

From where they stood in the back room—a den, maybe, although the heater and utility meter were in the room—Hoover could see the kitchen and the bathroom. As he peeked into both, they seemed unused, the bathroom almost barren—desolate—in its lack of use. While O'Malley shone the light in, Hoover looked in the tub, and then the toilet. Sometimes, traces of blood or hair would be residually left behind while being washed away (*Once a cop, always a cop, even while perpetrating criminal acts*), but Hoover didn't spy anything in either receptacle. In fact, there wasn't even water in the toilet bowel, only glossy porcelain. He tried the faucet. Other than a clanging noise in the pipes, nothing came out.

"Why is it all so empty?" O'Malley asked.

"It's his killing field. And he's scared of it" was Hoover's impression.

"I don't follow."

"Murder isn't an easy thing to do, Father. The taking of another's life is a galling piece of work *not* for the weak of heart. Every muscle and organ inside the body moves with life, twitches.

It's all covered in blood, everything hot and wet and slimy—the inside of a human body is *humid* It gives me the willies just thinking about it. And I bet it gives him the willies too. That's why it's empty in here—he's scared of being down here by himself when he's not doing what it is he does."

"How can evil be scared of itself?" the priest asked.

"When one is alone, imagination can have an immeasurable power over your mind. Haven't you ever lain in bed in the middle of the night and been scared witless, even as an adult, by something you've heard or some shadow that looked disconcertingly like something it wasn't?"

"Sure, I have."

"That's your imagination. When people die of natural causes in their sleep, how can we know it wasn't their imagination that scared them so bad in the dark of night that their heart burst in their chest? I've always thought people without imaginations were better off than those with. People like that are often labeled stupid or boring, but I consider them lucky. Without imagination, they aren't worried about every unaccountable minute of their wives' lives wondering whom she's sleeping with, or conjuring a fiery car wreck for their kids if they're ten minutes late coming home. The way I see it, imaginatively deprived people sleep like babes in the woods.

"But I don't think our guy's one of those; I think he's got an imagination. From the Laplin note, from the things he's said to me, and from the way he's set this whole murder-suicide thing up, I think he's highly imaginative, if delusional. And I think that imagination sneaks up and spooks him from time to time. My bet, that's what keeps him out of this apartment."

"That's highly intuitive, if you're right," O'Malley said, his own imagination starting to run wild in his head. The place was definitely spooky.

"On the force, we call it gut instinct. Come on, let's see what *is* here."

Walking a little farther in, following the beam of light, they found an empty bedroom; adjacent to the bedroom was a living room and a room with a closed door.

They chose the living room first.

Hoover knew this was the room—rectangular and longer than

it was wide—that faced onto Kennard Street because of the door. There were many locks running up and down it, including a steel pole that wedged into plates on both the door and the floor, not to mention the nails driven into the wood or the concrete lining the gaps. If he and O'Malley had tried this way in, they wouldn't have made it.

Every window was boarded up, save one, where blue-black curtains hung. Hoover knew that these same curtains were hung in the other boarded-up windows from his inspection out front. *Dedaker must've hung the curtains for appearance, then sealed them in when he nailed up the boards*, he theorized. The curtains were meant to keep curious onlookers from taking a closer peek, but his ruse hadn't worked—it hadn't been able to keep that Roberts guy from looking.

Standing in the middle of the room, on flattened gray carpet that looked as if something had been lying on top of the entire square footage for some time and then not vacuumed after it had been removed, was a podium. It was four feet high and made of wood, a spot on the front in which the color of the wood was lighter than the rest indicating that there might have been an emblem for a building or a company attached to it at some point before being given away or stolen. The top was slanted, and there were shelves in the back. Father O'Malley inspected its alcoves.

"Hoover, take a look at this," he said quietly.

Hoover walked around the side of the podium and looked in. Lying on the shelves were many different types of knives. There were boning knives and fishing knives, hunting and modeling knives, kitchen knives and operating-room knives—long ones, short ones, wide ones, thin ones. The only thing they all had in common was that they were sharp, and that they could kill.

Sitting amongst the knives was a white box, inside the box various-sized pieces of black chalk. Hoover reached in and picked up a piece. Fine grains of black dust powdered onto the rubber of his glove. He held the chalk up to his nose and smelled it. "Charcoal," he said to O'Malley.

"What does he do with that?"

"I don't know. The lab didn't report any traces of it on the bodies from the airport, but then they had been left exposed to the wind and rain and snow; the charcoal dust might've dissipated. Or it might be for something else entirely, and not have been used for the murders at all. Then again, two of them—Knoble and Fattore—haven't turned up yet. He could've used the charcoal for something with them."

"Like what?" O'Malley asked hesitantly, not sure if he really wanted to know.

"Medically, charcoal is used to pump stomachs, for overdoses and things like that. At hospitals, they tube it down so that it can powder the stomach, absorbing any poisons. He's put stuff into the other bodies; maybe he pumped something into Knoble or Fattore's stomachs." Hoover swallowed before saying, "Or out of 'em."

O'Malley was all eyes, wide and staring, unbelieving.

"There's a coat closet over there," Hoover said, pointing with a gloved finger. "Let's see what's in it."

Empty, except for a clear huge tarp folded in squares and pushed into a corner. Through the tarp they could see tiny prisms reflecting in little drops of moisture when the flashlight shone on them, the moisture beads of water sealed in the plastic from the last time the tarp had been washed off then stowed.

Hoover kicked the tarp over to see if anything was underneath it. Nothing.

They both turned around and looked at the only room in the whole apartment with its door closed.

Hoover started to approach it before O'Malley gripped his shoulder to stop him. "What's wrong?" Hoover asked.

"I don't know if I have the courage to go in there," O'Malley whispered, his imagination gunning on all cylinders.

"Why not; you've come this far?"

O'Malley held up his hands. Even through the gloves, Hoover could see them shaking. "Look at my hands; I'm scared to death."

"So am I, but we both know he's not here. There's nothing on the other side of that door that can hurt us," Hoover assured him.

O'Malley shook his head. "I was all right until you started in with all that imagination shit. Then you had to mention the missing bodies. John, I'm a priest; I've never seen a dead body before, except at funerals after the undertakers were done with them. What if those women are in there, all sliced up and stuff?"

"If they're in there, they're dead; they can't do anything to you. I'm creeped out myself. In order for me to be able to go through with this, I need you to toughen up and go with me. Besides, I'm hoping there's a set of stairs in there that leads to the second floor. If not, we're going to have to go back outside, and you're going to have to perform your unlock trick on the side door."

O'Malley swallowed, and it clicked audibly. "All right, I'll go with you. But you have to go first. Here, take the light." He handed him the flashlight, and Hoover turned toward the door, O'Malley getting into step behind him. Hoover could feel the man cowering, his rapid breathing warming the back of his neck. The priest was mumbling. Hoover thought it a nervous reaction, but it was too rhythmical—the priest was praying.

Hoover reached out to grab the doorknob, feeling sweat trickle against his palms from his fright and his skin being unable to breath within the rubber gloves.

He opened the door, and they entered the room.

8

$\mathcal{M}$ichael Dedaker backed the Ford Escort into his driveway using his good arm to turn the wheel. The hole the bullet opened in his other arm hadn't stopped bleeding yet, but it was thickening and gelling over with coagulation.

Using the rearview mirror the car manufacturer had glued at the upper middle of the windshield—a windshield that was intact and usable—he slowly lowered the car down the decline until it was a foot away from the rear door. He had to use his right hand to bring the gearshift to park, and when he did, a bolt of pain shot through the bullet wound as the silently and slowly forming clots tore. He grimaced and hissed because he was human, but he didn't mind the pain really. He took comfort in it, actually; it made him feel alive.

He got out of the car and pushed the button that activated the security alarm. *One can never be too careful*, he thought, as the shrill *cheep-chirp* acknowledged the activation. *After all, even I have managed to become somewhat of a car thief recently*. That gave him a chuckle as he walked around to the stairs leading to the second-floor apartment.

It had all fallen apart in Philadelphia, and now it was time to move on. He had been prepared for this since the Purser Street failure and was looking forward to renewing his ambition on a different playing field. The cop, his unwilling (and inadequate) accomplice and nemesis both, had a weak mind, but he had bested him, Michael Dedaker. Of all the possible ways it could've gone bad—one of the women getting away before he could release her soul, the site at the airport remaining unfound, the Laplin note being unable to be deciphered by the cops—he had never imagined that anyone faced with the decision Hoover had been at the Purser house would not have gone through with the requisite action. That thought depressed Dedaker. To further salt the wound, the damage the hearse had taken had rendered it unsalvageable. He had loved that car. It had saved his ass, and now it was rusting at the bottom of the Delaware River, in a hero's grave where it would be found in a year or two or not. It didn't matter. The hearse, with its whimsical irony, had served its purpose and had died a courageous death on the field of battle. He would miss that car, but there would be another; God always provided.

Could that be why he was sometimes referred to as Providence?

Dedaker didn't know the answer to that question, and frankly, was too tired right now to put any thought into it. And the night wasn't even over yet. He still had to go into his apartment to dismantle the computer, the organizer and brain behind his work. When he had it safely packed in the Escort, he would get in and take off, fleeing for safer pastures. Until he was a thousand miles from the debacle Philadelphia had turned out to be, he could not rest. Then, and only then, with this ruinous misadventure behind him, would he find a hotel or motel where he could hole up for a couple of days, letting the aches and pains heal, his heart knit. At least money would not be a factor; he had enough from his occupation—which he liked to think of as that of a carpenter, as Joseph had been, as Jesus probably had been. Did he, Michael Dedaker, not build wealth out of pyramids? It was amazing what you could buy and sell on-line to the greedy: useless stocks, junk bonds, false hopes. People were so gullible that they believed everything they read, and were so willing to be parted from their money. There's a reason why greed was not only a sin but one of the deadly ones—it'll kill ya.

But ruminations aside, there was still work to be done before he could rest. He had to collect the computer, then he had to scram.

There was nothing else inside he wanted or needed that he would not be able to reobtain after his rebirth in the next city.

Except for the renderings.

But they weren't his for the taking. As much as he loved to stand in their presence, gazing on them longingly as the art they were, he could not take them with him. They were a part of this stage, not the next. They would remain in this house as testament to his work here. Sooner or later, they would be discovered and marveled over, pondered, discussed, dissected. That was why they were here; that was why they would remain here. Besides, there would be more to be made in the next stage, wherever that ended up being. He hoped that when they were found, they'd be turned into a book, published. Originally, he had thought that might happen posthumously, but because of Detective Hoover's screwup, he might yet live to see their publication. He could envision the book sitting on a shelf alongside the Holy Bible, its compendium, and *Mein Kampf*, its (in his opinion) namesake. Who knows, his work might even get its own room in some Catholic museum one day.

No, he couldn't take the renderings with him, but there was time for one final look, a visitation for old time's sake.

He spun the ring of keys in his hand and fingered through them until he had the one that worked the locks on the second-floor door. He had them all keyed the same at a locksmith shop which was, ironically enough, located on Race Street, cattycorner to the police headquarters building.

He smiled to himself as he unlocked the first lock by the amber light of the streetlamp. Everything was going to be all right. He had been bested by an infidel, true, but even Christ stumbled beneath the weight of his heavy burden three times on his way to Golgotha and the culmination of his work. The Son had picked himself up and had continued on his long and difficult road. He had even enlisted the help of the innocent Simon while the mass of ugly faces lining his path jeered and taunted.

Maybe, in the next stage of my own path, I should employ a helper, a partner, someone to help carry the cross for me. A Simon, that sounds interesting.

Instead of being a defeatist, Michael was looking to the promise of the future. There was no need to dwell on a failure or a stumble. Pick yourself up, dust yourself off, shoulder your albatross, and keep on trekking down the path God set for you, simple as that. It was all about being right with yourself in your own mind. Dedaker felt that he was.

First a peek at the renderings, then the computer, then I'm gone, he thought as he entered what was soon to become his last known address.

9

There were no dead bodies in the room, but what was in there might have been even worse for Father O'Malley to experience. Had there been bodies, it might have sickened him to his heart. What was in there shocked him to his very soul.

The room was another bedroom, mostly empty like the rest of the ground-level apartment. The stairs Hoover had been hoping for were not there and thus were not in the apartment at all.

What the conical light of the flashlight did illuminate were walls that swayed in the gentle breeze the opening door had stirred, and the silhouette of a round tub on the floor. Sitting next to the tub was something the size of a large rock.

"What the hell is this?" Hoover asked, standing next to the tub. When he kicked it, a sloshing sound came from inside. He aimed the light toward it, but it was too dark to see what it contained.

"I'm not sure," the priest said at first, looking at the walls rather than the only objects in the room. "It looks like the wallpaper is peeling off." O'Malley ran a hand down the length of one of the loose papers. Through the rubber gloves, he could not feel the texture of the paper, but he could tell that it was not thick like wallpaper should be.

Looking around the room, in the glow of the light Hoover shone in the tub, O'Malley could see that each strip of paper ran ceiling to floor, with a gap of a couple of inches separating each piece. The strips were white with black patterns or splotches running intermittently down them. All three walls that were visible upon entry seemed to have these papers attached to them. The fourth wall, the one with the door, was the only one devoid of the strips.

"Oh my God," O'Malley said in a frightened, weirdly hushed tone.

Hoover shone the light directly into the priest's eyes. "What?" he asked, sounding spooked himself. O'Malley was unsure if the cop wanted to know what he thought was in the room or what had just given the priest the heebie-jeebies.

It don't matter, it's the same thing, O'Malley thought. Verbally, he said, "Can we turn on the lights in this room? Just for a minute. I want to see this with my own eyes."

Hoover didn't see why not. They were deep within the apartment, and the windows were boarded up—no one would see the light on. John shrugged his shoulders in deference to the request before realizing O'Malley couldn't see him in the glare of the flashlight. "Yeah, go ahead," Hoover said.

Shining the light back at the open doorway so that O'Malley would easily be able to find the switch, he thought he saw something move in the hall, a flash of white.

"Who's there?" he shouted, his gun already up. The priest let out a pathetic little yelp, and Hoover felt him step behind him, crowding him.

"What'd you see? Is it him?" O'Malley asked right in his ear.

"I don't know. Think I saw something out there move," he answered, scaring the priest even more. Together, they walked to the doorway like some two-headed, post-nuclear holocaust mutation.

Both men were sweating profusely from fright, causing a palpable smell to rise off them. They inched back into the hallway, and Hoover pointed the light first into the den to the left, and then, after what O'Malley thought was too long of a pause, to the right, where the living room was. They didn't see anything in either area; nothing moved. They waited, watched, and listened. Other than them, the house was still empty. Except maybe for the ghosts.

"I don't see anything," Hoover said over his shoulder. "Must've been the old imagination, eh, Father?"

They reentered the bedroom this time with O'Malley in the lead. As he walked in, he flipped up the switch. The room burst with dazzling brightness that temporarily blinded them. Hoover shut off the flashlight.

When his vision returned, Father O'Malley said, "I thought so." He sounded both awed and horrified.

Hoover looked around the room. The wallpaper wasn't wallpaper at all, unless you were talking in the literal sense, for it literally was paper hanging from the wall. The papers themselves were long white, continuous strips, like the stuff found wound in rolls at the foot of examining tables in doctor's offices. Only it wasn't waxy to prevent the spread of germs; it was thin, onion-skinned paper used for tracing impressions.

Now we know what he did with the charcoal, Hoover thought. *He made outlines of them.*

Hanging on the walls—from the ceiling, actually—were renderings of the women Dedaker had killed. They were hung opposite of how they had been murdered, with their heads up and toes to the floor. He had taken an eight-foot piece of the long paper and laid it on top of each woman, having done so after they were dead, as indicated by the dried blood smears that had seeped haphazardly through the papers like grease spots on drive-thru bags. Dedaker then applied pressure as he did charcoal rubbings of the deceased. The result was a very detailed and recognizable image of each woman, and the torment she had suffered.

The facsimile of each woman and, more specifically, the pain she had gone through at the end (which was somehow captured in the vivid details of streaky, hollow eye sockets and the abysmally deep contortions of the mouth) was eerie and quite grotesque to see. The misery visible on each charcoal countenance was an aberrant abomination of masochism displayed in a gallery along the walls. Hoover could sympathize, with deep compassion, the ordeal they had suffered. He had been there, lived it firsthand.

Father O'Malley and Detective Hoover had found Michael Dedaker's sepulcher—this bedroom was an office for the dead.

There were twelve portraits in all. At the bottom of each work, in steady block lettering, were names and dates. Starting on the left, Hoover read, Judith Kasay, May 5. Next to her, Haley Goldberg, June 6. Then, Tammy Allensworth, July 12. It went on down the line, all twelve in chronological order, ending with Amber Knoble and Natalie Fattore, once presumed dead, now confirmed. They were all there, all except Beverly.

Because she wasn't the one that was supposed to die that night, he was.

Each print hung from a row of four thumbtacks, the tacks perfectly straight and equidistant from each other, pushed into the ceiling about an inch from the wall, leaving breathing room behind each strip.

That's why they billow every time a puff of wind goes by. He likes the impression of natural, unpredictable movement. It gives them life, even in death. It was little things like that that had amazed Hoover at how much ingenuity a person could put into something that was so sick, so antisocial. *How do you think this shit up, you twisted freak?*

He hadn't even heard the half of it yet.

"What's in the tub?" O'Malley asked.

Hoover had forgotten about the tub until the priest mentioned it. He looked down and noticed that it was made out of metal. *It looks like one of those old movie-prop washtubs seen in Westerns, when the poor wife of the gunslinger has to stay home and wash the skid marks out of his underwear while he's out keeping the lawful peace in the one-saloon town.* It was half filled with a very deep, dark red—almost garnet—liquid. Hoover kicked the side of the tub again, and the liquid rippled. "It looks like blood," Hoover told him.

"It's wine," the priest said, still studying the walls, his back to Hoover. "Is there anything next to the tub?"

Hoover looked. When he saw it sitting next to the tub, he remembered thinking that it had been a rock.

"Is it bread?" O'Malley asked.

"How did you know?" Hoover asked, briefly wondering again about the priest's involvement in this. Sitting next to the tub was not a rock, but a half loaf of Italian bread that looked as if it had come from a bakery.

"Because I know what he's doing here, in this room."

"What?"

A chill ran up Hoover's spine as O'Malley turned to look at him. There were tears in the priest's eyes. "He's recreating his version of the Last Supper," O'Malley said. "That's why there're twelve rubbings; they each represent one of the apostles at the meal. He sees himself as the Christ figure. That's why he wanted you to kill him on Purser Street; it was right before Easter. Christ was put to death the Friday before Easter, not Saturday, but it's close enough. Our boy wanted the same thing to happen to him, to be put to death by the local law for what he saw as erroneous sins that he hadn't committed. It all makes sense now."

"If that's it, then the math's off. Those last two were still alive when he took them. If I had killed him, there'd only be ten, instead of twelve."

O'Malley shook his head. "Think of it: sketchy, black-and-white visions of his victims. That sound like anything to you?"

"The grainy images of the Internet footage from Purser Street."

"Right. The final two were to come from that room, and in essence, they did—Beverly's actual death and your 'sacrificed' life. But that combination wasn't the one he wanted, because he wanted it to be him."

"I fucked it up."

"You fucked it up; Judas to his Jesus, you sold him out. The last two he abducted, he probably did because it's what he does; at this point, he doesn't know any different. Either that, or he simply didn't know what to do with the women he unexpectedly found in his backseat, so his hand was forced . . ."

"By me, which infers that I played a part in their murders as well that damnable night." *You're no better than he is.*

"I didn't say that."

Hoover sighed; it wasn't the priest's fault. "So then, if he believes himself Christ, did he think he was going to rise again?"

"I have no idea; maybe. What I think is these renderings are supposed to represent the Shroud of Turin, the cloth that covered Christ's body when it was entombed. The shadowy image of Jesus was burned into the cloth, much like the charcoal images of these women."

Hoover was not a religious man, so this should not have affected him as much as it did, but damn if this whole thing hadn't just gone to another level. *It was one thing to piss on humanity, but God's territory was another area entirely. Or was it?*

Wasn't it said that God made humans in his own image?

"I see now why God wanted me to do this, why he wanted me to come here."

"Why's that?" Hoover asked, taking a closer look at the red-black liquid in the tub's basin. It wasn't blood—it was thinner, and there was a sweet, vinegary smell emanating from it. O'Malley was right; it was wine.

"Because this is sacrilege of the highest order," the priest said, pointing both of his index fingers at the floor, but meaning the room itself. "In the first Mosaic law—the first of the Ten Commandments—God stated that 'Thou shalt have no other gods before me.' Of all the rules in all the world, that is number one. It's even higher than that. The first commandment is rule number one on Earth and in the heavens. It's the biggest, highest, most powerful law of all. All other laws are second to it, and this guy is just going to say fuck that? Fuck Moses and his commandments; fuck the burning bush, casting himself as a false idol, some sort of gothic Christ figure. And then he has the balls to make a mockery of the Last Supper, when Christ knew that he was going to be betrayed and did not back down, but went freely to his death for our salvation."

Father O'Malley paused in his stupefaction at Dedaker's condescendence of God.

"I have lived such a sheltered existence," O'Malley finally said when he could speak again, tears freely falling down his face. "Hiding behind the shield of the cloth, which turns out to be only but a thin fabric. I see where I was wrong now. The church vestments aren't supposed to be a shield, they're supposed to be exactly what they are, cloth; cloth that has purposefully been constructed to be porous, so that things—ideas, beliefs, convictions—can seep in, and absorbent so that I may retain and learn from them. Only in that way am I able to pass knowledge on to others."

"What are you talking about?" Hoover asked, his brow furrowed. *This is what I must've sounded like earlier, when he came to my house and found me in a stupor.*

"In all my life, I had never known such a thing as this . . . this macabre sacrilege . . . was possible," O'Malley continued, answering Hoover's question as best as his confused mind could. "I've been a Roman Catholic priest for more than half my time on Earth, and do you know I thought that in all that time, I had been *helping* people? I hadn't, John. I'm not a priest; I'm a sham. I'm a sham of a man, a false shaman.

"I hold the position of the Pastoral Councilor at St. Tiburtius. The councilor's position is set up to help people through their times of darkness, when all looks lost. The desperate would come to me and ask for guidance, and I would give it from the comfortable cushion of my chair, not worrying about where my next meal was coming from or how I was going to pay my bills, just as you pointed out earlier tonight. Understandably, the one issue at the core for most people who sought the help of the Pastoral Councilor was death. Death of a loved one is a hard thing to accept. I did what I thought was the right thing at the time, I consoled. I felt bereft for them. I thought I was helping, when all I was doing was placating. Death—any death—is not what they should be worried about; death comes for every man. What people should worry about is eternity!

"It goes further than that. People would come to me and confess to their petty sins, and I'd absolve them, thinking I was being comforting yet stern. I was being bullshit was what I was being. I wasn't helping anybody. The sins the common people out there are guilty of are the equivalent of gnats flying around the head of a tyrannosaur. This guy, who does this," he jabbed his finger at several of the renderings, "this is that tyrannosaur. The people who came to me with their frivolous infractions came expecting me to free them of their guilt. I did it, just as I was taught to do. But now I realize that it didn't mean anything, what I did. My whole religion is wrapped around the concept of guilt. The guilt those people felt for their inconsequential sins was not wrong, but it was baseless. They should not be guilty of being human.

"It is I who am the guilty one," said Father O'Malley. "I am guilty of thinking that because I wear a collar, I am guiltless. Guilty of thinking I was living a sinless life, when what I was really doing was no different from what the man who killed these women and staged this Last Supper has done. I am guilty of thinking—no, *making*—myself godlike through what is only an occupation, the priesthood. I am but a mere man, an extension of God's covenant with the people. I am *not* his equal."

The tears were gone from O'Malley's eyes, and only the rage—

directed at himself—remained. Still, some of the salty moisture glistened on his cheeks in the glaring, harsh light of the sepulcher. Hoover stood rapt, listening to the man's soul-searching. He thought briefly of Agbalaya's accusation—*You're no better than he is*—and wondered what the priest would make of it. And how it might reflect on him, O'Malley.

"I hadn't known why I concocted the plan of events I've relayed to you," Father O'Malley said. "I only thought that it was God's will that I go through with this, even though I'd be breaking one of the Mosaic laws myself. Now that the scales have been lifted from my eyes, and I understand the complexity of God's plan, I see why it was that he wanted me to be a part of such a hideous act. This is a test of faith, my faith. A faith I thought I had, but I hadn't even been aware of the meaning behind that word. Now I know. It took a monster to slaughter thirteen beautiful young women for me to understand everything—to understand who I am, and who God is.

"What's to pass in the next few days is the Lord's idea of reparation. It's like when Abraham was asked to take the life of Isaac. For my penance, God has made it so that I must sin in order to understand the sanctity of the position I hold. My punishment for thinking I was equal to his grace and goodness is to be my very soul.

"And now I must finish the rest of the duty the Lord has set upon me. Let's go upstairs and wait for him to come home."

No matter what the priest's personal thoughts concerning his own life were, Hoover too was ready to go to the second floor. There was nothing left to accomplish here, and they had wasted too much time speculating over the horrors of Dedaker's killing field. Plus, Hoover was starting to get a queasy feeling being inside this house. It was like standing inside someone's brain—a sick, festering, homicidal brain. He needed a breath of fresh air, and the necessary trip outside before they would be able to gain access to the second floor sounded good to him.

Father O'Malley was already in the hallway when the sound of a closing door was heard. Someone was here.

That was no fucking imagination, Hoover thought.

O'Malley pointed to the gallery wall, silently asking if the noise had come from the neighbor's duplex adjacent to this one. Hoover shook his head. A thick, cinder block firewall separated such buildings, and there was no way the noise they heard had come from next door. If it had come from the neighbor's, it would have been muffled; they had heard it clearly—*too* clearly, in fact.

Either he's in this apartment with us right now, or there is a way upstairs from inside.

Hoover let the priest know what he was thinking by pointing first at the floor, then pointing upstairs, then shrugging his shoulders. He finished by putting a finger against his lips. Amazingly, O'Malley got it and nodded his head without moving.

They stood stock-still until they heard the footsteps walking around above them. He was upstairs. Once Hoover realized this, he tiptoed over to O'Malley, turning out the light of the sepulcher behind him. In the new darkness, he put his mouth so close to O'Malley's ear the cracked dryness of his lips brushed against the priest, tickling him, as he said, "The noises he's making are too loud; there has to be an opening in here somewhere that leads upstairs. He's got access to this level." O'Malley nodded again, having already figured that out.

"He's in the house, but it's us who are cornered," Hoover went on. "I think we should go outside, one of us waiting by the back door while the other goes upstairs."

"And do what?"

"Knock. When he answers, we grab him."

O'Malley shook his head, disagreeing. "We make some noise down here, draw him to us."

"What if he's got a fucking machine gun and shoots at us through the access opening? Even with my gun, it'd be him in the foxhole and us standing in the open field. We'd have no defense."

"All right, we do it your way. But how can we be sure it's him?" There was a sound of something dropped to the floor above them.

"Who else would it be?" Hoover asked.

O'Malley nodded again. "Remember, I haven't seen him."

"I'll make sure. Head for the back door as quickly and quietly as you can."

As soon as they were clear of the sepulcher, Hoover clicked on the flashlight and shone it at the living room ceiling. There was no hole, but there was a thick piece of black piping spanning the room.

That's what he hung them from while he cut them up. Then he probably used that tub to catch the blood. Christ, he thought, but then again, so had Dedaker.

The priest was already down the hall, and Hoover trailed behind, watching the ceiling and waiting for Dedaker to pounce down on them. When he got to the den, O'Malley was there, but he wasn't heading toward the door. Instead, he was looking at something a little off to the right. Hoover directed the flashlight toward it before he realized that he didn't have to; he could see just fine—there was light spilling into the room from the floor above. It was the access hole that O'Malley was looking at.

A not-quite-perfect square was cut into the ceiling of the den about a foot from the exterior wall. The edges of the hole were covered in handprints, which were stains from old dirt, clammy sweat, and wet blood. There were many of them, made over the course of the past year as Dedaker hauled himself in and out of the apartment.

Dangling down from the hole was a thick strong piece of rope, capable of holding the weight of a man, which had not been there when the priest and the cop had first entered the apartment. The rope was well used and caked with the same dirt that marred the edges of the access hole.

Hoover clicked off the flashlight and whispered, "Move," to O'Malley, nudging him on the arm. Before the priest could follow his order, a pair of legs emerged over the edge of the hole. Dedaker was coming down.

Reacting as quickly as he could, Hoover indicated that O'Malley should get on one side of the rope and he would get on the other. They would surround him. They shifted into position as Dedaker slid down the rope to land on the floor between them, facing Hoover.

"Hello, Michael," Hoover said.

Dedaker's commonplace brown eyes widened to the size of saucers. "How—," he began, and then the cold steel of Hoover's gun pressed against his forehead. In a comical, cross-eyed fashion,

Dedaker looked up at the gun through his glasses. He was enraged, but hid it well.

"Now we're playing by my rules," Hoover said.

"Don't kill him, John; not here," cautioned O'Malley.

A sly smile appeared beneath the frames of Dedaker's glasses. "So it's almost time," the Dandelion said. He ignored the unknown man who had spoken from behind him. He knew which one was weaker, knew in which direction escape laid.

"Yes, it is," Hoover concurred.

Dedaker closed his eyes, his arms hanging limp at his side, and said, "Then do it."

There was a click as Hoover cocked back the action.

"John," O'Malley warned again. "Not yet."

Time seemed to stretch as the three men weighed the moment. Finally, the spell was broken as Dedaker's eyes snapped open. He said, "This is the third time you've had me under the gun, *John*. Three strikes and you're out." With the gun pushing a small indent against his head, Dedaker took a step forward. "What are you waiting for? You've shot me once; why don't you shoot me now? We're in the privacy—or what I *thought* was privacy—of my own home. You could kill me now, and no one would ever know." He took another step, then another. "What is it about death that scares you so? Is it the pain? Is it the unknown? What?"

Dedaker was pushing him back down the hallway to the living room, to the darkness of the killing field, *his* turf.

"Are you a coward? Is that what it is, *John*? Is that why you couldn't save poor Beverly?"

Hoover's lips pressed together, and his eyes screwed down; a thoughtful worry line formed between his brows and ran to the bridge of his nose.

He's going to kill him, O'Malley's mind warned. *Do something!*

The fist of the man behind him struck the bullet wound in Dedaker's arm. Pain flared up into his shoulder and down to the tips of his fingers, making them tingle with numbness. He had been ready for it. Once he had discovered the infidels in his house, he knew that he wasn't going to be able to get out without some pain. He had expected the move to come from the cop, not from the nameless man behind him, but it had come regardless. Now he had to use the advantage.

When O'Malley struck him, Dedaker cried out in pain. Overly emoting, he grabbed the freshly bleeding wound and stumbled forward, into Hoover. Dedaker wasn't a large man, but when his weight crashed into the backward-peddling Hoover, their feet tangled up and they fell. Hoover lost hold of the flashlight, which came to life again when it bounced off a wall.

The two men went to the floor. Since Dedaker was on top, he had the better positioning. He raised himself up with his hands and brought a knee down hard on Hoover's wrist—the one holding the gun. The full body weight of a man pushing down on his wrist forced his hand open, releasing the .38.

Instead of picking up the gun, Dedaker shoved it off into the darkness.

It had all happened so quickly, O'Malley, who was used to serving wafers to shuffling old ladies on easy Sunday mornings, didn't know what to do. He tried to use his instincts as best he could, going for Dedaker's throat. He wrapped his arms tightly around and started choking.

With Hoover's wrist still pinned beneath his knee, Dedaker reached up and grabbed O'Malley by the shoulders. He bent forward, pulling the priest with him. O'Malley came off his feet and was hip-tossed over Dedaker's back. Forced to let his grip go, he landed on a hard piece of metal just inches from the door to the sepulcher. An exquisite pain flared in the priest's kidney, and he suddenly felt a pressing need to urinate.

Dedaker, in control, sprung to his feet and sprinted into the living room.

He's going for the podium, Hoover thought as he got to his knees, which were still hurting from his earlier leap onto the hearse. He hopped over O'Malley, who was writhing around holding his back, and charged at Dedaker.

Hoover ran into the living room, which was in absolute darkness this far away from the access hole and the light from the upper floor. He had an idea where the podium with its cache of sharp instruments was in the room, and he did not hesitate as he ran toward it, hoping that Dedaker hadn't had enough time to get hold of one of the knives; otherwise, he was apt to be gutted.

*   *   *

It was the Maglite O'Malley landed on, never experiencing such pain before. Along with the dull, overfull throbbing of his kidneys, he felt a sharp twinge along his spine in the area of his lower back. He wanted to lie still on the flat hardness of the floor but couldn't—Hoover needed help. Although O'Malley could not see a thing, he could hear the two of them scuffling about in the living room.

O'Malley reached behind himself and pulled the flashlight out from under his back. It was already on, and he shone it into the living room.

Hoover and Dedaker were throwing each other around in the beam of light like two people dancing in the strobe of a discotheque.

*   *   *

In the tussle, Hoover's hip caught the edge of the podium.

There was a crash like that of a silverware drawer pulled too far past its stops, as the podium was knocked over and the knives spilled out. Hoover had gotten to Dedaker before he could find a cutting blade in the darkness, but now he had to be even more wary because knives were everywhere.

The light from the Maglite flashed into the room, jerky and unsteady as O'Malley got to his feet. In one flash of light, Dedaker was five feet away, in the next three feet. The stop-motion effect of Dedaker's movement made him look like an incandescent leviathan rising from the abyss.

Having to prejudge his aim, Hoover swung blind, hoping that Dedaker would be moving fast enough to run into his fist. He was, but the timing was off by a hair, and Hoover wound up striking him behind the ear, at the base of the skull. The rigidity of the bone made the punch hurt Hoover more than it did Dedaker.

Untrained, Dedaker swung wildly, making good connections. His punches had impact, but Hoover was a bigger, thicker man, and could withstand the beating.

Hoover came back at him with a shot to the stomach and another to the chin. The man was wiry, but Hoover could tell that he was starting to get weary. Dedaker might have made a fool out of him with his pretentious shell games, but in a fair fight, he was no match for Hoover. And Dedaker knew it.

Gathering all his strength for one final move, Dedaker shoved off Hoover using the cop's body as a countermeasure. He wanted to get some distance between them so that he could go for one of the knives strewn about the floor.

Ironically enough, it was a knife that Hoover slipped on.

It was an X-acto, a knife with a round, pen-shaped handle and a razor blade tip—one of Dedaker's personal favorites. It went under the heel of Hoover's boot and he slid on it. Just like they say the stones for the Great Pyramids were rolled across the desert on logs, Hoover rolled across the room on the knife—

—And right into the only window Dedaker hadn't boarded up, the one left unsecured to let the ghosts out. It was that window which had brought Hoover and O'Malley to this house this night, via Darren Roberts. And it was that same window that had almost saved Dedaker's life from the execution O'Malley and Hoover had planned for him.

Almost.

Either way, it was certainly a window through which the winds of change blew.

Hoover's ass hit the window and shattered it. Slivers and fragments rained down on his back, cutting up his clothes but not slicing his skin, the broken glass landing mute on the new spring grass of the front lawn.

The window frame—which was the type that could be opened two ways by sliding a pane up or sliding a pane down—was constructed of wood and less than a foot wide. Smaller than his own frame, Hoover found himself wedged in on all four sides: shoulders, legs, and back. He tried to pull free, but his arms were trapped, and he couldn't reach the walls to either side for leverage.

He could only struggle and watch in the feeble, approaching light as Dedaker bent and picked up the X-acto knife. The smile across the madman's face was terrible and hideous, the rictus so wide that it seemed as if his mouth was eating the bottom half of his face.

He held the knifepoint upward as he approached—instead of stabbing, he intended to slash. And slash. And slash.

Hoover tried to shimmy himself free by thrashing from side to side. It wasn't working. The only thing left was the approaching, backlit knife in Dedaker's fist, his wrist flicking to the right, preparing to slice.

And then darkness descended upon the room again.

Hoover had been expecting searing pain to glide gently across his skin while tearing and ripping his flesh. What he hadn't been expecting was the sickening sound of meat being struck with a blunt instrument, followed by a metallic twang. The pain that had come after the strange sounds was not the slicing pain of a knife but rather the pelting of small, hard objects, somewhat like thrown stones.

The stones could only be one thing, D-cell batteries. Father O'Malley had hit Dedaker with the long, heavy shaft of the Maglite.

A few moments later, when O'Malley found a switch for the lighting fixture attached to the ceiling a foot away from the black pipe, Hoover saw Dedaker lying on the carpet, just beneath where his feet dangled from the stuck position in the window. Batteries and knives were scattered all around the unmoving form.

O'Malley still held the empty tube of flashlight when he came over to help pry Hoover loose. He let go of the Maglite and took hold of Hoover's hands. With a firm tug (and several deep, scrapped cuts on the rear of his legs from the broken glass), he was freed.

"Is it him?" O'Malley asked.

"It's him," Hoover said. "That's Michael Dedaker."

Hoover bent down to check on Dedaker. He was out cold; O'Malley had hit him a good one across his neck at the base of the skull.

From his crouched position, Hoover said, "Now what? We can't keep him here, sooner or later the cops are going dig up his name and address from among the Grapple Company's clients."

"We're not staying here. I know a place where we can take him."

Twenty minutes later, Dedaker was bound hand and foot. O'Malley had used one of the knives from the living room to cut down the rope Dedaker used to shuttle between the duplex units. The rope was moldy and stiff from the dried blood worked into the fibers. It was unpleasant to handle, but the gloves helped.

"I don't recommend using my car," said Hoover. "It's a city issue, from the department."

"I took the bus," replied O'Malley.

"You took the bus? Really?"

"Yeah, I didn't want anybody to notice me or maybe recognize one of the rectory cars. St. Tiburtius is only a couple of parishes away. Some of my constituents could live in this neighborhood."

"How were you planning on getting him out of here? On the bus?"

"I figured he must've had a car. I was going to use that."

Hoover opened the back door, expecting to see a very old and damaged Cadillac hearse. Instead, a completely intact late-model Escort sat in the driveway where none had been before. "All right, his car it is. Check his pockets for the keys."

"Here they are," O'Malley said after patting him down.

"Go open the trunk, then come back and grab his feet."

With some effort, they managed to lift Dedaker's dead weight into the trunk. Hoover rolled the gloves off his hands and shot them into the trunk like a rubber band, before slamming the lid. The Dandelion had been caught.

"You drive his car, Father. I'll follow in mine."

A third of the way down Kennard Street toward where he parked, Hoover remembered something. When he had first arrived at Dedaker's house, he had tried the front door—his fingerprints were on the knob. Jogging back up the incline, he grimaced with each step as the pain registered in the aching bones of his legs.

You're getting too old for this, John, his mind chided as he wiped the knob clean with the tail of his shirt. *Maybe it was time for a new line of work.*

He would be amused if he weren't so friggin' tired.

10

$\mathcal{J}_t$ was a greenhouse O'Malley led them to.

The Valley Green Nursery was located deep within the heart of a residential section of the city, the edge of the remains of the outer building bordering on Bustleton Avenue, which was a main artery and snow-emergency route for the city. What was left of the Valley Green sat on a large parcel of land across the street (Bustleton Avenue) from another large, open area known as Pennypack Park with its fishing creek and hiking trails.

In early winter of the previous year, a fire raged out of control, burning down completely three of the six buildings of the Valley Green, leaving the remaining ones soot-covered husks. It was still two hours before dawn, and the nursery grounds stood in ebony shadows.

"Why are we here?" Hoover asked as soon as O'Malley parked the car. The priest spun the knob, clicking off the headlights. They had driven to Hoover's house and dropped off the city car before heading out to the nursery. Hoover hopped into Dedaker's car, and they had driven on in silence, until the priest stopped in what had once been the driveway of the Valley Green but was now so overran with verdant grass and weeds that it looked like an extension of the woods surrounding the old nursery.

"This is where we're going to hole up until I can finalize the rest of the . . . the situation," O'Malley told him.

"You're not ready?"

"No, I'm not a hundred percent ready. I told you my whole itinerary got fucked when you let slip that you thought he was going to bolt. I still have to meet with some people, still need to get the rest of the things we're going to need."

"We can't do it here; it's too public. Burned out or not, people would notice thirty cars showing up in the middle of the night."

"I know. I've got somewhere else in mind," the priest assured him.

"Where?"

"A fire hall up in Brakes County."

"A fire hall! You're going to rent a hall to do this? Will there be an open bar and dessert table too?"

"No. The brother-in-law of one of the victims' families is a fireman there. He's in charge of running the hall. It's not booked for the next two weeks, so we can use it whenever we need it."

"How convenient. You've already discussed this with the guy?"

"Not him, the father of the dead girl. Her uncle who is the fireman there lost both his baby and wife while she was giving birth. Without them, he devoted his love to his only niece, his brother's girl. He loved her more than anything else in the world, doted on her. He wants to be a part of this."

"Which girl was it?" Hoover asked.

"Kasay."

Hoover nodded. "I met the old man. Edward, isn't it?"

"Yeah. His brother—Judith's uncle—is Stanley."

"They've both agreed to this, to what we're doing?" There was no question anymore about whose idea it had originally been—Hoover and O'Malley had become equal partners.

"Not only them, now I've got three other families from the original nine. I poked around the edges at the other one but decided I couldn't recruit."

"Why not?"

"They're religious, the father a strict Protestant minister."

"Dean Dasher?"

O'Malley nodded.

"That leaves seven families still to be contacted," Hoover said.

"No, only four. The three girls from Purser Street were all from out of the area."

"How do you know that?"

"After I left your house, I stopped back at the rectory for the tools I needed to get into Dedaker's. While I was there, I checked out the website for BarbeesDollHouse. All of the girls had been hired to live in the house by your Grapple Company through a talent search done over the Internet, according to their biographies listed on the site. Among other tasty tidbits, it listed their home states. One was from Houston, one from Seattle, the other from LA, but I can't remember which was which. I don't want to invite those families because it's too high risk. There's too much space between where we are and where they live; if they all come here on or around the same date, there will be travel records and receipts that can draw suspicion and possibly link them to us."

Hoover was impressed; the priest had his shit together.

"Maybe somewhere down the road, I'll drop them an anonymous tip to put their minds at peace. It's the best I can do," O'Malley said with a frown, unsatisfied at a job not fully complete.

"So how long do you think we're going to have to wait it out here?"

"Two days, three at the most. Just till I set up the hall and feel out the remaining four families."

"How we going to work it?"

"Twelve-hour shifts. I'll have to take the nights because of my duties at the church. As it is now, I'm going to have to break my ass to get cleaned up to serve the 6 a.m. mass. That leaves you the day shift, starting now."

"Great," Hoover, bone weary and hungry, groaned.

O'Malley pointed to his right. "There's a little shack—an old toolshed, really—that wasn't damaged too bad in the fire, over that way. We'll keep him in there."

"What if someone comes by; we're not exactly in Siberia here." Hoover indicated a gap in the still-sprouting trees where he could see Bustleton Avenue and the occasional early-morning car wiz by.

"We'll have to scare 'em off. Whatever, you know, play it by ear. What do you want from me? This is the best I could do. I'm not an organized crime leader, and we can't take him to my place. I live with a group of other men in what amounts to nothing but a straight-laced frat house. Wanna try your place?" the priest asked, a little more facetiously than Hoover would have liked, but it got his point across.

"No. We'll have to make this work."

"Agreed. Let's get moving." O'Malley pushed the dash button that popped the trunk.

Since Dedaker had gone in headfirst, he had to come out in reverse. Hoover wrapped his arms around Dedaker's legs, using the swell of his calves and the indents behind his knees as handholds. Walking backward, Hoover began to pull Dedaker out of the Escort's trunk. When Dedaker's back was resting on the lip, the latch having made his shirt hike up to reveal a pale, hairless torso, O'Malley could finally get a grip under the man's shoulders. Grasping the armpits, he used the large muscles of his legs to lift the man's weight.

Just as Dedaker cleared the edge of the car, and with his full weight spanning between Hoover and O'Malley, the priest dropped him.

"What—," Hoover began.

"He's awake," O'Malley said. As soon as the priest said it, Dedaker began thrashing around on the grass-covered macadam. "I could feel the tension in his muscles; they weren't as slack as they should've been."

Hoover pulled out his gun and aimed it at the bound man, this time butt first. He pistol-whipped him twice across the base of the skull. Except for the same involuntary twitching of a freshly beheaded chicken, Dedaker lay still. They picked him up again and started moving.

They walked across a slate and brick pavement, then under an arbor with green vines and purple and white wisteria, winding their way through the laths overhead and the latticework of the trellises on the sides, before O'Malley said, "It's to the right." Hoover angled, and before he knew it, they were standing in front of the remnants of the shack. With an ogee over the door, it looked as if it had been designed to resemble a rustic bower but was now only the burned-out skeletal remains of a toolshed.

Gentler than the last time, they lowered Dedaker to the ground. O'Malley gave a try at opening the wooden door of the shack, but it wouldn't budge, rusted shut.

"Give me a hand with this," he said.

Together, with their shoulders against the dry-rotted wood of the door, they shoved. With a screech and a shower of rust, it opened inward. Hoover walked inside and realized that he was still outside—the shack had no ceiling, the wooden roof being the only part of the structure to completely burn during the fire. The result was that the toolshed, with its climbing ivy snaking up the walls, looked like a bigger, grander version of the arbor they had just walked through. Hoover could see why only the roof had succumbed to the flames—the walls were constructed out of stone, and the floor had been left unfinished, its dirt hard-packed from many years of trampling feet. Other than the four windowless walls, the shack was completely empty, not even stray graffiti marring the stone.

"You know," O'Malley said, "back during the Depression, there were crudely built camps located along the edges of towns throughout the country, set up to house the destitute. I bet they looked a lot like this."

"Yeah, probably," Hoover said, not giving a fuck, but trying to be polite.

O'Malley turned to look him in the eye. "Those camps had been nicknamed Hoovervilles, after your namesake president. Apt, don't you think?"

Hoover said nothing.

Working furiously so that Father O'Malley could make the six o'clock mass, they broke one of the legs off a trellis from the arbor. In the center of the shack, they ran the arbor leg through the tightly bound loops of rope securing Dedaker's hands. While he lay unconscious, Hoover and O'Malley alternated turns driving the impromptu stake into the ground, using the flat metal of the bottom of the car jack they found in the trunk of the Escort.

When they were finished, Michael Dedaker was sitting upright with chin on chest and his lank hair hanging down in front of his face. He had been spitted.

"I have to go," O'Malley said. "I'm usually at the church more than an hour before mass. Today I'll be lucky if can even start it on time.

"What should I do?" Hoover asked.

"Sit here and stare at him. If he makes any kind of play, shoot him. Your life is more important than any agenda we have." What was left unsaid, but Hoover heard it anyway, was, *And so are the lives of any more women he kills if he gets away from us.* "I have a busy day ahead of me at the church, followed by attempts to contact the other families, as well as the Kasays to let them know what we have so that they can get the hall ready. When I get a free minute, I'll dig up some food and bring it over here. I'll try and relieve you for the night as early as I can."

O'Malley turned to leave. "Father," Hoover called.

"Yeah?"

"When you're at mass, would you do me a favor?"

"What?"

"Pray it doesn't rain."

O'Malley smirked and looked up through the roofless building at the clear night with its fading stars.

11

Something had startled him, and he jolted awake. Hoover looked at his watch. 3:48 p.m.

O'Malley had stopped by earlier with a couple of cheeseburgers from a fast-food place, teeming with lettuce, tomato, and grease. Hoover had never tasted anything so good, downing both burgers in a total of eight bites. With the fatty lunch weighing heavy in his stomach, Hoover sat down facing Dedaker in the angle of a corner created by two adjoining walls. He must have dozed off because when he opened his eyes, two hours had gone by, and Dedaker was awake.

"Detective Hoover, whatever are we doing in a place like this?"

"We're waiting," Hoover said, his tired and unused voice cracking as he rubbed his eyes.

"Waiting for what? Not Godot, I suppose."

"The bell to toll."

"Ah, then this would be death row," he said, looking around at the paltry surroundings. "Was it the license plate?"

Hoover was surprised at the straightforward manner with which he accepted his fate, a fate of his own devising. "Yeah, it was the license plate," Hoover concurred.

"I wasn't sure whether to boost a tag from somewhere or keep it legit. There's a strong argument to be made either way. Go legit and possibly have someone track you with it, just like they did with Berkowitz in New York, just as you have done with me," Dedaker said, drawing a parallel between his fate and that of the famous Son of Sam. "Or steal one and run the risk of being pulled over for a stolen tag or a routine traffic stop and have the whole thing blow up in my face. I decided to go with my own, since I wouldn't be in the game long. It seemed safer that way. At least with the real tag, I would know when the heat was on. With the fake one, I would always have to keep my fingers crossed."

Hoover didn't congratulate Dedaker on his foresight, which had failed anyway. Instead, he pushed himself to his feet, sliding up the wall for support. He had to shake his head to clear out the grogginess before he circled Dedaker and hunkered down to check on the bindings "Why'd you pick my city?" Hoover asked.

"Philadelphia's the cradle of liberty, where the new world was started and governed, where the evil and decadence began."

The rope was tight, but Hoover noticed that the post he and O'Malley had driven into the ground was looser than it had been. He examined the hole and saw that there was some space between the wood and the ground. Dedaker had been trying to wiggle the post free.

That's what must've woke me, Hoover thought. "Michael, have you been a bad boy, trying to work your way out?"

"Me? No. I woke up with a screaming need to go to the bathroom and tried to stand up to take care of business, but inconveniently found myself shackled to this pole."

"I think you're lying to me."

"I'm not. Let me out so I can pee and I'll show you."

"I think not."

"Then where am I supposed to go?"

"You're sitting on it," Hoover told him. Dedaker looked down between his legs at the hard, brown earth.

"Detective Hoover, don't you think this is a bit uncivilized?"

"Not for you, I don't," Hoover said. He opened the door to the shack and walked out, going to find some rocks to wedge down between the wood from the arbor and the ground. If he pushed them in there tightly, they would only slide deeper down and pack the post even tighter if Dedaker continued to try to wiggle it free.

And besides, if he kept talking at Dedaker in the quite seclusion of the woods, Hoover might do something he would not be proud of. Something inhumane.

12

*H*ow's he doing?" O'Malley asked.

"Better than he should be," was the answer Hoover provided. O'Malley wasn't sure what he meant by that. It was quarter of nine, and Hoover desperately needed sleep. The priest had brought some more food with him, this time a loaf of bread and a pound of tavern ham from a deli. To drink, there was water.

They made sandwiches and ate while standing outside the toolshed. A family of wild cats came by with their green eyes glowing in the moonlight. Hoover tossed some slices of ham to them. There was some hissing as the cats snatched up the pink meat and ran off with it.

"He dumped the other two back at the original site, out in the woods by the airport," Hoover said.

"Who? Knoble and Fattore?"

"Yeah."

"How do you know?"

"He told me."

When Hoover and O'Malley had finished eating, O'Malley made another sandwich and went into the shack with it. Hoover watched through the open door as the priest fed it to the shackled man. They were silent while Dedaker eat. After O'Malley upended the water bottle for Dedaker to drink, the priest came back out to Hoover.

"All right, go home and get some sleep."

Hoover handed him his gun. He could see that O'Malley intended to balk but cut him off by saying, "He tried to get loose earlier today. I caught him at it and reinforced the pole he's tied to. Just like you told me, I'm telling you, use the gun if you have to."

O'Malley nodded his head. He took the gun and could feel the awesome weight of it in his hand. If the time came, O'Malley wondered if he would be able to use it. Hoover wondered likewise.

"Keep the talking to a minimum, Father, lest you get charmed by the snake," Hoover cautioned.

O'Malley nodded again and said, "I understand."

"How did things go with the planning?"

"The hall is ready, but I've got two more families to talk to yet. We've now got six out of the eight possible families, discounting the Dashers."

"What two are left?"

"Allensworth and Hustead."

"Forget Hustead; it's a dead end."

"You sure?"

"I'm sure," Hoover said, remembering George Hustead's ignorant remarks regarding his late daughter's life. Mr. Hustead wouldn't care one way or the other what happened to Dedaker.

"Then there's only one left," O'Malley said. "I'll try to recruit them in the morning, after mass."

"When is it going to happen; when are we going to do this?"

"Tomorrow night."

There was nothing to say after that. Hoover got into Dedaker's car and drove away from the Valley Green Nursery.

Father O'Malley watched the taillights of the car through the trees until Hoover turned left onto Bustleton Avenue. He went back into the shack and sat down cross-legged a good distance away from Dedaker. "Hello, Michael," he said.

"I heard him address you as 'Father.' Are you a priest?"

"Yes, I am. Father Thomas O'Malley. I'm a Catholic priest from St. Tiburtius."

"St. Tiburtius, huh? Executed in 286 for his faith, sentenced to death by fire, but it didn't work—he emerged from the flames unscathed only to later be beheaded. His feast day passed but recently, on the fourteenth, I believe."

The priest was impressed with the man's knowledge of Catholic lore; O'Malley himself had to look Tiburtius's name up after he had been assigned to the parish.

"I must say that your being a priest puts me at ease, Father. Are you here to administer Last Rites?" Dedaker asked, unknowingly echoing Hoover's question from the night before.

"In a manner of speaking."

Dedaker was sharp. "You don't mean you're involved in this."

"I conceived it."

"How is that so; you're a man of the cloth?"

"It was his will, son," O'Malley said. That seemed to make sense to Dedaker, and he was quiet for a while.

"I have to go to the bathroom," Dedaker said the next time he spoke.

"I can't untie you," was all O'Malley offered. Dedaker knew the rest, but the dirt he sat on remained dry.

For the next couple of hours, silence reigned, until finally the curiosity got the best of O'Malley. "How could you do it?" he asked Dedaker.

"Same as you; it was God's will."

"You can't believe that."

"Why not; you do?"

"Because we're different. I'm an ordained priest. My actions *are* the actions of God," O'Malley argued, but it sounded ridiculous when he said it. To clarify, he tried, "Murder is not an act of God," but it came out accusatory.

"Will I not die by your hands?" was the rebuke.

"What I do, I do for the greater good," O'Malley said, angered. "I am deliberately breaking a commandment—and sacrificing my own soul—so that others may live in peace, free of the fear of a madman like you."

"Then we are more alike than you could know, Father. I have also felt a calling to sacrifice my life for the souls of others."

"Butchering women—practically *girls*—stripping them of their dignity, and then their lives. Is that what you consider helping others?"

"They were sinners, infidels, one and all. If it weren't for me, they would be spending eternity in hell. Because God has chosen me to give my life, they will be granted the serenity of heaven. By my giving up of my life, they will be saved."

Father O'Malley was enraged. "How can you have the balls to envision yourself a Christ figure?"

Dedaker swiveled his head slowly and took in the nursery toolshed. "Are we not in a modern-day Gethsemane, on the eve of an execution?" he asked, his intelligence gleaming in his eyes as if he were not strapped to a broken shaft of wood in a burned-out hut waiting to be executed.

O'Malley didn't justify his statement with a response, so Dedaker went on. "How do you know I'm not him? What if the Second Coming really is now, and *you* were the one chosen by God to take the life of the Messiah this time. Suppose you're Pilate and Hoover and his police department are the Romans. How do you know it's not supposed to end this way? Because you didn't receive official notification? There was no North Star to guide you to a manger? The people in Christ's time didn't know it for sure, either. They had to *believe* it.

"I'll tell you what, Father, religion is all about faith. Anyone can say they believe in God, but to really *believe* they believe is something entirely different." Dedaker grinned. It was an intelligent, feral grin, and it made O'Malley sick to his stomach.

Dedaker was a strong orator, the way that Hitler must've been. And while he didn't have O'Malley believing what he was saying, he had him doubting himself, doubting his faith. Dedaker was silent, letting him mull what he had said. While Michael waited, he used the heels of his sneakers to draw a pattern in the dirt.

O'Malley believed that God worked in mysterious ways, and what Dedaker had said about belief and faith was entirely true. *What if something like what Dedaker described were possible? Hadn't God already proven that he would do such a thing once before by giving his son life, only to take it from him through pain and suffering? Wasn't the promise of God's salvation for the entire human race wrapped around a core of death?*

O'Malley went over it all in his head, playing with it from every angle.

Theoretically, it could be true. But what his mind kept returning to was the sepulcher. And the staged Last Supper. That room, with its bread and wine meal and its rubbings of dead apostles, debunked every argument that Dedaker had presented to justify his warped crusade. That grotesque gallery proved that Dedaker was not the Second Coming of Christ. It proved that he was a vile, murderous creature, the antithesis of Christ—the Antichrist.

"You've committed murder. The commandments expressly forbid such a foul act," O'Malley said. "Because of such heinous acts, you will be denied what you sought for those women."

"The commandments are rules for humans. God is exempt. He must be; otherwise, how do you explain the plagues he had Moses release on the Egyptians?" Dedaker asked, his feet still working the dirt.

"He wasn't killing those people; he was punishing them, scouring the earth of evil."

"What evil could babies have committed when their only faults were being born first among their siblings?"

O'Malley had no answer. But Dedaker did. He said, "God is exempt."

"Then, in some form of twisted logic, you think you're exempt."

Dedaker nodded once, slowly.

O'Malley looked at the ground, noticing that Dedaker had traced the form of the Chi-Rho cross in the dirt. Usually found on holy vestments and altar linens in the form of the letter X superimposed over the stem of a capital letter *P*, it is the Greek cruciform monogram for Jesus Christ.

13

$\mathcal{T}$he alarm clock had been playing music for over an hour while Hoover slept through it, incorporating the songs into the soundtrack of his dreams. Groggy and still slipping in and out of sleep, he finally switched the dial to the off position.

Every muscle and more than half of the bones in his body ached from the abuse he put them through yesterday.

And he smelled.

He had driven home from the greenhouse in a state of semi-consciousness. Bleary eyed, he stripped naked and crawled into bed without taking a shower first. Now that he was awake he could smell the poisonous fumes of the bourbon remnants that were still escaping through the pores of his body. He also smelled like the garbage and refuse of the alley behind Fiona's building, the odor of old sweat and adrenaline cloying.

Underlying it all, Hoover could still smell the decaying offal of Dedaker's apartment.

It had been a long day yesterday, and today was apt to be even longer.

Against the screams coming from his body's muscles and joints, Hoover pushed himself to his feet. He shuffled into the master bedroom's bath and turned the water on. Before the water was warm, Hoover stepped under the shower. Minutes later, lathered, rinsed, and smelling much better, he padded back to the bedroom with a towel wrapped around his waist.

After the better part of a week, he still couldn't get over how quiet the house was without Lauren and the kids. Up until Father O'Malley had appeared on his doorstep, Hoover had lived his life in silence, only moving from room to room as it was necessary. It was a sorrowful silence with the rest of the pieces of his family missing, the likes of which reminded him of a mortuary.

He dressed in comfortable clothes: jeans, sweat socks, sneakers. Reaching into his shirt drawer, he pulled a T-shirt from the top of the pile. Once he had it on, he looked at himself in the mirror. The shirt was navy blue with a police badge over the left breast. Without looking at the back, Hoover knew it said Philadelphia Police Academy. With what was planned for tonight, it would not do well to announce what his occupation is. Or was. He peeled the shirt back off and reached for another, this one plain black without any markings on it. It would do.

There was a safe in the closet. He turned the dial the required number of times and then pulled open the fireproof door. Along with insurance papers, the series EE bonds relatives had bought for Pammy and Janey on their birthdays and Christmases, and the collection of love notes he had written to Lauren in high school, which she had kept, was his gun.

The gun he gave O'Malley at the Valley Green was the department-issued .38 Detective's Special; this one was his personal weapon, which he had bought some three years back. It was a nine-millimeter Glock with a fifteen-round clip. Made from a plastic resin, it was lighter than the Detective's Special. A semiautomatic—as opposed to a revolver—the nine millimeter was stronger than the .38 calibers. It was an all around better weapon than the Special, but Hoover was from the old school; he preferred the metal heft of the older gun. One has to wonder, though; if he'd had the extra rounds in the alley, this might all be over already.

He looped the holster around his belt then closed the safe. After a pause, he redialed the combination and once again opened the door. After putting his wedding band inside, he descended down the stairs. He checked the answering machine by the phone in the living room. There was one message. He played it. Captain Korzenowski's voice politely demanded that he return the department's car, right now.

Five minutes later, after having dry-chewed four Tylenols and stuffed two more into his front pocket where they could mingle with the lint, he tossed a well-used and cracked leather jacket into the backseat of Dedaker's Escort, and left to relieve O'Malley at the nursery.

14

*H*e found the priest pacing back and forth in front of the toolshed, much as he had been when O'Malley had shown up to relieve him last night.

"You were right; he's a wily one," O'Malley said.

Right away, Hoover was nervous. "What happened?" he asked, and poked his head in to check on Dedaker. He was there, seated in the same position and still bound. His head was hanging down, and it looked as if he was sleeping.

"Nothing happened; everything's fine. I just let him get into my head. It's like you said, the imagination can play tricks that are mean."

"Wicked," Hoover said. "Nothing else?"

"I thought I heard something out here a little while ago but didn't see anything when I checked."

After quick-glancing around the perimeter, Hoover reached into the plastic bag he brought with him. He had a quart of orange juice and three bacon, egg, and cheese bagel sandwiches. He took one himself and gave another to O'Malley. The other one was for Dedaker; he would feed it to him later, after the priest was gone.

O'Malley unwrapped the wax paper and took the top off his bagel. With fingers as gentle as a mother removing a splinter from a child's skin, O'Malley peeled the bacon from its bed of cheese. There were three slices, and he dropped each of them to the ground.

Around a mouthful of food, Hoover inquired, "Don't like bacon?"

"I love it, especially when it's crisp and overcooked enough that it crumbles like that. But today's Friday. No meat on Fridays, even if Easter has already passed. A hard habit to break, you know." He put the lid back on the bagel and took a huge bite. They passed the OJ container back and forth.

"For a minute there last night, he had me believing he was the Second Coming of Christ."

"How did he manage that?"

"The tongue of the devil is a forked one, my friend. He told me that he killed those women to save their souls. I spent the whole night trying to figure out what that all meant."

"That's where your problem is, Father. There is no rationale for murder. Motivation is all you can guess at, and even that's usually unclear. People who do the things Dedaker has done are off in their minds; there's something missing from their original genome sequence."

"Normally, I'd agree with you, but this is different. *He's* different. The types of people that you're talking about are psychotic and insane, prone to random acts of violence. This guy's not like that. He's constructed a whole design, given it meaning, and made it real."

"What's this all about, Father?"

"It's about the human soul. Yours, mine, his, the dead women's. Each taken individually defines only that singular person. But all of us are wrapped up in this together, connected on a spiritual level. Each of our souls is but a single piece of the puzzle. Collectively, they add up to make one picture. That man in there is the catalyst of our little group. He's the artist who sketched this particular picture."

There was a pause before Hoover asked, "Yeah, but what are you getting at, Father? Have you lost your resolve, backing out of tonight's activity?"

"No, I'm in. For good or bad, right or wrong, I'm in this thing to the end. But I am saying that—maybe not for each person who has committed an unspeakable crime, but for some—there may be reasoning behind the deeds that were committed that need to be evaluated, rather than simply writing the perpetrator off as a sociopath or a lunatic."

"That still sounds to me like you're backing out."

"I'm not backing out," the priest stated. "I've had a calling. I must do this."

"You realize that you're going to commit murder."

"I know," O'Malley said, chewing. "Dedaker believes that he's Jesus Christ. I do not believe that. I believe him to be a confused man turned zealot. Probably somewhere along the line, another zealot taught him to be such, programmed him."

"Did you ask him about his past?" Hoover asked, more for his own curiosity than about what drove Dedaker.

"No. I didn't want to make him any more human than necessary, in light of what we're going to do. He is what he is. At God's behest, I'm willing to correct that matter—and save countless other lives in the process. I'm going to sacrifice my own soul to save his. It will be my soul that pays for his sins."

"Why would you feel the need to do that?"

"It's my job, I'm a priest."

"What if it's a trick? What if he's Mephistopheles or something, here to trick you into making a mistake that'll cost you your soul?"

"Now it sounds like you're the one who's backing out."

Hoover shook his head, thinking of Beverly, thinking of Lauren and the kids, and of his lost profession. "I'm in to the end," Hoover said. "The only thing keeping me from going in there and slicing him to pieces is your promise of delivery."

"What you've just said—the peace that I will have helped provide for you—is why I'm doing this. More than anything else, that's it. For you and for the others."

There was another pause as they both considered what they were going to do, and why.

After a minute, O'Malley said, "I've got work to do; I'll see you back here tonight," and left.

15

$\mathcal{I}$t took three blows to the back of the head before Dedaker succumbed to unconsciousness. When it was done, Hoover barbed, "If we continue hitting him in the head like this, we won't have to go to the fire hall at all."

When they were sure Dedaker was out cold, Hoover clamped one side of the set of handcuffs he brought with him specifically for this around Dedaker's wrist. When it was on securely, O'Malley used a knife and cut the ropes. Dedaker slumped to the side as Hoover closed the other cuff on him.

They lifted him up and shuffle-carried him to the trunk. Dedaker's pants were damp with urine, and there was a pungent odor about him; he smelled like piss and something else that resembled moldy cheese. Hoover took a sniff of the gunshot wound in the man's arm. He drew his head back sharply as the stench of the hole filled his nostrils. Hoover was no doctor, but he thought gangrene had begun to set in.

Together, they got Dedaker to the trunk and stuffed him in. After making sure that they had left nothing behind, they got in the Escort and drove off. It was 9:17 p.m., and the crowd had already started to gather at the Brakes County Fire Hall. At ten o'clock, O'Malley and Hoover would arrive with the guest of honor.

16

The buzzer sounded, and he pulled open the door.

The night had progressed to the small hours after midnight. He had gone home and showered, but he couldn't clean the stench out of his mind. Or the screams. Hoover, along with a priest and a vigilante group, had put a man to death tonight. It was the third person he had killed—two in the line of duty, and one very far outside the lines. The two were to save his life, the final one to get it back. He felt justified, but he would never be able to do such a thing again. Or would he, if pushed to such extremes another time?

Three soft raps on the door and she opened it. Along with the spill of her black hair and her wide, round eyes, there were three new narrow red lines running along her neck.

Yeah, he would be able to do it again. Michael Dedaker had taken so much from him—from them all—and tonight they had taken it back.

He cupped Fiona Oswald's face in his hands and kissed her forehead. She wrapped her arms around his waist, buried her face in his chest, and asked, "Is it done?"

"Yes."

"I was so scared for you. Are you all right?"

"Everything's fine," he said, and for the first time in as long as he remembered, he really felt that way. Everything was going to be fine. "Do you remember how we met?"

Without having to pause to recall, she said, "My father died, and I was in a flower shop looking at displays for the funeral. You were in the shop buying flowers for someone. When you saw how sad I was, you gave the flowers you had just bought to me. I asked in a choked voice, 'What are these for?' You said—"

"I said, 'They're a little bit of happiness to brighten up your day.'"

She smiled against his chest. "I was surprised. 'What about the person you bought them for?' I asked. You said, 'She doesn't need them as much as you do right now.' And then you walked out of the store. I was so touched by your kindness that I asked the guy at the counter who you were. He told me your name and that you were a cop. Giving me those flowers was the nicest thing anybody has ever done for me. I was very close to my father. When he died, it was the worst time of my life. What you did for me that day helped me get through a very dark period in my life."

He could feel the warm tears of memory wetting his shirt.

"Would you be able to do the same for me? Would you help me through this dark period of my life?"

Still holding him in her embrace, she looked up at him. "How?" was all she asked.

He didn't know if he was capable of love, but he was willing—finally—to try. He knew that he had feelings for Fiona, and Dedaker's actions had proved to him that they were strong. He wanted her to teach him how to learn to love; he wanted her to teach him how to be a better person.

"I know I'm not bringing a lot to the table," Hoover said. "I have no job, no prospects, and I'm staring down the barrel of a lengthy and bloody divorce. In short, I have nothing to offer you except my heart, a heart that has never been true to anyone—including you. I don't want you to forgive me; I don't want you to forget. What I need you to do is help me. Help me be a better person; help me be a better husband. What I'm asking is for you to give me a second chance. I'm asking if you will marry me."

Her eyes were shining, brimming with the moisture of her tears, making the blue look azure. They were as wide and staring as those of a newborn marveling at the enormous new world it was born into. And just as frightened.

With every new life, there is but the first step. A newborn, amazed by the prospects of what life has to offer, will always take that first step. Unable to know what's in store for it, the newborn walks hesitantly on into the future. It might fall, and it might hurt, but even that is an accomplishment.

"I will marry you, John," Fiona said.

It had taken a monster to show Hoover the monster lurking inside himself. *You're no better than he is*, Agbalaya had said, comparing the two. But he was. Both he and Dedaker had used women for their own personal satisfaction. The difference was that he, John Hoover, could recognize the monster that he had become, and change it. Monsters have no responsibility for their actions—they're animalistic. People have control over their abilities and their emotions; it's called evolution; it's called civility. They can think; they can rationalize; they can learn; monsters cannot.

What separates man from beast? Animals have instinct; humans have thought—that little voice somewhere inside the mind, the consciousness of the soul.

17

At 10:55 a.m the next morning, a call was made to 911 from a payphone at the corner of Twenty-first Street and Girard Avenue. From that phone, the police have a recording of a man's voice stating that there were two dead women in the woods next to the Northern Philadelphia Airport. He declined to give a name before the phone was hung up.

Twenty minutes later, Detective Sako, working the desk in the homicide office of the Roundhouse, notified Captain Korzenowski that the bodies of Amber Knoble and Natalie Fattore had been discovered. There were in the exact same place the rest of the bodies had been found.

18

Eight days after the last two bodies were called in, Detectives Holmes and Meltzer arrived at the Kennard Street residence.

With the coming of the warmer weather, the police force was heavily laden with work. In every major city around the world, crime escalated with the temperature.

Although inundated with a large workload from their revolutions on the wheel, Holmes and Meltzer still managed to squeeze in a few minutes here and there to check out the addresses of area subscribers to the BarbeesDollHouse website, which was provided for them by the conscientious owners of the Grapple Company after the court had ordered it so.

As soon as they arrived at 573, and found the broken downstairs window and the askew drapes lying at a slant, they knew they had something. They knocked on the door to the house listed as belonging to a Michael Dedaker. When there was no answer, Meltzer looked in the broken window. After seeing the knives scattered across the floor and the black pipe running along the ceiling, Holmes went back to the car and radioed dispatch.

Armed with a warrant, Holmes, Meltzer, Whaat, and Korzenowski entered the duplex and found the sepulcher.

19

*U*ntil this day, the whereabouts of Michael Dedaker are unknown. The case remains open.

Metempsychosis

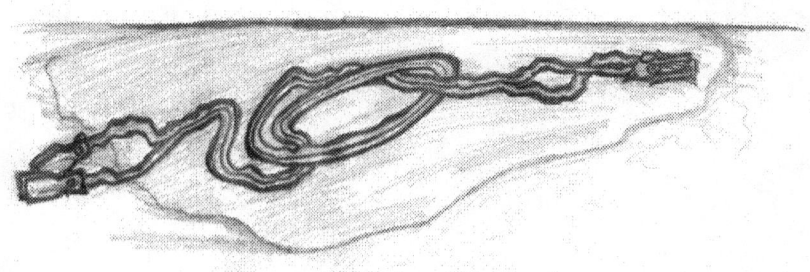

1

*W*hen she looked into his eyes, he could see the disturbance on her face, and maybe even a little bit of fear as well. That was to be expected. Edward Kasay wasn't an easy man to look upon. Not anymore. Not since the last time he was in attendance at the Brakes County Fire Hall.

She hadn't been paying attention to where she was walking. As a result, she ran into the slow-moving Ed Kasay. Realizing what she had done, she immediately turned to say she was sorry. When she got a clear look at the man she'd run into, rather than an apology, a quite little scream escaped her lips.

A husky-sized woman, what in Ed's day would have been termed "big-boned," she was in her early twenties, with hair a pretty shade of blond that lacked style. Her dress was pink, inexpensive looking, and perhaps a wee bit too small for a woman her size. In her hand she held a Styrofoam plate with roast beef and salad on it.

This was her; he just knew it.

Ed Kasay was a firm believer that karma and physical attributes went hand in hand. When one was good, so was the other. When one was not . . . Looking at this woman—and projecting her karma from her stature—he knew without a doubt that she was Emma Anderson, the name written on the placard. Destiny was one mean bitch.

"I'm sorry," Ed said. Using his two handheld orthopedic crutches, he began to shuffle out of her way.

"Oh my God, no; it's my fault. I wasn't watching where I was going," she said, horrified that she had almost ran over a handicapped man.

"No, my dear, it is me who is in the wrong. I was off daydreaming right in the middle of the damned floor, standing in everybody's way," he said, and he was. But more specifically, he was standing in *Emma's* way. When he had found the chair—a chair he knew would be here, was *destined* to be here—he stood as close to it as he could, waiting. He wanted to meet the woman whose name had been placed on the table before that particular chair, indicating that she was to be the one to sit in it. The one *chosen* to sit in it, you might say.

In a fine calligraphic hand, the black lettering against the bone-white background of the seating card read, Emma Anderson. It did not say "and guest," as most all of the others in the hall did. Emma was going to be in attendance alone, and the chair knew it.

Edward gave Emma the most pleasant smile he could, but it still felt rueful on his lips. "Have a good evening," he said to her, even though he knew it would be anything but. He then walked off, using the lightweight crutches that had become extensions of his hands ever since the night of Michael Dedaker's execution.

Emma watched the strange little man fuddle his way through the smattering of tables spread throughout the single large room attached to the Brakes County Fire Department (Engine 12, Ladder 33) and called a "hall."

The man she had almost run over with her bulk (*You should have one of those alarms installed in your ass*, she thought with self-depravation, *the kind that beeps to let others know when a truck is backing up*) was older. Emma had never been one to link status with age, considering it as a form of prejudice. Among the heavy hitters like color, race, and religion, ageism tended to be overlooked, as if it were the redheaded stepchild, ha-ha. Normally, she wouldn't immediately categorize someone as old as the man with the crutches was (he could be in his sixties, but barely) as a senior citizen, but in this case, it seemed to be an accurate assessment.

Based on the structure of the man's body, he seemed to have been powerfully built at one time. The muscles and the mass had aged, but they were still there. It wasn't the structure of the man that made him seem older than he was; it was his mind. He looked as if he had been beaten down, used up, deflated. The contrast of his mind and body made him come off as weak and frail, while physically, he was not.

It's the handicap, she thought. *I know if I were twisted up like that, it'd be a labor on my mind too. Besides, did you get a load of those eyes? They looked haunted, more than half psychotic; the poor thing must've been driven mad by his handicap.*

The older man—the *senior citizen*—walking away from Emma struggled along, using his forearms instead of his legs to walk. The crutches he used were Lofstrands, which were the type that had straps looped near the top so that he could slide his hands through to grasp the handles; this she knew because an uncle of hers had needed them after he took a bullet in the knee in Vietnam. In height, they only came up to the rounded mass of muscle below his elbow, rather than all the way to the armpit. His back was rigid, and when she had bumped into him, she felt hardness under his sport coat, a brace perhaps.

He was completely bald and had the face of a high school disciplinarian, only withered.

As she set her food down in front of the placard with her name on it, she wondered what kind of disease he had that had caused his personality to shrink like that. He was alone at the celebration, as she was. There was no one to help him, she could tell, not only from the absence of visible accompaniment, but also from his demeanor.

He pulled up three tables over from the one Emma was stationed at. The bouquet on his table had a silver reflective plastic number 5 stuck in the middle of it. Emma's had a 3.

Using the crutches for support, the man eased himself into a seat. There was already food on the table in front of him. Someone else had either gotten it for him, or his relation in the wedding party had prearranged with the caterer that he be served so that he might forgo the infernal buffet line.

She felt saddened as she watched him slide out of the crutch straps, leaning them against the side of the table, then shuffle some silverware around, preparing to eat. His seat faced Emma's, and she caught his eye when he looked up. He raised his hand in a half wave, which she returned, embarrassed at having been caught staring.

She reached for her own chair to pull it out. There was a crackle of static electricity as her hand touched the metal.

"Ouch," Emma said, immediately retracting her hand. She had to fight the need to put the newly tingling fingers into her mouth.

Must've built up a static charge as I walked across the rug. The Brakes County Fire Hall was completely carpeted, except for the fifteen-by-fifteen dance floor, an area that also included the DJ and buffet tables. *That's what you get for buying nonrubber-soled shoes.*

She rubbed the offended hand on her dress and wondered if such an action would produce another charge. She reached, more tenderly this time, and grabbed hold of the chair. Nothing happened. She pulled it out a considerable way—far enough for her to fit between chair and table—and sat down without giving the chair a second glance.

As soon as Emma sat down, she knew something was wrong. Dreadfully wrong.

She received another shock; only this one wasn't like the first. This one was actually *two* shocks. They had been produced between her rump and the seat of the chair at the moment of impact, and then branched in different directions. The first one started in her shanks and ran up her spine, as if it were a tuning fork. At her head, the static electricity ran around the circumference of her skull. When it could not penetrate the thick bone to get to her brain, it dissipated to nothing.

The second electrical charge was shorter, but more intense. It ran right to her loins. While it was there, it gave her a vibrating feeling that washed over her entire vagina, inside and out, creating an instantaneous, short, painful orgasm. It was unlike any orgasm she had ever experienced before. The past orgasms, both passionate and impassionate, were more acute, fuller. The one she got from the chair was fervid in its heat but devoid of passion.

"Oh," she said, and this time her hand did go to her mouth. The small moment of biting sensuality caused her to gasp in surprise, and a slight blush arose on her cheeks. She glanced around at the other members of dinner table number 3, hoping that no one noticed anything out of the ordinary. The people around her were all still trying to get situated after the trip to the buffet; no one seemed to notice what had just happened. The thing was *what had just happened?*

Emma had no idea, but it gave her pause.

She knew that something was severely wrong, but she also knew that it felt right to be sitting in this chair. On some level, she knew that she was supposed to sit in this particular chair, and not just because the placard with her name on it indicated so. Now that she was seated in it, she felt drawn to the chair, if indeed someone could be drawn to such an unremarkable piece of serviceable furniture.

Steadying her nerves with a deep breath, Emma looked down at the chair itself, expecting the unexpected. Of course, though, there was nothing to see. The chair was just that—a chair. It had a dull brown finish with gray metal showing through in the spots where the paint had flecked off. Sturdy looking (even under Emma's weight) but definitely not the top of the line in folding chairs, it was one of a thousand clones surrounding the tables at the BCFH.

Not satisfied with her inspection (and wanting an explanation for the odd emotions that had come upon her when she sat), Emma lifted an overlap of skin from her thigh so that she could check out the chair's cushion.

What she saw was that there wasn't much cushion left on the one square foot of seating; she was practically sitting with the pink nylon covering her ass touching the metal of the frame. Clearly, this lack of quality preparedness was something that should have been dealt with by the people who ran the fire hall, but this wedding being of the no-frills variety, it was probably something that could go overlooked in preparation. Or something that just didn't matter in the bigger scheme of things. Rule of thumb: you get what you pay for, and Emma's metal folding chair had economy written all over it.

Regardless of how it had come to be, her chair was a chair without a cushion. What was there instead was a dark lump that could've once resembled a cushion but now only resembled misuse and neglect, dirty in a way that suggested homelessness.

And it was torn in the upper right-hand corner.

Still holding her dress back, and on an impulse, Emma thrust an index finger into the hole, searching. Inside, she moved her finger in an arc pattern, but there was nothing to feel, nothing but air in this part of the cushion where there had once been spongy stuffing.

Still curious, and leaning to the right on her seat, Emma retracted her finger from the hole and poked it directly into the cushion itself. There was no resistance as her finger slid with ease through the cracked leather covering, the inside she encountered feeling worse than the outside looked. As she was regretting her curiosity (as most are usually apt to do once they uncover the nasty secrets they had been dogging), the inside of the cushion felt moist and warm, repugnant. And it felt dark. If you could feel evil, this is what it would feel like.

Emma guessed the warmth was from her own body heat being absorbed by what little was left of the cushioning, supposing that she had sat on the chair long enough for the seat to be warmed by her mass. But the texture of the inside of the seating was not something that she could explain. Verbalization failed her; what she was left with were vivid pictures in her mind's eye.

Inside this part of the cushion, there was a viscous wetness. She turned her finger in another pivoting arc and felt the wetness separating. It was not ripping like the inside of a normal cushion would, but instead it was *parting*. It felt as if she were giving a gynecological exam. Or prodding blood clots.

Disgusted, Emma jerked the probing digit out of the impromptu opening she had poked in the cushion. As it came out, it made a popping sound much like that of a corked bottle being opened. Before Emma could look at her finger—and the residue she had pulled out of the cushion with it—she heard someone talking to her.

She looked up at the other people seated around the table with her. She knew none of them, but they were all staring at her, their food forgotten for the moment.

"What?" Emma said to the woman sitting directly across the table from her. Emma wasn't sure who had spoken to her, but after she had pulled her finger out of the opening, this was the person she happened to be looking at. From her right, she heard someone say in a shrill, high-pitched voice, "I asked if you were all right, my dear." Emma turned and found herself looking at an elderly lady who could've passed herself off as Barbara Bush, if she wanted to.

"What?" Emma asked again, still disorientated.

The positively ancient-looking man, with eyes so squinty they seemed shut, accompanying Mrs. Bush tonight, said, "Young lady, my wife asked if you were all right."

Emma was nodding her head, but staring off into space. "Yes. Yes, I'm fine. Why?" she replied.

"Because you were pokin' holes in your seat cushion and moanin'," said the man, who looked nothing like the ex-president, and every bit like Mr. Magoo.

"I was moaning?"

"Yes, dear, you were."

Emma was still nodding her head, but not really seeing the man, as she addressed the whole table. "I'm so sorry. Please excuse me for the way I was acting. I don't know what came over me."

The meal resumed with Emma picking up her fork with her left hand. She kept the other one, the one she had been poking the chair with, under the table. She ate. But for one of the only times in her life, she was not thinking about the food she was consuming. She was thinking about the cushion. And the warm wetness it contained. She imagined that she could feel it pulsating beneath her. If not pulsating, then she knew that it was squishing around with every move she made.

The absurdity of the cushion squishing under her actually brought on a smile. She rarely did it, but when she did, Emma's smile lit up her face. Everybody has that one feature, Emma's smile was hers.

Sitting among strangers at Sheila Oswald's wedding, a very painful reminder of her fleeting youth and her own lack of marriage prospects, Emma Anderson was smiling. She was smiling because she had seen a clever bit in something repulsive and awful: *If the icky stuff inside of a* cushion *were* squishy, *shouldn't it be called a* "squishion?"

The tackiness of the substance on the tip of her right index finger brought her back to reality.

Reality?

As people all around her made conversation between bites of roast beef and broccoli-cauliflower medley, Emma summoned up the courage to take a look at her soiled finger. She quietly set down the fork, and was starting to bring her other hand out from beneath the tablecloth (more like table *paper*, since it was made out of the same stuff napkins were made from, cheap napkins, at that) where it was hiding when another shock hit her.

If the previous shocks had been but small jolts, this one was an immense lightning bolt.

Emma's head snapped to the side, where it squeezed tight against her shoulder, trying to block out the pain. Her mouth went so dry that it felt as if she had been force-fed a whole bag of cotton balls. Very faint, as if from far off, she heard people yelling at her. She couldn't hear what they were saying, but she had the distinct impression that it was her they were yelling at. But that wasn't quite right, either. It was hazy, as if in a dream, but it seemed like the people were yelling in her direction, but not at her, Emma.

It all made her feel distant, outside herself, like she didn't know where she was.

Focus, she thought in a loud, commanding voice, *I've got to bring myself back from wherever I've gone. I must have fainted. Or I must have choked on something, and am now lying on the dirty rug of the Brakes County Fire Hall. Will someone start pounding on my chest? Am I going to die?*

"You are going to die," someone concurred. It was faint, not a whisper, but at the edge of her aural range. But even as low as they were spoken, they were the most powerful words she had ever heard. Those words had confirmed her worst fear. There was nothing more frightening in Emma's hard-luck life than the fear of dying. It was that fear that brought her back from the dark depths she found herself in after receiving the latest electrical shock from the folding chair.

As the current momentarily ceased flowing through her body, Emma was able to pull her head up from her shoulder. Still sitting straight up in her chair at the reception, she realized that it had all happened in a split second, and that no one had noticed.

Keeping her head still but scanning with her eyes, she looked over the other people at her table. There were eleven others beside her. And not one of them had noticed that she had fainted, or blacked out, or something.

Then who told me I was going to die?

All very weird, and not one other person in the whole hall aware that something strange had happened. *Wait a minute; that pathetic bald guy with the crutches and scary eyes—the one I almost ran over—is he looking at me?*

He was, right at her.

From three tables away, where he was holding a bowl up to his mouth and slurping soup directly from it, he was staring at her. So hard, she imagined, that he was able to see her very soul.

It wasn't your usual amorous leer—there was no lust in his eyes, only interest. He wasn't a *dirty* old man, just a pathetic one.

He set the bowl of soup down on the table, not pulling his eyes off her even though he knew she had seen him staring. Instead, when one of his brows shot up in a gesture reminiscent of Mr. Spock ("Fascinating, Captain") from the old *Star Trek* series, she knew that he had seen her black out.

Except it was more like a "blankout" than a blackout. She had still been awake and aware and had still sensed things while in that state but just didn't think she could react to them.

It all seemed so surreal. Had she really heard a voice in her head tell her she was going to die?

You've got to get a grip, woman, she berated. Heeding her own advice, she decided to act as if nothing were wrong and began to eat again. This time she used her right hand to pick up the fork.

Emma skewered a piece of roast beef from the congealed gravy, then raised the fork to her mouth. Before she pulled the food off the tines with her teeth, she noticed a foul odor. As she retracted the utensil from under her nostrils, she remembered the warm thickness inside the "squishion."

The index finger of the hand she was using to serve herself the cold roast beef was covered, from tip to second knuckle, with a mixture of blood and a lumpy brown substance that looked like feces.

2

*W*hen John Hoover awoke Friday morning, he had been in a great mood. He was off from work for the next three days (his regular days off were Saturday and Sunday, and he had taken a personal day off today for the candlelight wedding this evening), and he had been waked not by the incessant buzzing of the alarm clock but by light, warm kisses from his wife, Fiona. To make the beginning of his day even more pleasurable, the light kisses progressed into a passionate tumble before breakfast.

"Mmm, that was fun," he told her, "I could fall right back asleep."

Fiona playfully slapped him on the chest. "Get up, big boy. The ceremony is at six, and we've got a lot of things to do before we get ready."

The bright May sun was shining in the bedroom window, warming him. "Looks like Sheila will have good weather," he said.

"The TV said clear and sunny, no rain," Fiona agreed. "She got lucky; you know how fickle rain can be in the spring." She got out of bed, and he watched the lithe stride of her bare thighs as she walked into the bathroom. A minute later, the shower started running.

He smiled. How content he was. At three years to the plus side of forty, he finally thought himself mature.

The divorce had been finalized for a while now. It had gone civilly at first. He was of the mind that he had wronged her, and when their day in court came, he hadn't contested anything. Lauren had taken him for everything that he had, but fuck it, she had been entitled to it after the unknown philandering he had put her through over the years. Then she hit him where it hurt. She had taken the kids and moved to western New York, nearly five hours away from

Philadelphia—far enough that it was not some place he could just drop in. Her brother was there, and he had gotten her a job.

In one swift stroke, Lauren had turned him from a weekend dad into a biannual relative. It had infuriated him, and he had fought her every step of the way for over two years, amassing a staggering amount of debt in lawyer fees. His lawyer had been good, but he had still lost. Thanks to the infernal, infamous Purser Street video, his infidelity was known nationwide.

He didn't regret the loss of the marriage—it had never really clicked anyway—but Janey and Pammy were the innocent victims of his indiscretions. For that he would always be sorry.

Accepting his mistakes as unchangeable facts of life—and not about to let sour memories ruin his mood—Hoover got out of bed with a sigh and went about his daily duties before getting ready for his sister-in-law Sheila's wedding.

*   *   *

Hoover's good mood lasted right up until the moment the ceremony began. Then trepidation set in.

As the joyful organ music filled the rafters of the Church of St. Tiburtius, Father Thomas O'Malley appeared from the sacristy. Hoover hadn't thought about O'Malley, or the night at the fire hall, for over six years. When he saw the priest, the memories of that night—and the week that preceded it—came flooding back.

Midway through the ceremony, Fiona, resplendent in a bright, red dress that was low cut in the front and even lower cut in the back, leaned over and asked him in a whisper, "John, are you all right? You look pale."

What could he say? He couldn't be straightforward with her and tell her what it was causing his hands to shake and his palms to sweat. Fiona knew that something had happened between the night he dove out her window onto the fire escape and the night he proposed to her, but she had never asked. God bless her, she had never asked.

"I'm fine. It's a little hot in here, that's all," he said, when what he really wanted to say was, *Honey, let's get the hell out of here right now* How would he be able to explain why he wanted to ditch her baby sister's wedding? He could never explain. As far as she knew, he didn't even know Father O'Malley. He was an atheist, for Christ's sake. This was his first time in a church since his own wedding— his second wedding, when he married Fiona.

He could do nothing. He would have to sit and watch and wait, the nerves beneath his skin squirming. He had never asked Fiona where the wedding would be held because what difference would it have made to him? Over the years he had forgotten that for those three fateful days, he had been closely associated with the Roman Catholic Church of St. Tiburtius and its representative, Thomas O'Malley.

They had been through death together.

For the most part, O'Malley looked the same. Except for the expanse of gray at the temples, the years hadn't aged him; he was still trim and healthy. But the sight of the priest was enough to frighten Hoover that he felt twice as old as he actually was. According to Fiona, it scared him so badly that the blood had drained from his face. In his chest, Hoover's heart beat hard enough that it hurt. The usual *lub-thrump, lub-thrump* felt irregular, as though there was an extra quiver at the end of each beat.

But it wasn't just the sight of O'Malley, was it?

No, there was more; Hoover could feel it in his bones . . . because he thought he knew where this day was going to end.

"Let us come together and join these two people," Father O'Malley was saying from the altar.

He leaned over to Fiona and whispered in her ear. "Where's the reception going to be?"

She gave a sighing sound of disapproval under her breath. "They've rented some run-down place. I offered to help pay for it and get something better, but Sheila's too proud to have let me. It's being held at some shithole called the Brakes County Fire Hall. You know it?"

"Yeah, I know it," he said.

He was now sure; a day that had started out with love and passion was going to end with pain and suffering.

3

*T*he weather report had been wrong; the sky was beginning to overcast as twilight approached, the bloated clouds rolling in stained grapefruit pink by the setting sun.

Father O'Malley got out of the rectory's car and pushed the button on the key to activate the alarm. The lot was crowded, and he had to park at the severe edge of it, above a steep decline that led to the street below.

It wasn't required for the priest who had said the mass and consecrated the vows to attend the reception, but it was customary for Father O'Malley. He liked to celebrate with his parishioners, liked to share in the couple's joy and expectations for the future. He had taken two separate lives and made them one today. He wanted to be there when they greeted the world for the first time as a single entity.

In the semigloom of dusk, he turned and looked at the fire hall.

He hadn't been here physically in six years, but he had never really left. There had never been a place of such haunting as this. For O'Malley, the BCFH had stayed with him. It was where he went in his nightmares.

* * *

After the night they put Dedaker to death, O'Malley had waited for a sign from God. He had hoped, begged, and prayed for it. He had pleaded for it with his actions, by striving to become an exemplary priest. He had embraced the church. There wasn't an undertaking, no matter how daunting, that he would not try to accomplish in the name of the Father. For his struggles, when Father Anthony passed away from colon cancer, O'Malley had been chosen to succeed him by being awarded the pastor's position.

But no sign had ever come, nothing but the gruesome memories. The sights, the sounds, the smells, they had all been kept alive within him.

Now he was looking for absolution as he grew older. He understood what he had done was a sin, but it was at God's behest, his request; there had to be a salvation in the future, didn't there? Hadn't God stayed Abraham's hand? *Yes, he did,* a voice inside his head assured him. Then it bit him with, *But hadn't he also denied Moses the Promised Land after letting him wander the desert all those years, baking in the intense heat, looking for that exact goal, only to, at the last, make him climb Mount Nebo so that he could lay eyes on that which he was denied because of his questioning faith, before being struck dead?*

Yes, he had. Moses had asked of God for water for his followers while crossing the desert. God instructed him to strike a rock once, and only once, and water would be provided. Moses doubted and struck the rock twice with his staff. God was angered, and he prevented Moses from entering Canaan after the laborious trek across the desert.

O'Malley had been wandering the desolation of his own desert for the last six years. And it had brought him full circle. It had led him here again, to this fire hall, because of his questioning faith, with no promise of heaven to come for his efforts.

Is this fire hall my Mt. Nebo? Have I been led here to die?

4

O'Malley had recognized Hoover among the guests at the church, so he wasn't surprised to find him at the reception.

When O'Malley entered the hall (which had been decorated for the gala in light blue pastels to match the gown worn by the only bridesmaid in that party), he scanned the room, looking for Hoover. The cop was seated at a table just to the left of the door. Sitting next to him was a stunning-looking woman with black hair and a red dress. While the woman was in an animated conversation with the other people at the table, it appeared that Hoover had been staring at the entrance, awaiting his, O'Malley's, arrival.

After the priest made eye contact with Hoover, instead of going over to him, O'Malley roamed around the room, meeting people and shaking hands, congratulating the parents of the groom and the mother of the bride.

Father O'Malley continued making the rounds until after the bridal party was introduced to thunderous applause. Once the bride and groom had gotten their food, the DJ began announcing table numbers for the buffet.

Standing a few feet away from the small alcove that acted as a bar, Hoover found O'Malley sipping beer from a plastic cup.

"Well, if it isn't old Tom O'Malley, the Alley Cat," Hoover said in greeting. He was smiling, but from the inside, it felt like a cringe.

"Hello, John. How have you been?" From the tone, Hoover knew what he was really asking was how he had been coping since the last time fate had brought them together.

"I've been . . . good. Yourself?"

"Unfortunately, not as good, but I'm coping. Been dealing with it in my own way, thrown myself into my work. I'm now the pastor of St. Tibby's," he said, taking a mouthful from the cup.

"Good for you, Father," Hoover said, hoping it was the right sentiment, and clasped him on the shoulder.

"Thanks," the priest muttered, then more happily, "hey, you know, there was one thing that I promised myself I'd ask you if I ever saw you again."

"Yeah, what's that?"

"Whatever happened with that reporter you slugged?"

"Nicos Agbalaya? Didn't you hear about it; it was all over the television for a while there?"

"I don't watch that much TV," O'Malley said.

"Agbalaya dropped the charges then wrote a true-crime book about Dedaker and the murders," Hoover told him. "He christened the killings 'The Messiah Murders' after the room with the charcoal rubbings was found. Agbalaya's book turned out to be a national phenomenon three summers back. The mixture of graphic violence and sex, along with the mysterious disappearance of Dedaker, caught on with the college kids, cybergeeks, and strangely enough, a demographic of housewives and career women; from there it steamrolled across the country until every second person lying on a beach or in a hammock was reading it. Read it myself, and even I've got to admit that it was pretty good, up there with Capote's *In Cold Blood* After the popularity rage of the book, the whole thing festered into sort of an urban legend, with the threat of Dedaker still out there somewhere. Even heard an epic miniseries was in preproduction. I guess the book and movie rights were a lot better option than sitting through a lengthy trial against a guy who was pretty much out a job anyway."

"You still lost your job, even though there was no lawsuit?"

"After the assault case was dropped, the commissioner still decided to pin the 'conduct unbecoming' on me, and I was bounced, just as I figured. He said I was 'neglectful in my duties to protect the citizens.' What could I do? Honestly, I couldn't really blame him. After the pawnshop fuckup, the assault, and what happened with Beverly, I'd fire me too."

"So what are you doing now?"

"I'm a theft investigator for a department-store chain." At that point, people usually asked him which chain it was, curious to know if it was one they shopped at, but O'Malley didn't. *Oh, well,* Hoover thought, and continued, "Banker hours, weekends, and holidays off. Full benefits, and I'm building up quarters so that I can collect Social Security when I retire."

"Cops don't collect Social Security?"

"No, they have a pension fund which excludes them from Social Security."

"I see," Father O'Malley said. Their talk was only filler, like that of old friends who haven't seen each other in a while and have found that, in their absence, they've grown apart. Worse, their conversation was banal and stilted, as if they were both consciously trying to *not* talk about something.

Reaching for something to say to fill the void, Father O'Malley asked, "You're not eating?"

"Not hungry. I'm not big on buffets; I don't like a lot of other people putting their hands in my food."

"How about that?" O'Malley asked, pointing his chin at the cup of beer in Hoover's hand. "You handling it okay?"

"What? Alcohol? Since that . . . outing, I've cut it out entirely. This is the first beer I've had since you found me on the couch, and I'm only having this one to calm my nerves, know what I mean?"

O'Malley closed his eye and nodded. "Only too well do I know." Trying to steer the conversation away, he said, "But forget that; how's things with your wife? Last I heard she'd taken your kids and left you."

"That was my first wife, Lauren, and she did take the kids and leave me. We divorced. Since then, I've gotten remarried to that lovely woman right over there. Her name's Fiona."

"Won't she be missing you, standing over here talking to me?" O'Malley said, now looking for an escape route.

"Nah, she won't miss me for a while yet. This is her sister's wedding; she's busy talking to her relatives. I'm not much in the mood to celebrate, anyway; I haven't been myself today, as you can imagine."

Tom had no response. After a minute, Hoover asked, "Why did you come back?"

"You know me," the priest said. "I'm always looking for answers. You?"

"Combination of ignorance and magnetism."

There was another uncomfortable silence as they stood side by side looking out over the crowd sitting down to feast. They were strangers to each other, except for a momentary shared act not unlike a one-night stand, a deed done under the cover of darkness.

"Can you feel it, Father?" Hoover asked in a hushed voice.

Without knowing that he was going to answer, O'Malley said, "Yeah, I can feel it. It's tense, like a calm before a storm."

Hoover nodded. "Something's happening, Father. I don't think it's ended yet."

Just then, a heavy-set woman in a pink dress at the center of the room began to scream.

5

*E*mma looked at the discoloration on her finger without really seeing it. Instead, she was looking past it and into another night entirely. She was seeing a night in which this hall and, more specifically, this chair were in use.

In her vision, the guests seated on all sides of her at Sheila's wedding were fading out, being replaced with a different crowd. As the change occurred, her sight did not shimmer, nor was there a sudden change from one place to another. It happened more like what happened to a car radio when one signal was lost and replaced by that of another closer station. A change that was not only noticeable in reception, but also in format. It was like going from smooth jazz to raunchy rock and roll, from adult contemporary to rap. As the change happened, there was an overlapping of individual entities, a sort of doubling, as each separate presence occupied the same space simultaneously. And of course, there was the burst of static.

The change went from one crowded event to another, with only the hall remaining the same. The doubling would have been a smooth blend, like the splicing of two different photographs to make one panorama, except for the static.

It radiated throughout her body, making her muscles contract and jerk spasmodically. Her eyelids fluttered, and the tips of her fingers began bleeding where the nails met the soft pink skin beneath. In her head, she could hear—as well as feel—the bursting pulsations of the static. It was loud, the pitch high, like standing inside an amp while the guitarist wailed feedback. It caused the coils of her inner ears to vibrate, and the drum of her left to pierce.

A small trickle of blood flowed from the canal into the cup, directly above the lobe. Emma would never know it, but the crossover left her with partial deafness in her left ear.

As the static began to fade and then diminish, so too did the pain she experienced during the transmigration—it was no longer entire, having localized in the biceps of her right arm. There, it was a swelling, merciless agony. And it itched so much that it felt like it was burning.

Things had changed.

Emma found herself in the same room, but she was no longer with the same people, that much was obvious. What wasn't so easily detectible was that she wasn't in the same *time* That could only be seen in the subtle differences, like the clothing or the hairstyles of these new people.

Emma had gone to the past. Not far, but too far for her liking, because when the people had changed, so had the mood. The people in this past were angry. The gathering that she had somehow found herself in was not festive, as it was at Sheila's wedding; it was hostile.

She could feel their anger directed at her. Surprisingly enough, this was not a feeling Emma was unaccustomed to. Growing up as she did—an individual isolated from the world because of the person she was . . . the *fat person* she was—she began to notice the feelings the people around her gave off. Because of the lack of much-needed and desired attention, her senses became fine-tuned to the emotions of others. As a virtual outsider in her own skin, Emma enjoyed watching other people, and she absorbed their emotions like a chameleon took on the color of its surroundings. Emma became a human mood ring—an instrument that displayed the feelings of others, happy or sad, jealous or tolerant, friendly or mean. Throughout most of her life, she was bitter, angry with herself, and angry with others, because that was how people felt toward her. Without being able to control it (or even know what it was she was doing), she had built that anger up and stored it, because it was the most dominating emotion offered to her from others around her. People hated her, and she absorbed it. People were disgusted with her, and she absorbed it. She accepted being a not well-liked person, but could all of that anger and hatred actually be only because she was overweight?

It was that same anger and loathing that she felt as soon as she arrived in this room, providing comfort in its normalcy, and at the same time, appalling in its animosity. Just as her feelings were being pulled in two different directions, so too were the anger and loathing she experienced coming from two directions. They were coming from the outside, as well as from the in.

Although used to being a conduit for animosity, Emma had never before experienced that rancor coming from within her. But then again, she had never before met Michael Dedaker, either.

A wave of nausea hit her, causing her head to spin; paradoxically, she felt as if she were going to faint and throw up at the same time. In her mind, her own being repulsed her. She had always been depressed by her weight, but never before had it made her physically ill. When the urge to vomit passed, there was an instant when she felt as if she were *thinking* someone else's feelings about her, that someone else was disgusted by her and yet, at the same time, accepting of such limitations as those of a person the likes of Emma—a woman. It was a very brief thought, almost fleeting, then it was gone. Not gone as in disappeared, gone as in moved. The feelings of revulsion didn't leave her; they seemed to push her—

My what . . . my being? My essence? My soul?

—out of the way, to shove her thoughts into the background, while the malevolent thoughts took over, took command.

"You are going to die," said a man standing in front of her. He said it in a hissing, vengeful voice. Emma saw him, but he was distant, almost two-dimensional, like she was watching an actor in a movie from behind the screen, rather than in the audience. The man was tall and well built, wearing jeans and a black T-shirt. His hair was mussed, and his eyes were red from exertion or exhaustion or both. She had never before seen this man in her life, but from deep in her mind—deep in *front* of her mind—she recalled his name. John Hoover. He was a cop . . . a detective. *How do I know* that?

"How does it feel to be the one in the corner, you sick fuck?" the guy named Hoover asked. Behind him, there was a crowd watching with frightened—yet anticipating—eyes.

Even for Emma, with her high resilience level, this Hoover's rage was a lot more anger than she was used to dealing with. She wanted to ask this man—a man whom she had never even *met* before—why he would want her dead.

But she couldn't ask. She couldn't even move.

With her eyes, and only her eyes, she looked down to see why she couldn't move. When she saw, two disconcerting things assaulted her already-laded mind:

She couldn't move because she was bound and gagged—shackled—to a brown metal folding chair.

And she was in a different body. A man's body.

A cold splash of liquid caused her to look back up at the crowd gathered before her. She guessed that there were maybe thirty people present, none of whom she knew, but who all seemed to know her.

Or him.

What the hell is going on here?

There was another cold dose of water thrown in her face. Her head shook to clear her eyes, producing a dizzying effect, as if she were watching roller coaster footage in one of those room-sized IMAX theaters designed to induce motion sickness.

The worst part was that a second before she decided to turn her head to see who had thrown the water on her, *her head turned itself.*

Hoover was still standing in front of her chair; the person who had thrown the water standing to his left, unknown, unlike Hoover, to the mind she shared. The man splashed it at her again and again until she was saturated. When the clear plastic bottle was more than three quarters empty, and the contents wouldn't splash anymore, he upended it, and the rest of the water ran down over her head and into her eyes.

What was that all about? Why was he throwing water at me?

Or should it be us, *now?*

Her eyes blinked several times to get rid of the water that had found its way in when the bottle was upended. The water stung, but it was nothing compared to the flaring, itching, pulling on her—their—right arm.

As the rivulets continued to run, she looked down at the arm causing her—them—so much agony. There was an open wound about the size of a half-dollar seeping blood and pus and caked with dirt and a green fungus. It itched because it had been left untreated and was now festering, but it hurt because of the angle in which the arm had been placed when she—no, *he*—had been bound. The arm had been bent back when his hands were tied behind the chair, causing the wound to tear open. The pure whiteness of the newly purchased rope stood out in stark contrast to the grunge of the sore as it wound around him beneath the opening. Trying to sniff the wound for the rotten-egg-like smell of gangrene, she could only detect the stench of old urine coming from the man's grimy clothes that she was also, by proxy, wearing.

For a moment their eyes slid close. Inside, Emma felt the thoughts of this man centering. He was accepting what was to come. And he was at peace with it. He was ready to meet God.

Meet God? I don't want to meet God. I want to get the fuck out of here! I don't know who you are, or what you did to get in this situation, but you better not give up on me. Didn't you see Frankenstein? *That's one angry mob of townspeople out there looking to kill a monster, and they think it's you . . . us!*

Her complaints went unnoticed. While she ranted, the man whose body she shared, in a serene mood now, opened his eyes again. A third man had separated from the crowd and joined Hoover and the water thrower.

"Hello, Michael," this newcomer said with a grim expression on his shallow face. "I've waited a long time to meet you."

The mind of the man that Emma was sharing didn't know this person personally but acknowledged him as a relative of one of the dead women whose souls he had released.

Dead women? Souls he had released? Huh?

The thought was interrupted as the man—a dead woman's relative, apparently—punched them with a closed fist. He had hit them right on the jaw, causing this Michael's head to recoil, taking Emma's with it. Emma was frightened by the way she saw this escalating. She tried to scream, but it didn't work; Michael's mouth was gagged.

As Michael sat silent, the crowd inched closer. When they got near enough, fists began to rain down, hammering. They struck repeatedly. Again and again, fists hit Michael's tethered body, pummeling them. They struck him about the face and neck, in the stomach, on the sides, in the crotch. Everyone in the room had their chance. The beating was merciless.

All the while, Emma screamed unheard within the other's mind.

The final fist flew and connected with Michael's nose, breaking it. Blood rained out, causing the nostrils to clog and respiration to slow.

The trauma of the beating and the lack of oxygen caused Michael to pass out, taking the hapless Emma with him.

6

Floating on a sea of blackness, Emma drifted, watching the private thoughts of the man whose mind she swam. She didn't know how she had gotten into his head, or even who he was, for one does not tend to think of oneself by proper name, but instead as the center of the universe. There is an old cliché that says the world does not revolve around you, but it does. It revolves around us all individually. We are the lead actor, the main character, the protagonist of our own lives.

Emma watched the lifetime activities of the man called Michael as he drifted alongside her in his state of unconsciousness. She saw him living and complacent; she saw him routine and depressed; she saw him vibrant and working. She watched as he planned and abducted, then killed and committed necrophilism.

The visions were not the abstract non sequiturs of dreams, but the continuous reels of memories; it was like watching home movies of a friend.

A murderous friend.

Emma Anderson now had an understanding of what was happening in that rental hall, of what was happening to this man, and consequently, what was happening to her.

And she didn't know if she wanted it to stop.

7

$\mathcal{A}$nother splash of cool liquid and she was back—they were back.

Along with consciousness came blurred vision; Michael's eyes wouldn't focus correctly. His head was tilted backward, and Emma could see his reflection blurrily in the mirrors attached to the roof above the dance floor. The mirrors had been placed overhead to reflect the multicolored strobe lights and the celebrating dancers. Emma saw no celebration; what she was witnessing was a damnation.

She looked upon the face of the man whose body she was in. It was the face of a killer, and it looked the part after what the angry townspeople had done to it.

Michael was a bleeding mess held to a metal folding chair by nylon rope and gagged with a wide, frayed piece of gray duct tape. His hair was matted down with sweat and water and the natural oils from not being washed. There were open cuts and scrapes on every bit of exposed flesh.

His face, while unfamiliar to Emma, might be unrecognizable to anyone who knew him, it was that puffed, cut, and bruised. His neck was so covered with discolorations that it made him look like a man in the last stages of cholera. His left eye was red and glassy, the right one with a mouse so large over it that it was almost completely swollen shut. While she looked up at the mirror, she could see the overhang of the mouse's black-and-blue bubble expanding slowly. It looked like a malignant tumor getting ready to burst through the skin.

Between the infection raging in the hole in his arm and the

savage beating he had taken, Michael needed a doctor big-time But none was going to come; no one here was going to call for one. And Emma couldn't blame them for it.

More water came, and this time she grasped an understanding about what the water was for. It was meant to revive Michael. Revive him for the next step on his path to Golgotha, a step that she, the unwilling hitcher, was going to be forced to take with him.

If he dies, will I die too?

Sure, she would die. She reasoned that if she could feel his pain and hear his thoughts then . . . but wait, *could* she hear his thoughts? Well, no, she couldn't. The only voice that she had heard inside his head was her own. She could feel his moods, and she had watched the things that he had done in the past, but they had been displayed before her like noninteractive videos. They were facts, not thoughts. They had only been memories . . .

They were his memories!

Memories, that's it; nothing more. All the things she had seen him doing, from the mundane to the mutilations, had only been but memories. She wasn't sharing his brain, just its space inside his skull; her mind was squatting in his brain's house.

But that wasn't quite right, either. Something was still bothering her; what was it?

Squeak.

It had something to do with her not having control over him.

Squeak.

She had control at one point, and then he had shoved her mind out of the way. She had felt—what? Intentions of her own?—and then he pushed her thoughts to the rear, where she no longer felt the pressures of life weighing on her, or the need to achieve anything ever again.

Squeak.

Her mind had been in control of itself, of her ideals, her hopes and dreams, and then he had taken that control from her. But why? How? It was impossible. This whole thing, this nightmarish vision, was nothing but a large memory that the smaller ones compiled to make up, a memory mosaic of Michael's life displayed for her enjoyment . . . or her torment.

That's why everything looked so abstract, so two-dimensional—it wasn't real. I didn't go into the past, I've been watching a memory movie, his memories, but in my head.

Then it struck her with complete clarity—he was in *her* head, not the other way around.

She was still at Sheila's wedding, sitting with her roast beef in front of her and the other more placid guests around her. Nothing had changed, except a killer with the first name Michael had somehow taken over her body and was now recalling his last memories of life.

Squeak.

It's the chair. He came in through the chair somehow. It's got to be the same one in both time periods; that's the only possible explanation. Maybe it was the shock; maybe he rode the electrical currents into me.

Squeak.

Emma's reeling mind suddenly became distracted by the squeaking noises she heard approaching from behind and off to the left. *Squeak, squeak, squeak.*

"Is he awake?" someone close by asked. The memory said it was Hoover who had spoken.

A woman's face came into Michael's view, as he still leaned back, staring at his own reflection in the mirror above. "Yes," she said in a hoarse, stressed voice.

That was the only bit of conversation Emma heard as a hushed pall came over the crowd. In the quiet, she heard a final squeak followed by the thump of something heavy being lowered to the ground.

Emma didn't know if Michael had the strength to lift his head anymore. He wanted to just lie down and die, but she could feel him summoning the energy that he needed to see this through to the end. Michael forced his head up.

They were looking at the crowd again.

The anger hadn't dissipated with the abuse, but it had subsided. A new emotion had surpassed the hatred. Fear. The crowd had known what was going to happen, but now that the point of no return was upon them, their suburban faces revealed ghastly surprise.

There was something else: most of the people gathered in the fire hall weren't looking at the ravaged remains of what used to be a man strapped to a folding chair; they were looking off to his left. They were looking at the squeaking thing.

Emma watched as Michael's head turned to see what was more interesting than the raw red clot of meat he had become.

When Emma saw it, she was shocked too, shocked more by what she saw to Michael's right than anything else she had seen on this strange night.

She had known since the beginning that this vision wasn't going to end until the man strapped in the chair with her was dead. But the sickening thing that was being prepared—and even worse, who was doing it—was more than Emma's mind could take. She felt as if she were being driven insane.

As the last tattered remains of any innocence Emma had left in her young life were stripped away, she screamed across time.

$$8$$

At Sheila's wedding, Van Morrison's "Brown Eyed Girl" had just reached the part when he starts singing "Sha-la-la-la-la-la-la-la-lala-gida, ladi-da" when Emma screamed.

As far as anyone at the wedding could tell, they thought she was screaming at the lingering piece of roast beef skewered on the fork poised in front of her mouth. That thought quickly changed as Emma dropped the fork but continued ululating the high-pitched feminine screech at her discolored finger.

Just as unexpectedly as she had started screaming, she stopped, gasping for air. The stunned crowd around her watched in mute silence as the song ended and the music died out. The only sound to be heard throughout the hall was the sound of Emma's rasping breathing.

With no one having really taken notice of the fat chick before this, there was no way they would be able to notice that the features of her face no longer belonged to the overweight but pleasant woman she had been. Her features had transformed, having become wickedly evil.

9

$\mathcal{A}$s her own screams died out in her head, but her heart continuing to gallop, she noticed a man standing to Michael's left, a man she didn't recognize right away because he had a full head of hair. He stood less than a foot away from the chair and looked directly into Michael's eyes. What he was looking for, she didn't know. Perhaps he sought justification for what he was about to do; perhaps he wanted to see the fear of God in the person he was about to kill; perhaps he wanted to see what a dying man saw in his final minutes.

Can he see me? Emma wondered.

It was the staring that sparked the recognition for Emma. The man with the penetrating eyes, the man who had wheeled in the squeaking thing and was now gazing into the depths of a killer named Michael, was the same man who had been staring at her at Sheila's wedding.

He's the man I bumped into. The one who was now—or will be in the future—sitting at table number 5, slurping soup right from the bowl; the same man who had been looking directly at me when I snapped out of this reverie the first time.

Emma would never know Edward Kasay by name, but she would know him as their executioner.

As he stared at Michael/Emma, she heard another of those mysterious squeaking sounds come from behind the chair. With a final squeak, Kasay pulled the thing into view.

It was a generator.

The squeaking noise had come from the single rusty axle that ran the length of the rear of the machine, its hard rubber wheels serving the dual purpose of making the machine portable and supporting the heft of the industrial engine's overhead valve and gas tank. Instead of wheels, a single black metal bracket with two rubber feet supported the front, where the on button and the receptacles for the plugs were. The metal frame that housed the generator was dinged and weathered from outdoor use. The engine itself looked well used but still fairly new. The brand name and model number on the housing were unreadable, worn off.

Michael swallowed as he looked at the machine. Emma agreed.

Printed in menacing bold black letters on the switch and plug panel was the description that the machine was "contractor quality with 6,500 rated watts and 8,125 maximum watts."

8,125 maximum watts of electricity!

There was going to be an electrocution.

When Emma looked back up at Kasay, she had a newfound understanding about why he had been staring at them so intently—he was trying to memorize every detail of the execution so that he could forever remember it, burning the images into his mind, freezing them in time, immortalizing the face of the killer. He was inhaling the coppery smells of blood and sweat, as well as the acrid odors of urine and gangrene, while caressing the tangible power of the generator and the chair with his mind, enjoying the power of finally being the righteous, instead of the victimized.

And Emma was sure that if Michael was somehow at Sheila Oswald's wedding and remembering this event, then so too was this man, the executioner.

That's why I bumped into him; he was standing in front of my chair, waiting for me. It's the same chair, and he knew it, she thought, confirming her suspicions. *Oh God, how did I ever get in an electric chair?*

Wrapped tightly around the generator's handle so that they wouldn't slip loose during transport were a set of battery jumper cables specially designed with spring clamps on only one end and a three-pronged plug on the other. The prongs were also not the normal two flats and one round of a household male plug. This one had *three* flat conductors on the head, each slightly curved to the circumference. A household plug conducted 120 volts; this brute could handle 220. Plugs like this were generally used for large industrial-strength, package-unit air conditioners.

Kasay uncoiled the cables with slow methodical movements, never taking his eyes off Michael. When they were free, he stretched his arms high above his head, letting the cables dangle at their length to work out the kinks, the prongs of the plug making tiny tinkling noises as they bounced off the hardwood dance floor. With an intent gaze and arms open in a wide, threatening Y, Kasay was the image of an Olympus god poised to cast lightning bolts at the fallen.

With the spring clamps in his hands, Kasay took a cautious step forward and sank to a knee. Emma watched in horror as he attached the black negative cable to the thin bar that ran perpendicular to the chair's front legs; as the teeth closed on the metal, a piece of brown paint chipped off. It was the same flecked spot that Emma's internal clock told her she had inspected just fifteen minutes ago in real time, but years in the future from when it actually happened.

Suddenly, Emma could feel the body in her mind start to lurch against the binds that held it. He thrashed about, yelling incomprehensibly behind the striated tape, all to no avail, the nylon rope having been tied too tightly to break or slip.

Michael was finally scared.

Not of dying—he was all right with that. It was the pain that frightened him. Emma could sympathize, but she didn't know if she would help him, even if it were physically possible for her to do so. This man had shown no remorse when he had tortured all of those women; why should he see any?

Nonetheless, the struggle for freedom was a short one. The loss of energy from the beating—and whatever else it had taken to get him here to this hall, strapped to a chair—made it so.

When the fight left Michael, the rest of the process started up again. At no point during the hookup did the soon-to-be-bald Ed Kasay say anything to Michael. Instead, he continued to matter-of-factly untangle the end of the positive cable with a patience that belied the moment. When it was straight enough, he opened the spring clamp with his callused fingers and sank it into the tender underbelly of Michael's calf, the pain of the clamp's teeth biting into the meaty flesh exquisitly.

The weirdest feeling of Emma's whole, woeful life was feeling another person's skin crawl—from the inside. Goose pebbles rose up along Michael's arms and legs, and the skin began to undulate over the muscles it sheathed.

The crawling skin had freaked her out so much that she hadn't noticed the man who had stepped forward from the crowd until he started to speak.

10

*P*eople at the wedding were beginning to react to the convulsions Emma's body was going through. Their reactions, of course, were not to help, but to move away from her as far as they could. The other members of dinner table 3 had been the first to go, so they had the benefit of being the farthest away from her when the sparks begin to fly later. But they were also the closest to the exit door, and would be the ones to get trampled to death when the exodus began.

As Emma's body was being rocked from Dedaker's memory of the brief escape attempt before the electrocution, a brave woman grabbed hold of table 3 and drag it away from Emma. The woman stumbled and twisted her ankle at the same time that another person, who was trying to get out of Emma's vicinity while still gawking at the convulsing women instead of looking where he was going, ran into the round edge of the table, jarring it. All of the food on the ceramic (not china, definitely not china) plates, glassware, and utensils, as well as the bouquet of flowers in its filled, two-gallon vase, slid to one side of the table.

There was a thunderous crash as the table upended, depositing its contents onto the floor and the poor woman who had twisted her ankle.

Sheila Oswald was standing at the main table, a palm to her mouth, gibbering over and over again, "No, no, no, no," behind her hand. Her groom, a dimwit by the name of Paul Reed, whom no one in the Oswald family could understand Sheila's attraction to except Sheila herself, was still snarfing down a roast beef sandwich on kaiser as he enjoyed the outbreak with wide eyes and brown gravy dribbling from the scraggily whiskers of his thin beard.

Hoover and O'Malley watched, rooted to the floor, as someone's elbow took a huge divot out of the wedding cake on the table next to the bar alcove, the piece of cake sacrificed from the middle layer of the three tiers. Before the yellow cake and white icing hit the dance floor with a splat, the second tier lost its foundation, and the whole cake collapsed in on itself like a concertina.

Hysteria set in as metal folding chairs were strewn across the floor while guests of Sheila's wedding were trying to get out of the way of the once-screaming, now-shaking woman. Every chair in the place was on its side or leaning; all except Emma's, which stood right where it had been placed and now occupied the center of another crowd whose sole attention was directed its way.

"Let me through! Let me through!" came a gruff voice from deep within the semicircular throng. "It's that chair; we've got to get her off that chair!" People began parting like the Red Sea to get out of the way as a bald man with two arm crutches pushed through. He was moving as fast as his handicap would allow, balancing himself first to one side then the other. The swaying gave his movements the appearance of slithering.

"Isn't that—," O'Malley started.

"Ed Kasay," Hoover said. When Hoover had first recognized Kasay among the crowd in this fire hall some six years ago, he had had mixed feelings about the man's presence. The priest was a sympathetic fellow, but Hoover had been glad to see someone he knew in attendance at that time that had shared the pain of losing a loved one to the Dandelion as he had—Kasay would understand Hoover's convictions. But Hoover had also been just as happy that no one else amongst the mob could have recognized him, for the obvious reasons. Of the three victims' families that had originally been assigned to Hoover and Beverly Farrell during the investigation, Kasay was the only one present at the execution—the priest didn't ask the Dashers because of their religion, and at Hoover's warning, the loveless George Hustead had been skipped over, omitted admittance. The reason Hoover was slightly apprehensive at first upon finding Kasay among the crowd was that the man could readily identify him if the shit hit the fan later;

he had to rely on Kasay to keep his mouth shut. But after the festivities, Hoover's worriers had been waylaid, since Kasay had been the one who had fired Dedaker up that night.

Now, as it was all unfolding again, one of the people that Hoover had desperately not wanted to see here was Edward Kasay. All of the people who had watched Michael Dedaker cook that night had come out spiritually changed by the experience, Hoover was sure, but Ed Kasay was the only one to emerge from that night *physically* changed. Kasay had walked into this very fire hall those years past as an able-bodied man in his late fifties and had been carried out as a handicapped burn victim, with only partial movement remaining in his legs.

Now Hoover watched along with everyone else as the man he had helped carry out that fateful night—soaking wet, smelling of burnt skin, crying in agony, and laid in the back of Dedaker's own car for O'Malley to take to Holy Redeemer Hospital—shamble on his almost listless legs toward the possessed woman.

"Somebody help me knock her out of the chair!" Kasay yelled.

Hoover tossed his cup full of beer toward a trash can, missing the wide hole by an inch, striking the rim. Foaming beer splashed all over his back and the guests standing next to the buffet tables, behind which befuddled servers looked on with questioning eyes.

"It's showtime, Father," Hoover said, picking up his pace.

11

The man who stood before Michael in his impromptu electric chair was a Catholic priest, his white Roman collar gleaming above the black cassock. The crowd watched him as he kissed a purple stole before bowing his head and draping it around his neck.

They knew his name, for he had gathered them personally, but not one of them knew his heart. Father Thomas O'Malley knew the fear of God—the Hebrew God of the Old Testament, not the more accepting, forgiving deity of the modern era—because he had been taught it in prison.

As a young adult, Tom O'Malley had been straying outside the lines, dabbling in theft, burglary, and larceny. Who knows how far it would've gone if it hadn't been for his father, Bryce O'Malley.

Bryce had been a loving father, but he had also been a linear, no-nonsense guy, a serious person who believed that the line between father and friend should not be a blurred one. If that line were to be crossed, he would lose the respect necessary to guide his three boys into manhood.

He had worked two jobs since the day Tom, the eldest of his sons, had been born. That left his wife, Deirdre, to be the eyes and ears of his house, in which he was the law. He was not an abusive father, having raised his hands to his children in only the most extreme of cases. What he had had was fear; it was Bryce's most useful tool. That fear was rooted in the respect that his children had for him, but mostly it had come from having a good woman behind him.

Not a mother who would belabor the hollow threats of "I'm telling your father" or "Wait until your father gets home," Deirdre watched, looked, and glowered. With her eyes she said more than any threat could ever promise.

Deirdre O'Malley was a fiercely smart woman in a time before such a thing was recognized, but that didn't matter to Dee; there was only one thing in life that she had wanted more than anything else, and that was a family. Even if there were a possibility of being the first woman on the moon, she would've given it up to have children. Her love for her children was unsurpassed. It was that love that let her know Tommy was starting to screw up. It was also the money.

How did a sixteen-year-old without a job have enough money to do the things Tommy was doing? There were expensive clothes for the lavish parties he and his friends would host. There was always money in his pocket for a movie or to go get something to eat. Jewelry started popping up in the form of rings on his fingers and chains around his neck. Dee had noted all of this and—the night after she had been washing dishes and looking out the window over the sink and saw Tommy driving by in a car she had never seen on the street before—informed her husband.

Bryce listened to it all, giving no sign of outward emotion by exploding in rage or blurting expletives. When Deirdre was done, he calmly rose from the table, walked over to the entranceway, and took his hat off a coat peg, then he left. Deirdre hadn't asked where he was going or what he was going to do. When he climbed into bed late that night, he said, "I took care of it." Curiosity ate her up inside, but Dee had never asked what he had done. The next time she saw Tommy, there was a fading lump on his forehead and a healing cut under one eye (the scar of which could still be seen today on his fiftyish cheek), along with a marked difference in his attitude.

From that day forward, Thomas O'Malley, the Alley Cat, began to straighten up and fly right. A year later, after graduating high school, he flew right into the St. Charles Seminary.

That night had changed his whole life, and he would never forget it. Or never forget his father, and the brave thing he had done to save a son from the streets. It wasn't until fifteen years later, as Bryce lay dying from black lung, a disease he got from working the coal mines of Allentown, that he told his son he had gone home and laid awake, silently crying in the bed he shared with his wife.

"I laid there, seeing it over and over again as those men gripped you roughly, beating on you," he said in a voice phlegm-choked from the pneumonia. "Men I had *asked* to do that to you. Those cops had been friends of mine, and I was the one who had told them to do what they did. It was hard for me to watch, and I had to hold back the tears as they dragged you from the corner and threw you in the rear of that squad car, bleeding and crying in front of those hoodlums you called friends." Bryce began to cough. When he was done, Tom wiped his mouth for him, coming away with phlegm and saliva and blood. Black lung was a disease that came from long-term exposure to coal dust. Inhaling it formed a lining on the inside of the lungs, as well as the pores of the skin, depriving both of oxygen, a disease that once acquired, you could never get rid of. The skin doesn't sweat and the lungs can't breath. Old miners die from pneumonia that leads to suffocation—if the cancer doesn't get them first.

"I never told your mother about what I did, because I was ashamed," he said.

"There's nothing to be ashamed of, Dad," his son consoled. "If it wasn't for what you did, I would've been lost."

Bryce gave a weak little laugh that came out as a wheeze. "I've never asked you, but please, appease a dying man, and tell me what it was that changed you."

Sitting by the old man's bedside, decked out in his priestly outfit, Thomas O'Malley leaned forward and said, "I learned the fear of God."

Bryce's eyes went wide above his choked, pale skin.

Tom nodded. "They threw me in a holding cell, where I spent the rest of the night and the whole next day." Tom looked down at his intertwined fingers, rubbing the balls of his thumbs together. "Inside that cell was a huge black man. I'm talking big, a bear of a man. He never told me his name, and I damn sure wasn't going to ask. As I got older, and would think back on it, I'm not sure if he even was a criminal, or only a cop who took an interest in setting me straight. Either way, it worked."

"What did he say to you, son?"

"I don't want to tell exactly. The things he said to me, I hold dear. His words were my revelation. When he was finished talking, I was scared like I never was before. I was scared of God and Jesus and hell. I was also scared of the world. That man illustrated to me, in the deepest voice I have ever heard, a voice that sounded like it was from the pits of hell itself, what the penal system could do to me, laying out examples from minor infractions, to the torments—both psychological and physical—of incarceration, and all the way to the death penalty. With those things already scaring the bejesus out of me, he then turned it up another notch and demonstrated that no punishment man could ever inflict on me would be worse than when I had to stand in judgment before God.

"You taught me fear of my father; he taught me fear of the Father.

"He had no Bible, he had no props—only his voice and my imagination. For the first time in my life, I was alone. I was locked in a cage with a man who could've been a murderer or rapist—and he might have been, for all I know—and there was no one to help me if he chose to take me next. My mother wasn't there; my father wasn't there; my friends weren't there. There was only me. All I had was fear. And he fed on that.

"But he gave me something else that night, something I don't think he expected. When I was let out of that cage, I took this with me: I took sympathy for the victimized.

"It dawned on me that there was no champion for victims; that there were no heroes in today's world, only in legends and myths and movies. Whose job is it to look out for the little guy? The answer: no one. I know this because I was becoming a person who fed off the weak and unwary. At the age of seventeen, I was victimizing people. My cellmate showed me this without having to show it to me. I was turning into somebody that I hated; I was becoming my own enemy. The next day, when I was let go, I decided to change that. I wanted to become a champion for the people, someone they could come to for help. But also, I wanted to be someone who could comfort.

"I found those things in the priesthood."

"Should I say I'm sorry?" his father asked, not knowing if he had inadvertently taken away his son's free will.

"No, it's me who should say I'm sorry," Tom had said, thinking about the way his father had stood with his arms crossed, watching as the cops beat on him in front of friends for whom respect was hard won. They had laughed and snickered as he was shoved into the back of the patrol car, finding it amusing that the Alley Cat's own father had gotten him locked up. Tom had hated Bryce that day, wishing him dead, as he looked at him through the cigarette-smoke-coated, fingerprint-smudged rear window.

His father had been standing there, unmoved, his jaw set as the car pulled away, carting his son off to jail. At his father's bedside all those years later, less than a month from the funeral, Tom realized that Bryce's jaw had been set so tightly because he had been trying to keep from crying.

Tough love, man; tough love.

In that cell, with the smells of stagnant water and old piss strong in his nose, Tom O'Malley became a man. And although he hadn't known it then, he had become a priest as well. The vows he had spoken at graduation were but a ritual; he had taken his true vows in the bowels of a police-district house that had since become defunct and was torn down as the city lines were redrawn and the districts moved to adjust. He had said his vows to himself in the presence of the largest black man he had ever met, making his commitment, not to the priesthood as of then, but to God. O'Malley had vowed that he would never stand aside when someone called on him in their time of need.

He had forever since stayed true to those vows.

But he had never suspected that it would be God who would come calling. Or of what he would ask him to do.

In a society where everyone has inviolable rights, everyone from the common criminal to the mass murderer is expected to be treated civilly. By law, the uncivilized things that such people do to their victims are not supposed to come full circle. Instead, these monsters are housed in jails, supported by taxpayers—among which were the monster's victims themselves—where they were sheltered and fed three meals a day, along with a healthy dose of violent entertainment dispersed through the prison's cable television subscription.

When God had said an eye for an eye, prison was not what he had meant.

Michael Dedaker would soon know his true meaning.

On the day of the execution, Father O'Malley had made an excuse to get out of the rectory after his duties were complete. The other priests he shared residence with were beginning to become suspicious about what he was up to—he had been spending a lot of time away from the church and, more incriminating, had been missing dinners. The priests of St. Tiburtius always ate at exactly six sharp on weekdays. Father O'Malley had missed two consecutive meals, and was going to miss a third that night. What was going on?

A sick friend.

Who? Most priests were personally familiar with their congregation.

She's not Catholic.

Where does she live? O'Malley hadn't been using a rectory car for his excursions, so it had to be close.

Not far had been his answer.

Fine, Father Anthony, St. Tiburtius's pastor, had said. *But Thomas, remember to keep an eye out for the North Star in your travels.* It was the old priest's way of asking if he, O'Malley, was questioning his faith. The North Star, also known as the Guiding Principle, is the only star in the sky that never moves; it is unwavering in its location. It was the North Star that had led the first people—the Wise Men—to Jesus.

O'Malley left the rectory to go meet Hoover dressed in street clothes, on his back a school bag containing the uniform of his profession. He had walked two miles to a bus stop, then took the bus three more miles before getting off and unlocking Dedaker's car. During the whole trip to the Valley Green Nursery, he recited Our Fathers, never once regretting what he was going to do.

When Father O'Malley stepped out of the crowd, with his heart and soul, he believed that he was doing the work of the just. He was doing the work of God.

"Michael Dedaker," he began, "the families of the women you tormented and murdered are present before you. They are your jury, and they have found you guilty of murder in the worst degree. For your crimes against God and humanity, you have been sentenced to death by electrocution." O'Malley turned to Hoover. "Remove the tape," he said.

Hoover stepped to the opposite side of the chair from the generator, making it look like he and Kasay were flanking the condemned. He grasped a tiny edge of the tape that was sticking up, feeling the friction of Dedaker's unshaven cheek as he did so. With one swift pull, the duct tape was ripped from the man's face, leaving behind an angry red welt the size and shape of the binding of a thick hardback book. Beneath the tape, Dedaker's lips were cracked and dry.

"Michael, would you like to say a prayer?" Father O'Malley asked.

He tried to say something, but only a small wheezing sound came out of Dedaker's mouth. He swallowed twice then said, in a rusty, unused voice, "Father, I do not need an oracle such as you to speak to God."

"Do you have anything you would like to say then, as your last words?"

Dedaker's good eye scanned the crowd before him, the eye full of hate. The families of the victims stood in shocked silence as they waited for his testament. "I only have but this to say," Dedaker started. "What I did, I did to help those women, your women. By taking their lives, I have saved them, saved their very souls from infidels like you." Finished, there was a smug, holier-than-thou satisfaction on his face.

With his words, members of the crowd (mostly women) began to cry. For the rest, the heat of a slow boil had been turned up; pent anger and frustration—which had not been slaked by the beating—beginning to spill forth. Swears and oaths emanated from the mass. Fists were being waved, fingers pointed, and the crowd was starting to edge forward. They wanted blood; they wanted Dedaker's life.

They're getting unruly, O'Malley thought. *We're going to lose them soon, and they will tear him apart. This asshole sure knows how to liven up a party.*

Hoover and Kasay were looking to O'Malley. The priest pointed at Kasay and said, "Get ready. When I point again, hit him with the electric." Hoover took that as his cue to step back.

Using the volume that he had used on the altar for almost thirty years, O'Malley cast his voice above the outrage. "Michael Dedaker, for Judith Kasay, Haley Goldberg, Tammy Allensworth, Heather Plunkett, Andrea Hustead, Melissa Griffin, Kristen Fiorella, Leta Hirsch, Sherry Dasher, Michelle Laplin, Amber Knoble, Natalie Fattore, and Beverly Farrell, may the Lord NOT have mercy on your soul!"

In the air before the condemned, O'Malley made the sign of the cross. When he pointed at Kasay, he said, "And may you burn in hell!"

He was more right than he knew.

12

*N*O, NO, NO, Emma tried to scream at the top of her lungs, not for the life of this man, but for herself, for the uncertainty of what would happen to her when he was fried. But no one at the Brakes County execution chamber could hear her plea; even the person whose vision she shared was deaf to it. Not that that mattered; as the juice was about to be applied, the killer the priest called by the surname Dedaker made not one move to avoid it.

The executioner—and future reveler at Sheila's wedding—held the three-pronged plug up in front of Dedaker's good eye for his final inspection and introspection. In his last moment at the front of the tribunal that had cast him as the devil, the self-christened Christ figure sat mute.

Ed Kasay plugged him in.

13

$\mathcal{A}$t the wedding, horrified guests watched as Emma raised bunched fists, contracting the biceps in her fatty-padded arms and parting the seams of the tight pink dress from her elbows to her shoulders, trying to fend off some invisible attacker. While right in front of her, the bald man with the crutches, balancing himself with his left, raised up his right, preparing to strike the seated woman.

From the other side of the room, a priest and another man began to run toward the excitement.

With her eyes squeezed tight enough that tears seeped from the corners, Emma violently shook her head from side to side and screamed, "NO, NO, NO!"

Then hellfire erupted.

14

As the three prongs slid into the female receptacle, 6,500 watts, divided by 220 volts, conducted slightly more than 29 amps of electricity through the body of Michael Dedaker, causing it to stiffen against the nylon rope holding him to the chair.

The members of the crowd held one expression on their singular face as they watched the chair begin to vibrate in place: abhorrent disgust. None of them—some white collars, some blue—had ever seen a man die before. Screams and retching sounds resonated from the group who had once had a bloodlust for Dedaker's life, but now only looked on in horrified disbelief. Melissa Griffin's mother fainted; no one helped her up, every eye held mesmerized by the violence of death.

As soon as the wave of electricity washed through Dedaker, he lost control over his voluntary muscles, dropping all of the excrement he had been holding since the greenhouse. Feces was forced to ooze through Dedaker's pants by the convulsing bouncing of his weight upon the seat, a stream of urine expelled through the fabric to form a puddle on the floor in front of Father O'Malley; blood was mixed with the normal yellows and browns from internal bleeding, a result of the beating he had endured. On the seat of the chair, the cushion sopped it all up.

From the pressure the electricity was putting on his brain, Dedaker's eyes bulged in their sockets. They shifted quickly from side to side, as if watching a ping-pong tournament. The skin of his cheeks began to quiver, and the ropes bit into his chest, his arms and legs from the strain. The water (a natural conductor of electricity, which had originally been poured on him for that exact principle, not to arouse him as Emma had guessed) that had soaked his body was boiling off into steam.

Inside Dedaker's consciousness, Emma's mind writhed in agony.

Out of the crowd, a man approached the chair, wanting to make it all stop. Before he was ten feet from the generator, Father O'Malley grabbed him and pushed him to the floor. The priest yelled at the interloper, but it could not be heard above the crackling of electricity. Hoover read it on his lips, though. The priest had warned the man that the electricity would fry him too, if he were to touch Dedaker.

The juice flowed uninterrupted.

People in the crowd were vomiting as the skin of Michael Dedaker began to turn waxy and then blacken. The combined odor in the air smelled like burnt-out ballasts and barbecued chicken; the folding metal chair—completing the circuit and absorbing the same flow of lightning as Dedaker—thrummed with vibration.

Why doesn't it stop? Emma's mind beseeched no one, anyone. *Why doesn't a fuse blow?*

What she could not have known was that while preparing, Ed Kasay and his brother Stan had removed the GFCI safety outlet from the generator and replaced it with a receptacle that did not have such a safety feature built in. A ground fault circuit interrupt outlet worked exactly as a fuse box in a house: if a circuit was completed by the same electrical current coming into contact with the same object, it would overload and trip the fuse, interrupting the flow of electricity. By attaching both of the cables to touching surfaces—Dedaker and the chair—the circuit was completed. If the GFCI outlet was still in the generator, it would not have shut it down, but it would've cut off the 220-volt flow of electricity.

With the new receptacle Ed and Stan had bought from the Home Depot on Bristol Pike, the electricity would continue to flow until the generator was shut off manually, or the mounting wattage exceeded the maximum 8,125, causing a meltdown.

Having no circuit breaker to stop it, the electricity continued to course through Dedaker, causing his teeth to chatter and the metal of the chair to hum. There was a crackling noise followed by a shower of sparks as a stray stick of electricity escaped through the bullet wound on Dedaker's arm. Blue and white flashes of light hissed as the stick flicked back and forth like the tail of an irritated cat until the bolt touched the chair's backrest. When it came in direct contact with the metal, there was a loud popping sound like that of a firecracker set aflame inside a house. The electricity coiled around the pole of the backrest, magnetizing the metal, and ran down the length of the chair, past the seat and its new "squishion," to where the pole crossed another to become one of the front legs. So many lightning bolts radiated out of the man's arm, electrifying the entire chair with incandescent whites and blues, that if the throng were the angry townspeople, then the chair looked like a prop from the laboratory of the mad doctor: *It's alive; it's ALIVE!*

Each of the four feet of the folding chair ended in a in a rubber cap. Were the leading end of the electricity coil to strike a cap, the rubber would've grounded it out. Displaying an intelligence that it could not possibly have, the end of the stick derailed from the metal an inch from the rubber and arced into a pool of standing water that had collected beneath the chair from what had been poured over Dedaker's head.

The people watching in various states of revulsion backed up, afraid of being struck with a stray bolt of lightning. But no one left the hall. They couldn't; the electrocution was just too disgusting to miss—and too appropriate for the likes of Michael Dedaker.

After many steady minutes of electrical flow, Dedaker's skin began to crack and peel off. Flakes fell to the floor where they turned to ashy dust. His eyes, which never had shut (perhaps they couldn't because of the voltage), finally melted back into his head, blinding him, as well as Emma. Since the dying man had been rendered unable to see, his final memory of the moment before death could only be recalled as a sensation; that sensation was of his hair bursting into flames.

Following suit with Dedaker's hair, the well-fastened rope became alight. The nylon had been chosen (and purchased at the same time as the generator's new GFCI-less receptacle) because of its resilient nature—its synthetic polymers were of a high strength, ensuring durability under intense conditions. But to endure the electricity and the flames was too much to ask; the rope broke, and Dedaker's body leapt from the chair.

Emma had no knowledge of this, other than a feeling of vertigo.

Michael Dedaker was completely dead, and his soul had exited his body, before the ropes broke. It was the unending current from the electricity that caused him to rise up out of the seated position. The crowd, which had started out as a vengeful lynch mob, cowered against the farthest wall, scared that the fiery devil was trying to come get them, just as he had gotten their daughters. More than a few of them wondered if this nightmare would ever end.

Ed Kasay, however, had no doubt that the end had come for Dedaker. When he'd seen Dedaker's skin begin to flake, Kasay had donned a thick pair of fire-retardant gloves he had gotten from Stan, his brother the fireman. Ed had positioned himself next to the chair, ready if things got out of control.

When Dedaker's body rose out of the chair, Kasay grabbed the metal housing at the front (for some reason, the company had put the handle of the machine on the same side as the control panel and the receptacles) of the generator. He gave it a hard, quick yank, intending to either unplug the cord or pull one of the cables free from its contact point.

It didn't go as intended.

Instead of the cables releasing their grip on one of the ends, they pulled taut, the inertia of Kasay's yanking motion causing the separating paths of the electrified chair and the flaming body to be redirected. They both were now coming toward him.

15

The wedding guests stood and watched, no one knowing what was happening or what they should do. The heavy-set woman was having some type of epileptic seizure, and the handicapped man, positioning to strike her with one of his crutches, was yelling that it was, of all things, the fault of the chair in which she sat.

Emma's convulsions had graduated into violent shakes. She had spread her arms wide when the electricity hit, making her look like a seated high diver preparing for the leap, her hands beginning to flap up and down, as if she thought she might be able to take flight rather than plunge into a pool below. The forgotten fork that was once clutched in her chubby fist lay at her feet, gleaming in the light from overhead.

Mirroring the past, a man broke from the horde and tried to approach Emma. He wasn't sure what he was going to do, try CPR maybe. He wasn't trained for it, but he had seen it on TV enough time to get the gist. He had to try something because he was damn sure that he wasn't going to stand around and watch an old man club someone who was choking to death. Before the man was within reaching distance of Kasay (who had managed to stabilize himself in a tripod position and was just now raising the crutch above his head), someone grabbed him from behind. It was the priest.

"Look," a man with the priest yelled.

There was smoke rising from the sides of the chair. Because of her excessive weight, the metal bars had burned into the back of Emma's thighs where they overlapped the seat. Her dress began to first smolder and then catch fire. The guests stared with utter amazement at the woman who, as far as they knew, was spontaneously combusting. Emma opened her mouth to scream, and the people before her were given the special treat of seeing electricity arc between her fillings.

That was when Ed Kasay hit her with his crutch. He swung it like a baseball player trying to move the runner over, hitting her with a flat whack in the ribcage. She didn't budge; instead, electricity hissed and cracked as it bridged across the crutch and into Ed Kasay.

He felt it run through his entire body, hitting every nerve end and organ, until it centered in his heart, where the rhythm quickened until it was racing. The feverish pace continued until, in a burst of pain, the large muscle seized up for a moment, giving Edward Kasay a heart attack.

The conduit crutch twisted like a rubber band, the air within its misshapen hollow tube becoming superheated and expanding, blowing the foam handgrip off Ed's end. There was a clap of explosion, and Kasay was flung to the floor.

He lay fallen next to the chair, clutching his chest, watching as the rest happened in lazy, slow motion.

16

$\mathcal{A}$s Dedaker's body and the metal chair came hurling at him from his own doing, Kasay thought for a moment that he could manually unplug the cable, but it was too late, they were already upon him.

Kasay felt the heat before he felt the impact of bone and flesh and metal. It came baking off Dedaker's flaming body like the swell of hot, rank air trapped inside a subway line in the middle of August. The temperature of the heat made him break out in a sweat as it sucked the breath from his lungs.

The impact came next.

The chair, which was lighter than the man, flew past him, continuing forward until it reached the maximum payout of the cable attached to the pole between its front legs. When it reached the apex, the teeth of the clamp slid along the pole but did not let go. With a twang from the sudden stop of the semi-elastic jumper cable, the chair reversed direction and came back toward Kasay. It struck him behind the knees, just as the burning mass of Michael Dedaker slammed into his chest. The cable whipped around the two of them, tangling them in a fiery embrace, as Ed tried to avert his face from the flames he had mistakenly brought upon himself.

The frontal impact had been much harder than the rear, and the inertia of the dead weight caused Kasay to lose his balance and fall to the right. Kasay, Dedaker, and the chair fell directly on top of the generator.

Dedaker's body struck the leading edge of the housing and ricocheted off, finally jarring the jumper cable's plug from the outlet. The electricity ceased to flow, sparing Ed Kasay from electrocution, as his side impacted with the metal edge of the generator's engine, breaking his hip and injuring a cluster of nerves inside his spinal column, an injury that would forever after plague him with arthritic pain and make him dependant upon crutches and a stiff back brace for mobility. Because he had been facing away from the flames, the fire did not injure his face, but his clothes and the skin of his back were burning. The follicles at the nape of his neck were singed up past the occipital bone, and no hair would ever grow there again, forcing Ed to opt to shave his entire head forevermore. After his recovery, he decided that he would rather be bald (as he would be when he met a young lady named Emma, six years hence) than look like a mop-topped Moe Howard or a Liverpool-era Beatle for the rest of his life.

Edward Kasay laid broken and burning, tangled up in a web of his own weaving, ready to accept death when it began snowing.

17

*N*ow, lying on the floor in the throes of a heart attack, he wasn't just ready for death—he longed for it.

After Dedaker was executed, Kasay had thought he would finally be able to exist in relaxed peace for the rest of his days, knowing that the abuse and murder of his daughter had been avenged. He anticipated closure coming on a wave of electricity.

How wrong he had been.

Instead of drawing together the fissures that the Kasays had been living with since Dedaker stole the life of their only child, Judith, eleven months before, it widened them. His daughter was dead, his loving wife a shell of her previous self. Living under the same roof, but estranged from him, the woman he had married all those years ago when the future was long and promising had become a recluse, hardly ever stepping outside the house. Their friends too were gone, being unable to find things in common with him or Miriam after Judith's taking.

Compared to those losses, the injuries he had sustained that night from Dedaker's death waltz were only nagging reminders of his continued shallow existence. His hair was gone, and he had lost a kidney to renal failure from the impact. The constant arthritis in his hip and back made him weary and had crippled him up enough to get a handicapped plate for his car. He was in pain whether walking or sitting or lying; he could not bend with the range of motion of a normal person. Hell, he almost couldn't bend at all. The most embarrassing thing about not having flexibility was eating. Until you can no longer do it, you don't realize how much bending is required to eat. No one outside of a finishing school eats with a rigid back; they slouch, they lean, and they bend. For Ed, eating had gone from a pleasure to a chore, with one of his favorite foods being the most difficult thing to partake of—soup. Without being able to bend to the spoon, it was impossible to get the hot liquid into his mouth without spilling it. Therefore, when eating soup, Ed had three choices: have it cold, wear a bib, or drink it directly from the bowl. Without doing one of those three things, he got burned, something no one likes to do, but something Ed especially didn't like to do.

So why not just skip the soup? Because in the listless coma (trapped in his own body, not quite here, when he should rightfully have died with Dedaker) that his life had become, eating soup was the only challenging stimulation left for a mind that was once active and analytical.

That was why when Ed saw the food that his brother Stan's stepson Paul (the groom of this fiasco) had one of the buffet servers prepare for him, he smiled to himself. He knew there would've been soup; there had to be. In this hall (funny that it should be a *fire* hall, isn't it?), with the chair they had used for their evil retribution sitting there like an accusing albatross, difficult and challenging were the way of things. In this building, the mecca of his misery, things would always be hard.

Looking down at the bowl of brown, watery minestrone, in the same building where he had murdered someone in cold blood to cool his own, he had smiled. Food was one of the three things needed to survive, with the other two being water and oxygen. Set before him was a bowl of soup, a symbol of the need to sustain life, embedded deep within the double entendre of the handicap imposed on him while taking life. A dose of his own medicine that was literally hard to swallow.

Let's eat, Kasay had thought sitting down, prepared to embarrass himself by slurping his soup, wanting to display an outwardly visible scar representing to society how he had had a hand in regressing mankind in the eyes of both God and America's forefathers by undermining their explicit laws of not taking the most sacred of things, life. He had wanted to be looked at, to be talked about and ridiculed for his uncouth actions. It was, in his mind, a public penance.

Before he ate, he leaned the crutches against the table and took another glance at the woman who had been assigned the chair that they had used to off Dedaker. The *exact* chair. *How the hell was that possible?*

He didn't know.

After he had gotten twisted up with Dedaker's body and landed on the generator, things got a little hazy. He drifted in and out of consciousness, catching snippets of events, like photographs that relate but a single action, not the whole story. He remembers being carried out of the hall by the burly cop who had been investigating his daughter's murder and a couple of others; exactly who those others where, he wasn't sure. He remembers the jostling ride in the car, making the bones in his body grind like broken glass. He remembers the brightness of the hospital and the tubes and the masked faces looking down at him. He remembers the pain.

What he can't remember is the chair. He knows that it was involved in the collision between Dedaker and himself, but then nothing. *How could they have forgotten to take the chair with the body?*

Putting his lips to the bowl, Kasay slurped his soup in thought.

18

The snow fell as it always did, in silence, and the fire went out.

One minute Ed Kasay was joining Dedaker in a fiery end, and the next he was being smothered by snow. Years later, recalling the incident in a pathetic drunken stupor one Christmas Eve, Stan told him that it wasn't snow that put out the flames, but a fire extinguisher. What Ed had thought was snow was a substance called Purple K, a dry chemical that put out fire by taking away its oxygen. John Hoover had run across the dance floor and pulled the extinguisher from the wall, hoping that it wasn't the normal type of extinguisher used to put out wood or paper fires by spraying water, which would only worsen the electrical fire burning up Kasay and Dedaker. It wasn't; it was a dry, A/B/C chemical extinguisher that worked on any type of fire: wood, grease, or electrical. Hoover pulled the pin and sprayed the white powder over the clumped mass of burning metal and flesh. As the Purple K snuffed out the flames, it clogged the carburetor and exhaust system of the generator. It never worked again.

Later that night, not wanting to answer questions in the building next door about why the extinguisher needed replacing, Stanley Kasay exchanged the used A/B/C can with one charged with water.

When the extinguisher was empty, Hoover tossed it aside and began to issue orders to the traumatized lynch mob comprised of middle-class Caucasians.

"Help get them apart before he suffocates from the chemicals," Hoover yelled at O'Malley, et al. It took eight people, moving with an urgency that showed they knew there was no way for them to explain why there were two dead men attached by battery cables to the generator that baked them. Hands were blistered from handling the still-hot metals, and another person, the grandfather of one of the dead girls, cut open his palm on a sharp edge somewhere in the confusion, needing stitches.

Father O'Malley knelt down next to Ed, his fingers probing for a pulse under the seared skin. It was weak, but it was there. O'Malley gave a quick prayer of thanks. "He's alive," he said to Hoover.

John nodded, looking over the crowd where the women were standing. "Is Mrs. Kasay here? Miriam Kasay?"

"Yes, I'm here," came a frightened voice, not unlike that of a child made to go to sleep alone in a dark room. The crowd parted to let her through, not wanting to touch her, treating her like a leper. Miriam was crying and hadn't bothered to wipe her face, her cheeks glistening with the sad moisture.

"Ed's alive, but he's in bad shape," Hoover said, gripping her shoulders. "We have to get him to a hospital, and I need you to help us. I can't take him because of my previous association with you and your husband through the investigation. If a cop got a whiff of that, he'd know something was up. Father O'Malley will take him. Do you drive?"

"Yes," she said.

"Good. Drive your car home, and I'll have Ed's brother meet you there. Now listen to me, this is very important to all of us," Hoover said. "Whatever Stan tells the cops, you agree with it, okay?"

"Yes," she said again.

Hoover squeezed her shoulders. "Good. We'll take care of Ed; you take care of the things that Stan tells you to. When everything is done at home, go to Holy Redeemer Hospital; Ed will be there."

"I can't leave."

"Why not?"

"Ed has the keeeeeeyyyys." Her control broke, and she began sobbing.

"Wait here," Hoover told her. He made his way to O'Malley. "Father," he said, "get his keys out of his pocket."

The priest grimaced, wondering why he always got this job, but did not hesitate or complain. Less than a minute later, Hoover was holding the still warm keys out to Miriam. She took them and left crying.

"Tom, Stan," Hoover said, "let's get him out of here." Someone had found an old, stained tablecloth, and they wrapped Kasay in it. The three of them picked him up as gently as they could, Hoover at the head, the other two at the legs, and took him to the parking lot. Ed tried to say something as they loaded him in the back of Dedaker's car, but it was unintelligible.

"Stan," Hoover said, "O'Malley is Ed's parish priest; they're friends, so there shouldn't be any questions about why he's with him at the hospital."

Stan Kasay glanced at the priest. "He's my brother. Why can't I go to the hospital and O'Malley go to the house?"

"Tom doesn't know them, their lifestyle. You do. It'll be easier for you to think on the fly rather than him."

"All right, then. What do you want me to do when I get there?"

"Go into Ed's house, out in the garage maybe, and blow out a receptacle. Use a screwdriver insulated with a rubber handle so you don't shock yourself, then call the rescue squad and tell them what happened, that Ed was working in the garage when he got zapped. Ed's got some electrical burns among the rest, and that's the best cover I can come up with right now. If you think of something better, go with it. Say whatever you think will be easiest for you to cover.

"As soon as the rescue squad arrives, tell them that O'Malley was visiting with Miriam when it happened, comforting her about Judith, and you guys didn't want to wait for the paramedics, so you sent Ed to the hospital with the priest while you took care of the wife. Let them see Miriam, but keep her in the background. She's the weak link in this, so you've got to make sure that her only role is as the worried wife. Don't let them ask her questions, understand?"

"Yeah," Stan said, white as a picket fence.

"Then go."

Stan Kasay took off at a jog for his own car on the other side of the lot.

Hoover turned to O'Malley. "Get him to the hospital and use the bones of the story. All you know is that you just stopped by to comfort Miriam about her late daughter when you found out Ed was hurt. You don't know anything else; don't embellish; leave the rest of the story for Stan. I'll take care of what needs to be done here. When you finish for the night, wipe the car clean of prints, then lose it in a hard neighborhood, got it?"

"I got it," O'Malley said and bent to get into Dedaker's car.

"Hey, Father?"

O'Malley looked at him over the roof of the car with the unconscious and burned Edward Kasay in the backseat. "Yeah?" he asked.

"Did you find what you were looking for in there?"

The priest shook his head. "No, I didn't. You?"

"Yeah, I think I might have," Hoover said. "Life is a precious thing, to be treated with respect, not taken for granted."

When Hoover went back in, there was almost no indication remaining of what had happened. The floor had been mopped (the electrical fire hadn't scorched the hard surface of the dance floor, as a wood fire would have), and the generator had been wheeled out. Most of the crowd had dispersed. Except for the body (which was wrapped in another soiled tablecloth) and the smell, no one who entered the hall now would know anything out of the ordinary had happened.

When the body had been removed and everything was taken care of, Hoover visually inspected the room once more, then flipped the light switch and locked the door before he left.

During the rushed cleanup, the chair used to electrocute Dedaker was scrubbed clean by the mother of Heather Plunkett. She cleansed it until the fluorescent lighting glinted off the areas of exposed metal that shone through the dull brown paint. Touching that chair had made her feel queasy, and she had remained in bed sick for ten days afterward, thinking that it was general malaise from the whole experience. After she recovered, she found that she was barren. At the relatively young age of thirty-nine, she had never had another monthly flow of blood.

After the chair was clean, someone else had pushed it out of the way so that the floor could be mopped. It had been folded up and moved back near the group of chairs from which it had first been randomly selected for the night's duties.

When Hoover shut off the lights, the chair was left sitting in a recessed corner of the hall where all the other chairs were kept until needed. That chair sat in the dark, forgotten long after the remains of Michael Dedaker had been buried deep in the ground behind the burned-out toolshed at the Valley Green Nursery.

It sat unused through event after event that took place in the hall. It sat at the end of a long line of chairs, waiting, for six years.

19

Ed knew that the chair would still be there when he received the invitation to the wedding of his brother's adopted son. He knew it even before he found out that the wedding reception would be held at the Brakes County Fire Hall. Logically, where else would it be held, since his father ran the hall?

Ed didn't even bother to call Stan and mention this to him. Stan was there that night; he knew what had happened. Even in light of the strange way history has of repeating itself, what could possibly happen at the wedding? Stan, who had played it cool and went on being a fireman in Brakes County while also continuing to run the fire hall as if nothing had happened, had probably not even given it a second thought when his son requested the use of the hall for the reception. It was only a building, after all. In life, death is the only certain thing, and people have been dying in buildings since the first structure was assembled out of animal hides. Hell, people die in hospitals 24/7; how come no one ever says anything about hospitals being haunted?

Because it just doesn't happen, Ed told himself, *ghosts are not real.* But he knew better. Ghosts don't haunt hospitals for one reason only: because there's no relation tying the recently departed to them. They hadn't lived there, and they didn't know anybody there. In fact, the strangers at the hospital had been trying to *save* them from dying. Hospitals are like Sweden to poltergeists; they're neutral.

But that's not so for this fire hall, is it? Ed thought, as he lay on the floor clutching his chest next to a chair that was most certainly haunted.

The invitation to the wedding had been a date with destiny, he knew. He insisted on going anyway, even after Miriam had flat out refused to accompany him. It made no difference to him that he had to go it alone—he had been doing everything else alone for the past six years, anyway. Especially living alone in the house he shared with his wife.

Even if Miriam's defiant stance could have swayed him, he still would have had to come tonight. He had been living on borrowed time since his dance with Dedaker. That was supposed to have been his last dance, but it had been interrupted. Now it was time to pay his bill and wind the music again. There was no way he would survive another confrontation with the chair.

Ed had arrived at the hall an hour before everyone else, not having attended the wedding ceremony so that he could look for the folding chair his heart told him would be there. Forgoing the ceremony didn't matter to him, he did not know the bride at all, and hardly knew his brother's wife's son from her first marriage. Ed had only been invited because he was Stan's brother, no other reason. To Paul whatever-his-name-is, he would never be Uncle Ed.

The hall had been unlocked long before the ceremony had begun so that the caterer could set up. Using the dexterity he had learned from countless hours of physical therapy after the "accident," Ed opened the heavy glass door and let himself into the hall, crutches and all.

It was decorated with wedding bliss, but nothing had changed. The streamers hung from the same paneled walls, and the fresh bouquets on the guest tables surrounding the dancing area livened up the muted colors, but nothing could mask the odor of burnt flesh Ed smelled in his mind. Some of it had been his own flesh burning, and that was a hard thing to forget.

Long tables had been set up for the buffet, small tins of Sterno used to keep warm the food sitting on them, unopened. The employees of the caterer were not there yet, off doing whatever they did before beginning work for the evening. Ed had the hall to himself.

Starting along the wall closest to the door, he deftly used his crutches to circle each table, like a dog looking for a place to lie down. The chair he was searching for would be set up for use tonight, he was sure.

At the front table of the middle aisle—closest to the spot where it had sat on the dance floor for Dedaker's death—Ed found it. He knew the chair instantly. Wrapped up in the cables and the flames, it had become a part of his life. He would never forget it—the greasy look of the aging brown paint, the underlying stench of its evil, the slight thrum of its power.

Ed stared at it with respect, surprised to find that it hadn't been placed in front of his own name card. Trying to find meaning where there shouldn't be any, he wondered why the chair hadn't picked him. *Who was its quarry? What was it up to?*

With the chair pushed in, he studied its back, its sides and its legs. He got down on his knees (not an easy thing for him to do, and his back screamed at him for it) and, without touching it, looked at its bottom. Underneath, there were scorch marks from when the current ran down the leg and grounded in the puddle. The scratched, sooty marks had obliterated half of the manufacturer's name stamped into the metal. What was left read,—Textile Folding Chairs, 684 East Street, Corpus Christi, Texas.

Ed Kasay had never heard of a folding chair company whose name ended in "Textile," which was irrelevant since he had never heard of *any* folding-chair companies, but didn't textiles have something to do with cloth?

Using the muscles of his arms and the handles of the crutches, he pulled himself back up. When upright and balanced again, he couldn't resist the urge to touch the chair. The mind and the eye can work together in collusion to delude the brain, but touch makes something real, gives it definition.

With a tentative, reverent touch, Ed traced his finger along the curved metal of the chair's back—smooth as the devil's tongue. Thinking he was safe after taking his baby step, Ed wrapped his hand fully around the cylindrical bar to pull the chair out from where it was hiding beneath the table so that he could get a good look at its topside.

A good look he did not get.

What he got was a jolt of electricity that ran up his arm and around the metal strips encased in the leather of his back brace. He quickly let go and jumped back a step, displaying an agility that he hadn't possessed in years. The metal of the brace was warm from the electricity, but not painful; it felt like a heating pad pressed against the small of his back. His heart and his lungs were in a race to determine who was the fastest. Ed's money was on the pumper.

Frightened, he looked around to see if anyone else had arrived at the hall. No one had; he was alone. Alone with the chair.

His reaction had moved the chair, and it was now (what do you call a chair when it's partially pulled out from under a table? Ajar? Drawn?) slightly exposed. Ed could see the dark lump that was its cushion. It looked as comfortable and as inviting as an iron maiden.

He kept trying to tell himself there was nothing to fear; he was here because of this chair, and he was going to let it take his life, so why not just get it over with? The faster it was done, the sooner he could rejoin his daughter, Judith, in the afterlife. If there proved to be no afterlife (which Ed seriously doubted since Judy had been taken from him—if there was a God, how could he let such dreadful things happen?), then Ed would at least, at last, be free of his misery. It was win-win.

But it was not to happen that way. The chair—or whatever evil inhabited it—had seen to that.

If it wanted his life, it could have taken him when he had touched it. It hadn't; it had only shocked him. The chair did not want him . . . yet. It was waiting for someone else. Whatever the chair had in mind, he was sure it would be grandiose.

Ed would have to wait for the salvation from what his life had become a little while longer.

He would have to wait for someone named Emma Anderson.

20

$\mathcal{A}$s it turned out, it wasn't exactly Emma he had been waiting for; it was Michael Dedaker himself. He was here, inside of the Anderson woman, his soul somehow transferred there by the chair. Even before he/she spoke, Kasay knew it was Dedaker. The woman's body was the same as it had been when she had bumped into him, but her face was different; the features had changed, the new demeanor hateful.

Those glaring, evil eyes were turning Kasay's way when they were blocked out by the arriving form of Detective Hoover. The cop was looking down at him, his back to Dedaker.

"He's alive," someone said from his other side. It was Father O'Malley, repeating the same words he had said the last time Ed had seen him, six years ago and flat on the floor, hurt.

Hoover opened his mouth to respond just as a guttural voice arose from behind him. If Kasay hadn't witnessed the transformation before Hoover stepped in the way, he would've thought the ventriloquist act expertly done.

"Well," said a deep and rumbling masculine voice, the double consonant tinged with a higher, feminine pitch, "it seems the troika of damnation was unable to do its job properly."

From the floor, O'Malley, Hoover, and Kasay looked and found themselves staring up into that changed face, the rest watching transfixed from a distance.

"The judge, jury, and executioner have failed, and now cower before the Lamb of God," Dedaker/Emma chuckled. It sounded heavy with phlegm, on the verge of coughing, as if the bass were too much for the woman's vocal chords to handle. "And now it's my turn," it said.

Father O'Malley rose to his full height, while Hoover remained crouched low, supporting Kasay. "We did not fail, Michael," O'Malley said a little whimsically, "we killed you."

The larva laughed at him. "Then how am I still here? How haven't I ascended?" it asked, a cackle of lightning coming from the still-charged chair.

"I was going to ask you that very same question, Michael. Take a look around; things have changed." Above the grimace of a smile, Dedaker slid Emma's eyes in her sockets, noticing the wedding revelers.

"Take a look at yourself, Michael," Father O'Malley urged further.

He did as requested, looking over the slope of bosoms at the mountainous shape below.

21

*S*he heard her own voice, deeper and darker, speaking, but she wasn't talking. She heard what was being said, but paid no mind to the meaning behind the words. Nor did she care about what was happening to the three people on the floor in front of her. They were men, and that meant they didn't matter, not now, not in this new state of mind.

When the memory-movie ended, having survived the electrocution by some impossible, improbable miracle, Emma found herself back in her own body, and she was furious. Michael was still inside of her, in control of her. This was her body, and a man had somehow relegated her to the rear of it, as if she were a passenger. How all of this had come to happen didn't matter; their coexisting immediate future looked bleak—she smelled death on the air, to come in the forms of lightning and flames. But there was still something, even here, at the sure end of her life, that she did see the importance of.

All her life, men had treated her as a second-class citizen simply because she was fat. They had used her body in ways she found objectionable, never once treating her as an equal. Or even as a woman. They had treated her not as a human being with feelings and intellect, but like the meat *they* thought she was.

No more. It ended now, here. The line has been drawn.

If I'm going to die with this bastard, I'm going to die with dignity. I'm going to die in possession of my own body.

22

$\mathcal{I}$t seems as if the joke's on us, Father," Dedaker said in his strange combination voice, cackling just like the electricity. "Apparently, there's no such thing as a soul, as indicated by my not ascending."

"Ah, but there is," O'Malley disagreed. "You yourself are physical proof the soul exists. If the soul were not real, then how would you be inside that woman, if not transposed, then reincarnated?"

After a beat, Dedaker asked, "What is this, some kind of trick?"

"No, Michael, it's no trick. It's your purgatory," O'Malley told him. "What you had sought to save for others cost you your own. We *did* kill you, Michael. Look at my face, look hard. Look at all three of us," O'Malley said, waving an arm behind him at Hoover and Kasay. "Can you see it? We've aged. Six years, to be precise. That's how long it's been since we ended your life. And it has been six long years since the Lord you had so hoped to please, in his infinite wisdom, chastened your soul to a metal folding chair. Befitting, don't you think, that a man whose ambition was to free souls through murder had his own jailed inside the very instrument used to kill him?"

"NOOOOOOO," Dedaker roared, distracted by the priest's statements, stretching Emma's arms wide in frustration.

Inside, Emma grabbed hold of him.

23

*M*ost people believe the soul to be of the same size and shape as the person, the true being that fills up every inch of the individual, making them unique. Emma had just found out that that belief was incorrect. The soul was the essence of the mind, not the physical life. It is the thoughts, conscience, and consciousness of being. And as such, it takes the form of a particle of energy harboring deep inside the intellect. It is but an electrical synapse alive within the mind, a ghostly spirit inside the machine.

With her own spirit, Emma pounced on Dedaker's, intending to snuff him out of existence.

24

When the move came, Dedaker felt as if his thoughts were being muffled, suffocated in a mound of dough. He wasn't so much as dying as he was disappearing, fading.

He could not let that happen. If it did, his soul would be . . . well, gone.

Gathering all of the inner—*spiritual*—strength he could, Dedaker fought back.

To the onlookers, it might have been humorous, if not for the electricity. To see two people struggle for possession of the same body was something right out of a slapstick comedy. Except that as the body thrashed from side to side in the chair—slapping, punching, struggling with itself—electrical sparks were being discharged.

Hoover's and O'Malley's first priority was to get Kasay out of the way. They started to lift him, but he was dead weight with the limited use of his legs and vertebrae (not to mention six years of little exercise, compounded with the diet of fatty foods he had to concoct himself when Miriam quit her wifely duties). Trying to help him stand would be cumbersome and slow at best.

"Grab him under the arm," Hoover said, "we'll drag him out of here."

O'Malley did as he was told, but before they had moved a foot, a horrendous ripping sound came from the chair. Turning, they saw that Dedaker had lifted the woman's bottom off the seat, the back of the pink dress and the flesh of her thighs having fused with the metal of the chair, remaining behind.

But the woman wasn't standing, or free. The long-ago current that still coursed through the chair had stiffened her body, making her posture that of a plank of wood propped across the backrest and seat. The watchers could see threads of electricity flash back and forth between the body and the seat, running up and down the woman's spinal column, making her look like a malfunctioning robot. Except you couldn't smell the skin of a robot burning.

Hoover and O'Malley stepped up their struggle, trying to pull Kasay to safety as fast as they could.

There was a loud burst of electricity, sounding as if a transformer had blown. A large buildup of current had reached out from the seat and, instead of hitting the meat hanging above it, veered backward, striking the metal of the backrest. The power was more than the folding chair could stand, crumpling beneath the pounding and the poundage.

Emma's full weight came crashing down on the chair. It hit the floor and squashed, the metal legs spread in wide, gymnastic splits. Sparks showered onto her, causing the tattered remnants of her dress to become alight.

In her mind, she had been able to deal with the pain of the electricity, figuring that if it didn't stop her heart, she would be able to live through it. The fire was another story entirely. It hurt, and it was doing damage quickly.

The tight fabric of her pink dress had been molded close to Emma's body, and the flames consuming it were boiling the epidermal tissue beneath. Her heated skin turned into a large, liquid-filled angry red blisters rising instantly.

She was being cooked alive, which took precedence over the inner struggle with Dedaker—the flames had to be put out. Flat on her back, Emma let go of Dedaker. She rolled to the right, hoping to douse the fire.

When she let go of him, Dedaker regained the reins.

Before he had full control, Emma managed to roll five feet from the ruined chair that had taken Dedaker's life and was in the process of taking hers. The short roll did not smother the flames from the electrical fire. Instead, the inexpensive and threadbare carpeting ignited, a trail of small fires breaking out in Emma's wake.

When Dedaker was again in command, he brought her body to a halt, coming to rest on her stomach beneath a table. A flame licked the end of the thin tissue acting as a table cover. In seconds, the entire surface of the table was engulfed.

The inexplicable nature of human beings will never explain the fascination people have with pain and suffering. That same magnetic draw that causes people to slow down for a good look while passing traffic accidents, or to watch operating-room exposés on public television, now held the wedding guests from fleeing while it was still possible to do. Some of them were even brazen enough as to sneak peeks under the table to catch a glimpse of the fricassee. No one had noticed that the flames rising from the floor were between them and one of only two exits in the room.

Emma was making a squealing noise (not unlike the noise the axle of the generator had made when it was wheeled in years ago) as Dedaker positioned her hands beneath her and pushed up. Together they erupted through the center of the wooden table grown weak from the heat of the fire like a phoenix from the flames.

Standing erect in an eclipsing pillar of rising flames, Dedaker swiveled the woman's head, glancing around the room looking for something. Emma watched as he looked over the buffet with its sweating, reheated food and past the head table where Sheila and her groom—along with the bridesmaid (one of her sisters) and the best man (his cousin), a tactfully small wedding party for such a cheesy shindig—watched insouciantly. Sheila's face showed no emotion or concern for her dying friend, as her new husband chose this moment to push past his bride, making a break for the exit. He gracefully leapt over a patch of burning carpet—the flames tasting his soles—and made it to the door, living to become a widower.

Spotting Hoover and O'Malley moving at a snail's crawl as they inched their way across the room, dragging the fallen old man to safety, Dedaker found what he was looking for. Knowing he didn't have much time left, he wanted to use what he had to its fullest extent. The woman was dying, and, for good or bad, without the use of the chair to hold his soul on the mortal plane, she was going to take him with her. The first time, he had been willing to accept the martyr's death for his Lord and the promise of his paradise; this time, he had no misconceptions of what awaited him after death. And if he had learned nothing in his servitude—

and apparently his six years of purgatory trapped inside some bourgeois electric chair—it was that he should've lived his life for himself, not for some unseen, idolatrous godhead.

But to that end, if he did have to go—and it seemed as if he did—then there were some people he wanted to take along for the ride.

25

*H*oover and O'Malley were still dragging Kasay when Dedaker came toward them, assessing the situation against his rapidly depleting amount of time—the old man was dying already, and the priest would wait his turn; it would have to be Hoover first. He had been the cause behind this whole aborted fiasco, to begin with, the one whose actions had denied Dedaker his entrance into heaven, so it should stand to reason that Hoover be first. *If he had killed me on Purser Street like he was supposed to, then I would be seated on the right-hand side of Christ, on the right-hand side of God the Father.* Yeah, Hoover would definitely be first.

In that grating, rusty-chainsaw voice with its highs and lows, Dedaker asked, "Detective Hoover, after all we've been through, aren't you afraid of the dark yet?"

Hoover wanted to tell him to go fuck himself, but he didn't think he had to—at the rate the flames were growing, Dedaker, along with the woman he was in, were fucked already. All Hoover had to do was get out of his way and wait for the unchecked element to do its job. Hoover knew this; O'Malley knew this, and Kasay knew this, that's why he started to wiggle free of their grasp.

"Leave me," Ed said. "Save yourselves and leave me here with him." He dug his heels in as best he could, trying to impede their assistance.

"What? You'll die," O'Malley said.

"I want to die; it's my time. Please," he said, doing a switching rumba from side to side with his shoulders, trying to free them.

Hoover said, "Stop it, Ed. You're gonna—"

But Dedaker was within reach, swinging the woman's thickset

fist at him. It stuck Hoover below his eye, the pain forcing him to let go of Kasay. Ready to finish Hoover with his (her?) bare hands, Dedaker moved Emma a step forward.

Father O'Malley, knowing it was a lost cause to try and drag the fitful man by himself, also let go. The woman's body was turned from him, Dedaker's sights on Hoover. With the flat of his foot, O'Malley kicked the back of the woman's left knee through the flames. It unhinged, and she started to fall.

26

This time it was happening in fast-forward.

Displaying the quickness of a striking scorpion, Kasay reached out and wrapped his arms around Emma's paunchy middle after the priest took her knees out. With the strong muscles of his upper body—developed from years of using crutches to drag around the dead weight of his legs—Kasay reached upward and pulled Emma down on top of him, the flames of her dress spawning on his tweed jacket. Expecting his longed-for imminent death, Kasay intertwined his fingers at the small of her back.

Coming face to face with Kasay, Dedaker rationalized the old man's intent and immediately began to struggle. He flopped like a fish, trying to use the woman's weight to his advantage, but the old fuck had him tight. Time was running out.

I have to do something, he thought, *he's willing to die to take me with him.* Panic wanted to seize him and take over, squandering his last precious few minutes. But then the woman's hand chanced upon what Dedaker hoped would be the answer, happening upon it on the floor.

"This is how it was meant to be," Kasay whispered into Emma's ear, talking to Dedaker. "You took a life from me, and I tried to take yours; somehow we both ended up as living dead men. But no more. Tonight, we both die."

Then the fork plunged into Kasay's neck.

It had been Emma's originally, and the piece of roast beef was still on it, above which the tines entered Kasay's skin. Dedaker pushed down on the utensil, working it deeper into the neck muscles. Once or twice it ground against bone, but Kasay did not worry, able to tell that it hadn't done damage to the spinal nerves because he still had control of his arms, and his grip was tight. He would endure the pain and not let go as if it were the last thing he would ever do, because he thought it would be.

The fire had spread to Kasay now and was making its way up his sides. It had burned the hair off his chest, and he could feel it eating into his stomach like acid. Still, he held the embrace strong. It was all about to end; he could see the resolve in the not-quite-dead eyes of Emma Anderson. The fork hadn't worked, and now the end drew near, nearer. The flames would engulf them, and the husk of a man that was left after Judith was murdered would burn off, freeing him of his torment. This unfortunate, innocent woman was going to be his savior. She was going to deliver him to the gates of heaven after six long years in hell.

How ironic that his salvation from hell would come in the form of flames.

Then it started raining.

27

$\mathcal{A}$ billowing cloud of smoke was forming near the ceiling.

Oh my God, we're trapped in here, Fiona thought. *John!*

In all the confusion and disorientation, she did not know what was happening. After the woman combusted, she saw Hoover and a priest try to pull the handicapped man who had hit the poor thing with his crutch away from the fire. Fiona hadn't rushed over to help because it had all happened so quickly, and there were already four hands helping—men's hands, which were stronger than hers.

That changed when she saw the rotund woman attack her husband.

Fiona had heard the woman say something to Hoover while she was still seated, but it had been garbled. John hadn't replied to her, so it must not have meant anything to him, either. But now Fiona was sure that the dying woman had been singling Hoover out from the other two—when she pried herself from the chair, her body sparking electricity, the first thing she did was go after John, striking him in the face.

Fiona wasn't about to let that happen.

She pushed her way through friends and family so that she could get to her man. "Excuse me. Let me through," she said, using her hands to widen gaps. Before she made it to the front of the pack, the priest had taken the woman down.

But unfortunately she had landed on the cripple, and now both of their bodies were fueling the flames.

Midway between the throng and the burning people, Fiona saw a fire extinguisher hanging on the wall with its black hose and bright red cylinder. She pulled it from the mounting brackets, wondering why they would paint extinguishers such a color, red being too close to the color of flames, and possibly causing the safety device to be accidentally camouflaged from sight during a fire, when it was needed most.

She pulled the pin with the inspection tag attached to it. Loosening the nozzle, she ran over to the burning man and woman.

Squeezing the two silver handles together, Fiona let loose with the extinguisher that Stan Kasay himself had hung on the wall when he replaced the one used at Dedaker's execution.

28

From the corner of his eye, Hoover saw Fiona come racing over.

In the melee, he had forgotten all about her. Perturbed with himself for such neglect, he wondered, *How could I be so stupid?*

He looked and saw that Kasay had Dedaker in his arms. The old boy was on fire too, and was as good as dead, but at least he was taking Dedaker with him. It would all be over soon.

The building itself was another matter. The fire was really rolling now. Two of the walls were ablaze, and decorations and streamers were falling like flaming confetti. They had to get out of here. The fire was blocking one of the exits, but the other one behind the voyeuristic guests was still clear.

That's our way out, he thought, and stood to retrieve Fiona. Once she was outside and safe, he would help O'Malley clear the others. That's when he noticed Fiona had an extinguisher in her hands.

A water extinguisher.

It wasn't technically an electrical fire anymore, but Hoover knew what would happen if she hit the woman's body with discharge from that hose.

"*Fiona, no!*" he shouted, but it was too late. She had sprayed the water.

29

*H*er aim was true, the stream hitting the burning woman squarely on the back, fountaining off her. Fiona was surprised at the force such a compact extinguisher managed to put behind the flow.

"*Fiona, no!*" she heard her husband yell. Turning to see what he was warning against, she was the only one in the hall that didn't see the stream of water turn from clear to blue. The electricity that had been the constraints of Dedaker's soul—and what had preyed on Emma's weaknesses—had still been inside the fallen woman. When the water hit, it produced a conduit on which the electricity could ride free.

Fiona squinted her eyes in the haze, not understanding what her husband wanted. "What—," she began.

There was a crack of thunder that resonated off the walls as the electricity followed the water trail to its source and entered into the compressed extinguisher, exploding it. Shrapnel bit deep into Fiona's thighs, the middle and ring fingers of her left hand sawed off, the stumps immediately cauterized by the electricity. The concussion of the explosion knocked her cold, unconscious.

Sparks and bolts of electricity bounced playfully around the puddles that had formed on the floor from the gushed water. Parts of the rug on this side of the room caught fire. The electricity, seeming to contain a life of its own now, arced and flew, spanning the open area. It struck curtains, and they erupted into flames; it struck onlookers, burning faces and skin and clothes.

Screams and frightened shouts rang from the crowd of guests who finally decided that they had seen enough. With only one exit unimpeded by fire, the gathering began pushing and shoving their way toward it. There were two doors, and two people reached to depress the long crash bars at the same time to open them. The man on the left was lucky, the one on the right not. To secure the fire exit doors, there was only one key lock, which was on the left-hand door. The right door was held secure by dog-ears—two metal flaps mortised on the side of the door near the top and the bottom so that when pushed up, they slide two bolts, one into the jamb and the other into the floor. When Stanley Kasay unlocked the fire hall for the reception, he had not lowered the dog-ear latches.

The door on the left pushed open, and the man exited out into the damp, misty night air. The man on the right—who had been running and expecting the door to open just as its compatriot did— broke his wrist and tore tendons when it did not budge and his weight came down on the bar, crushing the wrist between it and the steel of the door.

Three seconds later, the other 150 guests crushed his ribcage, collapsing his lungs, as they too tried to flee from the fire and lightning. The nonworking crash bar was driven up into the man's abdomen, grinding his liver to pieces. Unable to breathe, bile soaking into his bloodstream, the man died. Held up by the pushing crowd, he did not fall to the floor.

With only one serviceable three-foot-wide exit, the panic level reached incoherence quickly. One woman was shoved so hard up against the cinder block wall that her skull cracked open and gray ooze seeped out. Stanley Kasay died when the long, extremely durable stickpin of his corsage punctured his heart.

The pool of people piled at the door became so deep that it was impossible for anyone to get out. Men and women (thankfully, no children had been invited to the Oswald wedding) were being trampled to death in front of an impassable exit.

30

When the electricity ran upstream from Emma to the extinguisher, it crossed over the knuckles of Ed Kasay's intertwined hands. The voltage of the shock broke four bones in the eight fingers and was too much for him to handle; he lost his grip.

Before the water extinguisher had unwillingly set him free, Dedaker had brought the woman's fists up, ready to claw Kasay's face. Once he felt the tension ease from the old man's arms, he ceased his attack and, with her positioned hands, used Kasay's face to push Emma to her feet once again.

The movements of the large body on top of him had snuffed out the flames, but the four sharp points of the fork sank deeper into Kasay's neck, separating the C4 and C5 vertebrae and piercing the spinal canal and its thick cord of nerves. Dedaker had unknowingly used Emma's weight to turn Edward Kasay into a quadriplegic.

At six feet tall, two hundred and fifty-odd pounds, with her lower half in flames and electricity running up and down her arms, Emma was a nightmare. Her hair stood on end, and with the pink dye heat-faded from her shoes and the newly whitewashed leather burning, she looked like she walked on smoldering clouds of fire. Her skin was waxy and melting; blisters rose and burst, releasing a murky, oleaginous liquid.

The pain would have been too much for him to take, but it wasn't his body, so Dedaker pushed on.

"May the power of God smite you," he said to no one, to everyone, in his and Emma's harsh commanding voice, mockingly laughing all the while. Raising an arm, he pointed it at the crushing horde of people pushing for the door. Splaying her fingers, he relaxed her body, releasing. Feeling the electricity glide down her muscles and out the tips of her fingers, Dedaker wielded lightning into the multitude.

31

*H*oover had seen Fiona get injured, but there was nothing he could do about it. The herd had congested the only door, and Dedaker was rampaging. If he were to save Fiona and himself, he had to do something to cease the actions of the burning woman. Left unabated, Dedaker was going to outlast everyone else.

Hoover needed a weapon.

He spun in a circle, looking for something, anything, to hit Dedaker with. The only things close were chairs—metal folding chairs.

Fuck it, he thought and grabbed one by the backrest, mentally preparing himself to receive the same jolt Kasay had gotten through his crutch. Hoover hefted the chair and arched his back to swing when a hand reached out to stop him.

32

In the midst of chaos, a clam washed over Father O'Malley as he saw the meaning, as he understood.

Six years ago, Hoover had asked him if he had found what he was looking for when they electrocuted Dedaker. He hadn't. He'd spent the subsequent years after the debacle wondering what it had all been about, what his part in it meant.

Tonight, he knew. Tonight, he found the meaning.

At the Valley Green, he had told Hoover it was all about souls. Dedaker had said it; he had concurred it, and Hoover had bought it. But they had all been wrong. It wasn't about souls, plural; it was only about one soul, *a* soul.

The soul of the woman on fire.

When her body finally succumbed, Dedaker would die, but he would die in control. *He will die as her, and his soul will ascend, leaving hers behind, trapped.*

What happened to a soul if it was unable to ascend and left uncontained? O'Malley didn't know. Dissipated, he supposed. Whatever happened, the woman—whose name he would never know in life—would be gone, ceased to have existed in every state of being. Who she was will be lost forever, and Michael Dedaker will have hitched a ride into the afterlife on someone else's ticket.

O'Malley's instincts had been right. God *had* wanted him to expunge the evil that was Michael Dedaker. But not from life—from the *afterlife* What had happened six years ago was but the precursor to what was happening tonight. The execution had been a trial by fire—literally—given to him by God to see if he, Father

Thomas O'Malley, would be strong enough to make the ultimate sacrifice when the time came.

He felt—no, *knew*—he was strong enough, and he knew what he had to do. The woman had showed it to him herself right before Dedaker had forced her to stand up from the chair. O'Malley had seen her struggling against the madman for control of her own body.

When O'Malley had confronted him with the loss of his own soul, Dedaker had become distracted *and lost control* For a brief time, the woman was once again in possession of herself. She would have to have that possession again when she died, if her soul was to ascend, leaving Dedaker's behind.

What O'Malley needed to do was distract Dedaker.

Hoover, his wife hurt and in agony, had picked up a chair, of all things, and was getting ready to clobber the Dedaker/woman/thing with it. O'Malley's hand halted him.

"You can't fight him," the priest said. "It's not his body; you wouldn't be hurting him. She's got to do it herself, from inside."

Hoover was an intelligent, insightful man, as O'Malley had once remarked to him in the bowels of Dedaker's slaughterhouse, and he quickly discerned the theory behind what the priest was saying.

"You asked me before if I found what I was looking for," O'Malley said, "remember?"

Hoover nodded.

"I didn't then, but I have now. It's her soul."

Hoover didn't say anything, the comprehension on his face enough to ensure O'Malley that he had understood.

"Take your wife and try to get out, John. I'll handle Dedaker."

Hoover knew what that meant for the priest but didn't protest. He dropped the chair and went to Fiona. She was light, and he picked her up in his arms. He said, "Godspeed, Father."

O'Malley nodded, then turned to Dedaker.

There was a terrible squeal of feedback as Dedaker used the woman's hand to hurl a bolt of electricity into Sheila Oswald, traversing her body front to back, and emerging to stab a speaker at the DJ table.

"Michael," O'Malley roared with the voice of God himself.

Dedaker turned to him, his fingers crackling with blue sparks of electric. "Hello, Father," he said. "Is it finally time for our confrontation?"

"Yes, it is, Michael," O'Malley answered.

Dedaker raised the woman's hands again, this time at O'Malley, looking over them in a hypnotic gaze. O'Malley saw the electricity jumping and popping. The fire had spread up the woman's back, lighting her hair aflame.

"This is the end for us, Michael," O'Malley said, smug and unafraid. "We both deserved better, don't you think?"

Dedaker gave pause, looking at him. He said, "I have become what I had not fully known I sought until you and the cop interfered. I have the power of God at my fingertips; there is no better."

Inside, Emma was waiting. She could feel the languor of her body progressing; the end was getting close.

She had heard the priest's words, as she had heard them earlier, and knew the effect they had on Dedaker. Her body was beyond words, and dying. The priest was backed up into a corner, the room filling with smoke and flames. They were all going to die; it was only a question of whose soul was going to be released by Emma's death, and whose was going to stay to burn with the carcass.

"Yes, there is, Michael; there's better," O'Malley said, "but not for us. The callous bastard up there used us, used us both. We devoted our lives to him, and what did we get in return? Nothing; we were pawns. For the work we did, the sacrifices we made, he has damned our souls; neither of us will be granted heaven. For our struggles, we will spend our eternity together, you and me, in hell."

The woman's shoulder's sagged as Michael considered what the priest said, the affront from God he suggested. Emma's mind— her soul—reached for Dedaker's and, grabbing hold, shoved him to the rear. She was in control, and the monster was boxed in, in the growing darkness within her consciousness.

Emma heard him wail in defeat as he realized what had happened. And what lay ahead.

The priest stood before her in his obsidian garb and alabaster collar—a man and a hero, a true savior, a true martyr.

Father O'Malley looked past the flames and burning eyebrows to the woman's lidless eyes—they had changed, her features were softer. He had won. Dedaker's soul was trapped and would die with the woman's body; she in turn would go on to God's grace. What the priest's own fate was, he did not know.

"Thank you, Father," she said, and it was solely the voice of a woman.

33

The first flames of the fire had reached the roof of the hall, setting off the overhead water sprinklers. Rather than dampen the electrical fire, the water worsened it. There was enough electricity—and evil—conducting through the water that if it could have been harnessed, it might have been able to power an entire city block, if but briefly. The temperature rose so high that the steel girders behind the cinder blocks began to warp and the exterior of the building began to crumble.

34

John Hoover saw the smoke and flames rising into the overcast night sky through the rearview mirror. It was raining, and the swish of the wipers kept time.

Dedaker had cleared enough of a pass through the crowd with his lightning that he had been able to carry Fiona through the fire exit of the hall before the building succumbed. She lay slumped over on the seat next to him, still unconscious. They were yet miles from the emergency room at Holy Redeemer, the nearest hospital. His wife was hurt, but other than the loss of two fingers, no major damage had been done; Fiona would live. She might never again be the same after tonight, but he would be there to help her with that.

He would be there for her.

35

*F*our hours later, the men and women of the Brakes County Fire Department had the fire in their own hall contained enough that they could enter the remains of the building. They searched through the smoking rubble, as by routine, not expecting to find any survivors. To everyone's surprise, a young African-American rookie by the name of Jefferson found someone.

"Over here," she shouted. "I've got a breather!"

Firemen and rescue workers wearing long black fire-retardant coats and rubber boots pulled bricks and masonry off the person lying in what would have been the exact center of the hall. It was a man, his face and neck seared, his features made runny from the heat of the flames. The fingers of his unmoving hands were no more than charred bone, making them look like charcoaled twigs, kindling. The skin of his chest had been vaporized to the point that striations of muscle beneath could be seen. There was no hair on his head, only blisters. A fork protruded from his neck, and he was rightfully moaning in pain. His body lay motionless, but he was alive; he was alive.

When they cleared him off enough, Jefferson got down on her hands and knees. She removed her helmet and said, "Hang on, sir. The paramedics are getting a stretcher."

As Jefferson leaned in close—gently, so as not to brush against the injured man—she could hear that the moans had a rhythm to them. "Oh my God," she said, "he's talking."

"How the hell did he live through that," asked a fireman standing behind her.

"He was covered with so much shit, the brunt of the flames

must have missed him," said another. "Plus, he was low to the ground, keeping himself from smoke inhalation."

"He's pretty beat up; you think he'll make it?"

"Who knows, it depends on whether or not whatever god has kept him alive up till now wants him to keep on living," was the answer. "What's he saying, Jeff?"

"I don't know," she said, "It's weird. It sounds like he keeps repeating the same thing over and over again."

"What?"

"No more soup."

www.ingramcontent.com/pod-product-compliance
Lightning Source LLC
Chambersburg PA
CBHW051507250626
47156CB00001B/1